Beware the Wolves

A Soviet WWII Story

By

Victor Moss

Llumina Press

© 2005 Victor Moss

All rights reserved. No part of this publication may be reproduced or transmitted in any form or by any means electronic or mechanical, including photocopy, recording, or any information storage and retrieval system, without permission in writing from both the copyright owner and the publisher.

Requests for permission to make copies of any part of this work should be mailed to Permissions Department, Llumina Press, PO Box 772246, Coral Springs, FL 33077-2246

ISBN: 1-59526-554-6 PB
      1-59526-569-4 HC

Printed in the United States of America by Llumina Press

Library of Congress Control Number: 2005938100

DEDICATION

This book is dedicated to my parents, Walter (Vladimir) Moss and Vladys (Vladyslava) Moss (pictured above in 1941, shortly before the war began). This novel is based on their lives.

ACKNOWLEDGMENTS

I express my sincere gratitude to Vincent Cole, an author, who suggested the title of this book and at what point to begin this novel. I also wish to thank my children, Paul Moss and Katherine Moss Stafford, for their discussions regarding the direction of the text. I am particularly grateful to my daughter-in-law, Rebecca Stepien Moss, for her initial editing of each chapter.

Enormous thanks are given to R.J. Black Schultz, Colonel, USAFR (Ret), and Charles Bedard, M.D. for their help with the medical aspects of this novel.

I thank my sister, Mary Moss Janssen, and her husband, Duane Janssen, and my nieces, Julie Janssen and Natalie Janssen, my son-in-law, Scott Stafford, and my friends, Gayle Branger, Melanie Tappen, Marsha Butkovich, Phyllis Koch, Gordon Hurne, Margaret Herdeck, Robert Bradley, and Richard Barr for their encouragement and useful comments and suggestions. And my appreciation to Cynthia Becker, an author, for her final edit of the text.

But above all, I thank my wife, Rita Moss, for her support and the many hours we spent discussing each segment of the story. Her suggestions and editing were truly invaluable.

NAMES OF CHARACTERS

Except for Vladimir, Slava and their families, all other names of characters are fictitious.

Beware the Wolves

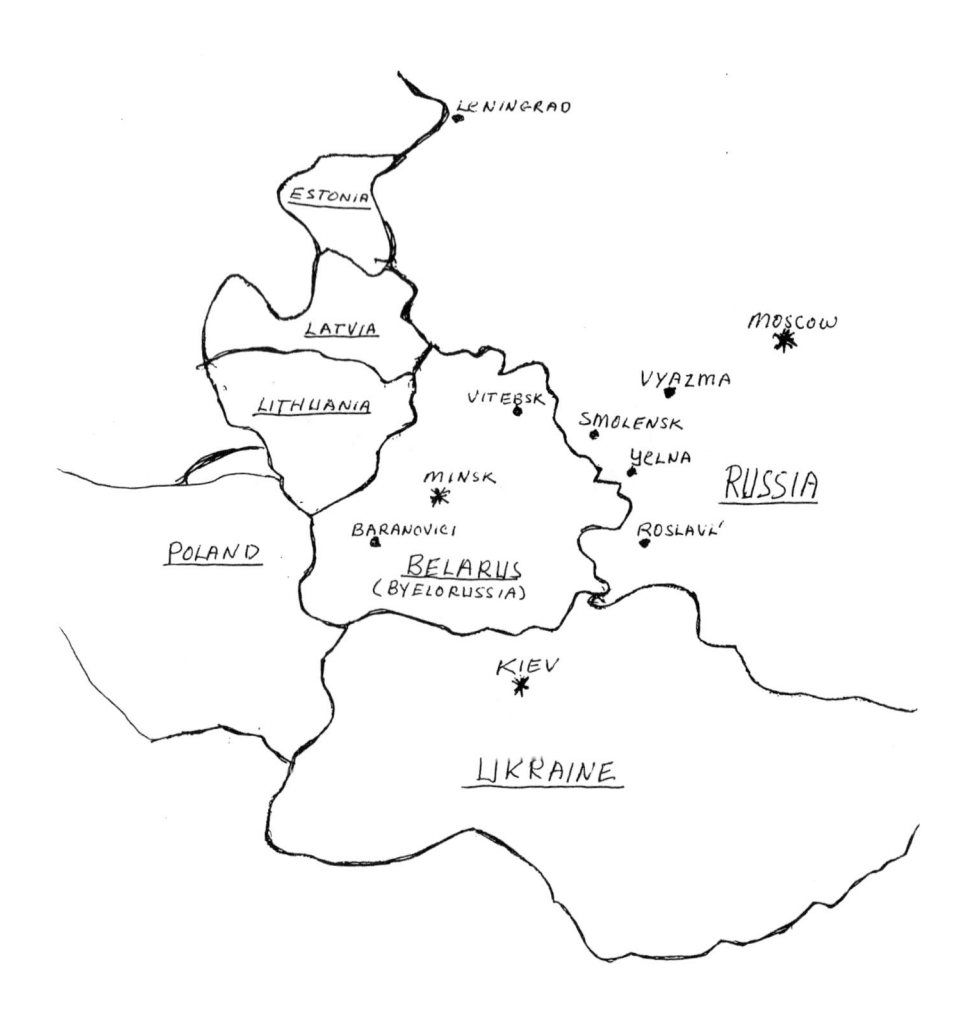

CHAPTER 1

Hitler called his invasion *Operation Barbarosa;* the Soviets called it a nightmare. On June 22, 1941, at exactly 4:00 a.m., Hitler broke his non-aggression pact with Stalin, and Germany, unexpectedly, invaded the Soviet Union. In defense of their motherland, over twenty million Soviet citizens lost their lives during the war years of World War II (1941-1945).

◆ ◆ ◆ ◆

He could still smell the smoke. Another village, one of hundreds, once alive with flesh, blood and bone, was deadly quiet. Captain Vladimir Moskalkov stood at the edge of a previously vibrant community that had turned into a graveyard of homes. Silence surrounded the chaos. Fire had destroyed the wooden houses, with their tree-limb fences and gardens that once lined a gravel street. Stone or brick stoves with their chimneys pointing toward heaven remained as forlorn monuments to the former residents. Scorched fields surrounded the collection of homes. A lone wooden outhouse survived, its door swinging in the breeze. In the distance, at the end of the village, Vladimir saw the charred remains of a brick building.

What have we done to deserve this? Vladimir asked himself as he gazed on the black landscape. *And what have I done? Who would have thought that this village would be evacuated and burned to the ground this soon?*

"What happened here? Who set the entire village on fire and where is everyone?" Asked Igor, one of the two medics who accompanied Vladimir. "Were the Germans here already and we didn't know about it?"

"Listen, Igor, you fool," Misha, the other medic responded. "Didn't you hear about Stalin's decree that residents must evacuate and destroy everything behind them?"

"Comrade Captain, Misha is not serious is he?"

"Actually, Igor, Misha is correct. It's a drastic order. Our Government decreed the destruction. The Czar long ago set the example of a 'scorched earth policy' to defeat Napoleon in 1812. And now Stalin followed suit, ordering the inhabitants to destroy their homes, take whatever belongings they could carry and evacuate east, toward Moscow and even beyond into the Ural Mountains bordering Asia."

"Well, what's the reason for that insanity?" Igor asked in disbelief.

Victor Moss

"So that the advancing Nazis would have less food and shelter."

"What if they had stayed?"

"They had no choice," Vladimir said. "The inhabitants had to obey the Government's decree or face arrest. Besides, who wants to live under foreign occupiers? But to us now, since the village was evacuated and destroyed, we have a huge predicament."

A serious dilemma faced Vladimir. He had disobeyed his commander's direct order not to leave the camp. With the village destroyed, his personal mission appeared to have failed. Waves of defeat continued to streak through his core as he stared at the ruin. *I made a big mistake. I should have complied with Colonel Popov's order. What have I done?* Vladimir's mind reeled as he thought of the consequences of his action. He had heard that Popov was a malicious and unreasonable man. His friend, Ivanov, had told him that their Colonel was a fanatical communist with a violent temper. Popov had shot his own brother twenty years ago, killing him on the spot, when his brother threatened to join the White Army and fight on the side of the Czar. And now he was in trouble with this man. Not only did Vladimir violate the order, but also it appeared that he would come back empty handed. The mornings's conversation with Popov revolved in his head:

"Colonel Popov, I request permission to go off base and procure medicines. We desperately need them. My wounded are in horrible pain. They require morphine and sulfa drugs immediately. I received information from one of the wounded soldiers that there is a village not far from here with a physician and a clinic. I could be back in no time at all."

"Your request is denied. You are not to leave this camp, especially on a wild goose chase."

Vladimir sensed Popov's annoyance, but he had to convince him of the importance of the drugs. *What is he thinking? I can't treat my patients without medications.*

"But Colonel Popov, the wounded are in dire straits. We have to do something. A village, part of a collective farm, is only about twenty kilometers from here. I believe the soldier. I believe that he is credible. He assures me that there is a good supply of medicines at the clinic not only for the village, but also for the surrounding farms. And as you know, I was told not to expect any new supplies for another 10 days."

"I don't want to hear any more about it, Comrade Captain. I specifically order you to remain in camp. Now get back to the hospital. I expect many more wounded in the days to come."

Popov's face was mottled red with anger. Vladimir's blood boiled, but he decided to back off before he lost his temper. *One more try,* he thought. *Then I'll have no choice but leave it alone, the bastard.*

"That's all the more reason why I need medications now. I can't treat without them. Please, Colonel, the injured soldiers need them now."

"No, get out of my office! Can't you understand an order! My mind is made up! I don't have time to mess with this. The wounded are not my priority."

Popov's eyes were cold and empty. Vladimir realized the futility of his insistence. He returned to the hospital. He heard the moans and whimpers of the wounded soldiers, transported from distant battlefields west of Smolensk. The delirious ravings and cries for help of those in excruciating pain cut through Vladimir like a blade. *I can help these poor souls with medication. I need to give them relief.* He had already rationed morphine, administering only partial dosages in an attempt to conserve the pain medication. But partial dosages were not effective. He needed additional morphine and antibiotics. *I can't wait another ten days. Dammit! Popov's order is unreasonable. If only that bastard could look into the eyes of the suffering. If he had any humanity, he would have agreed. I need to do something for my patients. Regardless of what Popov said, I need to go. It is my duty as a physician.* He made up his mind. He had to disobey the order for his patients.

Thus, after a long walk by way of a shortcut through the forest, Vladimir and his medics stood at the periphery of what used to be a village. *Why did I bring them just to get them in trouble?* Vladimir thought as he glanced at Misha and Igor, each with a cigarette hanging in his mouth. *What have I gotten them into? I didn't order them to follow me. They volunteered.*

"Captain," Misha had said. "The rumor mill is strong in this camp. No one can keep a secret. We heard you're going to look for medicines in a nearby village. Igor and I would like to volunteer for the mission."

"Yes, Comrade Captain," Igor added. "I'd like to get out of this camp. At least for a while, that is."

"You realize there may be danger," Vladimir said. "We will be leaving the camp without permission and walking into territory soon to be overrun by the enemy. But if you're willing, I suppose I could use your help to carry back any medicines we may find."

"We would enjoy the adventure," Misha quipped. "Isn't that right, Igor?"

Igor was slow to respond.

"Look, Igor if you are unsure, I don't want you to go." Vladimir said.

"No, I want to go. I can help you."

Now in silence, the three men viewed the scene in front of them. Vladimir's mouth was dry. Once outside the forest, the heat and mugginess of the day weighed him down. Vladimir missed the damp coolness of the woods. The still smoldering homes and fields added to Vladimir's discomfort. The acrid smell of smoke burned his eyes and made breathing harder.

"We'll never find any medicines here," Igor said. "If they left anything, it would be burned to a crisp."

"It doesn't look good, Comrade Captain," Misha said.

Vladimir shuddered again inwardly at the thought of failure. A terrible regret continued to assail him. He risked punishment for disobeying an order, and all for nothing. He thought of the consequences of his insubordination. *I could be shot for this.*

"Captain, should we go back to the camp?" Misha asked.

"I want to look around," Vladimir said. "That brick house at the other end of the village could have been the clinic. And who knows, we might get lucky and find undamaged bottles of medicines."

As he walked down the gravel road, Vladimir recalled his grandparent's village of Jazwino, Byelorussia. He had lived with his grandparents in that village of his birth until age seven. *Could it be that Jazwino was also burned to the ground? If so, it's a good thing my grandparents are not alive to see the destruction. I can't imagine setting fire to my own house, walking away and looking over my shoulder to see my home go up in flames.*

Vladimir recalled that the Jazwino clinic was in a small brick building with a metal roof. With his usual quickstep, Vladimir briskly proceeded forward. Misha and Igor lagged behind.

"Can you slow down a little, Captain?" Misha asked.

"Listen, you soldiers need to move faster," Vladimir said, raising his voice a little. "Time is running out and we have a long way back to camp before nightfall. Besides, I have this strange feeling in my gut that the Germans are nearby."

As he said that, he looked around. Toward the northwest he saw a cloud of dust in the distance. *I hope to God that it is the wind kicking up dust,* he thought. They soon stood in front of the building. Fire had charred the crumbling red bricks. The blaze caved in the roof. The scorched wooden porch barely stood. But still attached to the brick above the burned door a sign read "Clinic." Vladimir's heart beat with excitement. After all, he had found the clinic and with luck, he would find what he came for. *The trip will be worthwhile, in spite of everything,* he thought as he envisioned medications left behind.

Vladimir's eternal optimism and his unbound energy had propelled him from humble beginnings to a medical degree. He graduated from medical school only by sheer persistence, attending elementary and gymnasium (high school) sporadically while working full time. He was used to labor both as a child and later as a teenager. He studied on his own and tested out to enter Feldsher (physician assistant) school. After four years, he graduated as a Feldsher despite the competition for admittance and the arduous examinations. But he desired more. His dream was to be a physician. To achieve his goal, Vladimir studied day and night and at the same time worked as a physician's assistant at a clinic. He passed the grueling medical school admission examinations on his first try. Examinations did not come easy for him. He had to work hard at it. *That's pretty good for a poor peasant boy to become a doctor,* he thought proudly upon graduation.

He learned persistence from his grandfather. Vladimir's father died in the World War in 1917. His mother took him and his baby sister, Anna, and moved in with her parents until she remarried. Since he never knew his father, Vladimir's grandfather was his mentor. He lived by the old man's motto, "If you can't get through the door, then go through the window."

Vladimir climbed the two wooden steps that led up to a charred deck of the porch. The steps were solid, but only the center portion of the porch seemed secure. The edges were badly burned. The half open door still smoldered. Misha followed him, treading carefully on the charred porch.

Vladimir and Misha proceeded cautiously over the threshold into the brick structure. Suddenly, a loud crack like the sound of a gunshot broke the deadly silence. Vladimir jumped. A second later, an even louder crash accompanied the collapse of the porch roof. He turned back and saw Igor stretched out underneath the rubble. As Igor had stepped on the edge of the deck, his foot went through the burnt wood. In an attempt to keep his balance, Igor clutched the pillar holding up the porch roof. The pillar disintegrated into several pieces and a portion of the porch roof tumbled down.

"Are you all right?" Misha asked, pulling debris off Igor.

"Oh shit, now look at my uniform, it's black from soot and the shoulder's torn."

"Forget the uniform. Are you hurt?" Vladimir asked, feeling for broken bones.

"No sir, hopefully a roof crashing down on me will be the worst thing to happen today."

"Good, let's go inside," Vladimir said. "This time, watch your step."

The interior brick clinic walls still stood. The furniture was burned, but the cabinets, although scorched, were in fairly good shape. The flames singed some areas of the floor, but overall, it seemed strong enough to hold the three men. None of them was a big man. Vladimir was 170 cm. (5'8") tall and weighed 70 kg. (154 pounds) The other two men were slightly heavier, but not by much. The roof of the clinic had collapsed but portions fell against the brick walls allowing a passage for the men to move around the inside of the building. *The front room is obviously the reception area. This is the examination room and the back part was the residence of the physician,* Vladimir mused, proceeding forward. *Where would the medicines be kept?*

Vladimir inspected each cabinet. He moved quickly from one to the next. The cabinets were empty. There were no medications.

"Men, help me move some of this roof away, maybe we'll find something underneath it."

"Comrade Captain," Igor said. "We're wasting our time. It's obvious that there are no medicines in this place."

Vladimir's heart sank. The inner torment that began when he first saw the devastation intensified and gnawed at him. He had struggled intensely with

Victor Moss

whether or not he should disobey Popov's order for the sake of his patients. An inner voice had told him to stay put and follow orders. *I should have listened. Now it appears I made the wrong decision,* he reflected. *After the risk I took, we better keep looking. They may still be here.*

"Captain, should we head back?" Misha asked.

"No, men. We need to search the whole place. Let's move this big piece of collapsed roof. Let's see what's underneath."

With effort, the men lifted the debris and moved it over a meter. As they did so, Misha yelled out, "There's a body underneath."

Vladimir looked down and saw a man's body partially buried under the collapsed roof.

"Quick, let's move the rest of the roof over so we can see the body," Vladimir said.

"Do you think he was the doctor?" Misha asked.

"He could very well be," Vladimir said. "I wonder why he didn't evacuate with the others? He might have been trying to save something in this clinic."

Vladimir examined the body and realized that the man's right hand clutched an object. He pried the stiffened hand open and saw the handle to a trap door whose outline was not visible in the shadows.

"Look here, a cellar," Vladimir said. "Must be something important in there for him to either come back into the burning building or stay in the building with it on fire. Move the body so that we can open the door and look inside."

As Misha and Igor lifted the partially seared door, it crumbled and came off its hinges. Below they could see steps leading down into the cellar. They appeared stable enough. As the men descended the steps, the cellar darkened. Misha struck a match and the men, in that quick flare of light, saw a kerosene lamp on a shelf immediately to the right of the steps. Igor took his match and lit the lamp. As light filled the murky darkness of the cellar, Vladimir's optimism reawakened.

He scanned the room. Vladimir noticed wooden barrels along the far wall of the musty cellar. He stepped over to a barrel and raised the lid. A whiff identified the contents as salted cabbage. The middle barrel held a few salted herrings and the third barrel contained pickles. Vladimir picked up a pickle and chewed on it as he walked over to see what was on the shelves on the adjacent wall. He found glass jars of mushrooms, more pickles, more herring, and fruit and berry preserves. *They should have destroyed all of this,* he thought. *Or the physician forgot about the cellar in his attempt to evacuate and then returned only to have the roof fall on him.*

Vladimir proceeded carefully to examine each shelf. The cellar was full of food supplies. *Come on, where are the medicines? There must be some here.*

"Igor, I can't see in this corner," Vladimir said. "Bring that lamp over here."

As Igor approached with the lamp, Vladimir saw shelves that looked well stocked with familiar bottles.

"Here, here, Igor. Let me have the lamp."

Vladimir brought the lamp closer to the bottles and read the word "Morphine." His heart pounded rapidly. A sense of elation ran through his being. He grabbed another bottle on a lower shelf. It was a "Sulfilimide." Other bottles contained aspirin. Vladimir, flushed with excitement, grabbed his head and ran his fingers through his hair. He could not believe his luck.

"It's all worth it!" Vladimir exclaimed. But Misha and Igor did not hear him. They stood at the opposite corner next to a pile of loose potatoes on the earthen floor of the cellar. They were occupied, each tugging on a shinny object.

"You asshole, I found this samovar! Igor shouted. "It's mine. Take your paws off of it."

"You get your grubby paws off of it, you bastard." Misha retorted. "What does a peasant want with a fine item such as this?"

"I'm going to sell it." Igor said. "Now let go. I told you it's mine."

"Shut up, you fools!" Vladimir yelled. "We found what we came for and you're fighting over what? Some shiny object!"

Vladimir gazed at his medics, their faces red with anger and exertion. He walked over to them and demanded that they give him the samovar. The reflection from the lamp gave the samovar an appearance of gold satin. Bold spiral fluting in high relief graced the sides. It was, indeed, a fine piece of workmanship. Much nicer than any he had seen.

"Comrade Captain, I saw it first and by all right, I'm entitled to it," Igor said. "It's like, you know, spoils of war."

"No, captain," Misha interjected. "I saw it before Igor did and pointed it out to him."

"For God's sake! Get a grip on yourselves!" Vladimir yelled. "What's going through your minds? Here you're arguing over a samovar. We're wasting valuable time! What are you going to do with a bulky samovar, anyway? We have to get back to the camp before we are missed. Carrying that samovar will only slow you down. Anyway, who would you sell it to, even if you brought it back to the camp! Our political commissar? Look here, I found some medicines, enough for at least a week, possibly two. By then, we should get a new shipment from Moscow. Now, I'll put the samovar down and you help me put the bottles in these flour sacks we brought from camp."

As Vladimir and Misha began loading the sacks with the small bottles, Igor kicked the samovar with his foot.

"I'll smash this before I'll let the Fritzes get their hands on this treasure."

Vladimir looked at Igor and shook his head. There stood a twenty-year-old soldier in his torn and soot-covered uniform kicking a samovar, like a soccer ball, into a post. *This guy is a real piece of work,* Vladimir thought.

Victor Moss

Each of the men carried a bag full of medicine bottles as they began their ascent out of the cellar. Vladimir took two steps toward the front of the door and froze. He heard the distinct roar of engines rapidly approaching their position.

"Oh God!" Vladimir said. "Do you hear that?"

"I hear them," Misha whispered. "Those are motorcycles."

"Whose do you suppose they are?" Igor asked with a trembling voice.

The resonance grew louder and nearer. Vladimir felt a momentary panic. He remembered the dust. *That must have been a German column.*

"Get back into the cellar!" Vladimir commanded. "Those are German motorcycles."

The men looked at each other and dove back through the trapdoor and fell down into the cellar. Vladimir felt a knot in his stomach as the motorcycles passed by the clinic. The sound diminished in intensity, though they could still hear the rumble of the engines. Vladimir's breathing was quick and shallow.

Igor pulled out his cigarette and was about to light it.

"You idiot," Vladimir said. "Get rid of that cigarette. You can smell that foul-smelling makhorka tobacco a mile away. And what about the smoke? You want to send them smoke signals that we're here?"

"Who do you think they are?" Misha whispered, breathing heavily.

"They are probably German advance scouts," Vladimir said. "Means the Panzers are not far behind."

Suddenly, the snarl from the motorcycles increased in volume. *Oh shit! They've turned around,* Vladimir thought with dread.

"They're coming back!" Igor panicked.

"Stay absolutely quiet." Vladimir whispered.

Vladimir prayed that they moved on. But his prayer was not answered. The roar of the engines died in front of the brick house.

Vladimir heard voices, recognized the German language, but could not hear the details of their conversation. Suddenly he heard footsteps above, approaching the opening to the cellar. The sweat dripped from his brow and poured into his eyes. His could barely see. He could hear his heart banging and imagined that everyone could hear it. His knees felt weak.

The footsteps drew closer to the trapdoor. Vladimir pulled out his revolver and pointed it toward the opening. He had never pointed that gun at a man before and could not imagine shooting anyone, much less take a human life. *I was trained to save lives, not to destroy lives.* But in this situation, curled up between the barrels and the potatoes, the gun gave him some comfort. To save his life and that of his men, he would shoot. The medics did not have weapons, as only officers were allowed to carry a sidearm. Vladimir was an officer only because of his medical education. *It's my duty to protect my men and myself,* he convinced himself.

The footsteps were at the edge of the opening. Vladimir saw the silhouette of the soldier. A beam of light flooded the steps. Vladimir shrank back even

Beware the Wolves

further, as his hands shook. He wiped the sweat from his eyes. He held his left hand over the cylinder and hammer to muff the sound and quietly cocked the trigger of the revolver with his right hand. *What if he heard the click?* The German's boot stepped on the first step. Then there was a boot on the second step. Vladimr thought he heard gasps from his medics. His heart pounded, trying to escape his body.

Before the boot found the third step, he heard a voice yelling outside the house.

The painstaking lessons in German, the many hours of practicing with his young, multilingual wife were finally paying off. He recognized the words.

"Helmut, get back here, we have to go back and report. There's no one here. There is nothing left of this village."

The boots retracted and the footsteps became more faint. In a few seconds, the motorcycles started up again and were gone.

With his uniform totally drenched with sweat and still breathing heavily, Vladimir whispered as though the enemy was still there, "Let's get out of here! The Panzers cannot be far behind. Take those sacks of medicines and let's head to the forest as quickly as possible. We won't be spotted there."

The motorcyclists were gone and once again the street was deserted. Vladimir heard the thunder of engines. He felt a vibration in the ground underneath his feet. The cloud of dust that seemed so far away before was now only meters away.

"Oh shit!" Igor shrieked. "We have to get out of here."

Igor took off toward the forest, with Misha close behind. They ran doubled over down the middle of the street, hugging their booty to their chests.

"Hey," Vladimir shouted. "Don't run in the middle of the street in open view."

Either they did not hear him or did not want to. Vladimir chased them and grabbed their arms. He pulled them off to the side toward a surviving rock stove and chimney.

"Crouch and run behind this row of chimneys and debris," Vladimir ordered. "When you get to that tall grass, crawl your way back to the woods, understand!"

The growl of the approaching motorized vehicles intensified by the second. Vladimir and the medics stopped and hid behind the carcass of the last house. Just a few meters separated them from the field adjacent to the forest. Yet, with the column so close and the run to the field visible from the road leading into the village, the few remaining meters appeared kilometers away.

"The grass is tall enough to hide in," Vladimir said. "Let's go."

Suddenly, just as the men took a step for the field, the reverberation of motorcycles filled the air. *Oh no, not again..* He peeked out around the brick chimney and saw several motorcycles with sidecars making the turn from the road onto the gravel street of the village. He jerked his head back. His chest tightened. *Oh God! They might have seen me.* He held his breath as he waited a few seconds, expecting the motorcycles to come in his direction. His heart continued to beat erratically.

The motorcycles roared past them and stopped down the street. Vladimir decided that it was time to run toward the field before the rest of the column turned the corner into the village.

"Now run for it," Vladimir ordered.

The three men ran the fifty or so meters to the field. Once in the grassland they dove to hide themselves in the tall grass and wild sunflowers. Vladimir's heart pounded. The veins in his head throbbed. To make himself as flat against the ground as possible, he pushed his face into the ground and stretched his arms out and hoped that Misha and Igor did the same. *Did they see us?* He wondered to himself. More motorcycles and then the sound of a car crawled past them. The three men laid in the grass for a few seconds, then crawled through the field. When they looked up and saw that the coast was clear, they ran toward the cover of the forest as fast as they could. They almost made it all the way when the first tank came into view. They again hit the brush-covered ground and finally crawled into the forest.

"Let's rest a bit, Captain. I can't go any farther until I catch my breath." With that, Igor pulled out his makhorka and lit up as he sat on an old decaying tree trunk. Vladimir was anxious to run deeper into the forest. He was not sure whether or not the Nazis had seen them. But as he looked at the faces of his medics, he knew an order to proceed immediately was useless. *These men must have their smoke. They also need a rest.* He sat down and reflected on how close they had come to being discovered. The danger was there and he realized his close brush with death. *I can't die*, he thought. *I have to return to my dear Slava.*

With the Germans in this village, he realized that the enemy could also occupy his hometown of Vitebsk as well. *What has become of her?* He shuddered as he thought about her. His body was still tied up in knots. Tears misted his eyes. *It's just a release of nerves and stress,* he rationalized. He looked at the bags full of medicines and felt good about his success. *Now if we can only get back to camp without getting caught?* He was not an overly religious person, but now, at the edge of the forest, with the racket of motor vehicles entering the village, he crossed himself and asked God for help.

CHAPTER 2

The rumble from engines intensified. Metal tracks pounded the earth. The three men knew they had to get far away from the enemy, but curiosity got the better of them. Hiding behind the trees and brush, Vladimir and the medics crawled to the edge of the forest and looked toward the village. A long column of Panzers, enveloped in a cloud of dust, advanced into the village.

"My God! Misha mumbled, almost to himself. "How can we possibly defeat that?"

"Yes. It's frightening," Vladimir answered. "But we must."

"Yeah, sure," Igor said. "With our shitty army. Oh, I'm sorry Comrade Captain. Please don't report me. I just can't believe the number of those tanks."

"Watch your mouth, Igor. The political commissars don't want to hear negativism."

"You're not going to turn me in are you?"

"No, but again, watch what you say. Even trees have ears."

Vladimir continued to stare at the enemy. The tanks were mechanized beasts with their ominous black crosses painted below the turret. A shiver ran through him when he espied for the first time the German heads, covered with helmets and goggles, protruding from the tank hatches.

He dwelled for a moment on Igor's remark about the Red Army. In fact, the army was unprepared from the surprise invasion. His friend, Sergey Ivanov, had told him about their aircraft, still in neat rows on the airfields, destroyed by enemy attack before they could get up in the air. He remembered Ivanov complained that their mechanized units lacked tank, artillery and ammunition. *I even had to promise Ivanov that I would never tell anyone how he told me that Stalin, in one of his fits of paranoia, had executed almost all of the experienced military commanders and strategists in 1937 and 1938, leaving the army with no unity of command. We do have an uphill fight ahead.*

"Let's go," Vladimir ordered. "We have a long way to go."

Vladimir took his sunglasses off and placed them in his pocket. He would not need them in the dense shade of the forest. The soft summer breeze wound itself around the grove of birch, fir, pine and aspen trees. It felt refreshing as it played with his shirt. The thin rays of the afternoon sunlight pierced the branches. As the men walked down a path, the surroundings reminded him of the numerous walks he had taken with his grandfather through the forest.

Victor Moss

Vladimir's grandfather often took him to the forest near his house in Jazwino to collect firewood. He was seven years old and his grandmother dressed him warmly in his styoganka, a quilted cotton coat with heavy batting and a rabbit fur hat that covered his forehead and ears. She carefully wrapped strips of felt over this woolen socks and around his feet and legs to keep them dry and warm. The snow was deep. His grandfather dressed the same and the two would go off. It was always such an adventure for him. His grandfather would gather his old rifle, saying,"Protection from those damn wolves. Beware of wolves. You must always stay alert."

At that moment Vladimir, recalling his grandfather's advice twenty-one years ago, looked around the forest to see if, indeed, any wolves lurked. There were none, but then he did not really expect to see any during the summer day. His grandfather's words echoed in his mind.

"Even if they are not hungry, they'll turn on you just for the sport of it. But they are always hungry. If they can't find anything to eat, they'll eat each other. Those demons. They are only brave when they are in packs. One or two wolves will avoid you, but a pack of them will attack you."

The first fear Vladimir ever experienced was in the forest. Vladimir and his grandfather gathered wood one cold blustery winter day. They already had bundles ready to carry home when his grandfather suddenly stopped, dropped his bundle and grabbed the rifle that was slung across his back.

"Do you hear that Volodya, my little Vladimir?"

Vladimir heard nothing. He looked at his grandfather's face, so stern and so deeply creased around the eyes and mouth. He waited for his grandfather to tell him what was wrong, but the old man's lips were clenched tight and frowning. A breeze lifted strands of his grandfather's long hair and bushy beard. Standing still, eyes gazing at the distance, filaments of hair rising and falling, the old man looked like a leshii, the spirit of the forest, protector and destroyer, master of all wildlife, able to grow twice his normal size. Vladimir continued to stare up at his grandfather. He looked so different. It was as if some wildness seized the old man, a feral turbulence rising to the surface, distorting his features and darkening his eyes into black holes that absorbed all light. At that moment Vladimir knew what it felt like to be scared. He froze in his tracks, afraid to move. What caused his grandfather to act so peculiarly?

He sensed an unidentified danger and wanted to rush toward his grandfather for comfort and protection, but the old man leaned the rifle against the tree next to him and said,

"Be quiet. Stand still. Can't you hear them? Can't you hear them howling in the distance, a haunting cry of a lost soul tormented by hunger."

Vladimir did, indeed, hear the howling at that moment and then he heard another howl, closer, louder, a savage cry of desperation. A third howl echoed the others and then a fourth. Another joined in and soon it seemed as if the entire forest howled and snarled around them. He realized the wolves had

Beware the Wolves

surrounded them. Then it all stopped and the silence was more dreadful than the savage lamentation. Between the trees Vladimir was sure he saw piercing, yellow-gold eyes staring at him, ready to pounce. Many times, while sitting at home with his grandparents, he heard tales of wolves snatching children and eating them whole. He shuddered.

Suddenly, the old man grabbed the wood he had gathered. With a roar that echoed throughout the forest, his Grandfather began to throw sticks and logs in all directions. Ravens burst forth from a nearby tree and scattered into the sky. He stomped his feet and began to shout, "Damn you demons!"

He was a man possessed, hair flailing, eyes wide and angry, spittle flying from his lips. Vladimir saw gray outlines with penetrating eyes inching closer. He began to whimper and cry. His grandfather continued to bellow and curse the wolves. When it appeared the wolves were not backing away, he lifted his rifle, put it to his shoulder and shot in the direction of a gray shadow in the trees. Something yelped and struggled through the underbrush. Something else snarled and Vladimir saw fleeting gray shadows disappearing deep into the darkness of the forest. He could hear twigs breaking underfoot as the creatures scurried away.

Vladimir never forgot the forest and the dangers it held. Again he found himself in the woods. Today, he would not see wolves, not the animal type anyway. The wolves of the forest were more predictable than the human wolves. The hungry German army was a pack of wolves closing in, feeding on whatever it found.

Hitler is not content to live within his borders; he must invade our land and obliterate our lives at his whim, he said to himself. And there was yet another wolf to fear. After all, he left the camp without Popov's permission. He was in trouble with his superior, who awaited his return. There were wolves at his back and wolves ahead.

Some areas of the forest were dense and the shadows deep. Carefully, he listened for any sound not in harmony with the forest. All he could hear was the soft thread of Misha's and Igor's boots crunching on pine needles and decaying leaves. But at the same time the words of his grandfather revolved in his head, "Beware of wolves, terrible things can happen."

He remembered his grandfather as lean with a long gray beard. His shoulders were stooped from toil. Yet his stride was firm and determined. Every step he took was sure. He was a peasant named Aksenti Kuharenko living on land that was owned by the "Pan," a Polish term for lord.

"The land may belong to the 'Pan,' but the house I built by myself and it is all mine," his grandfather had said.

His grandfather took pride in his house. He believed it to be the best in the area, just outside the small community. His fine herds of cattle, goats and swine added to his comfort. He knew that his neighbors considered him very well off.

Victor Moss

Kuharenko was a man who understood the seasons. He knew the ways of nature. His knowledge came not from books but from the world around him.

"Everything has a time and a purpose," he used to tell Vladimir.

When his daughter Agafia, Vladimir's mother, tried to teach her father to read and write a few words, he dismissed her saying, "Why? Everything I need to know is there in the fields and forests. Life tells me all I need to survive."

His grandfather knew his world and had little interest in anything else outside.

"Let soldiers march, let battles be fought and let the victorious change national borders." He could not be bothered if one day he was declared to be Belorussian, the next day he became Polish, and the following day he was Russian. The old man just wanted to live in peace and work in the fields. He often used the excuse that he had to work hard just so the "Pan" could have his share of the crops. In reality, he worked hard because he truly enjoyed the labor. He especially enjoyed his work when his wife, Evdakia, worked by his side. But then, he would never admit it.

"Tell me more about my father," Vladimir begged his grandfather time and time again.

"All right, here we go again. His name was Grigori Moskalkov and he was a hero. He received the St. George's cross from the Czar for valor. He died during the Great War in 1917. You were only two years old at the time and your sister, Anna, was a newborn when he was killed."

"Tell me again why was he a hero," Vladimir begged.

"He fought off an attack by seven German soldiers, single-handedly with his bayonet and with his boot spaga, (boot bayonet). He killed them all except one. That soldier, while laying on the ground, lifted his rifle and shot your father to death."

"Tell me again, what was he like?" Vladimir insisted.

"As I told you many times, you look a lot like him. The same cheekbones, the same slant to the eyes, the same smile. He was a happy lad and a good worker. He was a stable boy for the 'Pan.' He knew horses and had a way with them. In just a few days, he could tame the wildest horse, one that was quick to kick and bite. Everyone liked your father. I liked him. Actually I was pleased when your mother took a shine to him. Agafia liked him from the time they went to school together. She would come home and tell us tales about him."

"Why did he go to war?"

"The 'Pan' was told by the Czar to send fifteen of his workers to the front. Your father was one of the fifteen. He had no choice but to go. Your mother cried for days. She must have had a feeling he would not come home."

Reminiscing about the past made Vladimir very morose. He gnashed his teeth. He wished he had known his father. Once he was older he realized that his mother had to remarry. But as a small boy, he hated his stepfather, Mikhail, because of his drinking, although he loved his half-sisters, Valentina and

Beware the Wolves

Maria. *He was a kind man when he was sober, but it was a shame that he was extremely abrasive and abusive when drunk. Unfortunately, he drank most of the time.* The only redeeming feature about him was that he taught Vladimir how to make and repair shoes. Mikhail, a shoemaker, had his own shop in Jazwino, but then moved to Shumilino, a larger village not far away. Business was good. Vladimir learned how to work fast and produced a high quality product. At just ten years old, he knew how to assemble a shoe from scratch. But he could hardly wait to get from under the control of his stepfather, move to Vitebsk, and get some education. He wanted to make something of himself. And at age thirteen, on his own, he moved to Vitebsk, the nearest city, and found work in a shoe factory.

The pungent, unpleasant odor of Mahorka tobacco filled Vladimir's nostrils and interrupted his childhood reflection. It always amazed him how often he had those thoughts when he was in a forest. Misha and Igor had fallen further behind, but the smoke from their cigarettes blew ahead of them. Vladimir glanced at his watch, and realized that it was later than he thought.

"Hurry up men, we have to step it up."

"We need to rest," said Igor. "My feet are too sore. It would be good to have a little vodka right now."

"You bastard," Misha complained. "The only reason your feet are sore is because you drank too much last night and danced the hopak like a Cossack until you collapsed. We had to drag you back to your cot."

"Get off my back, you son of a bitch, I'll be all right if I could just have a five minute nap, right here under this tree."

Vladimir turned back to join his medics. "I know you are tired, but we need to forge ahead. We still have a long way to go and we need to get back before supper."

"The supper is no problem," Igor said. " I know one of the cooks well. He'll give us something to eat when we return."

"I am not worried about the food, Igor," Vladimir said. "I'm concerned that we will be missed. I am sure that they have already looked for me at the hospital. I don't want them to think that we've deserted."

The men slowly unfolded themselves. Each took the sack with the medicines and started walking. Vladimir slowed his own pace so that they could walk together. He did not know these men well and did not trust them entirely. Especially Igor. Vladimir had the feeling from the start that Igor wanted to walk away. *All I need on top of the trouble I may be in for disobeying a direct order is to have these two medics desert under my supervision,* he thought. As an officer, it would have been his duty to stop a deserter or even to shoot him, if he had tried to run away. The idea was unthinkable.

"Comrade Captain," Igor said. "Where are you from?"

Victor Moss

"I'm from Vitebsk," Vladimir answered deciding that it is better to engage in small talk. *If Igor talks, there is less chance of him bolting.* "Where are you from?"

"We're from the same place. We're fellow countrymen. Actually, I'm from a collective farm about ten kilometers from Vitebsk. Did you leave family behind in Vitebsk?"

"Yes, my wife, her family and my mother and sisters."

"What's your wife's family name? Maybe I know them."

"I don't think you would know them."

"I know a lot of people in Vitebsk. What is their name?" Igor persisted.

The questions began to annoy Vladimir. "Igor that's not important. What about you? Are you married?" Vladimir asked, trying to avoid any further questions about his family. In the society created by Stalin, it was always wise to give as little information about yourself as possible.

"Yes, I left my wife, Lena, and our son on the farm. I don't know if they're still there. But if they are, they need me and I sure would like to see them. But tell me, what's your wife's name?"

Should I tell him more? Vladimir thought for a moment. *I suppose there is no harm in giving him her name. After all, it's just small talk.*

"Well, Comrade Captain, what's her name?"

"Vladislava."

"I bet she's beautiful. Am I right?"

Vladimir had it by now. He turned toward their quiet companion.

"Misha, you are more quiet than usual," Vladimir said. "What are you thinking?"

"Do you think our army knows that the Nazis are this close to our camp?" Misha asked.

"Of course, they know," Vladimir said. "There are scouting parties all around and even air reconnaissance."

With that said, all three walked quietly. Misha and Igor lit up their cigarettes again. Igor saw a stump and sat down, the cigarette dangling from his mouth. He dropped the sack of medications on the ground next to the stump and took off his boot.

"Go on ahead," Igor waived them on. "I'll catch up."

Vladimir, still suspicious of Igor's intentions, did not want to leave him, even for a minute. *That sack of medications would bring a healthy sum on the black market.*

"Get up Igor! It's an order. Put your boot back on. Pick up that bag and let's go."

Igor rose reluctantly. He grimaced, threw the sack over his shoulder and followed Vladimir and Misha, complaining of thirst.

"Chew on a tree twig like I've been doing," Vladimir said. "It will help keep your throat from drying out."

Beware the Wolves

They walked for several hours. Camp was now only a few kilometers away. Vladimir already pictured in his mind the edge of the forest, the open field and then a series of defensive trenches, some still under construction. *The Germans are not far behind,* Vladimir thought. *Those lines won't hold the tanks for long.*

Suddenly the men heard the sound of hoofs and laughter ahead. "Quick, quick, hide!" Vladimir ordered. The men darted off the path and crouched behind some fallen logs and shrubs. Through the brush they saw six Soviet soldiers approaching on horseback. *They're either a scouting party, or a search party for deserters, or both.* The thought of being found, hiding in the woods, tore at his insides. Once again, he broke out into a sweat. Out in the open field, returning to camp, he would not have been concerned. But found in the forest, without authorization, they could be considered deserters and shot. *It probably would not make any difference that we found the desperately needed medications.*

The men laid on the ground long enough for the patrol to pass.

"Whew, that was close," Misha said. "It is a good thing they were not paying attention."

"Yeah," said Igor. "Did you hear them laugh as they went by? Must have been a hell of a joke."

Vladimir urged them to hurry. The medics, however, had to light up. Vladimir shook his head in frustration for they walked slowly as if they were strolling leisurely in a park. *What is it with these soldiers? Don't they realize that the patrol could return at any time? Don't they comprehend that the sooner we get to the camp, the less trouble we may be in?*

Vladimir was a patient man, but by now his patience was wearing thin. He was tired and irritated.

"Don't you men understand how important it is to return to the camp as soon as possible! I've had it with your pace! I'm tired of you dragging me down. Now move your asses. I know you're worn-out. I, too, am exhausted. But we have to move along."

"Sorry, Comrade Captain," Misha said. "Come on Igor, you fool. You are the one slowing us down. Do what the Captain says."

As the men approached the end of the forest, the sun lying low in the western sky beat down on the shimmering grassy pasture. The light was a bright contrast to the darkened forest. In the distance, sappers worked on antitank trenches. Further on the horizon, past a vast meadow, rooftops of a few buildings of the camp could be seen between the trees. Vladimir positioned his sunglasses and stepped out of the cool forest onto the field. A stifling wall of heat and humidity hit him. At the same time, a cold shiver ran through his body at the thought of facing Popov. He felt good about finding the medications. On the other hand, he was fearful of the consequences of his action. *Was I impulsive? What's going to happen to me?* He took a deep breath and walked on, his medics following in silence.

"Look, captain," Misha said pointing to a column of trucks and horse-drawn carts approaching the camp. "Look at all those ambulances."

"More work for us," Igor said.

"Well, at least now we have some medicines to treat them," Vladimir answered.

He felt good about that. *They're a Godsend. Surely, Popov would understand and see the reason why I disobeyed his order?*

CHAPTER 3

The camp boiled with compressed energy and turmoil. Soldiers that survived and escaped the encircling Panzer forces in battles to the west poured in to make a stand against the mighty German war machine at Smolensk. In addition, reserves from across European Soviet Union rushed in as fast as the overworked railway system could bring them. Just as in the days of Napoleon in 1812, Smolensk was destined to be a major battleground of World War II. Smolensk was on the direct route to Moscow, along M1, one of the few paved highways from Brest to Moscow.

Vladimir felt the thrill of frightened anticipation that touched every soul in the camp. He had just seen the enemy in the burned-out village and felt the anxiety along with the others. The Nazi units of Operation Center were now only a few kilometers from Smolensk, positioning to encircle and attack using their tanks to devour everything in their paths. Much preparation for the defense still needed to be made.

"Give us a ride to the hospital?" Vladimir asked the driver of an ambulance. The driver nodded and Vladimir sat down in the cab with the driver while Misha and Igor jumped up on the running boards of the old 1930's gray GAZ truck.

Through the grimy window of the truck, Vladimir studied the small factory town on the southwestern outskirts of Smolensk that was transformed into a camp. *The evacuated inhabitants lost their homes to the military, all for the defense of the Motherland,* Vladimir thought as the truck made its way carefully up the dusty road, avoiding tanks, troop and supply trucks, horse pulled artillery and aimlessly marching soldiers. The homes of the residents became barracks for the officers and soldiers. One of the larger brick homes was converted into headquarters. *Oh-oh, we're passing past Popov's office. I hope he doesn't see me,* Vladimir thought as he turned his head away from the house.

Vladimir sat in the first vehicle in a column of ambulances transporting wounded to the field hospital from first-aid stations to be treated by him with the help of his five medics. The promised nurses had not yet arrived. Those wounded that required long hospitalizations or extremely specialized surgeries were transported to a large hospital in Smolensk.

At the hospital, as Vladimir walked away from the truck with Misha and Igor by his side, Lieutenant Sergey Ivanov, ran up to him.

"Volodya, Volodya, I need to talk to you. It's very important."

Victor Moss

Vladimir instantly read his friend's concerned face. Sergey's brows were drawn together in a troubled expression, his mouth tight and grim.

"What is it Sergey?" Vladimir asked spacing the words evenly, knowing that Sergey's answer would be unpleasant.

"You didn't see Popov yet, did you?" Sergey asked with a thread of warning in his voice.

"No, what have you heard?" Vladimir asked nervously, sensing that it appeared he was deeply in trouble with Popov. Sergey's demeanor suggested that something was terribly wrong. *It might not be as bad as he will make it out to be. Sergey tends to panic. He is a pessimist, always thinking gloom and doom. Hopefully, this is another exaggeration of misfortune to come that I have often heard from Sergey.*

"Popov is on a rampage, yelling and screaming all day long."

"He always yells and screams," Vladimir said. "That's nothing new."

"Well, he is more agitated than usual. He has been in such a foul mood that most of his orders made no sense. He had asked me if I saw you. When I told him that I hadn't, he called you a son of a bitch and said that when he sees you again, he will personally deal with you."

"Now, simmer down, Sergey," Vladimir said in an attempt to calm him, yet noticing a slight tremor in his own voice. "I am sure that I will be all right. Don't worry so much. You always worry about things that never materialize. You know Popov. I am sure his bark is worse that his bite."

"Oh, no, he has plenty of bite. Just a few hours ago, I saw him shoot a deserter. He didn't even arrest him, but shot him right in the forehead. He was only a kid, not more than 18 years old. A patrol found him hiding in the forest. He begged Popov to spare him, but seething with anger, Popov clenched his teeth and shot him with his revolver. He has a cold heart. I witnessed it before my eyes. He wanted as many as could to see him. He said he wanted to make an example of the poor soldier. Then he came over to me and asked me once again, his nostrils flaring, if I had seen you. Where were you anyway?"

Vladimir swallowed hard trying to manage an answer, but stammered somewhat from uneasiness.

"Look here at these sacks of vital medicines we were able to find," Vladimir said as he opened one of the sacks. "The wounded needed something now, not ten days from now."

"So where did you get these?" asked Sergey.

"We walked over to a village not far from here and found them in the cellar of a burned clinic. We were extremely lucky."

"Yeah, if it wasn't for us, we would not have any medicines for our patients," Igor said. "We took a chance and endangered our lives for the good of the wounded."

"Misha and Igor, take these sacks into the hospital, put them up on shelves in the pharmacy room. I'll be in shortly."

Beware the Wolves

"I don't know how lucky you were. Didn't you have permission to go out of the camp?"

"No."

"Well, your life is in danger from Popov. You need to run and get away from here. The way he looked, the vengeance I saw in his eyes, he is infuriated with you. You need to get out of here now. Hundreds have run off, what's one more?"

"Thanks for your warning and advice," Vladimir said. "You are a good friend to me. But I did the right thing. I knew I took a chance, but I had to do it. With any luck, if I avoid Popov today, he will cool off by tomorrow. He may even forget about it. I have no choice but to continue to treat. Sergey, thanks for your concern, but I need to go and tend to my patients. I'll be all right."

With a brave façade for his friend's benefit not withstanding, Vladimir's insides were tied in knots. He developed a tension headache. He gently squeezed the picture of Slava in his left shirt pocket. He cherished the photograph of his wife. She gave it to him the morning of his departure into the Army. On the back she wrote: "In memory of our first parting." He promised her that he would always carry it close to his heart. Just touching the picture now gave him consolation.

As he entered the ward, the wounded cheered and whistled. They called Vladimir a hero. His patients praised him for his efforts, considerably lifting Vladimir's spirits. *Word spreads fast around here,* he thought. The same reception was given him in every room that he entered.

Vladimir's smile grew wider as the praises and compliments continued. Popov escaped his mind. Instead, the thought of food became a priority as Vladimir realized that he was famished. *The rounds with the patients took longer than I thought and now it's probably too late for supper.* The food each day was mostly the same. Rations included shchi, a type of cabbage soup, and kasha, a mush made of boiled buckwheat. There was always tea or coffee, salt and bread. At times there was macaroni, salted fish and meat.

Vladimir went to the hospital kitchen only to find it deserted. The stove fires were out and the pots were empty. Food supplies were padlocked in cabinets. He remembered that all he had to eat for the day was a piece of bread with buttermilk in the morning and a pickle in that cellar. It was late. He was not only exhausted from the journey for medications, but also drained from the worry over Popov, fueled by the conversation with Sergey. He supposed that he could walk over to the officers' mess, but then he may run into Popov. *I'm starved, but on the other hand, I can wait until morning. Right now, I need a bed even more.*

He started back to his cot in the hospital when he saw Petya, the cook. Petya was staggering slightly toward him on his way back to the kitchen.

"Hey, Comrade Captain doctor, I heard what you did. That was absolutely remarkable," Petya said, slurring his words. "You should be given a medal. The whole camp is talking about it."

The words of encouragement gladdened Vladimir, even though they came from a drunk. For some reason, the term "comrade" grated on his nerves. He did not like it when he was called "comrade captain," as was the custom to refer to officers. But it was the custom and he accepted it. He did, however, refrain from using the term himself.

"Thanks for the kind words. As a doctor, I felt I had to do it. But Petya, can you do me a favor? I am very hungry. Can you get me anything to eat?"

"Sure, Comrade Captain, anything for you. I have some salami and bread stored in one of the locked cabinets. I'll get them for you. But don't tell anybody about it. If they knew I had some of this sausage, my clean kitchen would be ransacked."

Vladimir devoured everything that Petya gave him. Petya also offered him some vodka from his bottle to wash it down. Vladimir was not a drinker, but he did not want to disappoint him. Petya, like most drunks, never wanted to drink alone. He took a couple of sips from Petya's bottle and thanked him. As he was about to leave, Petya cautioned him, "Be careful Comrade Captain. I hear you are in trouble with the Comrade Colonel."

The warning from Petya was unwelcome. Vladimir had a brief respite with the praise of his patients and staff, but now Petya's remark brought his anxiety to the forefront again. He walked back to his room, shoulders slouching as though he carried the weight of the world. Sleep came instantly once he touched the mattress. However, his rest was short-lived. Popov seeped into his mind and suddenly he found himself wide-awake. He began to toss and turn, becoming increasingly uneasy. His fate was uncertain. He imagined the embarrassing arrest. *What would Slava think if she only knew? Would she have approved of what I did? She certainly would not have let me go. She is a person who pleases and avoids conflict, if possible. And she would have never disobeyed an order from her superior. If only I hadn't. But then the look on the faces of the injured made it all worthwhile. No, I would do it again. But why would they arrest me? They need doctors. This is just the beginning of the war and already the number of wounded is staggering. But then, what if they decide to send me to a labor camp in Siberia? What if they put me in front of a firing squad? Surely Popov will not want to shoot me himself just as he did with that deserter? But then Popov is crazy, who knows what he will do?*

"Captain, wake up." Tanya knocked softly on the door. Tanya was the only female medic under Vladimir's command. She was 23 years old, and well educated as a Feldsher (physician's assistant). She had a pleasant oval face, brilliant blue eyes and blond hair with an escaping curl that fell over her forehead. She looked rather delicate, although Vladimir was once amazed to see her carry an injured soldier on her back and shoulders. She was a flirt. Vladimir enjoyed the attention, but avoided giving her any encouragement. Although, he did notice that she liked to waggle her tail as she walked.

"I'm awake. I couldn't sleep. What is it?" Vladimir asked while his eyes burned from lack of sleep.

"We received another truck and a wagon of injured. I did what I could, but several need your help right away," Tanya answered speaking through the closed door.

Vladimir jumped out of bed, met her by the door and together they walked down the hall. His wristwatch showed 2:05 a.m. *It's going to be a long night*, he thought.

"Stepan and I triaged the wounded. The most severe cases are in ward 4," she explained.

Vladimir was comfortable with her assessment of injuries for triage. She was a very competent medic who should have been assigned to work as a physician's assistant, but for a bureaucratic mistake was delegated to perform duties of a medic.

The wounded required many hours of work. Several surgeries had to be performed, mostly the removal of shrapnel, repair of compound fractures and eye injuries. Tanya and Stepan, another medic, assisted Vladimir. At 6:35 a.m., Vladimir was in severe need of sleep. He gave orders, though exhausted and dreaming of his cot, to release those sufficiently recovered, back to the front. He finally returned to his room and collapsed into the cot.

A loud knock came at 8:00 a.m. Startled out of deep sleep by the knock at his door, he mumbled, "Yes, who is it?"

"Comrade Colonel Popov orders you to appear before him immediately. You are to come with us."

He felt his body slump in despair with a shiver of panic. *Oh my God! The bastard did not forget! I'm in deep trouble now.* Two soldiers with rifles slung over their shoulders stood at the door as he opened it. He recognized one of the men.

"You were my patient. How is your leg?" Vladimir asked trying to calm his nerves.

"Thank you, it is fine. Sorry I have to do this, but you know, orders are orders," replied the soldier.

Vladimir nodded and walked down the hallway accompanied on each side by a soldier. Hospital staff and ambulating patients gathered at the entrance to see Vladimir off. Tanya ran up to him. Tears streamed down her cheeks. She grabbed Vladimir, tightly hugged him and kissed him on his cheek. Not saying a word, she began to sob as the guards escorted Vladimir out the door. Popov's dark gray 1937 Moskvich automobile waited for Vladimir. At that instance Vladimir thought of his father. His father was a hero. He was brave. Vladimir also remembered his grandfather's words: "Never be afraid." So with those thoughts he straightened his shoulders, held his head high, put on his sunglasses and entered the car.

Popov waited at the gate. A large brick house with beautiful gardens was his headquarters. A wrought-iron fence with an ornate iron gate surrounded the house. *I can't believe it, he's outside waiting for me,* Vladimir thought to himself. *How angry can he possibly be with me? Can't he even wait for me inside?*

"You bastard, you son of a bitch, how dare you disobey my direct order not to leave this camp."

Vladimir never saw such fury in a human being before. Popov's face was twisted and red with rage. His hands shook as he screamed at Vladimir. He shoved his face just inches from Vladimir's. Popov was a volcano on the verge of eruption. At that moment as Vladimir looked at Popov's eyes, he realized he had seen similar eyes before. They were those of the wolf peering at him in the forest.

"I will not stand it, you bastard, having one of my officers disobey me. I take it personally. Do you understand, you scoundrel? I've shot men for lesser infractions than the one you committed. Do you understand me? You son of a bitch, I'll make an example out of you. I'll shoot you right here and now so that everyone will know not to disobey my orders."

At that instant, Popov unsnapped his holster and pulled out his black revolver. Vladimir's breath ceased and blood gushed to his head. A chill swept through his body. Vladimir's eyes were fixated on Popov's. Popov eyed Vladimir with cold triumph. An instant later, Vladimir felt hard steel against his temple. Blood pounded in his head even stronger and caused a roar in his ears. Vladimir felt weak kneed and faint. He began reciting the prayers his grandmother taught him. At the same time, visions of Slava, his mother and his grandfather appeared. Then Vladimir heard a click. Popov pulled back the hammer of the revolver. *Oh my God! Dear Blessed Mother, help me in this moment of death.*

At that moment they heard the sound of a plane approaching their position. Popov lowered the gun as he turned his head to look up in the sky. The sun from the east was bright, disguising the aircraft to a silhouette. Holding the revolver, still cocked in his right hand, Popov put his left hand on his forehead and squinted his eyes to get a look at the plane.

"Damn, I can't see if that's ours or not."

Vladimir resumed his breathing. His breath was labored and his chest heaved. He could not take a full breath. His head spun out of control. Yet, for some unknown reason, he took off his sunglasses. *I need to give them to Popov.*

"Here, Colonel Popov," Vladimir blurted out. "Take these glasses, I will no longer have a need for them."

Stunned, Popov took the sunglasses, put them on his face and gazed quickly at the plane as it flew overhead.

"Oh good, that was ours. We would have been in a hell of a fix if it wasn't."

Popov turned to Vladimir and lifted the revolver toward him. Vladimir closed his eyes, anticipating the end. *Be strong, be strong,* he told himself. An eternity later, although only a minute passed, Vladimir heard the release of the hammer. He opened his eyes and saw Popov put away the weapon.

Oh my God! He didn't do it. He didn't shoot me!

The two men stared at each other. Vladimir saw the tension in Popov's face soften.

"The devil take you. Hell, here are your sunglasses. You've escaped the bullet this time. Go back to work."

Popov quickly walked through the gate and up the walk to his office. Vladimir thought he heard a few cheers from the spectators. Vladimir's head still twirled and his head and chest ached. A river of blood continued to flow through his ears. He could taste the bile in his mouth. He stumbled back and flopped down on a large stone. He grabbed his head with his hands and sat slumped over for several minutes, feeling as though he would vomit. After his breathing became normal, although his body was tied in knots and still shaken, Vladimir stood up and started his long walk back to the field hospital. *I'm alive! I'm alive! Dear God, I'm alive. Slavochka, I'm alive!*

CHAPTER 4

The monster with its outstretched tentacles was at the door of Smolensk, ready to envelope the city. The defenders, who fought with great tenacity and valor in their attempts to stop the invasion, up to now, were chewed to shreds. The Germans called their efforts "savage determination" and they were taken by surprise at the Soviet resistance. Over time, it was their desperate, heroic and crude efforts to defend the Motherland that gradually eroded the German war machine. But, on this day, the enemy basked in the knowledge of their irresistible power and with smug delight they had conquered the territory up to and surrounding Smolensk. Their goal was to surround the city and with those tentacles, completely encircle the Red Army and obliterate it. Marshall Semyon Timoshenko, commander of the central front, knew he could not stop the enemy at Smolensk, but he could slow it down, giving the defenders of Moscow additional time to prepare for the invasion.

The Stukas swarmed without warning. The planes, giant birds of prey, swooped down on their victims. They dropped their deadly payloads onto soldiers and civilians without discrimination. It was not just the front lines that suffered from the onslaught, but also the City of Smolensk. The planes were used to soften up the defenders for the attack, followed by the artillery barrage, the Panzers and then the infantry. Smolensk was attacked on July 10, 1941, just eighteen days into the war. The defenders were not prepared for the encirclement. The number of dead and wounded was staggering.

Vladimir glanced at his watch. It was the morning of July 12, 1941, and the time was 4:00 o'clock. *How many hours has it been since I had any sleep?* He lost track of the hours since he slept. *It must be at least forty hours.* It started with the sleepless night before he was summoned to see Colonel Popov. Since then, the hectic pace with a never-ending stream of wounded had tired Vladimir to the point of exhaustion. His eyes burned. As he splashed water on his face and glanced into the mirror, the reflection stared back at him with eyes hollowed out with fatigue and red rimmed. *I need to see one more critically wounded patient, and then perhaps I can sleep.*

The patient took longer than he thought. By 6:15 a.m. Vladimir felt senseless. He could no longer concentrate.

"Misha, I can't do any more for my patients unless I get some sleep. I'll be in my room. Don't come and get me for at least a few hours unless it's more than urgent. You should get some sleep yourself. We can do no good unless we get some rest."

Beware the Wolves

"I know I need to go, but I'm waiting for Igor to relieve me," Misha said. "He should have been here an hour ago. Actually, he went to get some breakfast. Thanks, by the way, for asking Petya to keep the kasha on all day for both the wounded and for us. But did you hear? Petya says that his supply of food is running out. Maybe you should get down there before it's gone."

"Sleep is more important than food right now," Vladimir said with a wide yawn. "Let's hope that Igor returns soon. You need to lie down. But come back in a couple of hours. Where is Tanya, Boris or Stepan?"

"Comrade Captain, except for Igor, we are all here. Although I don't know how long we will last. The wounded come in as fast as the carts can bring them. As soon as they unload, they head back to the trenches. Even the horses are tired and dragging. Have you heard that an artillery shell hit our only medical truck and it was destroyed full with our wounded? There're all dead. We need some help here. The wounded are stacked on bunks, lying on the floor, and even in the halls. We can't keep up with even changing their blood soaked bandages. No one is around to wipe up the blood from the floor. Sorry, Comrade Captain, I am just rambling, but we can't go on like this."

"Misha, calm down. I'll call Popov as soon as I rest up and see if we can get some help. Right now, I have to go sleep."

Vladimir's room was a supply closet in the small factory hospital that, before the war, was used by the factory workers and their families. It was hurriedly taken over by the military for its wounded. He collapsed into his cot, but was too tired to fall asleep right away. He was agitated and strung out. As was his habit, he thought of Slava. Thinking of her was at least something pleasant in the grim surroundings of misery and pain. Certainly the war, the injured, the long hours were events he had to push out of his mind, at least for awhile, to keep his sanity. His thoughts about Slava, or Slavochka, as he liked to call her, were the escape that his mind needed. He took her picture from his breast pocket, looked at it for a few minutes and started to wonder if she was safe or whether she was still in Vitebsk. At this point, his eyes closed and he fell soundly asleep.

◆ ◆ ◆ ◆

The explosion was fierce. Plaster from the ceiling fell on Vladimir as he slept. His cot shaken, Vladimir jumped out of bed. He was groggy from the sudden awakening and staggered to the door. Tanya came running up to his room, careful not to step on the injured lying on the floor in the hall, and cried out, "Are you all right?"

"Yes, were we hit?" asked Vladimir.

"No, but the building next door was hit and apparently the concussion from the bombs damaged our building. Some of the windows on the south side were blown out. Do you hear the planes coming back?" Tanya asked in a panicked tone.

27

Victor Moss

"I hear the planes, but what about the patients in those rooms?"

"Igor and Stepan are moving them out of those rooms now. Come on, hurry, let's head for the basement," pleaded Tanya. She grabbed Vladimir's hand and began to pull him toward the basement.

"Wait, we can't leave these patients like this," Vladimir said. At that moment a bomb whistle came toward them followed by a deafening explosion. The building shook, plaster fell from the ceiling and walls. Pieces of glass showered on them.

"Come on, we have no choice," screamed Tanya. "We can't save all the patients. We have to save ourselves. What good are we to them if we are dead? Come now! The next bomb may hit this building."

"You go ahead. I'll be down soon. I need to see what can be done. Misha, Igor, Stepan," Vladimir yelled out. But no one answered. Vladimir tried to get away from Tanya's firm grip and run down the hall, but Tanya would not let go. She grasped his hand even more firmly and pulled with both hands. "Can't you hear the planes coming again? Let's go downstairs now! There is nothing you can do!"

Blasts of artillery shells became prominent as gun batteries opened a furious barrage on the City.

"All right, all right. Let's go," said Vladimir, "I just want to make sure all that are able get to shelter."

At that moment another explosion shook the hospital. More plaster fell to the floor. Tanya again pulled on Vladimir. Vladimir started to order her to let go, but then decided that perhaps she was right. He would be of no use if he were dead.

As they approached the basement steps, he was surprised and glad to see how many of the wounded scurried for shelter. The basement was full of patients and staff, including his medics. In the corner, he found room to sit and wait for the bombing to stop. Tanya huddled next to him. *She is sitting too close to me,* he thought fleetingly. She grabbed his hand and squeezed it. Vladimir enjoyed the occasional attention and the flirtations from Tanya, especially in the dreary hospital. *She is going too far.* He pulled his hand away and moved away from her as much as he could without pressing against a soldier on the other side of him. *I need to have a talk with Tanya,* he thought.

Tanya patted the hand that Vladimir pulled away and pointed to his gold wedding band. "Tell me about your wife?" she asked. At that moment, there was another bomb blast. The building shook and the lights went out. They sat in darkness. The cascade of bombs became less intense, and the bursts appeared further away, closer to the center of Smolensk.

"Come on, tell me about your wife. What's her name?"

"Her name is Vladislava Szpakowska. She is a medical student at the Vitebsk Medical Institute," Vladimir answered.

"How did you meet?"

"I was in my last year of medical school, already interning at a clinic. She was in the second year of medical school. Vladislava, or Slava as I call her, was sick at home for a few days and needed a note from a physician excusing her from school. I went to her house and it was love at first sight," Vladimir answered.

Tanya fell silent and moved a little further from Vladimir. Vladimir sat in silence waiting for the shelling in the distance to cease. Thoughts of the first meeting with Slava lingered in his mind. The day he was sent to visit with her at 107 Bebel Street was a most glorious day. He took the streetcar to the railroad station and then walked about 3 kilometers. *Quite a nice system for the patients, where the doctor was required to make house calls,* he thought. *There are probably no doctors now left in Vitebsk to make those calls.*

As Vladimir first approached the seven steps to Slava's house, he was amazed at how beautiful the house and the surrounding orchard looked. The stained-glass windows on an enclosed veranda, wrapping around the side of the house, impressed him. The big house sat at the crest of a valley where vegetable and flower gardens and fruit trees flowed gently down the slope of the valley. A stream meandered through the trees at the bottom of the valley, then more fruit trees ascended the rather steep grade to the crest on the other side. Two large barns stood back of the house.

After he rang the bell, a heavy-set lady in her late fifties and with graying hair pulled back in a bun opened the door. She introduced herself as Suzanna Szpakowska, and asked, "Are you the doctor from the clinic? My daughter, Vladislava, is ill. Please come in."

The room looked comfortable. A large green overstuffed sofa with a matching chair and two gold colored side chairs were placed on a green and gold Persian carpet. An upright piano stood gracefully against a wallpapered wall. On the opposite side of the room a gramophone was positioned between a standing radio and a large bookcase overflowing with books. Past the sofa was a large red mahogany dining room table surrounded by eight intricately carved chairs and a matching buffet. Curtains hung over the window portion of the door leading into the kitchen. Vladimir was amazed at the beautifully ornate chandelier over the dining table. He had never seen one quite like it. A large icon of Jesus hung on the wall in the living room while the dining room contained an icon of the Blessed Virgin Mary.

"I see you are looking at our Catholic icon," Mrs. Szpakowska said. "That is the icon of the Virgin Mary of Chestgohov in Poland. I always pray to her whenever any of my children are ill. Slava is in her room. This way, please."

The bedroom was small with a double bed in one corner of the room. On the opposite wall from the window hung a colorful Persian carpet. A desk loaded with books and papers sat underneath the carpet. A highly polished wardrobe was located next to the door.

A young woman sat up in bed. She gave Vladimir a shy little smile. Her short brown hair surrounded a sweet face. She had a slightly patrician nose and looked as delicate as a flower with those graceful wrists and fingers. He could see the intelligence behind her fever-clouded, beautiful hazel eyes.

"I'm Vladimir Moskalkov from the clinic. I understand that you need an excuse for school?"

"Yes, please. I ordinarily don't miss school, but I haven't been able to get out of bed for the last two days because of fever. Must be the flu that's been going around."

She was sick, yet her voice had a bright ringing tone. Her mouth widened in an infectious smile. Vladimir felt tongue-tied and awkward. Being suddenly spellbound, he realized that he had been staring at her for several seconds. He finally thought to ask her about her condition.

"It started last Sunday with a sore throat. Then the coughing began with a running nose and the fever. My mom took a measurement and said it was 40 degrees Celsius. She has been giving me aspirin. I feel better now. I think my fever is gone. I still have a stuffed nose and my cough is horrible."

Vladimir took her temperature. It was 37 degrees celcius. He measured her blood pressure. It was 110 over 70. He looked in her throat and then looked in her ears. He felt her throat for swollen glands. He took her pulse. It was 60.

"Your blood pressure is excellent and your throat is still a little red. I need to listen to your heart and lungs. Is that all right?"

He listened to her lungs, asked her to cough, and found they were clear. He listened to her heartbeat. *Funny thing,* he thought, m*y heart at this moment is beating faster than the patient's.*

"You do have a nasty cough," Vladimir said after Slava finished a series of coughs. "You have a slight fever and I suggest that you continue with the aspirin. I will prescribe some cough syrup for you. As a matter of fact, I'll bring you some tomorrow when I come to see you."

Vladimir did not know what possessed him to blurt out that he would be back. *She certainly will be all right in a day or two. I don't need to come back. But I want to.*

"Oh, it's all right, doctor. You don't need to come back. I may even be able to go to school tomorrow."

"Listen to him Slavochka, if he feels that he should come back, then let him," said Mrs. Szpakowsa who remained in the room throughout the examination.

"No, no, I would like to come back, just to make sure you are all right and have no lingering throat infection. I don't like your cough. We have to watch out for bronchitis. I think you should stay home at least one more day. I'll be back sometime tomorrow."

"Really, I do not want to burden you," Slava responded. "You must have so many patients to see. All I need is that slip of paper excusing me from classes due to illness."

"No problem at all. It is not a burden, but something I need to do. I'll give you the excuse later."

"I have some special tea from India, would you like some?" Mrs. Szpakowska asked. "It will only take me a few minutes to prepare."

"Thank you so much, but I need to return to work as soon as possible."

♦ ♦ ♦ ♦

The next day, her smile was warm and her eyes sparkled as Slava opened the door for Vladimir. He was so anxious to see her again that he ran all the way with his medical bag in hand from the streetcar to her house. She wore a white blouse with black polka dots and a black skirt with a narrow red belt hugging her trim waist. She appeared even more delicate and ethereal than he remembered the day before. Her exotic and striking face overwhelmed Vladimir. He felt a flush staining his cheeks and perspiration in his armpits.

"Please come in. As you can see I am doing so much better, except for the cough. We have tea ready. Are you hungry? My mother made some delicious piroshki, (a meat-filled pastry)." She laughed gently after she spoke. Her laugh sounded of sheer joy, a teasing laughter that infatuated Vladimir.

"Yes, please, that sounds wonderful. You do look much better. It's amazing what one day can do. As promised, I brought you some cough medicine. It should help. Let me look at your throat. Also I'd like to listen to your lungs."

Vladimir looked in Slava's throat with his tongue depressor. He also took out his stethoscope and listened to her lungs, first from the back and then from the chest. He knew that he was breathing heavily. He hoped that Slava did not notice.

"Your throat is perfect and your lungs are clear," Vladimir said. And then trying to sound official, he said, "You will be able to go to school tomorrow. By the way what are you studying?"

"I'm studying medicine. I'm in my second year at the Medical Institute."

"You are in your second year? I would have thought you are much younger. How old are you?"

Slava could not control her burst of laughter and responded in amusement, "I have just turned eighteen last week, on October 31st. I was born in 1921. I was lucky enough to test out of two years of school. I finished a ten-year gymnasium in eight years. I laughed because everyone thinks I am younger than I am."

Vladimir enjoyed her company. Her mother served them tea with the piroshki, then returned to the kitchen leaving them alone in the dining room. Vladimir did not want to leave, but after glancing at his watch, he knew that he had already spent too much time with Slava.

"I must go. I have more patients to see. It really was a pleasure meeting you."

"Thank you very much for coming to see me again," Slava said. "I'll go to school tomorrow. Could I have my slip for school now?"

"No, actually, you have to come by the clinic in the morning and pick it up. I'll be there from 7:00 o'clock."

Victor Moss

Vladimir felt a little guilty for asking her to come in. He could have given her the excuse right then, but he wanted to see her again. *The clinic is on the way to the medical school, and it would not put her out of the way that much,* he reasoned.

He tossed and turned all night as the thoughts of Slava danced in his head. He had calculated that he was only six years older than she and reasoned that was a good age difference. He further decided that he would ask her on a date when she came in. The next morning, Vladimir dressed in his best suit and favorite tie. He took pains to shave extra well and carefully combed his hair to look as neat as possible.

At the clinic he felt anxious and nervous. He kept watching the clock. *Where is she?* he wondered. Every time someone walked in, he glanced at the door. Finally at *8:46,* Slava walked in. Vladimir felt joy and yet apprehension. *What if she declines my invitation?*

As he walked up to Slava, her smile and a quick laughter settled his nerves.

"Please come into the examining room with me," he said.

"Oh, do you want to examine me again?" she asked.

Yes, over and over, Vladimir thought to himself, but said, "No, no, I see you are doing well. I have your excuse for school, but I would like to talk to you in private."

She looked radiant, her eyes were compelling and she continued to appear in perpetual merriment.

"Vladislava, there is an excellent ballet at the City Theater. You might have read about it. It's the *Coppelia.* I have two tickets for the performance this Saturday night. Would you like to go with me?"

Tanya pulled on Vladimir's sleeve interrupting his reminiscence of his first meetings with Slava. "Wake up, Captain, the bombing has stopped. Some of the people have already begun to go upstairs,"

"Oh, I wasn't sleeping, I just had my eyes closed," Vladimir answered. "But a few more minutes and I would probably have fallen asleep."

As they stood in line, moving slowly up to the steps leading out of the basement, Tanya asked Vladimir, "Do you think your wife is still alive? I mean, do you think she is still in Vitebsk? My family lives in Kaluga. I received a letter from them last week that they are being evacuated to the Ural Mountains, probably to Chelyabinsk. Do you think your wife was evacuated to the Urals? Have you heard from her at all?"

"No I have not heard from her. I don't know if any of my letters reach her. For all I know, the Germans may occupy Vitebsk. I pray she is fine. She is resourceful and will do whatever she needs to survive."

"Realistically, do you think you will ever see her again," Tanya asked.

Vladimir did not answer. He felt overwhelmed with sadness.

CHAPTER 5

Slava sat in the organic chemistry class. At the blackboard, the professor lectured on cycloalkenes. Vladimir had asked her on a date earlier that morning of November 23, 1939 and her mind was elsewhere. She played out the scene—how he looked, the exact words he used and the way he looked at her. Instead of taking notes, she found herself doodling the word "Volodya" in the margin of her paper.

Oleg and Richard, Slava's friends, studied at the same table in the chemistry laboratory. The large room contained several tables and chairs. In the back of the room were counters overflowing with Bunsen burners, test tubes, vials, bottles, petri dishes, titration tubes, and flasks containing liquids of various colors. A table of elements and blackboards with chemical formulas surrounded the room. On the front blackboard the professor had drawn a pentagon representing an organic ring with hydrogen and oxygen molecules in various positions around the pentagon.

"Cycloalkenes and cycloalkynes are normally prepared from cycloalkanes by ordinary alkene-forming reactions, such as hydration, and dehydrohalogenation," the professor droned on and on.

Slava had encountered the same problem of lack of concentration in her earlier classes, histology and physiology. *I can hardly wait to tell Valentina about the invitation to see Coppelia with a handsome young doctor. She'll be surprised.* Her best friend, Valentina, was also a medical student. Growing up together, they had been friends since childhood. She was one year older, yet she was in the first year of medical school. Slava was ecstatic when she found out that Valentina was accepted to the Vitebsk Medical Institute. Acceptance to the school was extremely competitive as the list of applicants was long. Excellent grades and high marks on the entrance examination determined whether the applicant became a student. The interview process was grueling. But once accepted and the student continued to receive good grades, the Government paid a stipend of 150 rubles per month for the entire five years of medical school.

The future looked bright for Slava. After all, she was the youngest student at the medical school. She liked school and liked medicine and imagined that some day she would become a famous physician. She had decided that once she obtained her degree, she would keep her maiden name as her professional name, if she ever married.

Victor Moss

"I will now pass out the results of the examination you took last week on alkyl halide chemistry," Professor Szpakowski said. "Generally, the class did well on the exam. One of you did exceptionally well."

Everyone, except Slava received the result of the examination. After dismissal of the class she approached her teacher and asked, "Professor, I did not receive my examination. You must have forgotten to give it to me."

"No, Vladislava, I did not forget. I purposely kept it from you so that you would come up after class. Here it is."

Slava looked at her paper and saw the grade of 5+++ (5=A).

"Wow, thank you so much for the grade," Slava said.

"You did remarkably well on this essay examination. Your understanding of the reaction of a halogen with an alkane was superb. You are the only one who discussed the effect that heat leads to the formation of haloalkane. Now, I want you to go and tell your friends your grade. They are probably waiting for you in the hall. I want you to tell them what I gave you."

Slava was flushed with joy at the terrific grade. As she walked out of the room she saw that the professor was right. Some of the students from class waited for her outside the door.

"Did you get your examination back?" Asked Oleg.

"Yes, I did."

"Are you the one that did exceptionally well?" Richard asked.

Slava suddenly felt embarrassed. *Why did the professor place me in such an awkward position? That's mean. It would only upset them and make them resent me. What is he up to?*

"Well, what did you get?" Oleg asked again.

"Oh, ahh, I did all right," Slava said. "Let's get some lunch, I'll see you this afternoon."

"You are the one," Richard said. "I knew it. So what did you get?"

"Why do you think that? Just because I'm hungry and want to go to lunch?"

Slava felt boxed in. The students were persistent. *I have to get them off my back and just give them a grade.*

"I received an A- and am very pleased to have done so well. Now can I go to eat?"

At that moment, Professor Szpakowski, who stood by the door, opened it wider. He glared at Slava and said, "I can't believe you didn't tell them your true grade. What are you afraid of? You don't want to hurt their feelings?" Looking at the other students, he continued, "I gave her an excellent with three pluses. You should know that you can do it too if you try. I expect that from each and every one of you." With that said, he closed the door and went back into his laboratory.

"Well, congratulations," Richard said. "It doesn't hurt to be related to the professor, does it? He's your uncle, cousin, what?"

Beware the Wolves

Richard was teasing, but Slava took it seriously and immediately became defensive. *I can't believe that the professor would place me in this position. What's wrong with him? And these people think I'm related to him.*

"No, he is not a relative. Szpakowski is a very common name in Vitebsk. You know that. As a matter of fact we have a Szpakowski family living three doors down from our house, and we are not related."

"Don't get upset," Richard said. "We are pleased for you. Can I look at your paper to see what you wrote?"

Slava felt a little better after that remark and agreed to show them her exam later.

"Now can I go? I have to meet Valentina at the cafeteria."

The cafeteria was a huge room in the northwest corner of the first floor of the building. All the tables appeared full, even those with standing room. Large posters with slogans hung on all the walls: "All Power to the Soviets," "Peace to the People; Land to the Peasants; Factories and Mills to the Workers," "The Party—Brain, Honor and Conscience of our Epoch;" "Proletariat of all Nations Unite;" "KPCC (Communist Party of the Soviet Union)."

Valentina was nowhere to be found, so Slava sat down at a long table where two chairs at the end were vacated. She was troubled at the notion the students thought that she received a high grade because she was related to the Professor. *Why didn't they ask me whether we are related a long time ago? They just assumed.* She sat there with her nerves on edge. *It's no big deal,* she thought. But then her mother's arrest crept into her mind.

A loud knock on the door in 1937 had startled the family as they prepared to go to bed. Slava's father, Vladislav, saw two men in khaki uniforms as he opened the door. They identified themselves as NKVD agents (People's Comissariat of Internal Affairs).

"We have come to arrest Mrs. Szpakowska," said one of the agents as both of them barged into the room.

"What for?" Vladislav said tremblingly. "What do you mean? Must be some mistake."

"We don't know, all we know is that we have orders to take her to jail."

"But she is sick with a heart problem and has difficulty walking. She has been in bed for several days. Please leave her alone," her husband pleaded.

"Where is she, in there?"

The door to the bedroom was open. Suzanna had already sat up, baffled at the commotion. The men entered the room. Suzanna pulled a blanket over her nightgown.

"Are you Szpakowska? You must be."

"Yes." Suzanna answered, horrified. Her chest heaved from labored breaths. "What do you want with me?"

"Get dressed. You're under arrest."

Victor Moss

"Why? What did I do? Oh my God. O Hail Mary, full of grace, help me. Oh, Mother of God, there must be some mistake. I did not do anything. What do you want with me? What did I do?"

"Hell if we know. Now come on, let's go. We have our orders."

"Can't I accompany her?" Vladislav said as they began escorting Suzanna out the door. "Can't you see she can barely walk? Her knees hurt."

They allowed him to help her to the car. Slava watched as her parents holding on to each other, limped down the sidewalk. As the men followed her parents, she overheard one say to the other, "I just can't understand what they need with people like this. They're making us arrest all kinds of worthless souls."

After shoving Suzanna into the car, the men drove away. Vladislav stared in the direction of the vehicle for several minutes. Slava joined him in the street. Both sobbed at the thought that they might never see Suzanna again.

Days passed with no word about her mother. For the first four days, Slava and her father made the long trek to the local jail for information. Each time, the authorities refused to give out any information of the arrest, Suzanna's condition or her whereabouts. On the fifth day, they were told very emphatically not to come back and bother them. Slava cried herself to sleep every night. She prayed to her favorite saint, Saint Anthony, for her mother's safe return. She received comfort in her prayers and was pleased that her parents continued to observe Catholic traditions, even though the Communists converted the two Catholic Churches in Vitebsk into museums and banned all religious services and observances.

Her mother's absence overwhelmed both Slava and her father. Neither had any appetite. Slava had wished that her two brothers and three sisters still lived at home. Slava was the youngest in the family. The next youngest was seven years older while the two oldest siblings, the family twins, were seventeen years older than Slava. They had their own families, lived far away in Leningrad, Russia, and could be of no help to calm her nerves. Her father sat around and moped all day. It was unusual to see her father so inactive. Ordinarily, when not working as the chief engineer on the railroad, he was constantly occupied with some activity. His favorite hobby was cross-pollinating plants in his garden and orchard.

Neither Slava nor her father could fathom a reason for Suzanna's arrest. With each day of no news, their concern that they would never see her grew. Their fear was legitimate. Under Stalin's orders, individuals were arrested, and never seen or heard of again. Rumors circulated that those who were not executed were sent off to prison camps in Siberia.

Five days after her mother's arrest there was again a booming knock on the door. Icy fear twisted around Slava's heart.

"We have a doorbell, so why don't they use it, those devils," grumbled her father with his face clouded with uneasiness. "They purposely knock with that authoritarian manner just to scare us to death. It must give them great pleasure."

Beware the Wolves

At the front door stood three serious-looking men, dressed in the same khaki uniforms worn by the arresting agents.

"We are here to search the premises."

"What for?" Vladislav asked. "What are you looking for?"

"Anything subversive," was the reply and with that they searched the bookcase, looked in all the drawers, in cabinets but found nothing. On the way out, one of the agents stopped and stared at the icon of the Mother of Chestohov. Slava's heart stopped. Her hands sweated. Her temples throbbed.

"You know that you should not have these icons. We could arrest you all for displaying religious material in your house," said one of the agents with an appearance of one who demanded instant obedience.

He looked carefully at Slava. He certainly must have seen the fright in her eyes. Slava could sense that he was deciding whether to arrest her and her father. Dread knotted inside her.

"Take that down," said the man and with that he and the other two walked out of the door.

"I am not taking the icons down," Vladislav said to Slava defiantly. "Your mother would never hear of it."

"But, Papa, we should do it," Slava pleaded. "We should remove the icons. It is too dangerous to leave them up. God will understand. He must know what we are going through. Next time if they return to search our house and see them, they will arrest us. The next one may not be as nice."

Her father would not budge on this issue.

"As good Catholics we will keep the icons up. We'll just have to chance it."

◆ ◆ ◆ ◆

More than a week later, Slava sat on the veranda, working on a calculus problem. She lifted her head and could not believe her eyes. Her mother was hobbling up Bebel street. Her limp was worse. She looked old and had lost much weight. Slava ran down the steps and down the block to greet her.

"Mama! Mama! Mama! We thought we'd never see you again," screamed Slava as she hugged and kissed her mother. "Here, let me help you home. Tell me what happened to you?"

"Shush. Not here. I am not supposed to tell anyone about my experience. They might be watching us right now," Suzanna whispered. "Oh, my little darling, if you only knew what I went through."

Slava could see how tired and worn out her mother looked. She was breathing heavily, gasping at every breath. She never had seen her mother in such shape. There was an unpleasant, pungent odor to her and her dress was wrinkled and dirty. Slava embraced her mother and kissed her once again.

"Let me help you, here, hold on to me. When we get home, we'll fix something to eat. You must be famished?"

37

Victor Moss

"Is your father home? He'll need to get the portable bathtub out of the barn and bring it into the kitchen right away. I can't stand myself the way I feel and must look. While he is doing that, you'll need to start boiling the water for the bath. Oh a bath sounds so wonderful."

While Suzanna cleaned up, Slava burned with curiosity about her mother's arrest. When the three sat down in the kitchen to eat, Slava asked her mother, "Mama, we are by ourselves right now. Can't you tell us what happened?"

Suzanna, looked around as though she expected someone to overhear.

"Now remember," she whispered. "They told me not to talk about my arrest and what I witnessed with anyone. So, don't you dare tell anyone what I went through." She looked frightened and yet Slava could tell she badly wanted to tell her story.

"They locked me up in this large, dingy, smelly room with both men and women. It was very noisy. There were few bunks along the walls. They had no mattresses, only wooden slats, and those were taken. There were also a few wooden chairs, but they were always occupied. No one offered an old lady like me a chair. I had to sit or lay on the cold floor. They did give me a blanket though. At first I didn't want to touch it. It was filthy and probably full of lice. Later, after I started to freeze, I took that blanket."

"Did it have lice? Slava asked.

"No, I was lucky. But don't interrupt. I have a lot to tell you. Now where was I? Oh yes, for a toilet, there was a large bucket in the center of the room that everyone had to use. Everyone, both men and women used it. It was awful; it was so grimy and smelly. But, you know, after a few days you get used to the smell."

"How many people were in the room?" Slava interrupted again.

"I'll get to that. For ventilation, there were two small windows that opened. Of course those windows had bars on them. Paint was peeling off the walls, and rats scurried about. I was afraid to sleep. I felt the rats would eat on me."

"Oh, my God!" Slava exclaimed. "But, why in heaven's name did they ever arrest you?"

"They thought that one of my daughters married a Pole and moved to Poland to live," Suzanna answered. "They mixed me up with Rosalia Szpakowska who lives four houses down. Can you believe that?"

"You mean that was the crime you were arrested for?" Vladislav asked. "I assume you explained to them their mistake."

"What do you think? Of course I did. I didn't lose my mind all together you know," snapped Suzzana, forgetting to whisper. "Only today, they came into the cell and took me into a little room with a table and four chairs. Behind the table sat some sort of NKVD and a communist party official. Out of the blue, they accused me of being the mother of Eleanor Szpakowska. They charged her as a Polish sympathizer. I told them that my daughters are all here in Byelorussia or in Russia. I told them that they all have higher education,

Beware the Wolves

educated in Vitebsk or Minsk or Leningrad. I told them that I love the Soviet Union, as does my family. Of course, they wanted to hear that. I told them we have a good life here. After all we were the first family to have indoor plumbing and electricity of any house in the area."

"They didn't talk to you before today?" Slava asked.

"No, I sat there rotting away for more than a week before I knew why I was there. Pass me some more ham, would you Vladyslav?" Suzzana asked. She had already finished off what Slava thought was an enormous amount of ham, boiled potatoes and pickles.

"I finally convinced them that I was not the woman they thought. I must have persuaded them that another woman's daughter ran off to Poland."

"Did they ask you if you knew who that other woman would be then?" Vladislav asked.

"Yes, they asked me several times. I knew darn well it was Rosalia, but I did not tell them. That poor woman, may Jesus help her."

"So, how many people were in that cell with you?" Slava asked once again.

"Slavochka, there were forty-two people in the room. You wouldn't believe who I saw there."

"Who did you see?" Vladislav asked.

"I saw Dr. Stalevski and his wife in the cell. I asked him why they had been arrested. He didn't know either. He thinks it's because he received a letter from a former patient who fled to Germany. What a crazy time we live in. Stalin's paranoia will kill off half of the population. The other half will be imprisoned. I had to tell them that we loved the Soviet Union to be released, but with this insanity, how can anyone? Do you remember the time that our son, Isaac, was arrested a few years ago in Leningrad just because he decided to list his nationality as Polish in his passport? He was lucky to have been released. This is total insanity. As they told me I could leave, they asked where I was born. When I told them in Rezitsa, Latvia, they got strange looks on their faces, particularly that communist official. I could tell he was thinking whether to lock me up again or not. If they knew that you, Vladislav, were also born in Latvia, and with both of us being of Polish descent, they probably would have locked all of us up. They would have locked us up, I tell you, even though we immigrated to Byelorussia years ago."

Slava could see how agitated her mother had become. She still appeared tired and haggard. Her face was pale and shadows deepened under her eyes. At that moment, Slava felt sorry for her mother and scared of the system. *To think, all of this happened because of the common name. They better not think that I am related to Professor Szpakowski otherwise every good grade I get, they'll believe it's because my "uncle" gave it to me.*

Suddenly, Slava saw her friend, Valentina and her mind was back in the present. It was unusual for her to dwell on the past. She was generally a happy

39

individual, both as a child and now as a young adult. She took her licks when something unpleasant happened, then moved on. *Today is another day, and tomorrow will be better,* she always told herself.

"Valentina, Valya, over here. I saved a seat for you," Slava called out.

Valentina came with a full tray of food. She had two cabbage rolls, two pieces of dark rye bread with a heaping portion of butter on each piece, two portions of boiled potatoes and two glasses of hot tea.

"You are certainly hungry today, aren't you?" Slava asked.

"It's not all for me," Valentina said, laughing. "I saw that you found some seats in this crowded room and I thought if we both go through the line, we would lose our seats. So I got enough food for both of us. I know you love these cabbage rolls. But then, you'll eat anything. You are not a picky eater like me. By the way, how are you feeling? You look much better."

"Thanks, that's wonderful. I am hungry and I feel great. I have a date this Saturday!"

"A date? Who is he? You were out with the flu almost all week, when were you able to get a date?" Valentina asked.

"He is a doctor, well actually still a student right at this Institute, but in his last year. Oh, he is so charming. He came to see me because I needed a doctor's excuse for school. Came back to see me again at my house, then he told me to come to the clinic where he was interning to get my excuse."

"Really, he made you go to the clinic to get the excuse? That's not the way it is done. He should have given you the excuse at your house during the visit."

"I know. But I really think he likes me and he wanted to see me again. Isn't that romantic?" Slava said excitedly. "That's when he asked me to see *Coppelia* with him this Saturday."

"Well, what is he like?" Valentina asked again.

"He is very charming."

"You already said that. What makes him so charming?"

"I don't know!" Slava said. "It's hard to describe. He is just charming. You know? His lips are curled as if always at the edge of laughter. He is very polite, a little bit shy, I'd say."

"He is not that shy, it seems," Valentina countered. "He's a pretty fast worker, asking you out on a date after he just met you. Tell me more about him. Is he tall or short? Is he good looking?"

"He is average in height, thin and I'd say very good looking. You should see how he dresses. Each time I saw him, he came in a different suit and tie. He even had cufflinks in his shirt. Today, for instance, he wore a double-breasted blue suit with a red tie. Let's see, what else?"

"Well, what color of eyes or hair does he have?" Valentina asked wanting to put all the pieces together.

Slava threw back her head and let out a great peal of laughter. She enjoyed every second of the conversation.

"His eyes are blue just like the sweater you have on, Valya. His eyes are gentle and contemplative. His hair is light brown. I am anxious to see him again, actually. Oh my gosh! Look at the time. We need to get back to class. I'll tell you all about our date on Sunday."

CHAPTER 6

The milk cart pulled by the old mare stood in front of Slava's house. It was Saturday. But this particular Saturday held a touch of magic since tonight was her first date with Vladimir. Slava had just returned from the anatomy laboratory and saw her mother on the porch with Lydia. Lydia and her husband had delivered milk, butter and cheese to the Szpakowski household for as long as Slava could remember. Slava knew the routine well. Lydia hauled a large milk can to the porch while her mother brought out a smaller container. Lydia would ladle out the portion that Suzanna asked. The milk was fresh that day from the three Holstein cows that the couple owned. Lydia's container was heavy, and Slava had always thought it odd that Lydia's husband remained sitting in the cart never helping his wife with the milk can.

"Oh, you're back," Suzanna said. "Good. I always worry when you go to that anatomy laboratory."

"Oh, mom, you always worry about everything. What could happen to me? After all, those bodies are dead. What do you think; they will jump up and grab me? Ha ha."

"Don't be so clever. Anyway, Lydia and I were talking that she doesn't know how much longer she will be able to supply us with milk and other dairy products."

"Yes," Lydia said. "We are afraid that those communists are going to take away our cows and put them on one of their collective farms. And worse yet, we could be arrested for having our own little business. You know what they say. Anyone who sells anything is a speculator and is therefore an enemy of the State. It's not that we are getting rich from selling milk. We, like everyone else are just barely surviving. But if they take our cows away and that little one-half hectare of land, we will have no choice but to go work on one of those collective farms. That is, if they don't arrest us first and send us to Siberia."

"Oh, those devils, those Bolsheviks, may they fry in hell,"

"Mama! Don't say a word more. If anyone hears we will all be arrested. Lydia, they have left you alone all these years and they'll continue to do so. It may not be as bad as you think."

"I think it's our neighbors who are jealous of us and want us destroyed. I saw the NKVD come and talk to them. I saw them pointing and looking towards our house. I thought that they would come right over and arrest us. But, for some reason they didn't. But I am sure that they will come sooner than later. We live with fear everyday of our lives."

Beware the Wolves

"Everyone lives in fear these days," Slava said. "But somehow we survive. Look how long they have allowed you to keep your farm and sell your milk products. If we lived in the Ukraine, you would have lost your property long time ago. It all depends on the individuals in the NKVD. It may very well be that they will leave you alone. It doesn't do you any good to worry about it. The worry will just eat you up."

Slava left her mother and Lydia on the porch and went inside. It was getting late and she had to get ready for the date with Vladimir. As she entered the house she looked around. *How lucky we are that we still have this house,* she thought. *Papa has brought so many nice things from his trips while working on the railroad. The communists have been taking property away, nationalizing it and moving in total strangers to share houses. So far no one in our area had property taken away. Maybe they will continue to leave us alone.*

Her parents had, in fact taken in a tenant for one of the spare rooms to help with the income. He was a nice young man by the name of Alexander who told them that he also worked on the railroad, but was somewhat vague about what he did for the railroad. Slava's father had never seen him there, but thought little about it. Many worked on the rail systems, and had different duties, schedules and routes. *At least my parents were able to pick and choose who lived in their house. Luckily, we are able to receive the rent as opposed to the Government moving people in against our will, or worse, moving us out of our home.* Slava thought to herself.

Slava looked at her watch again, and quickly changed her thoughts to her evening with Vladimir, she started to prepare for the date.

"What time is Vladimir coming, Slavochka?" Suzanna asked.

"He said he will be here at 7:00 o'clock and it's almost 7:00 now. Mama, so what do you think about me going out with him tonight? Are you excited for me?" While talking to her mother, Slava put on her red-shaded lipstick.

"Slavochka, we have been through this before. I told you I liked him from the start. He has class, something you do not see much of these days. I am sure you will have a good time."

"What will Papa think of him? Do you like this new shade of fingernail polish? Oh my gosh! There's the doorbell. He is right on time. Papa! Tell Vladimir I will be right out," Slava yelled out to her father from her bedroom.

Vladislav sat in the parlor reading the government newspaper, *Pravda.* He loved to read and study various subjects. He even learned and taught Esperanza, an international language that was meant to unite the people of the universe. Unfortunately, the new language did not catch on around the world as he had hoped. And now it was banned by the communists. He finally gave up the new language because of fear of arrest and banishment to Siberia.

Vladislav was lean, Sixty-one years old, four years older than Suzanna. He showed his age with his gray mustache and gray hair that was cut short around his bald head. His face was work-hardened, yet he gave the general appearance

Victor Moss

of an intellectual. He heard the door bell, put down the newspaper and round-rimmed glasses and quickly rose to answer the door.

"Come in, welcome. You must be the young doctor I've heard so much about. It's a pleasure to meet you. I'm Slava's father, Vladislav Ivanovich," Slava overheard her father tell Vladimir as she came out of the bedroom into the parlor. She wore black low-heeled shoes with a black woolen dress that had a white collar and cuffs.

"You look absolutely stunning," Vladimir said, as he gave her a smile that sent her pulse racing. As their eyes met she again felt the attraction, and was captivated by his kind blue eyes.

Slava noticed that Vladimir held his left hand behind his back. She immediately knew that he brought something for her.

"What is your favorite flower?" Vladimir asked, still smiling widely.

"Oh, I love roses the best, but then I love all flowers."

"I guessed correctly. I thought that roses would be your favorite and I brought you seven red roses from the flower shop on Zamkovaya Street."

"Oh, thank you so much. The flowers are beautiful." Slava said as she took the flowers and smelled them. "Now that you met both my parents, I'll get my coat and overshoes and then I'll be ready to go."

Slava asked her mother to place the flowers in water and walked back into her bedroom. She pulled out her dark red coat from the wardrobe. The coat was dear to her, as it was a gift from her sister, Maria, who had it sewn especially for Slava's birthday. The maple wardrobe, a handsome piece of furniture, was polished to such an extent that she could see the reflection of her face. The beautiful woolen coat was trimmed with a white rabbit collar and matching fur cuffs. She loved to rub her cheek in the soft fur. Maria also gave her a matching rabbit fur muff, but she decided against wearing it that night. She put on her black overshoes made of heavy felt material that was not only warm, but also waterproof. She threw the coat over her arm and walked back toward Vladimir. Vladimir was explaining to her parents where he lived, yet she could feel his eyes swing to her as she entered the room.

"May I help you with your coat?" Vladimir asked as he turned on his heel and strode toward her. His arm touched her shoulder and lingered there for a second, as he placed the coat across her back. Slava felt the electric shock of that lingering touch on her shoulder. She turned to thank him, glancing at him from beneath her eyelashes. Their eyes met, but only for an instant, for she dropped hers and turned toward the door, her heart beating fast and a blush staining her cheeks.

"We better go," Slava said as she put on her white mink cap. "We have quite a little walk to the streetcar, as you know."

"Actually, I tried to hire a cab. But wouldn't you know it, there were none available at the railroad station. They must be either so busy or all the horses decided to take the evening off since it's so cold," Vladimir said laughingly.

"Oh, that's all right," Slava said. "It is silly for us to ride in a cab. I am so used to walking that strip to the railroad station and catching a streetcar from there that I don't even think about it. The only time we ever hire a cab is when my brothers or sisters visit us here in Vitebsk. We have to get their luggage here somehow."

"They will replace the horse-drawn cabs with motor vehicles soon, I imagine," Vladimir said. "We're making such progress now. Life will be easier, you'll see."

"I know. At least that's what they tell us—that our lives will be better. But I still like the old ways. I think riding in a Hansom cab with its hood down and the clomp, clomp, clomp of hoofs on the street is so romantic."

"I agree. That is why I was hoping to hire one tonight."

◆ ◆ ◆ ◆

The street was crowded with pedestrians. It was, after all, Saturday night and people, especially the young, were out and about. Slava and Vladimir walked up Bebel Street toward the railroad station. There, they could catch a streetcar on Vokzsal'naya Street that would take them onto Zamkovaya Street and then finally onto Lenin's Prospect to the City Theater. They walked in silence, their footsteps crunching on the snow that had fallen the last two days. A gusty wind blew on their backs. Slava pulled up her fur collar to cover her neck.

"It's really cold tonight, isn't it?" Vladimir asked, breaking the silence.

"Yes, it is, but I like cold weather; it gives me more energy. For instance, look how fast we are walking. We will get there in no time at all."

"I really enjoyed meeting your parents, they seem like such nice people," Vladimir said.

"They are good parents, and they can be very funny at times."

"How so?" Vladimir asked.

"Well, for instance, my father had just last month purchased a dozen special hens from someone at the market. They were like no other ones I've ever seen. They were huge, almost the size of a small turkey. They laid the most delicious brown eggs. He was quite proud of them. My mother enjoys canning vegetables, fruit and berry preserves. We have so many fruit trees and berry bushes in our orchard that we can't possibly eat them all. As a matter of fact, my mother goes around the neighborhood and gives away jars of vegetables and fruits to the neighbors.

"There were a few jars that were left in the cellar far too long, so mama decided last Wednesday to feed the preserves to the hens. She spilled out the contents on the ground, saw that the hens pecked at the berries and went inside. A few hours later, she looked out of the window and to her horror, saw the hens lying on their sides, lifeless. She screamed and yelled out. I ran outside with her, all the while she kept screaming that she killed the hens. 'What will your father say? He will have a stroke. He is so proud of these stupid hens."

"You should have seen her, running around the yard in her pink and blue apron, panicked that the hens died. I saw them too. They, indeed, were motionless. 'What story should we make up for your father?' she asked. A few minutes later, my father came home. She reluctantly told him that she must have killed the hens with her berry preserves.

"My father looked distressed and then angry, but did not say a word. He is like that, you know. He is even-tempered. He never raises his voice. I think he only yelled at me once in my life."

"Oh, I can't believe anyone would ever yell at you. What did you do, anyway?" Vladimir asked as both of them started to laugh. Slava could see that Vladimir was interested in her story.

"I was a real brat. I was about seven years old and my mother left to go visit her friend and I didn't want her to go. So I went out in the middle of this street and started to yell to my mother to stay. People started to stare at me, but I kept on screaming. My father came out to the front steps of our house and it was the first and the last time I heard him raise his voice at me."

"Are you serious?" Vladimir asked. "The only time?"

"I know I deserved to be yelled at more often. But that's the way he is."

"So what did your father do about those hens?"

"He rushed to the back, saw them on their sides, shook his head and said, 'I better get the shovel and bury them.'

"As he came back from the barn with a shovel, and my mother stood there feeling guilty, the hens suddenly came to life. First a few, then each and every one of them stood up. And as they tried to walk, they actually staggered. My father laughed, then my mother and I laughed as well."

"What happened to them?" Vladimir asked joining Slava in her laughter.

"They were drunk from the berry preserves." Slava said, still laughing over the incident. "The berries fermented into alcohol."

Slava was pleased that Vladimir was interested in her story. She thought she had a good sense of humor and liked to entertain. After all, she laughed all the time. She liked Vladimir's pleasant laugh. She peeked at him under the brightness of the streetlight, and saw the charming way his upper lip curled when he laughed. *He is especially cute when he laughs,* she thought to herself.

"There sure are many people walking around tonight," Vladimir said. "Where do you think they are going in this cold night?"

"Well, some are going to the cafeteria that we just passed. See those girls walking arm to arm. I bet they are going to one of the three movie theaters. The closest is the First of May Theater by the railroad station. I hear there is a very good movie called the *Foundling* playing at that theater. It's about a child left abandoned on a doorstep."

Beware the Wolves

"Maybe we could go see that movie next Saturday?" Vladimir asked.

"That would be nice." Slava answered immediately.

"Do you go to the movies often?" Vladimir asked.

"My friends, Valya and Galya, and I go occasionally. But I don't have much time. My parents always force me to study. As if medical school wasn't enough, I have German and French lessons. I also attend the music conservatory."

"What do you study at the conservatory?"

"Piano."

"You must be good at the piano then?"

"I try, I've studied piano since I was a little girl. I am very tired of it. Before I entered the conservatory, I had private lessons from a very strict teacher. She would rap me on my knuckles if I made a mistake. She was Madame Schumann, a relative of the composer, Schumann. But then, I'm just rattling on, aren't I? I feel so comfortable talking to you. It is as though I've known you all my life and I can tell you anything. Do you play any instruments?"

"I studied the violin a little. I wasn't very good at it. I do like to sing though. And I actually played in a symphony orchestra, holding a trumpet."

"Wow, I'm impressed, a symphony orchestra. What do you mean, you're not very good? But then, what do you mean, 'holding' a trumpet?"

Vladimir laughed heartily. "I happened to be walking by the theater when the conductor grabbed me from the street and asked if I'd sit in during the concert. All I had to do was hold a trumpet and pretend to play it when the other trumpeters played."

"Why?"

"Evidently, one of the trumpet players couldn't make it, so they needed a live body just to sit and pretend that he was a member of the orchestra."

Both Vladimir and Slava were deep in laughter. Slava slipped her arm into Vladimir's arm. She enjoyed the closeness as they walked in matched steps over the bridge spanning the many railroad tracks that run through Vitebsk. The railroad station was just over the bridge and to the left she could see the streetcar.

Lenin's Prospect was a wide street lined with trees, apartment houses and government buildings. Government stores were located on the first floors of the apartment buildings. As they boarded the streetcar, all the seats were occupied, and Slava and Vladimir were forced to stand. With every stop, as the streetcar proceeded up Lenin's Prospect, more people got on than off. As more passengers got on, they pushed Slava and Vladimir toward each other melding their bodies together. They no longer felt cold. Their breaths intermingled and Slava could feel the beat of Vladimir's heart against her body. It was noisy, conversation was impossible and both stood silently, communicating only through their eyes.

The City Theater, a three-story brick building, was built in the Renaissance architecture with rows of large windows. The middle row consisted of arched

Victor Moss

windows in Romanesque style topped by keystones. It was a beautiful structure and the pride of the residents of Vitebsk. The area bustled with activity as the streetcar stopped in front of the theater. A pedestrian plaza with a huge statue of Lenin surrounded by rectangular flower and shrub planters was situated on the left side of the theater.

As Slava and Vladimir entered through the large metal doors into the lobby, they proceeded directly to the coat check area. Several retired ladies earned extra rubles from the government taking care of the patrons' coats, overshoes, hats, bags, and umbrellas. Everyone was required to leave these items with the ladies in return for a numbered stub to reclaim their personal items. This was a free service, and as everywhere else, tipping was not allowed.

Slava was thrilled and impressed that Vladimir was able to obtain tickets in the center section, ten rows from the stage. She felt as if all eyes were on her as she sat down next to Vladimir. To her right sat an extremely heavy woman whose left shoulder and arm took up the entire armrest along with part of Slava's seat. Slava did not care. She enjoyed every minute of her date thus far, and besides it only meant that she could sit that much closer to Vladimir.

"Do you know anything about this ballet?" Vladimir asked.

"Not much at all, except that it's about a girl named Coppelia who turns out to be a doll and not a real person."

"You're right," Vladimir said. "I didn't know that until I read about it in the newspaper. Except for her father, no one realized that she was not a real person until almost the end of the ballet."

"I imagine it, like most ballets, is a convoluted story," Slava said. "It will be fun to see how they will tell the story with their feet, won't it?"

"Yes, it's always more interesting to watch ballet if you have some idea of the storyline. Oh look, I guess they are about to start."

The orchestra started playing. The music was wonderful. They sat with their shoulders touching and their arms sharing the armrest. In the darkened theater, Slava felt Vladimir's little finger of his right hand rub softly against the little finger of her left hand. *Should I remove my hand?* Slava thought to herself as her heart beat erratically. *No, I like it.* The ballet became inconsequential at that point as she was focused on the sensation of Vladimir's finger on her hand. Gradually, Vladimir's ring finger joined the little finger and both were on her hand. She again thought that maybe she should move her hand out of the way, but did not. A few seconds later, Vladimir's hand held hers. He squeezed it gently as he slowly rubbed his thumb over the palm of her hand. Slava's breathing became more rapid as a strange sensation filled her body. She looked at him and their eyes met once again. Both smiled at each other. They were content.

At intermission, most in the audience rose and rushed out to the lobby. At one end of the lobby were long counters with platters filled with tiny sandwiches made with salami, some with cheese, some with eggs. The meat

Beware the Wolves

sandwiches were the most expensive and cost as much as thirty kopecks. One counter was filled with pastry items of cakes, napoleon pastry, creampuffs and cookies. At another counter women served tea, champagne, cognac, vodka, juices and mineral water. The cost for a glass of tea or mineral water was only five kopecks.

Slava had never seen such pandemonium. The public pushed and shoved to get to the counters for the food and drink. They acted as though they had never eaten before. The servers worked as quickly as they could to keep up with the demand. She overheard one of the servers snap at a customer, "Hurry up and make up your mind, can't you see the line behind you?"

With an intermission of only twenty minutes not much time was left to purchase food and eat it on one of the many small, round tables set up to stand around. There were not enough tables. The theatergoers stood anywhere they could to eat their treats. Food and drink were not allowed inside the theater.

"You must try the napoleon pastry," Vladimir said as the pair stood in line. "I know that the cream filling between the phyllo dough is absolutely delicious."

Vladimir bought a napoleon and a cup of tea for each of them and looked around. Slava was sure he was looking for a place to set the food down to eat.

"Oh, look. There's my mother and sisters standing at that table," Vladimir said. "Let's join them."

His family is here too. I bet that was planned, Slava thought.

Slava and Vladimir pushed their way through the crowd. Slava carried her tea and napoleon, barely avoiding a man who stepped back and almost knocked the teacup out of her hands. The tea sloshed but, fortunately, most of it remained in the cup.

Vladimir gave his mother a hug.

"What are you doing here? This is certainly unexpected. Slava, I would very much like for you to meet my mother and my sisters," Vladimir said. "Mama, this is Vladislava, the wonderful girl I told you about. Slava, I am very pleased to introduce you to my mother, Agafia Efdakeyevna, and my sisters Anna, Valentina and Maria."

Vladimir's mother was a woman in her forties, of medium build and dressed rather plainly. Anna, the oldest, resembled Vladimir. The two younger sisters favored their father, Agafia's second husband, Mikhail.

"We are so glad to meet you." Maria, the youngest sister said. "All we heard from Volodya was Slavochka this, and Slavochka that. He even bought us tickets for this performance just so we could get a chance to see you."

"Maria, hush! That was supposed to be a secret," Vladimir said, laughing.

"Well, we approve. Slava, what a pretty girl you are. Although, maybe a little bit skinny," Agafia said, chuckling along with the others.

The rest of the evening went by very pleasantly for Slava, as they sat close to each other again holding hands throughout the second half of the performance.

49

Victor Moss

◆ ◆ ◆ ◆

Vladimir and Slava stepped off the streetcar and began their walk back to Slava's house. As they started to cross the bridge over the tracks, Slava grabbed Vladimir's arm and pulled him along as she ran up the bridge.

"Hurry, hurry we can still catch it!" Slava exclaimed as both were running.

"Catch what?"

"The steam off of that train engine."

"The what? What are you talking about?"

"You'll see. It's a lot of fun."

At the top of the bridge Slava stopped, let go of his hand and looked at the bewildered Vladimir. At that moment, as the train chugged beneath them, the vapor enclosed them in a semi-real, ghostly fog.

"Doesn't this steam feel good against your face, especially on a cold night like this? I've done this since I was a small girl. Sometimes I even yell out as the train goes by."

Both Slava and Vladimir giggled and laughed. Slava thought that perhaps she should not have acted so childishly, but she could see that Vladimir enjoyed her antics. And she found that she enjoyed his company. As they walked back to her house she began to wonder whether he would kiss her. She was nervous at the thought. She liked the idea of a kiss, but then this was their first date and it was just inappropriate. *If he tries to kiss me, should I let him? I would love a kiss. But it just isn't right. I'll have to turn away. Should I invite him in for a cup of tea?*

"Would you like to come in for a cup of tea?" Slava asked as they approached her house. "After all you have a long walk back. Come in and warm up before you start back."

"Thank you, but it is getting late. It is after midnight and I am on call early tomorrow at the clinic."

On the porch of the house, Vladimir removed his otter fur hat and his gray leather gloves. He smiled and looked intently into Slava's eyes. *Is he about to kiss me?* Slava removed her gloves as well and Vladimir took her hand, softly blew onto her hand and kissed it. His moist firm lips dwelled on her skin for several seconds. Slava shivered deliciously and felt new spirals of desire coursing through her body as Vladimir said goodnight.

◆ ◆ ◆ ◆

The letter from Vladimir was very unexpected. It appeared on Wednesday, four days after Slava's date with him. Slava saw his name on the envelope and her heart began to pound. She ran to her room, took out the envelope opener and hurriedly slit the envelope and pulled out the letter.

Beware the Wolves

My dearest Slovochka,

I enjoyed our date so much last Saturday. I do not remember when I had a better time. You are truly a treasure that has come into my life.

You are in my thoughts from the moment I wake up in the morning to the time I drop off to sleep. I want to see you, to be near you and touch your hand once again. I never thought of love until I met you. And I desire the experience of the joy of love.

I want to walk arm in arm with you and play with the steam vapors over the railroad tracks.

I can hardly wait until this coming Saturday to see you again.

We had planned to see the movie at the First of May Theater. It is not so much the movie, but the excuse to be near you that I look forward to.

See you this Saturday at 7:00 o'clock.

Volodya.

CHAPTER 7

Eerie silence followed once the rain of bombs stopped. Smoke filled the air as Vladimir stepped out of the basement of the hospital. Glass, from broken windows, and plaster lay on the floor. A fine plaster dust covered everything. Vladimir was concerned for the patients unable to seek shelter in the basement once the onslaught by the German Stukas and Ju88s began. He rushed past the ambulating patients returning to their wards. Tanya was at his heels, staying close to Vladimir as he dashed from ward to ward. To Vladimir's relief, the patients had survived, mostly with minor cuts from the flying glass. The hospital building itself had endured. Vladimir looked out the glassless window and saw fire raging in many of the buildings around the hospital. One of the factory buildings down the street had collapsed, falling on itself. In the distance toward the center of Smolensk he saw a mass of flames with black billowing smoke.

"Looks like all of Smolensk is on fire," Vladimir said to the patients in the room. He glanced at Tanya who brushed plaster dust from a patient's hair. "It's a miracle that we are alive and that this building is still intact. They will be back, and we had better prepare to evacuate. I need to see Colonel Popov about a plan as soon as possible."

At that moment, Misha came into the ward. He, like everyone else, was covered with white dust on his clothes, boots, hands, face and hair.

"Comrade Captain, can you step out into the hall? There is someone to see you, sent here from headquarters."

◆ ◆ ◆ ◆

Waiting for Vladimir was another officer in the medical corps. He was short, youthful, slight of build and wore thick glasses. He appeared extremely nervous.

"Comrade Captain Moskalkov, Vasyli Buryanev, pleased to meet you. I have been ordered to replace you at this hospital. I should have reported in yesterday, but the chaos of the bombing delayed me."

"Oh, I knew nothing about this."

"Sorry. I thought Comrade Colonel Popov had informed you of the change."

"No, the fact that I am being replaced is completely new to me. I guess I had better call Popov."

Beware the Wolves

Vladimir walked down the hall to a desk used for admission work. It had the only telephone in the building. Buryanev joined Vladimir.

"Will you help me get up to speed?" Buryanev asked. "The bombing has left the hospital a wreck. What shall I do?"

"Well for one thing, I think you need to prepare to evacuate the wounded as soon as possible," Vladimir said.

"How am I supposed to do that?"

"You need to find out the general plan for evacuation. I assume it is toward Moscow. You must commandeer anything that has wheels to get everyone out of here—trucks, horses and wagons, carts, anything. This building may not make it next time, and believe me, there will be a next time soon."

"Where am I supposed to get that information and where in the hell am I supposed to get the transportation?"

At the desk, Vladimir grabbed the telephone, and while he waited for someone to answer his call, he looked at Buryanev.

"You know, my dear colleague," Vladimir said, "you have to be very resourceful around here. I suggest you send the medics, nurses once we get them, even patients that can walk and scrounge up anything that moves. You may want to grab any soldiers you see walking around to help you. Oh, damn! The phone is dead. I'll have to walk over to see Popov in person."

At that moment, Tanya ran up to Vladimir. She had a perplexed look on her face and asked him what was happening.

"Tanya, I'm not sure. I'll let you know. I have to see Popov, but in the meantime, this is Captain Buryanev. He says that he is now in charge here. Give him the help he needs."

Tanya's eyes widened and her mouth dropped. She looked at Buryanev in disbelief. Vladimir nodded goodbye to both of them and went out the door to see Popov.

Walking toward Colonel Popov's office, Vladimir stared at the smoldering ruin along the way. He stepped over bricks, boards, roof tiles, uprooted trees, downed power and telephone lines and walked gingerly around bomb craters. He took out his handkerchief from his back pocket and held it to his mouth and nose. The smell and the smoke were overwhelming. He marveled at the tireless efforts of the firemen and rescuers determined to save life and property.

Under a collapsed house Vladimir saw a hand protruding from the rubble. He rushed over to help. He separated a beam, bricks, plaster and pieces of lathe from the body, only to find that the hand belonged to a dead woman. He shook his head with deep sadness.

◆ ◆ ◆ ◆

Popov's headquarters had survived the bombing. Vladimir saw the wrought-iron gate, the same gate in front of which he almost lost his life at the hands of Popov. The thought made him shudder. He dreaded walking into that house and facing Popov. He imagined that Popov still had it in for him and his game of replacing him with Buryanev was part of his punishment. *No good could come of this.*

"I'm here to see Colonel Popov," Vladimir said to Popov's clerk, a lieutenant in the Army.

"Comrade Colonel Popov is extremely busy," said the lieutenant emphasizing the word "comrade." "You know, don't you, there is a war on. I don't think he has the time to see you today. He is in high level meetings."

"I absolutely have to see him. I walked here all the way from the field hospital—you know the one at the sewing machine factory. We must evacuate the patients and, besides, Popov had me replaced and I need new orders."

"I know where you work. Your hospital is not the only problem we have right now. The whole area is in peril. There is talk of more evacuations of civilians and that is probably what they are discussing in there right now, along with military strategy. High-level mucky mucks are here from Moscow. You might as well sit down and wait. If they get through with the meeting, I'll ask Comrade Colonel Popov if he wants to see you."

Vladimir sat down on the wooden bench next to Popov's clerk. Officers were scurrying about the house going from one room to another with worried looking expressions. The door to the house seemed never to close as officers were either entering or leaving. The scene reminded him of Slava's father's beehives with the bees buzzing around in every which direction. Oh, how much, right now, he would love to stir a teaspoon of that honey in a cup of tea. In fact, he remembered that he did not have anything to eat yet and he suddenly felt hunger pangs.

"Do you have any tea or anything to eat around here?" Vladimir asked the clerk

"You'll find something in the kitchen, over there."

Vladimir went to the kitchen and on a big black coal-burning stove found a large kettle with boiling water. Next to the stove stood a table with cups and a small teapot with steeped tea. He poured the tea into a cup. It looked strong, so he filled the cup one-third of the way and then diluted the rest with the boiling water from the kettle. He looked for some sugar cubes, but did not see any. Next to the cups was a towel lying over some plates. He lifted it and to his delight saw a piece of slab bacon. Another towel covered dark rye bread. He cut a piece of the bacon, placed it on the bread and devoured the meal in a few minutes, washing it down with the tea. He returned to the bench and continued to wait for Popov.

He was startled when artillery and tank shells began exploding in the distance. The explosions came rapidly, one after another. Popov's door opened and two generals, another colonel and two men in civilian suits hurried out. Popov was the last to exit the room and headed straight for the front door without looking in Vladimir's direction. Vladimir jumped up and ran after Popov.

Beware the Wolves

"Colonel Popov, please, it is very important that I talk with you. I have been waiting for you here for over an hour."

"What are you doing here? Why aren't you in the trenches."

"What do you mean, the trenches?"

"I sent you an order yesterday, by courier, that you are to report to Comrade Captain Savitski's battalion. We need a doctor in the battlefield. Take your gear and report to Savitski. You'll find him at the rear defensive line, the one closest to the camp. Supplies and surgical instruments have already been delivered and they should be all set up today."

"Yes sir," Vladimir said. But what shall we do about the wounded at the hospital? They need to be evacuated. The hospital is damaged and it's a sitting target."

"That's not your problem any longer. You need to be at the battlefield immediately. And take the medics with you. I've ordered nurses to work the hospital and the medics should be where they belong—on the battlefield. You have your work cut out for you. The wounded are mounting. So get the medics and your gear and hustle back here as soon as possible. There'll be a truck waiting for you, but it must leave for the front in less than an hour."

◆ ◆ ◆ ◆

As he hurriedly walked back to the hospital, Vladimir felt discouraged because he knew that the conditions at the battlefield would be desperate. The supplies and equipment would be inadequate. *On the other hand, it makes sense having me near the injuried. If only I had received some battlefield training. Oh well, I'll do the best that I can.*

Suddenly, he heard hoof beats on the street. Vladimir turned around and saw a medical wagon full of injured soldiers on its way to the hospital. As the wagon approached, he asked for a lift and sat next to the driver. The wounded in the wagon moaned with pain. He remembered the street was under rubble and deep bomb craters. He knew the horse and wagon could only travel so far before the street became impassable.

But, to his surprise, the firemen and rescue workers had cleared a path wide enough for the horse and wagon and they were able to navigate around the rubble up to a block away from the hospital. The driver of the wagon began cursing the Germans for the misery they brought on the Russian soil. Vladimir asked him to wait while he went for help to transfer the wounded to the hospital.

Upon entering the hospital, Vladimir saw Buryanev. He was in the hallway talking to eight nurses in army uniforms. They looked young and scared. Vladimir knew that they, just as he, were recently drafted. The nurses nodded their heads as Buyanev gave them instructions. *They'll learn quickly,* he thought. *Just as I did.* He had been drafted less than a month ago, but it felt like a lifetime. The nurses' presence relieved the guilt he felt for taking away the medics.

55

"We need some help with the wounded." Vladimir said. "They are stuck in the wagon about a block west of the hospital."

Buryanev, trying to appear in charge, ordered the staff, including Misha and Igor, to fetch the wounded from the wagon. Vladimir stopped Misha and Igor, as they headed for the door.

"Come by my room as soon as you are through. We will be shipping out in less than an hour. Where are the others?"

"What do you mean we will be shipping out?" Igor asked.

"I'll explain later. You need to help them with the wounded right now. Where is Tanya, or Boris, or Stepan?" Vladimir asked again.

"They are in the wards," Misha said.

Vladimir found the medics and asked them to finish up what they were doing and join him in his room within the next ten minutes. He went to his room and began packing his belongings into a canvas bag. He did not have much to pack as he wore most of his clothes. It was summer, so everything issued to him was of summer weight. Following custom, he placed his stainless steel soupspoon inside the edge of one of his black leather jackboots. He had two belts. The black belt that he wore over his tunic was also made of leather, as was the belt around his size thirty-inch waist. His holster with revolver was attached to his waist belt. The belt over his tunic was extra long so that it could fit over the telogreika (overcoat) in winter. That belt was designed to carry any gear that was not thrown over the shoulder or carried in his rucksack. His headgear was a pilotka (side cap). On the inner flap he pushed through a sewing needle with some thread wrapped around for mending clothes.

He placed his civilian dark blue woolen coat in the bottom of the bag. Slava had insisted that he take it with him when he left for the army. "You never know," she told him. "It's always better to be warm than cold." They assumed that he would be issued an overcoat, but you could not rely on the Army issuing what it promised. He next packed his khaki cotton socks, boxer underwear and a summer weight tank top issued by the Army. He had one extra pair of pants and an extra tunic, both in green color and also of summer cotton weight. Lastly, he packed away his razor, soap, comb and a towel that he brought from home. He left his bag and his greatcoat on the bed prepared for travel.

"What's going on?" Tanya asked, as she entered his room.

"We have been reassigned to the battlefield," Vladimir said. "You need to pack up as soon as possible. We need to be out of here within the next thirty minutes."

"Are we going to be together?"

"Yes, I assume so."

"Good. Then I feel better about it," Tanya said quietly, squeezing Vladimir's arm. At that moment, Buryanev came up to them.

"I'm glad I found both of you. I would like very much if Tanya would stay here. I will work it out with the higher ups. I just found out that she is educated as a Feldsher (physician's assistant) and I need her experience."

Beware the Wolves

"Actually, Tanya, that may not be a bad idea," Vladimir said. "Not that anyplace is safe from danger, but remaining here until the evacuation has to be safer than a medic in the trenches. Medics, many times, are the first to be killed."

"No, no, I can do more good in battle. Besides, as far as I understand, my orders are to go with Captain Moskalkov. Please take me with you."

Vladimir saw that her eyes were tearing up, pleading to take her with him. *What a fool she is,* he thought. If she had decided to stay, he would have readily agreed.

"My orders are that all the medics are to go with me," Vladimir said to Buryanev. "Until ordered otherwise, Tanya will go with me."

◆ ◆ ◆ ◆

They walked back to Popov's headquarters in silence. In the distance they could hear the thunder of exploding shells. Vladimir did not know what was in store for him. He assumed that each one of the medics had the same thoughts in his or her mind. He was uneasy with the nervousness of the unknown. He could hear the unrelenting noise of battle ahead and knew he would be soon in its midst. That worried him, but he told himself that he must be brave. Again, he remembered his father, a hero, and that gave him some courage.

The silence among them was broken when Igor took out a cigarette and asked Vladimir what was in store for them. Misha and Stepan also began to smoke and Vladimir noticed that their pace of walking slowed. Igor sat down on some debris in the street. Boris and Tanya did not smoke and, along with Vladimir, seemed to be irritated with the delay.

"Comrade Captain, I have to rest a bit," Igor said. "Can we take a short break?"

"No, if you have to smoke, walk along. We only have a short way to go. We will be there in five minutes. You can rest in the truck."

"Yea, truck to Hell. That's where we're going you know."

"You dumb shit, you're always complaining," Boris chimed in. "We're doing a great service to Stalin and the motherland. We have to chase those damn Germans from our soil."

"Shut your mouth!" Igor shouted at Boris. "What do you know about anything? You know nothing but what propaganda is fed you."

"Simmer down," Vladimir said. "I advise you to keep quiet before someone gets into deep trouble. We have a job to do and we're going to do it well. Our job is to save lives. Let's not get politics involved; it will only interfere with our work. Do you understand?"

Vladimir did not expect an answer. They walked in silence to Popov's headquarters. *I hope that Boris or one of the others doesn't report Igor's comments to the political commissar. We could all be in trouble.*

Victor Moss

❖ ❖ ❖ ❖

The truck waited for them. It was packed with folding cots, blankets, a table, kerosene lanterns and a can of kerosene. Boxes labeled "buckwheat grain" and barrels of water stood in the back. In addition to the supplies, soldiers sat packed closely in the truck. Vladimir looked to see if any room remained for his five medics, himself and their gear. *We can make it, if we squeeze in.*

Popov's clerk, the lieutenant, appeared irritated that Vladimir and the medics had arrived a few minutes late. Vladimir paid little attention to him. After all, they had packed up and walked back without delay.

The group hopped onto the truck. Vladimir noticed that Tanya was very careful to make sure she sat next to him. He liked Tanya. She was a competent medic, hard working, and a very good assistant. However, her increasingly obvious flirtation made him nervous. She knew he was married and deeply in love with his wife, or at least should have known. Yet she pursued him. He secretly wished that she had indeed chosen to stay at the hospital.

He looked around to make sure all the medics were on board. Igor was missing. *Well what do you know? He actually did it. He ran away, the bastard.*

"Captain, I don't see Igor," Tanya said. "You think he bolted?"

"It looks that way."

"Are you surprised? I mean did you expect it?"

"No, Tanya."

Actually, he was surprised that Igor waited this long to run away. The engine started up, there was a clang as the driver put the truck in first gear and they were on their way. Except for the engine, there was deathly silence. The shelling had stopped and no one said a word. Each face was glum. The spectacular sunset ahead projected its rays through the smoke and dust of the day's battle. Vladimir saw no beauty in the sun's display. Instead the scene was disturbing, as though the crimson sun presented an ominous warning of the future.

The ride took twenty-five minutes with two checkpoints on the way. As they jumped off the truck, a loud speaker blared a message from Stalin:

"Comrades, citizens, brothers and sisters, warriors of our Army and of our fleet, I am speaking to you my friends.... The enemy is out to seize our lands watered by the sweat of our brows, to seize our grain and oil, secured by the labor of our hands....Russia is fighting a national patriotic war, a war for the freedom of the motherland....Scorch the earth before yielding any territory to the Germans....The enemy must not be left a single engine, a single railway car, a single pound of grain, a single gallon of fuel. All valuable property that cannot be withdrawn must be destroyed. Sabotage groups must be organized to foment guerrilla warfare everywhere, blow up bridges and roads, set fire to forests, stores and transport."

Vladimir heard this speech for the first time on July 3, 1941. And he had heard it replayed at least twice again. This speech, the only one in which Stalin addressed his people as brothers, sisters or friends had moved him. He lifted his gear off the truck and followed the others into the trenches.

CHAPTER 8

The sappers (engineering troops) had been busy. Vladimir entered the maze of trenches and was astonished at the work they had done to hold the Germans back. He was faced with an intersection at the bottom of the entrance ramp. A narrow interconnecting passage to his right led to several support trenches or bunkers. Those contained ammunition stores. Straight ahead was the interconnecting passage to the defensive lines beginning about 400 meters away. To his left were other bunkers. The command staff occupied the first bunker. The second was the kitchen and the third one for medical aid. The interconnecting passages were shoulder high and barely wide enough for two soldiers to pass by sideways. In some places, small tree trunks stacked in neat rows lined the passages to prevent cave-ins.

The medical aid bunker, just as the other support trenches, was a dugout lined with larger logs on all sides, including the roof. Soil was thrown over that part of the structure that protruded out of the ground giving an appearance of a large mound of dirt. An open door made of log casings and an open, narrow, horizontal window opposite the door were the only sources of ventilation for the dugout.

The appalling stench of infected wounds, blood, feces, urine, sweat, and vomit assaulted Vladimir's senses as he entered the bunker. He was not sure, but he thought he stepped on a rat. The wounded either sat or lay on about six inches of straw that covered the floor of the twelve by twenty foot bunker. Blotches of blood seeped through the bandages around the soldiers' heads. Those who could, weakly waved away the pesky flies. The insects were thick. The moans and groans were like a chorus from hell. Medics were busy beside certain wounded, bandaging away. Kerosene lamps, this late in the evening, were the only source of light. Vladimir considered the mixture of kerosene and dry straw and shuddered. He placed his gear next to a metal box on the floor.

"Hey, out of my way!" yelled a medic to Vladimir and the group of medics accompanying him. Tanya and Misha stood behind Vladimir in the doorway, while Stepan and Boris were still in the passageway. "Can't you idiots see that I'm bringing in an injured soldier?" He carried a soldier on his back. The wounded soldier's arms were draped around the medic's neck and shoulders.

After laying down the wounded man, the medic rushed over to Vladimir and his group ready to confront them, until he noticed that Vladimir was an officer.

"Oh, excuse me, sir. I didn't realize who you were. I didn't mean to call you an idiot. It has been a miserable day. We can't keep up with the injured.

Victor Moss

Please forgive me." He was a short, older looking man, probably in his forties. His round face had a bulbous nose and narrow brown eyes. His body looked strong as an ox. His tunic was stained with dirt and blood.

"It's understandable. After all, we were in the way," Vladimir said. "I'm Captain Moskalkov, your physician. What is your name?"

"I'm Evgeniy, the senior medic here. We keep asking for transport and can't get it. Some of these wounded need surgery immediately."

Vladimir looked around at the wounded more closely. He walked over to the men who sat up erect and asked each one to lie down. Neither of them was able to lie still for long. They gasped for air.

"Hurry, bring me some tubes and a surgical bag," Vladimir commanded Evgeniy. "I need to stick a tube in those men because they can't breathe. Also bring me some alcohol to sterilize the instruments."

Evgeniy looked puzzled but hurried over to the doorway where next to the opening stood an old heavy metal ammunition box with metal handles and a lid that clasped down.

"They brought some supplies yesterday." Evgeniy pulled out some rubber tubing and a worn-out bag with a circled red cross displayed on both sides. He brought the tube and the bag to Vladimir. Vladimir in the meantime tapped the chest of the wounded.

"It sounds hollow," he said.

He opened the bag and found a scalpel and a pair of scissors. Vladimir cut a piece of tubing and laid it aside.

"Where is the alcohol?"

"Oh, I forgot to tell you that we don't have any."

"Run over to the command bunker," Vladimir barked. "Tell them it's an emergency and get a bottle of vodka. Tell them I ordered you to get one for sterilization of instruments. I am sure you will find one there, but hurry."

"Just in case he doesn't find vodka," Vladimir said to Tanya. "See if you can scrounge up some water and start boiling it. I saw the kitchen next door."

As Tanya was about to leave, Evgeniy and Lieutenant Sergey Ivanov, Vladimir's friend who warned him about Popov, ran in the bunker. Ivanov held a half full bottle of vodka.

"I can't believe it's you," Ivanov said. "Popov really has it in for you to send you here. Well, at least you are still alive, for now, anyway."

"Hello, Sergey," Vladimir smiled. "I see you haven't changed much. You are the same cheery self here in the trenches as you are above ground."

Vladimir took the vodka from Ivanov, poured some on the chest of the wounded, stuck the scalpel in the bottle, held it there for a few seconds, poured some on and in the tube and quickly punctured a hole in the patient's chest. Instantly, he pushed the tube into the chest of the wounded individual. Air hissed out from the chest cavity, the patient's color improved immediately and he was able to breathe.

Beware the Wolves

He quickly performed the same procedure on the second sitting individual. Except this time, he carefully inserted the tube in the bottom of the lung from the back. He grabbed a tin cup that was lying around in the straw, and blood poured out of the tube into the cup. That patient also improved immediately.

"How did you know where to put the tube?" Evgeniy asked.

"The first patient had hollow sounds in his chest, which meant that the chest cavity was full of air. The second had a solid sound most likely meaning that blood had collected in his lungs."

"Well, the old dog learned a new trick," muttered Tanya.

"I don't need that from a woman," Evgeniy countered with a seething look mounting with rage. "This is no place for a damn woman."

"What's the problem here, Evgeniy?" Vladimir asked.

"I don't like having a woman on the battlefield. Again I tell you that this is no place for a woman. Women interfere with battle. Sorry, Comrade Captain, but I always say what's on my mind. I've been in the Army for twenty-two years and know that a woman in this environment is nothing but trouble."

"You old, ignorant, peasant." Tanya's voice shook with anger. "Go to hell. I can do more work than most men and better. Just you wait and see. I'll make you eat those narrow-minded, pig-headed words. Stupid!"

"Simmer down, girl," countered Evgeniy. "Did I say anything about work. I'm sure you can do a fine job. What I meant was that a woman takes men's minds off their duties. These young bucks are going to fight each other to get your attention."

"Well, they will just have to live with it. I'm here to stay."

"All right. That's enough. We all have a job to do," Vladimir said. "Tanya, is a Feldsher and will be my main assistant in surgery. The other medics are Boris, Misha and Stepan." Vladimir pointed to each. "They will also help with the wounded here. How many medics are there in this battalion?"

"We started out with fifteen, and lost two already," Evgeniy said.

"Are you in charge of the medics?"

"Yes, comrade Captain Savitski put me in charge."

"Fine, carry on," Vladimir said. "You and the medics that you've worked with will give first-aid on the battlefield and bring the wounded back here. Now let's take care of the wounded."

"Yes, Comrade Captain," Evgeniy replied.

"Can we get something to eat first?" Stepan asked. "I am famished. I can't go on without something in my belly."

"The kitchen is in the next bunker," Evgeniy said. "All we have had for the last two days is buckwheat mush. There is probably a pot with mush left. But where are your mess kits? You do have your spoons?" They all nodded, including Tanya who had her spoon tucked in her boot as the others. "I don't see your mess kits. That's all right, the kitchen has some taken off the dead."

"I wouldn't even call it mush," Ivanov said. "You may be better off not to eat anything."

Vladimir's medics looked disturbed, but left for the kitchen anyway while Vladimir began to examine the wounded.

"Evgeniy, have these patients been triaged?" Vladimir asked ignoring Ivanov who seemed to be huddling around him.

Vladimir saw by Evgeniy's expression that he had no idea what triage meant.

"By triage, you determine which of the wounded need immediate help first, then who needs attention next and so forth."

"Well no, we just do what we can to stop the bleeding or splint broken bones before the trucks or wagons come to take them to the field hospital."

"Well, part of triage is to determine priority for certain procedures, including surgery. If a surgery requires four hours for example, we do his last. Instead we work with the one whose surgery requires the least time. That way we can save more people in the same amount of time."

"I don't know why you are so concerned about saving every one of these wounded?" Ivanov said. "Our latest information is that the Germans are ready to strike a heavy blow on us. Their artillery has caught up with their Panzers. And soon their infantry will catch up. The tanks will roll over us and the infantry will finish us off. Our intelligence is that their pinchers are close to encircling the entire city of Smolensk. And there is nothing we can do about it. Our defensive position will not stop the planes and tanks. The defensive line at the Dnieper River was shattered five days ago on July 7th. We cannot hold out here any more than another day or two. We will all be killed or captured. There is a lull in their bombardment for now, but watch out, once they start, it will be our end."

"Sergey, please," whispered Vladimir. "Keep your voice down. You are making matters worse for the wounded and scaring the hell out of me. You could be executed for such defeatist words. Don't you have anything better to do? What is your assignment here anyway?"

"I am in charge of one of the artillery companies of this battalion."

"I'm surprised and deeply upset with your attitude. Learn to keep it to yourself. In the meantime you better do a hell of a job with your artillery. You never know what will happen in battle. Our boys are tough and mean enough to at least delay the Germans from reaching Moscow. If they are coming at us from all sides, then their forces have to be spread out and therefore vulnerable."

"We are spread out as well," Ivanov replied. "And our troops are probably concentrated in the wrong places. We are totally outmatched. What other scenario can there possibly be? You will see I was right. Anyway, you didn't report to Comrade Captain Savitski yet, did you?"

"No, I'll do that as soon as I can stabilize the wounded."

"You are going to be in trouble again. You know the procedure. You must report in as soon as you arrive."

"I will Sergey. Just let me examine the wounds first."

Beware the Wolves

Ivanov left and Vladimir and Evgeniy looked at each other in disbelief. Evgeniy started to say something, but bit his lip. Vladimir realized that Evgeniy knew better than to criticize an officer in front of another. Vladimir kept working looking over every wounded. He counted twenty-three and knew he could only help a few. Five laid in head wound related comas.

Vladimir had to find a location for surgery. As he thought about what to do, Tanya came into the bunker with a mess kit strapped about her belt and another in her hand.

"I washed the pot out as well as I could and brought you some of this mush. It isn't as bad as they made it sound." When Vladimir stretched out his hand, she placed the kit into his and gently rubbed his hand. He noticed the touch, but was very grateful for his stomach churned with hunger. He took a spoon out of his boot and hurriedly gulped down the mush. It tasted like sawdust, but at least it filled his stomach.

"Thanks so much, Tanya," he said. "Try to find a safe place for our kits as we certainly can't work with them hanging off of us. Well, I guess, I better go to see Captain Savitski now."

◆ ◆ ◆ ◆

The meeting with Savitski was short. He did not appear to be at all concerned that Vladimir did not report immediately. He was distracted studying charts with his lieutenants and did not pay much attention to Vladimir. Vladimir asked him where he could perform the surgeries that were needed.

"You need to talk to the chief medic. He will help you."

◆ ◆ ◆ ◆

When Vladimir returned, Evgeniy was placing a bandage over a soldier's right eye.

"Bandage both eyes, Evgeniy, not just one," Vladimir said.

"He only has a wound in one eye, why waste the bandages. We are already running short on them."

"We need to start reusing the bandages by boiling them. But you need to bandage both eyes, as it will be less painful for the soldier. Each time he moves the good eye, it hurts the wounded eye. Any suggestions where we can set up for surgeries? Can we bring up a table above ground? A tent would be ideal."

"Not a good idea, Comrade Capitan." answered Evgeniy. "Shells spew cast iron chunks 360 degrees and you'll be cut to pieces. That's the reason for the trenches. Besides, we don't have any tents. But that's taken care of. Comrade Captain Savitski had the sappers dig out an area next to this bunker and we set up a table for surgeries. They didn't have time to put a roof on it, only camouflage netting."

"Why didn't you tell me that from the beginning?"

Victor Moss

"You never asked, Comrade Captain," Evgeniy replied.

Vladimir and his medics proceeded to the area designated for surgeries. It was pitch black, but with the light of a kerosene lamp, they saw four more lamps standing on top of an ammunition box. Misha took one of his matches and lit the area up with the lamps. Sandbags stacked up at least half of a meter higher than the top of Vladimir's head provided some protection. The floor was of dirt and the netting was of a fine mesh. The table was made of newly sawn boards. Another metal ammunition box covered with a lid stood in the far corner. Stepan raised the lid and discovered that it contained six sheets, a blood pressure monitor, an old worn stethoscope, several bottles of ethanol, sponges, bandages, towels, soap and other odds and ends useful in operations.

"Fantastic!" Vladimir exclaimed. "This is better than I had expected. And if Evgeniy had looked, he would have known that we even have alcohol right here. Misha and Stepan, let's go back to the bunker and I'll point out the patient you need to prepare for surgery. Tanya, clean off the table and place one of those sheets on it. We'll be right back, ready to work. Oh, Boris, go find a bucket of clean water."

The first surgery was on a soldier with a bullet in his shoulder. Vladimir removed the bullet and drained the surrounding blood clot as it caused pressure on the nerve. The next several operations were of a similar type involving bullets or fragments of shrapnel. They did not require a lengthy procedure. Vladimir left the more complicated to last. It was after midnight. He looked at his assistants and saw how exhausted they appeared. Tanya worked by his side, providing any help he required. Stepan, Boris and Misha held the kerosene lamps about the table and moved the light where necessary. Vladimir felt drained and thought he could no longer keep his eyes focused on further procedures. He needed to do one more surgery, however, on a soldier that had positive response to his taps on the stomach. He diagnosed that to be a perforated large bowel. *If he showed no response to my tapping, then it would have been shrapnel in the stomach and he could have waited.* They brought the soldier in. Vladimir worked on him for two hours. He found the perforation and sewed it up. The result was good, but Vladimir was totally exhausted.

"That's it for now," Vladimir said. "Grab your greatcoats. We'll sleep right here on the floor."

CHAPTER 9

Ear splitting explosions shook the ground. The clatter was unbearable. There was a symphony of racket that only the devil could orchestrate. Planes delivered bombs and strafed the ground. The enemy's artillery batteries opened an enraged barrage on Soviet positions. Clusters of bombs, incendiary shells, chatter of machine guns, and grenades added to the disharmony.

Vladimir jumped up from the ground. Dazed from his sleep, covering his ears with his hands, he was astonished at the dirt that showered down from the explosions. Some of the dirt filtered through the netting above, but most remained and weighed it down. As he looked up to see if the net would hold underneath all the weight, another explosion shook the ground and a geyser of dirt and shrapnel assailed the net. One piece of shrapnel cut through the netting and struck Misha's right arm.

"Oh shit! I've been hit."

"You're all right, Misha," Vladimir shouted over the hurricane of commotion after he examined Misha's arm. "It's just a scratch."

At that moment a plane that flew overhead, dropped a bomb just a few meters away. Another fountain of dirt and shrapnel poured on the netting, with more sharp pieces of metal cutting through. Vladimir quickly looked around at his medics crouched in one corner of the dugout.

"Head for the bunker next door, now!" Vladimir yelled.

The medical-aid bunker was jammed with soldiers. Not only were there many more wounded than Vladimir remembered from the night before, but now there were medics waiting for the bombing and shelling to subside. Evgeniy shook his fist at the enemy yelling, "We'll drive you out, you bastards!"

The others were silent. Dirt from each blast filtered through the logs of the roof and fell on everything including the wounds of the patients. Their faces and bodies were covered with the fallen dirt. Vladimir knew he needed to do something to help the wounded, but could not force himself to move. This was his first time in a combat zone and he felt so very vulnerable. He had some close calls in the last few days. His life could have been snuffed out in the village with the German scouts, then the Soviet scouts, later Popov's gun to his head and then bombs falling out of the sky at the field hospital. Now the extreme noise volume and the fear in the faces of men and Tanya around him was paralyzing. He felt torn apart as though a bomb had exploded within him. He was disoriented as he kept his hands over his ears. He breathed with shallow, quick gasps. He thought of his father, a war hero, and again of his grandfather, who always told him, "Always be brave, never be afraid." Those thoughts again gave him strength.

Victor Moss

As abruptly as the bombing and shelling began, it stopped. Vladimir lowered his hands. In the near distance, he heard gunfire and machine guns with an occasional artillery discharge. He stood up, feeling shaky on his feet. There was work to be done. He began evaluating the wounded. As Evgeniy yelled out to his medics to bring in more wounded, Vladimir wondered where they would place them once they were carried in from the field. He had just asked Stepan and Boris to clean up the surgical dugout so that he could begin to remove shrapnel from a wounded soldier when Ivanov came up to him.

"Come with me now. Comrade Captain Savitski wants to see all the officers, immediately!"

"Sergey, what's this all about. I need to be here. We're ready to operate on this soldier," Vladimir said pointing to a soldier who looked ready to pass out.

"I don't know. You must come with me right away, or both of us will be shot for disobeying a direct order." With that said, Ivanov grabbed Vladimir's arm and tugged at it for Vladimir to follow. "You have to come. Your patients must wait."

"Listen, Sergey, I need to do this now. It won't take long. I'll be there in a few minutes. Tell Savitski that I'm in the middle of a surgery and I'll join him as soon as I can."

"He won't like it. Hurry, will you? He told me the meeting is extremely urgent."

Vladimir finished the surgery and washed his hands. So many more needed his immediate attention. *I don't have time for meetings, but I better go.*

Vladimir did not know what to expect when he entered Savitski's dugout. *Am I in hot water for not reporting immediately to the Captain? What is this meeting about? If this meeting concerns military strategy, why would they need me, a medical officer?*

Pointing to a map spread out before him, Savitski stood bent over a crude wooden table surrounded by Ivanov, another lieutenant and a Communist Party commissar. Savitsi was a lean man in his late thirties with a kind-looking narrow face and a thin mustache. He was a striking man, with an outer shell of a professional soldier. He stopped talking and straightened up as Vladimir approached the table. An annoyed look swept his face, but he did not say anything about Vladimir being late.

"Moskalkov, I was telling these gentlemen that our line of defense at the Dnieper River has been overrun. Our valiant fighting men were either killed or captured. Now our line of defense here is collapsing and shortly will be crushed by the Panzers. In a few hours we will be overrun. We must retreat to save whatever men and equipment we have left. Comrade Commissar objects to a retreat."

"I strongly object," the Commissar said. "You all know very well, that our great leader, Stalin, decreed that retreat from defensive positions is not allowed. Every man must fight to his death. We are to hold our ground to the last man."

Beware the Wolves

"I know the decree," Savitski responded. "And if you insist that we hold our positions, we will. But I respectfully disagree to hold onto these trenches that will not stop the Panzers. We can be better utilized somewhere else where we can do more good. Why commit suicide? The Germans are encircling us and soon there will be no escape. They are rolling in from Orsha, to the west from us, and from Mogilev, to the southwest. In other words, their pincers have begun their stranglehold around Smolensk and the neighboring areas."

"You're bordering on subordination, Comrade Captain," the Commissar interrupted. "On the other hand, if you feel so strongly, and we are no use here, I'll allow a retreat."

Vladimir listened intently to the dialogue. *Sure he agrees to a withdrawal, he, too, does not want to die.* At that moment, an aide to Savitski hurried into the dugout with a paper in his hand. He gave the note to Savitski.

"Well, gentlemen, our discussion here is no longer necessary. It appears that we are soon to be attacked from the direction of Vitebsk, from the northwest. Colonel Popov has ordered us to pull out for other deployment."

Vladimir had been tied up in knots since the bombing and shelling began, and his body was still unable to loosen up. But when he heard Savitski mention Vitebsk, he felt as though someone turned that vice tighter around his chest, several more notches. He had heard rumors that the enemy occupied Vitebsk, but to hear a report that the Germans were moving in from Vitebsk, confirmed the rumors. *Oh my God! Is Slava all right? How is she coping with enemy occupation? What about my mother, my sisters? Jesus, be with them. Maybe, they had all evacuated, and they're fine. What if they didn't survive the attack, and they're all dead? Oh God!* His head had felt heavy for days, but now a visceral pain in his temple started at his forehead and moved with a vicious grip over his skull to the base of his neck. Savitski kept talking, but Vladimir's mind was on the fate of his family.

"Moskalkov!" Savitski bellowed. "Pay attention. I asked you how many wounded do you have?"

"Oh, sorry, Captain. Last night I counted twenty-three. This morning it looked as though the number had doubled and they were still bringing them in when I came here. I can't give you a count right now."

"Well, you know, the wounded are a big problem for me," Savitski said. "I really don't know what to do with them in a evacuation. I guess I'm going to hand you the problem and let you figure out what to do. It will be impossible to take them all. Their fate is left to the Germans."

"They will shoot them all," Ivanov said.

"We have to get all of them out," Vladimir said. "Can't you get me some trucks?"

"Oh, that's rich." Savitski laughed and the beam of light from the narrow opening in the bunker reflected off the gold crowns in his mouth. The other officers also gave a hearty laugh. Everyone looked for any excuse to release the

Victor Moss

built-up tension. "Well at least you made us laugh. We have no motorized vehicles left and we're not getting any more. But maybe, I can get you some room on the wagons. Ivanov! How many artillery pieces do we have left?"

"Five, all 122 mm howitzers, Comrade Captain."

"How many horses, carts and wagons and where are they right now?"

"We have fifty-five horses, Comrade Captain, twelve artillery carts, seven ammunition wagons, two first-aid wagons and, oh yes, a cook wagon, all sheltered behind a hill in the woods about three kilometers from here, all being cared for by our two groomsmen."

"Well, that's the answer, Moskalkov," Savitski said. "We'll bring up the wagons and you can decide which of your wounded can fit into the two medical wagons."

"I can only accommodate a few in two wagons," Vladimir was aghast.

"Comrade Captain, that is all you're going to get. And you're fortunate that I decided not to use the wagons for ammunition."

Oh God! How am I to decide who goes and who stays behind for the fascists to kill. Everyone deserves to evacuate. Of course, those poor souls in a coma most likely would be left behind. They probably would not survive the ride. Damn! It's obvious that ammunition is more important than human life. That's a tragedy. But in the defense of a country, it's understandable. "How far are we to transport the wounded?" Vladimir asked Savitski. "I imagine to the nearest running train and then to a hospital, I hope."

"You are right. Except that the nearest running train would be at Yelna, eighty kilometers southeast of here. The rails on both sides of Smolensk have been bombed out. That, by the way, gentlemen, is our next deployment. We are to defend Yelna and you, Comrade Captain Moskalkov, will place your wounded on the train and proceed with them to Vyazma. Comrade Colonel Popov has assigned you and the medics to help set up a field hospital west of Vyazma. We need to fortify the city in anticipation of the battle for the defense of Moscow. History repeats itself, gentlemen. Hitler is following in the footsteps of Napoleon, and like Napoleon, will be sent back with his tail between his legs."

"What about the wounded?" Vladimir asked. "You said we are to help set up a field hospital?"

"I'm getting to that. The wounded will continue onto one of the military hospitals just outside of Moscow. That's all, gentlemen, I want our column ready to move out in two hours, at 0800 hours."

Vladimir rushed to the surgical dugout, by way of the first-aid bunker. Every space was filled with injured. It did not appear that there was a square centimeter left even to walk past the wounded. *Will I ever get used to the stench and the moaning?* There was no one tending to the wounded in the bunker. He stepped next door to the surgical dugout and saw more wounded men had been crammed into all available space. One soldier was on the surgical table with Tanya leaning over him after prepping him for surgery.

Beware the Wolves

"There's another bucket of fresh water and I found some more soap for your hands," Tanya said. "It's on the ammunition box."

Vladimir made his way to the box, stepping over bandaged men lying on the ground. It was hard to see the bucket as two injured soldiers sat slumped over on the box. Vladimir also had to get more surgical supplies from the box and he asked them to move over. One of the soldiers, with great effort, stood. The other was not responsive. Vladimir placed his fingers on the neck to feel the soldier's pulse. He was dead. *How many more are dead waiting for medical attention? But then, even with medical help, nothing could have helped many of these poor souls.* Misha and Boris entered carrying another wounded man and began looking for a place to lay him down.

"Where do we put them now," Boris asked. "We've run out of room."

"Take this one out. " Vladimir pointed to the deceased. "Find someone who can sit up and lay the new one down."

"Shit, this is like a puzzle," Misha said. "We have more coming in."

"The shelling has stopped for now," Vladimir said. "Take them to the mess bunker. I'll get to them as soon as I can. Misha, give me an exact count of all the wounded. I need to know how many must lie down, how many can sit up in a wagon and how many can walk. Also, how many are in such shape that they cannot be evacuated. Boris, find Evgeniy and all the other medics. Hurry, we have less than two hours to get everyone out of here."

"What do you mean?" Boris said. "What's going on?"

"I have no time to explain, just do it."

While Vladimir performed the surgery on the soldier, Tanya wanted to know everything that transpired at the meeting with Savitski. Vladimir explained to her their new assignment. He was almost done with the operation when he heard a whistle followed by a loud burst from a shell that hit nearby. Another, then another followed that explosion. The barrage had begun once again. Dirt cascaded all around them. Vladimir covered the patient with his body to keep the dirt from hitting the open lesions and waited for the shelling to stop.

"Those are artillery shells. But I hear shelling from the Panzers in the distance," one of the wounded soldiers volunteered. "They're getting closer to us, they'll run us over in no time. Then the infantry will finish us off."

The shelling diminished around them, but the ground continued to shake under his feet. At least the rain of dirt had stopped.

"That's our artillery and anti-tank boys now. We'll get them. We'll slow those sons of bitches down," another soldier said.

Vladimir did not have enough experience on the battlefield to know the sound of the different weapons, but was impressed by the knowledge that these soldiers displayed.

"The wagons are here, Comrade Captain," Evgeniy yelled. "They are loading the ammunition on them now."

"Evengiy, run up there and make sure that they don't use our first-aid wagons," Vladimir hollered back. "Misha, how many wounded do we have?"

69

Victor Moss

"Sorry, Captain, I lost count at fifty. They're all over the place. I guess at about sixty."

Vladimir inhaled deeply and his cheeks filled with air. His headache had subsided during the surgery, but now it was back with a vengeance. *There has to be a way to transport most of the wounded,* he thought. He finished stitching the wounded and looked around. All the medics were now by the bunkers, crowding the area even more. Evgeniy had brought them all in from the field. *What about all the wounded lying in or near the trenches on the battlefield? There is no one to help them. Will they have to be left behind? I'll have to send the medics out one more time shortly before departure.* Vladimir felt overwhelmed with the logistics, but told himself that he had to be calm and in control. *I need to do my own triage to determine which of the wounded would survive an evacuation and which ones would not.*

The battle continued. Vladimir suspected that Savitski gave his all to hold back the enemy so that they would have a chance to escape. He admired Savitski for that. After a perfunctory examination of each individual, Vladimir counted a total of fifty-eight. If he had to leave anyone, seventeen would be left behind, as they would not make it an additional day, with or without medical help. Of the forty-one who would be evacuated, seven could walk, twenty-three could sit up and the rest had to lay flat. Tanya followed him during his evaluation, and he asked her to remember the status of each of the wounded. He ran up the ramp and onto the adjacent field next to the bunkers and saw Evgeniy arguing with a soldier. Both of them seemed very animated and irritated.

"What's the problem here?" Vladimir asked.

Both soldiers immediately stood at attention, then Evgeniy said, "Comrade Captain, you ordered me to make sure these first-aid wagons are for our wounded. Well this fool wants to use them for ammunition and supplies. He said the wounded are goners anyway."

Vladimir gave the soldier a hard look.

"Never mind, forget it. I have orders that I am to grab all the wagons I can for our supplies," the soldier said angrily. He asked permission to leave and walked away.

"Good, now that's settled. Evengiy, you and the medics start bringing up the wounded. Tanya will coordinate which come out first. Tell her I want those that must lie prone first."

Vladimir looked closer at the wooden wagon. It was approximately three meters long and one meter wide and had a white canvas cover with a red cross painted on each side. Two draft horses pulled the wagon. At that moment, he heard the whistle of an approaching shell and he instinctly dove under the wagon for protection. The shell overshot the wagon and exploded thirty meters away, sending a shower of shrapnel and dirt in all directions. The horses reared up. They were frightened, but were tied down well and could not escape. However, the wagon lurched forward. *Oh my God! I'm going to get run over here.*

Beware the Wolves

Vladimir quickly rolled out from underneath. Shortly after the shell hit, he heard other gunfire and remembered one of the wounded pointing out the sound of an anti-tank gun.

As shelling and gunfire ceased, Vladimir began to inspect the other wagons. He discovered three first-aid wagons instead of two. He was certain that he could place six laying wounded into each wagon. It would be extremely tight, but it would work. He could place eighteen in the three wagons. But there would be no space left for the rest of the injured. At that moment, an idea struck him. He walked over to the wagons that were used for the ammunition and supplies and speculated whether he could have some of the wounded sit on top of the boxes or on artillery shells. He did not have permission to do so, but this was the solution he needed. He was certain that Savitski would approve. Four draft horses pulled the ammunition wagons and they should have the strength to pull the extra load.

◆ ◆ ◆ ◆

As the retreating column pulled out, six Soviet T-34 tanks moved onto the battlefield. Vladimir had heard about that particular tank. It was a superior tank in maneuverability to the German Panzers. Unfortunately, the enemy had more tanks. As he watched the Soviet tanks, he suddenly saw fire erupt from their turrets. Greatly relieved that they were there to cover their withdrawal, he realized that the lives of those in the machines of war would most likely be short lived.

At the front of the long column, Savitski rode a roan horse alongside with one of his lieutenants, also on a roan horse. Vladimir knew nothing about that lieutenant. He assumed that he was in charge of one of the three companies in the battalion, most likely one of the rifle companies Most of eighty soldiers in a group that walked in formation behind the officers carried rifles, but many carried machine guns, mortars and anti-tank guns. He remembered that in his week of basic training, the mortars were 107 mm Mortar M1938 and 82mm Mortar M1937. These were used for the heavy support of infantry. The anti-tank gun was so long and heavy that it took two soldiers to carry it. *How miserable it must be to haul that weapon on your shoulder for many kilometers.*

A company of riflemen followed in formation behind the first group of soldiers. Vladimir estimated that there were thirty of them. Immediately after the riflemen, the artillery battery rolled along. There were five cannons on axles and rubber tires. Eight draft horses attached to a two-wheeled cart pulled each artillery piece. On top of each cart sat two soldiers. Ivanov, as the officer in charge, rode his horse alongside the cannon. All of the draft horses on the left side of the teams pulling the cannons were saddled and carried a soldier. Vladimir thought it unusual for an artillery unit to travel together with the infantry, but he understood that the Soviet strategy, in some cases, was to integrate various elements. There could have been cavalry and tank units in a battalion. Following the cannons were seven wagons loaded with artillery shells, ammunition, or other supplies. Wounded soldiers balanced themselves on or among the cargo.

Behind the artillery battery, Vladimir found a place next to the driver of the first-aid wagon. Vladimir had offered his seat to one of the wounded soldiers, but Savitski insisted that he had to hold up the dignity of an officer and ride on the wagon. Tanya, the other medics, and those wounded soldiers able to ambulate, walked behind the wagons. The cook wagon brought up the rear.

♦ ♦ ♦ ♦

A few kilometers away, the dense forest was visible from the open rye field. The shelling and the chatter of machine guns ceased. The quiet, the first since dawn, lifted Vladimir's spirits. He felt at ease and looked forward to the escape and journey through the forest. The deep woods offered protection from the enemy. Then, the cook yelled out in panic. His warning worked itself down the column. Vladimir looked back and saw in the distance two Panzers approaching in a cloud of dust. They were still too far away for the shells to reach them, but the tanks were gaining ground.

Savitski ordered Ivanov's artillery to take a defensive position and stop the Panzers. He also commanded the anti-tankers and the sharp shooters to set up positions in the field. The rest of the column was told to spread out and run for the forest. The pace picked up as the horses galloped at full speed. Those on foot ran as fast as they could. The medics grabbed some of the wounded unable to run and helped them toward the forest. One of the supply wagons hit a rut and two of the wounded soldiers fell out.

"Stop the wagon," Vladimir ordered his driver.

"We have no room to pick anyone up," said the driver, looking back at the approaching tanks.

"Stop now! We'll stack them up on the others. Look there, two more fell out. We'll pick them up too," Vladimir shouted to the driver, pointing to the fallen soldiers.

The driver swore, but drove his first-aid wagon toward the fallen and helped Vladimir lift and stack them on top of the others.

"They'll be all right on top of each other as long as each can breathe. Besides, we are almost in the forest."

The dreaded thunder of battle returned. Vladimir glanced back just in time to see a shell from a Panzer hit one of the artillery pieces as it was being set up. Legs, arms, pieces of skull and other body parts of the soldiers manning the cannon flew into the air in thousands of pieces mixed with chunks of the cannon, axle and wheels. This was the first time that Vladimir had ever witnessed the power of one shell. He began breathing heavily and felt intense pressure around his chest. His own body felt as though the shell hit it. *Oh God! Ivanov! He could have been one of the men torn to pieces.*

Beware the Wolves

The German tanks pressed on. They appeared ominous and unstoppable, like dragons spewing fire from their nostrils. The four remaining artillery cannons were now in place and began their barrage of shelling in the direction of the tanks. They appeared to be no match for the tanks. One of the Panzers squarely hit another artillery cannon and again Vladimir saw pieces of body parts and pieces of metal flying into the air. At that instant, an artillery shell hit one of the Panzers and a ball of fire escaped from within. At the same time, the anti-tankers shot several volleys at the tanks and disabled the second tank. Vladimir saw the Nazis crawl out of the hatch, only to be shot down by the Soviet sharpshooters lying in wait.

The elation was short lived, however. In the distance at least three more Panzers appeared. The accompanying cloud of dust raised by the tanks covered the horizon. Whether there were more tanks behind the first three was hard to tell. Savitski ordered the remaining artillery pieces to retreat and commanded the column to regroup once shielded inside the forest. As the column, now disorganized, rushed toward the trees, Vladimir wondered, *Will the forest be enough protection from the Panzers?*

CHAPTER 10

A narrow trail in the forest was just wide enough for the horses and wagons to trek. Savitski hurriedly assembled the column and ordered it to move forward. Vladimir, meanwhile, helped the medics transfer the fallen wounded soldiers from the medical wagons onto cargo wagons.

"What's the holdup here, Comrade Captain?" Savitski demanded from Vladimir.

"I have wounded stacked on top of each other and need to get them back on the cargo wagons, Captain."

Savitski's cheeks puffed out and he was just about to speak when Ivanov rode up to them.

"I ask you again, Comrade Captain, allow me to place my artillery pieces at the edge of the forest. I'll stop those tanks."

Vladimir was very pleased to see his friend and, at the same time, surprised by Ivanov's request. *That's a gutsy move on his part. For a negative and cynical individual, he's showing some gumption.*

"Ivanov, I said no, and I mean no. I can't chance to lose those weapons in a fight here. We already lost two in that skirmish. My orders are to deliver the artillery pieces to Yelna within two days."

"But we stopped those Panzers on the field and we can stop the others."

"No, we are totally outmatched. Now get your ass with your men and move out now! As for you, Moskalkov, I can't wait forever for you to get your patients comfortable. Start moving out whether you're ready or not."

"We're ready Captain. The fallen wounded have been relocated," Vladimir replied seeing the go ahead sign from Stepan.

The steady growl of approaching tanks, with their squeaky, high-pitched tracks became louder by the minute. Soon they would appear at the edge of the forest. Vladimir felt the monster crawling under his skin. He heard the tanks stop, and he stopped breathing for a few seconds.

"They're being careful. They think we set up a trap for them," Vladimir's driver said. "We should have, you know. We have enough firepower and men."

"If they think we are lying in wait for them, maybe they'll back off," Vladimir said.

At that moment, he saw sharpshooters and anti-tankers running past him. He looked around and watched some take their positions in the cover of the brush and trees. Suddenly, the tanks opened fire. Vladimir was startled. His ears, once again, almost burst with the painful ring of explosions. He immediately covered his ears. Fortunately, the shells fell behind the column and out of the range of the anti-tankers and the sharpshooters. Vladimir smelled smoke, but the odor was distinctly unlike the smell of gunpowder he had become used to. He turned around. The trees behind them were on fire. The bombardment stopped, followed by the cracking and snapping of the trees. With a shudder, Vladimir realized that the Panzers were pursuing them into the forest. *How big does the tree have to be to stop a tank?* Looking around at the size of the trees around them, he thought, *Most of these trees would not be able to stop a tank. The Panzers will mow them down.*

The fires could not sustain themselves on the soggy coat that covered the trees. The undergrowth was mushy within its thick blanket of decaying leaves, twigs and pine needles. A thought occurred to Vladimir of the vast difference between the climate in the dry fields and the humidity of the forest. His mind blocked out the battle, as if to protect itself by diverting fear of danger into a stream of peace and pleasure. Just that thought of the difference in environment between the farm fields and the trees was his instant escape from the German wolves pursuing him. He was desperate for any relief from the dread. The stress had been unrelenting the past several days and he yearned to find a spot under the tree where he could just lay down and sleep. He fantasized about a deep, long slumber.

"They're getting closer," the driver said to Vladimir, forcing his mind back to the situation at hand. "We are moving as fast as we can, but they are still on our backs. The deeper we get into the forest, the bigger the trees become. That will stop them. It better because we can't go on much longer. The horses are tired."

Vladimir looked back at his medics. The wounded that had been able to walk, were no longer mobile. Evgeniy, Misha and the others each carried one of the wounded on their backs, struggling to keep up. Tanya, like the others, looked worn out.

The boom of the anti-tank guns shook the ground. A burst of rifle fire followed a minute later. The sound of the engine that hounded the column ceased, as did the squeaking of the tracks and the snapping of the trees. Savitski and his lieutenants galloped past Vladimir between the adjacent rows of trees toward the sound of the clash. The column kept moving forward, but at a much slower pace. Vladimir was sure that the pursuing tanks had been disabled. He felt a release, as though a boulder fell off his body. Vladimir's mind, once again drifted to the beauty of nature about him. Rays of the late afternoon sunlight streaked through the brilliant leaves of the birch trees. He became aware of the noisy birds, the fresh smell of the damp trees mingled with the musty smell of decaying logs and old leaves.

Vladimir glanced back when he heard the officers' horses returning to the column. The men had smiles on their faces and Ivanov held up his thumb. He knew that the danger, at least for now, was past.

"We were lucky," Savitski stopped to tell Vladimir. "There was only one Panzer that followed us. But we got the miserable bastards. The other tanks must have turned back to Smolensk. There should be a little open area up ahead. We'll eat and rest up for a few hours."

Vladimir was pleased to hear that the column would stop. He was concerned about the wounded, whose chorus of moans and groans increased with each passing moment. Lying on those hard wagons was difficult at best, certainly not a good situation for those suffering. The bandages had not been changed and almost all of them needed their aspirin or morphine or sulfa drugs as soon as possible.

At the small clearing in the forest, the cook wagon took a prominent place among the resting soldiers. The cook was a short, thin fellow with a constant smile on his face. Vladimir thought him to be no older than eighteen. His head, like most of the soldiers, was shaven.

"Well, everybody, listen up, you have a choice for supper. You can have cold buckwheat mush right away or warmed up mush in half an hour," said the cook laughing hard as he stepped down from the wagon.

"I am sick and tired of buckwheat," said one of the soldiers. "There are plenty of mushrooms in the forest. Why don't we gather up some and you cook them."

"All right, if you bring me enough mushrooms," the cook said. "I'll perform a magic show for you with potatoes and a little bit of slab bacon. It will be a meal you'll never forget. Make sure you write home about it. And for dessert you can graze the forest for the berries, just like our horses."

Vladimir laughed along with the others and his mouth started to water with the thought of a mushroom soup. But he did not trust the hungry soldiers to know the difference between edible or poisonous mushrooms. He told the cook that he wanted to look at the mushrooms before they went into the soup. He knew the difference in mushrooms because his grandfather had taught him well.

The medics helped the wounded off the wagons and laid them down on the ground. The earth was springy and slushy. The many years of fallen leaves had created a brown spongy mattress. It was very comfortable to lie on, but the mass of rotting material was filled with insects and spiders. There were insects in the ground and in the air. Large mosquitoes feasted on the soldiers, as did the huge horse flies whose painful bites would later fester and leave scars.

Tanya and Vladimir immediately tended to the wounded. Vladimir expected help from the other medics only to see that they and most of the wounded and the rest of the soldiers were smoking their Makhorka cigarettes. The men rolled their own cigarettes out of cheap tobacco made out of the stems of the tobacco leaf. The soldiers used whatever paper they could get their hands on, mostly newspapers. The stink was awful. Vladimir could no longer smell the forest. *If the Germans searched for us now, it would not be difficult,* Vladimir thought. *All they would have to do is follow that stench.* Vladimir, however, could not be too critical of the smokers. He discovered that the effect of tobacco on morale was critical. Therefore, he let the medics take their smoke before ordering them back to work.

Beware the Wolves

One of the wounded concerned him more than the others. His leg was not getting better despite the sulfa drugs. His foot had turned black and he had lost feeling in that foot and lower leg. Vladimir diagnosed gangrene and made the decision that the leg would have to come off.

"Soldier, what is your name?

"They call me Ilya."

"How old are you?"

"I'm nineteen, Comrade Captain."

"Where is your home?"

"I'm from Roslavl, Comrade Captain."

"I've heard of it. It's a beautiful city, isn't it?"

"Yes, sir, it is. I miss it so much. I have a girlfriend there waiting for me."

"You're lucky. What's her name?"

"Her name is Svetlana, sir."

"You realize that you have to do everything in your power to survive so that you can go back to your Svetlana?"

"I know, Comrade Captain. I want to see her so much."

"You realize that you must have the strength and the will power to live, don't you."

"Well, yes sir, but what are you telling me?"

"Your leg is badly infected. The medicines I have here can't fight the extent of the infection. There may not be any medicines that can. You have gangrene. Do you know what that is?"

"No, is it bad?"

"Yes, Ilya. It is a very dangerous situation. Your leg is dead and the dead tissue is spreading up your leg. The infection will get into your blood stream. Do you understand what I'm telling you?"

"I think so. You're telling me that I will lose my leg, aren't you, sir?"

"Yes, Ilya, we need to take it off right above the knee."

"And if you don't what will happen?"

"Ilya, you will die a very painful death. But if we do the surgery, your chance of living and going home to Roslavl and to Svetlana are very good."

"But, I won't be able to walk. I will always be a cripple. People will make fun of me or feel sorry for me. No, I'd rather just die."

"You don't mean that. Look at all the people around us dropping dead and all the misery and suffering. We need to preserve life. Life must become even more precious in these times. Once you get to a hospital, you will receive an artificial leg. You will be just fine. You'll learn how to walk with it, even dance. You have to do it for Svetlana, and for yourself."

Ilya agreed, though reluctantly. Vladimir shuddered because now he would have to perform an operation that he dreaded. He almost wished that Ilya had refused. He had performed an amputation once before, but at a hospital with a surgical table, lighting and surgical tools that he needed. But to perform such a difficult surgery under these primitive conditions, and a surgery that was so difficult on him personally, brought a knot to his stomach. He hated the notion. It repulsed him to saw off a limb from a human being.

Vladimir asked Misha to bring him the saw from one of the ammunition boxes used by them for their medicines, supplies and tools. The boxes were still on one of the supply wagons. Misha brought him the saw and Vladimir heard absolute silence from the soldiers sitting around, smoking and waiting for the meal to be prepared. They noticed the saw and their jokes and laughter stopped.

"Good, Misha. Tanya has some water boiling. Put the saw in the water along with my scalpel and forceps and let them boil for at least ten minutes. Oh, yes, I also need a good steel knife with a wooden handle, see if you can find one."

"Where are we going to do the surgery?" Tanya asked. "Not here right on the ground, are we?"

"Where else?" Vladimir answered. "We'll do it right here. Start giving him morphine and then roll up his pant leg, and boil his sock."

"Boil his sock? For what."

"We'll put some weight in his sock, like that stone there," Vladimir said pointing to some stones on the ground. "We'll put the sock over his skin so that it will pull the skin over the stub and keep it pulled."

"Oh, God!" Tanya exclaimed as she put her hand over her mouth and went to get the morphine.

Vladimir cut the skin all the way around the young soldier's leg several centimeters below the point where he was to cut off the leg. He pulled the skin back and then proceeded to cut the meat and bone with the saw. Ilya screamed until he passed out. The sweat rolled off Vladimir's forehead in rivulets. Tanya's shaking hand tried to wipe it away so that Vladimir could see. He pulled the knife blade from the fire and cauterized the blood vessels to keep the blood from seeping out. The soldiers, including Savitski and the officers, stood mutely gawking at the procedure.

It was done. The part of the leg that he amputated was so infected that Vladimir knew that he made the right decision. He felt bad, but then he was also elated. He had saved Ilya's life. *Ilya will be all right,* he thought to himself. After the procedure, Savitski approached him.

"Good job, Comrade Captain," he said and walked off.

After the adrenalin rush passed, Vladimir ate greedily. The mushroom soup was delicious and a nice change from buckwheat mush. Vladimir was still hungry so he took his mess kit to the cook wagon and asked for a little more. Unfortunately, none was left so he returned and sat down on a fallen log next to Ivanov.

"Couldn't get any more, huh?" Ivanov said. "Oh well, we should be out of this forest shortly and get back on the road to Yelna. Maybe we'll find some chickens or pigs on the way. That is, if the damn Germans don't get them first.

Beware the Wolves

I think they are everywhere now. You know, Volodya, we are lucky we were sent out of the Smolensk area. General Yeremenko is supposed to bring in fresh units to Smolensk. The Smolensk garrison was ordered to hold every building or die. But we were sent to Yelna. Do you know why?"

"No, I don't. Why, Sergey?"

"Well, because in Smolensk they will have a battle from building to building. They will not need artillery. Yelna is going to be next. It is a road juncture surrounded by high ground. It is an important strategic position as a jumping off point to Moscow. They want Savitski there because he is a good strategist. But it won't make much difference. We won't be able to hold off the Germans there either. If Smolensk hasn't fallen yet, it will do so before the end of July."

Vladimir thought that Ivanov's pessimism was destructive. *He talks too much. One of these days, if the Germans don't get him first, he will probably be arrested for his big mouth.*

"Let me tell you a story my grandfather used to tell me," Vladimir said. "There was this head lying on the side of the road. A peasant came by, saw the head and asked, 'Hey, head, what happened to you?'

"The head replied, 'The Pan (landlord) cut me off from my body because of my tongue.'

"Sergey, you have to be careful what you say," Vladimir continued. "It's a good thing the Commissar is not here with us. One has to be optimistic about the outcome, otherwise why even bother to defend your homeland. After all, battles may be lost, but the war will be won. I can't imagine living under the Germans, can you?"

Before Ivanov could give a response, he heard a group of soldiers singing one of his favorite songs.

"We'll talk about this later, Sergey. You know how much I love to sing. Lets join in the song *Katusha*.

"As the apples and pear trees are blossoming
And the fog flows over the river,
Katusha comes out to its banks,
Its high and steep banks.

"She comes out and sings a song
About the gray eagle of the steppes.
She sang about the one she loved,
Whose letters she had saved.

"Let the song of the maiden
Fly toward the bright sun
To the soldier at the far away post,
And let the song carry a greeting from Katusha.

Victor Moss

"Let him remember the simple girl.
Let him hear how she sings,
Let him guard the motherland
And Katusha will guard their love."

After supper and one more smoke, Savitski allowed the men another two hours to sleep. Vladimir appreciated the free time. He went to the first-aid wagon and took his duffel bag and rain-cape from underneath the seat. All the soldiers were issued these capes that were worn in horseshoe fashion over their shoulders. Vladimir spread it on the ground, using the cape as a sheet on which to lie. He could wrap himself up in it if he needed to. It could also be used as a lean-to or if teamed up with a comrade, they could actually pitch it as a tent. For extra warmth, if necessary, he could use his great coat, but it was hot and he laid down on the cape. His duffel bag became a pillow.

Tanya came by and laid her rain-cape next to his.

"I am so exhausted," Tanya said. "Do you mind if I lay down here next to you?"

Vladimir thought for a moment before he answered, but before he could say anything, Tanya was already on the ground with her cape touching his. *Well, why ask,* he thought to himself.

"Tanya, you can lie down anywhere you want. All I know is I am dog-tired and I need my sleep."

Tanya laid there for a while on her back, then suddenly turned to her left side facing Vladimir.

"You aren't sleeping yet, are you, Volodya? I really admire how you handled that amputation. I pity the ones who lose their limbs. What do you think it will be like for us in Vyazma?"

"Tanya, I have no idea what's facing us in Vyazma. Every day brings something new to me. Let's get some sleep."

"Volodya, I'm too hyper to sleep. Let's talk a little. We never have a chance to talk to each other."

Vladimir turned his back on her and closed his eyes.

"Volodya, what day did you get married?"

"Tanya, please, I'm trying to sleep. We'll talk later."

"Volodya, what was the wedding day like? I really would like to know. For instance, what was your bride wearing?"

Vladimir rubbed his eyes and turned around and faced Tanya. He realized she would go on forever unless he talked to her. He could pull his rank on her and order her to shut up, but thought too much of her to do so. Besides it wasn't in his character. And actually, he liked to think and talk about Slava no matter how tired and sleepy he was. He also decided in his mind that if he told Tanya more about Slava, she would realize that there was no room for her in his heart.

Beware the Wolves

"We were married last year, March 2, 1940. She wore a white dress and held white roses tied with a pale white ribbon. We, as everyone had to, registered at the Records Bureau of Citizens' Civil Status since religious ceremonies are not allowed. I remember vividly Slava's face. It was full of happiness and excitement. She laughed so freely at the slightest provocation, as if the whole world was created for her amusement. Her laughter was a melody of bells, touching all who were near, surrounding them in a swirling celebration of life. When I heard her laughter I felt something warm in the center of my chest. It was like musical fireworks touching my soul.

"So there we stood at the counter to register our names and become husband and wife. I looked at her as she was signing her name, standing there, white roses pressed to her chest. She looked so pure, and appeared so untouched by the harshness of life. I felt so lucky to have found such love. We kissed and didn't stop kissing until the Army snatched me from her arms."

"Oh, that sounds wonderful," Tanya whispered. "I pray that someday I will find someone like you."

Vladimir looked at Tanya at that moment and under the rays of moonlight could see that she had tears in her eyes. He felt bad for her. He wanted to squeeze her hand to console her, but decided that would only encourage her. *What am I doing talking about this when I should be sleeping?* Neither he nor Tanya said a word. Then a few minutes later, Vladimir said, "Tanya, let's get some sleep. We will be moving out soon. Who knows what tomorrow will bring."

CHAPTER II

March 2, 1940 was Slava's wedding day. Slava's mother, Suzanna, was beside herself with anger. She had always dreamed of the day that her children would be married at Saint Barbara Church, a beautiful Catholic church that stood high on a hill before the communists destroyed it. Religious ceremonies were forbidden by the Soviets and there were no churches or priests.

"What sacrilege?" Suzanna said as she shook her head and raised her arms in disgust. "They want to make us a Godless society. Well it won't work. Jesus will always be with us, they can't remove Him from our hearts."

"Mama, we have been through this before," Slava said. "Only Eva was married in church. My other brothers and sisters had to register just like we have to do. You should be used to it by now."

"Oh, I'm used to it, but that doesn't make it right. I didn't like the idea of Eva marrying at sixteen, but at least a priest married her in church."

"Mama, it will be all right. I'm just thrilled to be Volodya's wife. Besides, I know you are excited about the wedding. You've cooked and baked for a week."

"Well, we can't run out of food. We have to be prepared. More people are coming than I expected. How many told you that they'll come?"

"Fifty, plus children, mama, and that includes our family. Don't worry about the food. You always prepare more that we need."

"What about the drinks? Has Vladimir brought enough liquor for the party?"

"Yes, mama, he has carried bottles in his briefcase for over a month now. Come and look at how many we have."

Slava opened the door to the sideboard in the dining room where the family's liquor was usually stored.

"It's amazing, isn't it, how he's always able to find things? Look, there are eleven bottles of vodka from Moscow, a bottle of vodka from Finland, six bottles of Armenian cognac, and seven bottles of Moldavian wine. He even found a box of Belgium chocolates. We're going to have so much fun. I only wish that all my brothers and sisters could come. Too bad they live so far away. Oh, well, at least Maria and her family will be here."

"Slavochka, you are chattering too much. You better get ready. Vladimir will be here soon to take you to register."

"Mama, call Vladimir, Volodya. Vladimir is so formal, especially since he'll be part of our family. Oh mama! I'm so happy right now. We're meant for each other and we're going to have a great life together, I know we will."

"If you're happy, I'm happy. You know, I wish you the best always. Now hurry and get ready. Maria should be here soon to help you with the dress. Be sure to thank your aunt Malania for the dress. That sister-in-law of mine really has a talent sewing beautiful dresses, doesn't she? Now get going and I'll continue with setting the tables."

Slava went to her room where her white satin knee-length dress was all laid out on her bed. Her brand new white shoes stood at the foot of the bed. They were a little big, but those were the only ones she found that she liked. She saw pictures of brides attired in long gowns with veils and long trains. She would really have liked a gown with all those trimmings, but the Communists forbade such apparel. She never really knew why, perhaps they considered them too decadent.

Slava just finished her hair and nails when Maria walked in with a white rose bridal bouquet she bought at the florist.

"Maria, these roses are just gorgeous. Let me smell them."

"Aren't they though? It's good to know the florist personally. She picked out the best white roses she could find. You know, it's difficult with white. They brown around the edges very quickly. Come on, let me help you button the dress."

"I know mama is happy for me," Slava said. "But I can't help but feel that there is something that troubles her, especially when I mention the relatives. Do you know what it is, Maria?"

"She goes through this with every one of our weddings. She mentioned her parents to me yesterday. She never talks about them. But when a wedding comes along and all the relatives arrive, she feels an empty spot in her heart because her mother wants nothing to do with her. Even I have never met them. They came to visit uncle Eshe and aunt Malania right here in Vitebsk all the way from Rejitsa, Latvia, before the border was closed, and never let mama know they were here."

"What exactly happened between them anyway? Slava asked. "Mama and papa never wanted to talk about it. You know, I don't even know my grandparents names."

"Their names are Joseph and Rosalia Tashkan. Evidently, papa was not considered to be of the same social class as mama. Mama grew up in one of the wealthy peasant families in Latvia. Papa came from poor Polish peasants in Latvia. They married without the approval of mama's parents and then moved to Vitebsk. Grandmother was so infuriated by this that she disinherited mama and swore never to see her daughter again."

"Because she moved to Vitebsk?"

"No, Slava, because she married papa. Uncle Eshe moved to Vitebsk shortly after papa and mama did, so they came to visit him."

"That must be really hard on mama, isn't it?"

"I know it is. She would love so much to have her parents here for your wedding. But then, she doesn't even know whether they are still alive. Her letters to them were never answered. Slava, you look absolutely beautiful. Volodya is so lucky."

"Oh thanks, you have always been my best cheerleader. You're really like a second mother to me. I will never forget the times when I was little that you would go out on dates and your boyfriends would give you chocolates. You always saved one or two for me, placing them under my pillow while I slept. In the morning it was such a thrill to reach under my pillow and find those chocolates."

"Well, after all, I am fourteen years older than you and I have to take care of my little sister."

As Maria helped Suzanna with the preparations for the reception and Slava stood in the living room, admiring the bouquet, her father returned from the store carrying two full cloth bags of groceries. He admiringly looked at Slava, came up and kissed her on each cheek and forehead.

"You're a vision, my little angel," Vladislav said. "I like Vladimir and know he will be a good husband to you. Your mama and I are old and someday we won't be here for you. But you will no longer need us because as in the cycle of life, you will make your own family. And through your family, a little part of us will live on. Be happy, my little one and try to survive no matter what the politics of the moment may be."

Slava looked into her father's brown eyes. It was obvious that he was holding back his tears. He was always sentimental, a man of very mild character. Her father meant to give her words of encouragement, but the message came across with sadness. She studied him closely, noticing that his hair was now grayer than she remembered. His face appeared to be more wrinkled and he had large bags under his eyes. She knew that age was suddenly important to him. She remembered that just recently he had begun to complain about how much he had slowed down. He was her rock, her stability in life. But she also felt that sense of strength and stability in Vladimir. He was her stonewall that she could lean on. After all, he even used those words in his proposal of marriage:

"My dearest and sweetest Slovachka. You have become the center of my existence. As the earth revolves around the sun, I revolve around you, for you are my sun. I love you so much and I have loved you from the moment I saw you. I know you love me too since I can feel it in my heart. Marry me. I will be your stonewall behind which you can always feel secure."

Remembering the words from Vladimir's proposal and how he held both of her hands in his, and then kissed each finger as he waited for her answer, brought a smile back to her face.

"Thank you, papa," Slava said. "You are the best father and I will always need you no matter how old I am. Besides, we are not leaving; we'll stay in this house with you until I finish medical school, and Volodya is through with his Ears, Nose and Throat residency. Oh look, I see a Hansom cab coming up the street. I bet its Volodya."

Beware the Wolves

◆ ◆ ◆ ◆

The Records Bureau of Citizens' Civil Status was in City Hall. It was a cold, impersonal structure with marble floors and walls. Slava, however, did not notice the coldness since she sensed a warm feeling throughout her body. She felt overwhelmed and giddy with joy. She laughed and giggled all the way from her house. Every little thing or word made her laugh. Their witnesses already waited for them. Her best friend, Valentina, came as a witness for Slava and Dodik, Vladimir's friend, for Vladimir.

The couples and their witnesses stood in line waiting to execute their names in a large ledger book placed on a highly polished mahogany table. The line was much longer than either Vladimir or Slava anticipated. Slava knew that Vladimir could be impatient, and observed him glancing at his gold watch with a brown leather band.

"Volodya, we'll be there soon. Lines are just a way of life. I remember the time my parents finally allowed me to travel to visit my brother and sister in Leningrad. I was only fifteen, and was excited to travel by train and see a big city. Volodya, Leningrad is so beautiful with its magnificent royal palaces that are now beautiful museums. It's an exciting city packed with people, automobiles and stores. But the lines are terrible. I went with Eva to the store to buy food. We had to wait in a long line just to pay and get a receipt to buy milk, yogurt and butter. Then we had to wait in line to pick up the dairy products. Next we waited in line to purchase bread, and then we got into another line to pick up the bread. On one particular day when we went to pick up the bread that Eva had paid for, they had run out of bread. We had to wait in the cashier's line once again to get a refund. Now that's waiting in line. This line is nothing at all."

"I know, Slavachka," Vladimir said. "To marry you I will stand here for a week, if needed."

It was finally their turn and Slava came up to the table. The clerk at the table was a stern looking woman in her forties. She did not smile and was formal, obviously pleased with her bureaucratic authority.

"Let me see your passports." She examined their papers carefully and compared their picture with their faces. "All right, sign the register and you are officially married." First, Slava signed her name as Vladimir watched, then Vladimir signed his name as Slava watched. As soon as the witnesses signed their names, the happy couple was married. Slava had enjoyed Vladimir's frequent kisses. She now waited for the ceremonial kiss, as was the custom after the registration. Vladimir held off briefly, teasing her, and then kissed Slava passionately on the lips, pressing her body to his.

◆ ◆ ◆ ◆

The accordion music provided by Slava's neighbor, Isaac, started to play as the couple and their witnesses came up the walk to the house. The guests

Victor Moss

lined up along their path cheering the newlyweds. Suzanna and Vladislav waited at the door. The moment Vladimir and Slava set foot in the house, the parents jointly held a round white-flour loaf of bread that Suzanna baked for the occasion. A small silver bowl filled with salt sat on top of the bread.

"I bless you both with this bread and salt," Suzanna said with a big smile on her face. "May you always have food in your house."

The crowd was noisy. Maria attempted to seat the visitors. If the guests squeezed together, the large dining room table accommodated sixteen. The two smaller tables set up in the living room held another sixteen people. The tables on the enclosed veranda held eighteen guests. The children had their own table in the kitchen. But this task of seating the guests as they milled around or talked in groups around the tables became too hectic and Maria gave up. She finally announced that they should sit where they liked. She made sure, however, that the side of the dining room table facing the living room was reserved for the newlyweds, the witnesses and their dates. Maria sat down with her husband, Feodor and their son, Vova, at the table in the living room with her parents and Vladimir's mother and his three sisters.

Each table held an arrangement of flowers made of pink and white carnations. The tables were laden with appetizers: herring, meat pies, potato pies, vinegret (beet and potato salad), slices of cold ham, jelled pigs feet, slices of cold boiled tongue, smoked fish, pickled mushrooms, slices of tomatoes and cucumbers, wheat bread, rye bread, and, of course, vodka, cognac and wines. Baked ham and roast pork with mashed potatoes were served for the main course. Dessert consisted of custard filled wedding cake, pirogi (pies) made with blackberry jams, cookies, and tea.

As the guests busied themselves with the serious task of eating, the conversation was trivial. First there was the usual talk about family, jobs and weather. Numerous interruptions to the important task of eating took place with toasts to health and happiness. The first toast was always to the newlyweds, then to the parents, then to brothers and sisters—then whatever excuse anyone could come up with for a shot of liquor. And every few minutes or so, one of the guests would yell out "gorko (bitter)" and Vladimir and Slava would be expected to kiss to make it sweet. Slava and Vladimir were more than happy to oblige. And with each kiss, there was the obligatory shot of vodka by the guests.

Topics of politics and religion usually were avoided because no one knew who would report to the NKVD. But as the vodka and cognac flowed, the tongues loosened. The conversations became heated and one of the neighbors banged his hand hard on the table causing silverware to fly down to the floor. Everyone in the house immediately became quiet.

"Maria, you're good at jokes," Suzanna said. "Start the jokes rolling." She knew very well that once someone told a joke, stories by the guests would follow for hours. And in between the yarn, the crowd would break into song.

"There was this fellow who moved into an apartment," Maria began. "He developed the habit of sitting down on his bed before going to sleep, taking off one boot and throwing it against the wall and then doing the same with the other boot. After several nights of throwing his boots, his neighbor came over, looked upset, and told him that he wakes them up every time he throws his boots against the wall and demanded that he stop. The fellow apologized to his neighbor and assured him that he will no longer do it.

"The next night he came home from work, sat down on his bed, as usual, and took off one of the boots and threw it against the wall. He suddenly remembered what he promised his neighbor and put the other boot down next to his bed and went to sleep. About an hour later, he was awakened by his doorbell and when he opened the door, he saw his neighbor standing there in his underwear swearing and hollering, demanding to know when he will throw the other boot as they could not fall asleep while waiting for the other boot to hit the wall."

Everyone laughed. The jokes began with each trying to outdo the other with a funnier story. The party continued late into the night. Several hours had passed since the dessert was eaten and Suzanna and Vladislav offered more food. Their offer was quickly accepted so, along with help from some of the women, they prepared another meal.

"They'll leave when the liquor is gone," Vladislav told Suzanna.

But when the liquor was gone, the guests still remained, drinking tea. The songs and jokes were fun, but Slava was anxious for the guests to leave. Vladimir told her several times during the evening that he wished they would all go home so that they could retire to their room. *Our room!* she thought to herself. *How strange that sounds? It had been my room for the last eighteen years and now it will be our room.* At first the thought of sleeping with a man terrified her, but she loved Vladimir so much that now, this afternoon, this evening, this moment she could hardly wait to go to "their room" and be with Vladimir.

She also thought how wonderful it would be to go away on a honeymoon. She would like to have gone to Leningrad or, even more so, to the Crimea. Her brother Isaac lived there, and all her sisters and her brother, Leonid, had visited Isaac. They came back with tales of the beauty of the Black Sea, the swim in the moonlight, and the picnics on the beach. She felt left out because she had been too young to go. *A honeymoon was out of the question as both of us have to study. Besides, it's too cold to go to the Black Sea this time of the year.*

◆ ◆ ◆ ◆

Fifteen months later, the wedding day was a fond memory. They each had settled into their daily routines. Slava continued with medical school, and Vladimir, who had graduated in June 1940, was busy with a residency in Ear, Nose and Throat and in addition worked as a doctor in two clinics in Vitebsk. Life was hectic for Slava, but she and Vladimir were happy and cherished each moment together.

Victor Moss

On June 22, 1941, Slava had invited her friend, Valentina, to her house to study physiology in preparation for the examination. They had strewn their books and papers all over the dining room table, and were sitting with their heads buried in books, when the parents' tenant, Alexander, entered the room.

"Don't waste your time studying," Alexander announced with a pale look on his otherwise robust complexion. "You will never finish the course because your school will be shut down and you'll be evacuated."

"What are you talking about?" Valentina giggled.

"The Germans have crossed the border. We are at war. You'll hear about it soon enough, whenever our government decides to inform us."

"What are you talking about, Alexander?" Slava asked. "You're joking, right?"

"I wish I were. I wish I were joking."

"How do you know this?" Slava asked. As his startling words began to sink in, she felt tightness around her chest, a pit in her stomach, and her smile faded.

"I wasn't supposed to tell anyone. But I guess it no longer matters. I'm not the railroad worker that you thought. I'm an agent for the NKVD and have access to government information. So you might as well put your books away and prepare to leave Vitebsk. Unfortunately, Vladimir will be drafted."

Slava was speechless. Her mouth fell open. She was dazed. *Is this a nightmare?* She heard the words but what Alexander told her was simply unbelievable. *How could this be happening?* Her mind revolved like a gyroscope. *War? Evacuation? Alexander is an NKVD agent living in our house for the last three years? He saw the icons. He saw us observe religious holidays in our house behind closed curtains. Yet he never informed on us or arrested us.*

"Where are your parents? I need to tell them that I will be moving out immediately."

"Alexander, I am just shocked. I'm sorry, what did you ask me?"

"Where are your parents? I need to say good-bye."

"Papa is in the orchard and Mama is in the garden."

Alexander left and Slava turned to Valentina who appeared to be in as much shock as Slava.

"I'm going to run home and tell my parents," Valentina muttered. "You better find Volodya."

Slava could not reply. Tears were streaming down her checks as she sobbed.

◆ ◆ ◆ ◆

Slava and her parents were on the veranda anxiously waiting Vladimir's return. As Vladimir entered, Slava flung herself into his arms and began to cry. She had cried for the past two hours and told herself she would be strong. She started to tell him everything, but could not hold back the tears. Vladyslav

Beware the Wolves

came to Vladimir and said, "Alexander has told us that the Germans have crossed the border and we are at war. A public announcement should be made soon."

Vladimir looked at Slava, then at her mother, then father and then in the direction to the west. He had a very sad look, one that was uncharacteristic for him. "Our lives, as we know them, will now change forever. It will never be the same. Our future is uncertain and fearful."

CHAPTER 12

Five days after the German invasion, Vladimir was ordered to report at 0700 hours to the local military garrison in Vitebsk for transfer to an unknown destination. Slava accompanied Vladimir to the military staging area. They walked silently, hand in hand. Nothing more needed to be said. Each had swollen eyes from the tears. Slava had been unable to sleep since the news from Alexander of the invasion, particularly, his statement that Vladimir would be drafted. His words were a knife twisting in Slava's heart.

The garrison building was in the old part of Vitebsk, not far from the apartment Vladimir had occupied prior to their marriage. Slava had walked by the military building many times never realizing that her fate someday would be sealed by the old rusty metal doors of the ancient tin roofed, squat two story structure. The closer they came to the building, the more their hands squeezed together. Slava could no longer hold the flood of tears.

"Slavochka, please," Vladimir pleaded. "You are going to make me cry again. I can't report for duty with tears streaming down my face. What will they think of me? We talked and talked about it and, remember, we agreed that our destiny will bring us together."

"Volodya, you know darned well that no one knows their destiny. We only talked about destiny to make us feel better. It's an escape from this miserable nightmare. Once you walk through that door, I may never see you again. I can't stand this feeling. I'm all torn up. It isn't fair. We just started our lives together, and now all our hopes and plans are ruined."

"Slavochka, Slavochka, my darling, it will be all right. You'll see. Life never goes according to plan. There are always roadblocks, detours and troubles. But trouble is our friend because it gives us strength, builds our character and, in the long run, helps us survive. We both have to become survivors, and you'll see, it will all work out."

They were in the courtyard of the garrison building. The double doors were just a few meters away. Two armed soldiers, stationed as guards at the doors, checked papers.

Slava and Vladimir looked at each other with sad eyes. Vladimir pulled her close in an embrace. He nuzzled his face in her neck and they remained in the embrace for several minutes. They separated for a moment, Slava kissed Vladimir's lips, and then they each kissed the other on the cheeks, then again a long kiss on the lips. Again they embraced.

"Don't cry, don't cry my little darling," Vladimir whispered. "It will be all right. There have been wars in the past. People have survived. We will also survive. I better go in, it's almost 7:00 o'clock. Slavochka, let me go."

Beware the Wolves

"A few more minutes. Please. A few more minutes will not matter."

They kissed again and Vladimir pulled away to leave. Slava held his arm, and as he pulled away, she grabbed his hand, walking with him to the entrance. Vladimir showed his orders to the sentry at the door and the soldier waved him in. Slava was still at Vladimir's side at the entrance, and the guard stopped her. The couple kissed again and hugged each other for a moment and Vladimir turned and entered the building. He glanced back at Slava as he took a corridor to his right and waived good-bye. Slava was sobbing out loud. She felt ashamed for her uncontrolled tears because she saw that Vladimir now had tears rolling down his checks. Just what he tried to avoid.

"Where are they going to take him?" Slava asked the sentry at the door.

"Only the devil knows, miss."

Slava stood at the doorway for several minutes longer hoping that she would catch another glimpse of Vladimir. But she stood there to no avail. Finally the guard told her to move along as the courtyard became crowded with more draftees and their families. The scene was desperate, and the tears of others made Slava weep again.

She walked from the building listlessly. Slava's feet barely moved. Her head throbbed and her eyes burned from the tears. People scurried about, but Slava gave them no mind. She felt numb. She had classes that day. The school was not far away, but she knew she would not be able to concentrate. She just wanted to disappear and be left alone with her sorrow. Her mind was so deep in thought. *Will I see Vladimir again? Oh, Dear Jesus, please protect him and bring him back to me.*

Loud speakers on police and military vehicles were blaring something. When at last, she focused on the words coming from the speakers, she cried out to herself, *Oh, my God! They want us to burn down our homes! They want us to prepare for evacuation!*

She was so alarmed with Vladimir leaving for the front that she had not paid much attention to the talk that Vitebsk could be in danger. Somehow that did not seem as important at the time. But, now, the danger hit home.

Through the window she saw a group of people gathered around a radio in a hardware shop. She went inside and joined them. The commentator advised the citizens that war had begun with the invasion by the fascists. The civilians must prepare to evacuate and burn all buildings, including residential houses and apartments, thereby depriving the enemy of shelter and provisions.

"Oh that's crap," someone in the crowd said. "We're far from the western border. Our army will stop them or at least slow them down."

"Yes, what's the damn hurry," another man said. "I'll worry about it when they are at the Dvina River. It will take them months to get here, if ever."

Slava calmed down a little, by listening to those men who sounded as though they knew what they talked about. Slava decided to hurry home to tell her parents of the evacuation order, but then decided that her father probably knew about it because he always listened to the radio. *Before I go home, I had* better see if classes would continue under this evacuation order. It would be simply awful to have spent a whole year studying and not complete final examinations.

As she entered the school building, the main hallway was filled with faculty and students. The radio in the administrator's office was turned up to full volume. Slava stood next to her histology professor.

"Professor Shapiro, is the school going to shut down?"

"They advised us to evacuate, but did not say how soon. The war just started. As far as I am concerned we will carry on with classes as usual until they shut us down. I think most of the professors share the same sentiment. I think that is the patriotic thing to do as the army will need the new doctors."

Slava was unable to react. She felt as if someone had hit her with a sledgehammer, one slam after another. She looked around and saw some students crying. Slava was out of tears and stood drained, her shoulders slumped. She had experienced one horrible event after another. Vladimir had left, she might never see him again. The school could be shut down, they could have to evacuate from home, and they might have to burn their beautiful house along with most of their possessions.

Classes were canceled for the day. Those students who were willing were told to come back the next day. It was, however, highly encouraged to listen to the government directive and prepare to evacuate. Richard ran up to Slava as she was leaving.

"Slava, what are you going to do. Are you going to continue to go to classes?"

"Richard, at this time, I just don't know what to do. I need to go home, talk to my parents and decide. It's a very confusing time, isn't it?"

"Well, I certainly will stay as long as I can. I need to finish and get that degree. Oleg feels the same way. I'd advise you to stay. What is your husband going to do? As a doctor, he'll probably be drafted, I suppose."

"He left this morning," Slava said with extreme despair.

Slava liked Richard as a friend. They met in medical school and immediately hit it off. He was tall and very thin with light brown hair. He had an oval, intelligent face and his round-rim glasses added to his studious and serious look. He always seemed to be at her side—in the hallway, in class and walking her to the streetcar on many occasions. She knew that he liked her, but so did Oleg, Richard's best friend. The three of them frequently studied together. Slava considered them friends, but knew that each wanted to be more than her friend. She saw how devastated each looked when she told them about Vladimir. She had noticed their absence at her wedding reception, even though they were invited and had promised to come.

Oleg was extremely handsome with dimples in his rounded face, wavy blond hair and naturally blushed cheeks. He was of medium build and loved to tell jokes. She was even infatuated with him and liked the attention and the flirtation that both Oleg and Richard bestowed upon her. That is, until she met Vladimir.

"Richard, I can't talk right now," Slava muttered as tears once again filled her eyes. "I have to get home."

"Let me walk you home."

"No Richard. I want to be alone."

"All right, then, I hope to see you tomorrow."

Slava was deep in thought all the way home. She always obeyed all government decrees and considered herself to be a good citizen. But to evacuate and leave Vitebsk was a difficult decision. *If I were to leave, how would Vladimir find me either during the war or afterwards? But what if I stayed? What would happen to me? And if I stayed, my parents would stay as well. Then I would be responsible for whatever happened to them. If I evacuate now, I would not be able to finish the year in school, assuming the school stayed open long enough.* The thoughts flowed throughout her head until she reached the house.

Inside, her father and mother were arguing. Her father was animated, gesturing with his arms and hands. Uncharacteristic of her father, she immediately realized something was wrong. Her mother's round face was flushed and her tone of voice was frantic.

"No! Absolutely not!" her father shouted. "I am not going to leave this house and I am certainly not going to burn it down! So get that through your head. I have worked too hard to make our home here just to see all my efforts go up in smoke."

"You old fool! If the Germans take over Vitebsk, who knows what will become of us? They may kill us all, and then who cares about this house. Maria and Feodor are at least reasonable and responsible people. They have packed up, ready to take the train to Moscow. We should be with them."

"Well then you better go with them, as I am staying here! Ah, Slavochka, you are back at last. Did you hear the horrible news? They want the citizens to evacuate."

"Yes Papa, but actually its just an advisement to prepare to evacuate, there does not seem to be any immediate urgency."

"Your mother is frantic, and wants us to leave. Maybe it's for the best that you and your mother pack up and leave. But, I am staying here."

"I am not going anywhere without you," Suzanna replied. "But Slavochka, my baby, I want you to go with Maria. They plan to take the late train out tomorrow."

"No mama, I've thought it over and decided to stay."

"Don't be as ridiculous as your father. I have agreed to stay with your stubborn father even though I think we are making a big mistake. We are old, no one needs us, but you, a young and an attractive girl—oh my God! Oh precious Mother in Heaven—you better leave; I shudder to think what could happen."

"Mama, we just have to take our chances. Besides, our troops may defeat the Germans before they even reach Vitebsk and life may go on as normal."

"You are always too optimistic for your own good. Why on earth would you stay in harms way?"

"How would Volodya find me if he had to? Besides, classes will continue and I need to finish the year."

"Vladislav! Do something! Order her to leave."

"Yes, Slavochka, I agree with your mother on this. Please start packing some of your things. It is better to be safe than sorry."

"No! Papa! I'm not leaving!"

"All, right, all right I'll burn this damn place down and evacuate. Now will you go?"

"No, Papa! I have to remain. But you and mama must leave. Just don't burn down this beautiful house. I'll stay in it until I hear from Volodya."

The argument continued into the night. Her mother was hysterical. But Slava would not budge. The next morning Slava woke up after a restless night with the acrid smell of smoke drifting throughout the house. She looked out of her window and saw flames pouring out of a house down the block. A truck and a few horse-drawn carts made their way down the street loaded with possessions of neighbors. Evacuation for some had already begun. A shiver of panic swept through her. She again struggled within herself whether or not she had made the right decision.

She hurriedly dressed and walked into the dining room. Her father sat at the table staring at the ceiling.

"Papa, have you changed your mind? Are you going to evacuate?"

"No, Slavochka. I'm not. We don't know what awaits us here if we stay, and we don't know what awaits us if we go east. But at least, I'll be in my home if I stay."

"Good, I feel the same way."

◆ ◆ ◆ ◆

Slava's heart pounded when she heard the thunder of anti-aircraft guns as German planes flew over Vitebsk. They were reconnaisance runs, but occasionally, bombs flew over the city and destroyed strategic Soviet targets. The planes circled the city as though they were buzzards awaiting its death. War had waged over and around Vitebsk since early July 1941, especially a large battle on the Western Dvina River. Slava heard rumors that the Vitebsk defenders stopped the German advance. However she remained jittery and terrified. No one knew how long the defenders could hold out or when the Germans would break through.

"Vitebsk will never be taken," assured Issac, her neighbor.

Those words comforted her and she constantly prayed to her favorite saint, Saint Anthony that Vitebsk would be spared from the invasion. In her prayers she always added, *And protect and keep Volodya safe and healthy so that he will come back to me.*

Beware the Wolves

The days went on and Slava continued to attend school. She was relieved that the Institute had remained open. This gave her some hope that all might not be as bad as it seemed. She was amazed that final examinations had continued in spite of the smoke throughout the city from residents burning their homes. Many evacuees left the city and most of them caught the train to Moscow. She had heard that those who arrived in Moscow were not allowed to stay but were sent further east into Siberia. Some fled to smaller villages where they thought they could escape.

The government had now issued strict edicts ordering the civilians to evacuate immediately, and to set their homes on fire. Her father still refused to leave, but he dug a deep hole in the orchard where he buried the family's treasures such as silverware, jewelry and silver platters. He hoped to retrieve them later.

Shortages became noticeable. It was difficult to find meat, bread and milk as more of the shops closed. Even potatoes, the staple food of Byelorussia, were scarce, as fewer stores remained open. The food products were horded or destroyed as instructed by the government. The large outdoor market on Lenin Prospect was no longer in business nor were the small neighborhood outdoor markets. A few of the residents, who had their own gardens, sold products at outlandish prices. The family used more of their food reserves. They were fortunate, not only because Vladislav had a large garden and orchard, but also they kept a good supply of meat in the smokehouse and canned vegetables and fruit in the cellar. The Szpakowski family could hold out for several months. Slava's brother, Leonid, somehow anticipated a shortage and delivered a full wagon of flour to them shortly before the evacuation order. He came all the way to Vitebsk from the Crimea, and quickly returned.

On Thursday, July 10, 1941, Slava was in class taking her last final examination. She heard commotion and the roar of numerous engines from the street below. The racket from the street was unusual, but then, in the last several days, nothing seemed normal in Vitebsk. For the past week, in the distance to the west fierce explosions from bombs shook the ground and rattled windows. And of course, rattled nerves. Those who had not evacuated began to panic and tried to grab any transport out of Vitebsk. The Germans approach was much more rapid than anyone imagined. They were already at Vitebsk's doorstep. Extra trains were not enough to keep up with the evacuations of a population of 250,000 inhabitants, although, by July 10th, many had left.

Slava hurriedly worked on her examination. She prayed that she would, at least, finish and get credit for the courses taken in the event that the Germans entered Vitebsk. The racket outside grew louder. She resisted the urge to look outside because the shades were drawn, and she still had several hours left on the laboratory portion of the examination. Everyone inside seemed to be engrossed in his or her test. *Probably the government has brought in more vehicles to help with the evacuation.* So she left the hubbub to itself without satisfying her curiosity.

Victor Moss

The examination took longer than she had anticipated. It was late afternoon when Slava and most of the other students finished. She gave her work to the professor and left, waving good-bye to some of her friends. Richard waved back and motioned as if he wanted her to wait for him downstairs. She really was in no mood to wait around for him. She had a long walk back, especially if the streetcars were not running. Lately, they seemed to be sporadic in their schedules. Neither that morning, nor the day before, had she seen any at all and had walked the five kilometers to the medical institute. Her feet were not only sore, but also on the ball of one foot she had a blister that bled. She gestured a "no" to Richard, left the room, and walked down the flight of stairs.

In the hall, she saw professors and students standing in line waiting to exit. That was unusual and she heard someone say that German guards were at the door. She laughed, thinking that that was not a very funny joke in times like these. But as she looked closer and saw the grim and frightened faces, she realized that they were not joking. She heard screaming and yelling outside the door. Blood rushed to her head, she felt light-headed and dizzy. She wanted to scream, but covered her mouth and refrained.

"What are we waiting for?" Slava asked Dimitri, the student standing in front of her.

"Oh God! German soldiers, checking our passports."

"Oh no! Can't be! Dear Jesus, save us."

"What's going on out there?" a student behind her in line asked.

Slava repeated what she had heard to him. At that moment, four German soldiers with rifles and a fifth dressed in a gray officer's uniform with a pistol holstered on his belt walked through the door and looked over the line of students. Slava's knees felt as though they were about to buckle. Her heart pounded. Her breathing ceased for a moment.

"Get your passports and all other identification out!" barked the officer in very broken Russian. Two of the soldiers pushed through the line and stood on the other side. The other two remained with the officer. The officer intently studied the faces of each individual in line. When his eyes fell on Slava, she immediately looked down. When she looked up a few seconds later, he had moved along and was looking over the people behind her in line. She pulled out her passport from her black leather handbag. The document with Slava's photograph, required by the Soviets to be carried by all residents for identification, contained information as to the name of the individual, date of birth, address and nationality. Slava's nationality was listed as "Byelorussian." She also carried with her, at all times, her medical student identification card with her picture glued on the left upper corner.

The line moved forward slowly. Closer to the door, she heard more screaming and shouting.

"What are you doing? What have I done? Where are you taking me? Let me go!" some man on the steps of the Institute yelled hysterically.

Beware the Wolves

"Can you see what's happening out there?" Slava asked another acquaintance three spaces in front of her and standing near the doorway.

"All I can see is they look at the documents and some they let through, while others they take away."

"What are they looking for?" Slava asked.

"Don't know, they're arresting people randomly."

"Silence! Keep your mouths shut!" bellowed the Nazi officer.

As Slava neared the soldiers on the steps by the door, with her knees still weak, she thought she would collapse. A heavy band pressed against her skull. Dimitri showed his documents. She glanced at his passport and under the heading of "nationality" she read "Jewish." He was detained, while the soldier motioned to two other soldiers standing nearby. They started to escort Dimitri to a waiting truck filled with people. Dimitri tried to free himself of the grip of one of the soldiers and screamed obscenities at him. The other soldier struck him on the back of his shoulder with the butt of his rifle, knocking him to the ground. Both of them lifted him by his arms and dragged him to the truck. All of a sudden, Slava found herself face to face with the enemy.

"Passport!" he barked at Slava. Before she could hand it to him with her shaking hand, he grabbed it from her. He looked at it, then at Slava, and waved her through. As she walked past the truck she recognized many of the students and some of the professors crowded in it. Professor Shapiro was one of them.

"Help us! Help us!" They shouted from the truck to anyone that passed by. Slava, in sheer fright, said nothing and quickly kept walking. The Nazis circled the truck. She felt awful for the detainees and powerless to help them. *Oh God! What could I possibly do? I must keep walking. I have to hurry home.* As she hastened home, the truck, now filled to capacity, drove past her. This time everyone in the truck was silent.

Invading soldiers with armored vehicles, trucks and tanks were everywhere she looked. *How did they get here so fast?* The combination of the enemy presence and the burned out shells of the familiar buildings all around her made her feel as though she were in hell. Her heart and her mind raced. She shook.

Slava neared the railroad station and saw many more German soldiers. Some strung wire fencing, topped with rows of barbed wires. In an area next to the sidewalk, a part had already been completed and men, women and children were shuffled behind the fence. The Nazis were unloading more people from the trucks that were lined up in a row next to the encampment. As Slava swiftly walked by with her head bend down, she heard her name called out. She quickly looked up and saw some familiar faces from behind the barbed wire.

"Help us! Please help us!"

A fellow student from anatomy class stood next to the sidewalk. He stretched his arm out of the fence with his palm out. "Vladislava, Vladislava, please help. Can you do anything to help! We're not animals! They call us Jewish swine. Everyone here is a Jew. Surely, they can't round up all 50,000 of us in Vitebsk?"

"Yasha, what can I do? Besides, I'm too scared."

"Can't you at least find out from them what they want from us and what are they going to do to us. Ask that guard over there."

An inner voice told Slava to keep walking. *Do not get involved with what does not concern you.* She could not. The desperate look of the student and the others caged up haunted her. She approached the nearest guard who was eyeing her intently.

"Why are those people there?" Slava asked in Russian. "What are you going to do with them?"

"Get out of here before I put you in there." The guard snarled in German to Slava.

Slava moved along and decided to ask an older looking officer who stood smoking a cigarette next to his gray, topless vehicle. A soldier stood on the other side next to the steering wheel.

"Can you tell me, please, what is going to happen to those people?" she asked, pointing to the fenced area. "Why are they there?"

"I don't understand Russian." The officer replied in German as he shrugged his shoulders and smiled. This was the first smile Slava had seen for days and she was taken aback.

"Please, can you tell me what is going to happen to those people?" Slava asked once again, but this time in German. It was easy for her speak in German as Slava's parents had insisted that Slava study German and French with a private tutor from the time she was a little girl. At home, the family, on numerous occasions, spoke Polish, but in public they spoke Russian. The Soviets demanded that the population speak only Russian. Polish and the native language of Byelorussian were prohibited in any official capacity. Now she saw an opportunity to utilize her knowledge of languages.

"You speak German," the officer said. "Show me your passport please."

What have I done? Oh Jesus Christ, what have I done! Slava instantly thought with terror as she scrambled to pull out her passport from her handbag. The officer took it and pulled out a piece of paper from the inside pocket of his jacket and scribbled down Slava's name and address and handed back the document.

"It is very good that you speak German. We need interpreters. Come with me."

Oh, my God, Slava's mind began to spin. *What a fool I am. What have I done? I need to learn to keep my mouth shut.*

"No, no," Slava answered. "My German is not that good. Please, may I go home?"

"Do you live alone?"

"No, I live with my parents."

"You have nothing to worry about, young miss. You and your parents will have many privileges. You will get paid for your work, and I'll guarantee you that you and your parents will not be sent away to labor camps."

"No, I can't. I will not do it. Can I go now?"

"You are being very foolish. I'll let you go for now. But I have a feeling, we'll meet again soon."

CHAPTER 13

The scolding was severe. But Slava did not need the lectures. She knew she had made a mistake by bringing attention to herself. Her insides twisted with the feeling of impending doom. *Why was my tongue so loose with the enemy?* That thought raced in her head. *My parents are right. I deserve to be scolded by them. I should have minded my own business and walked straight home. Now that enemy officer has my name and my address. He said we would meet again soon. What did he mean?*

Slava tossed and turned all night. Sporadic gunfire was heard in the distance, but it was the sight of the German army, the incarceration of Jews and her conversation with that officer that kept her awake. Her father and mother did not sleep either. She heard the sound of their voices, and her mother's muffled sobbing. *If only Vladimir was here by my side for comfort. He always made me feel secure. Whatever problem I had, he always seemed to have an answer and made me feel better.*

The morning arrived too soon and the first light of day streaked through the window. Slava heard a faint knock on the windowpane as she lay in bed. At first she thought it was the wind, but as the knocking persisted, she raised her curtain and was shocked to see Mrs. Gelman, the tailor her mother used on occasion, crouching in the blackberry bushes underneath her window. Her two daughters sat by her feet on the ground. Slava unlocked and raised the pane.

"Please, may we come in? I'll explain inside."

"But of course, I'll open the front door."

"No, please, the back door."

Slava's parents sat in the kitchen. Her father was dressed, but her mother was still in her nightshirt and robe.

"Mama, Papa, Mrs. Gelman is at our back door with her daughters and wants to come in. I'll let her in."

"What does she want?" asked her mother, with surprise.

"I don't know," Slava answered as she opened the door.

"Please help us," Mrs. Gelman pleaded. "We need a place to hide from the Germans. They are searching for Jews and locking up those they find. No one knows why."

"Yes, I know what they are doing," Slava said. "I saw it yesterday. Jews were plucked right out of the Medical Institute and forced behind wire fences."

"You see," Mrs. Gelman said. "That is why we had to escape. Your family has always been kind to us. I know that some Byelorussians would never help a Jew, but please help us."

Beware the Wolves

"Of course, but where would you go?" Vladislav asked.

"We have relatives in a village not far from here. If we could stay the day, then we will run into the forest under cover of darkness and try to get to the village. From there, we will try to go east into Russia. We should have listened to the government and evacuated. Now it's too late."

"Where are your husband and sons?" Suzanna asked.

"They were drafted into the army. They are fighting those bastards, the sons of bitches. May the Nazis fry in hell a thousand lifetimes."

"Of course I agree with Vladislav, you can stay," Suzanna said. "You can stay as long as you want. We have enough food for everyone."

"If they come looking for you, we can hide you in the cellar," Vladislav added.

"Thank you, thank you so much. We don't know what else to do. We spent last night in Panasenko's half-burned barn. Of course we could not sleep knowing they were looking for us. We saw a German vehicle drive past. We thought for sure, they would stop and find us. But, luckily, they drove on. Oh, what a nightmare? Can it really be happening? We are hunted. Words can't describe the feeling that my daughters and I are going through."

"Here, have some breakfast," Suzanna said. "Then, afterwards, you need to lie down and rest."

"Slava, come and help me move the dining room table," Vladislav said. "We need to keep the trapdoor to the cellar more accessible in case they come here."

Slava helped her father move the table to the side. Her mother called Slava to breakfast, but she could not eat. She felt sick to her stomach.

A haze of smoke and dust filled the early morning air. Only two houses remained on the street—theirs and Isaac's, the neighbor next door. All others had been burned to the ground. The residents fled. Alexander, Szpakowski's tenant, had left Vitebsk a few days ago on some secret mission. Before he left, he warned them again of their huge mistake in staying and not destroying the house. He cautioned them that they would be arrested by the Soviets for disobeying orders when Vitebsk was reclaimed. That is, if they should survive the German occupation. His advice troubled Slava, but she reassured herself with the thought that even though the government was able to remove most of the manufacturing and industrial equipment from Vitebsk, it was unable to evacuate the entire population. *Surely, not everyone would be arrested?* However, the Germans were the immediate threat and Slava wondered what would happen to her family and the remaining populace in Vitebsk. *Will we all be herded behind wire fences like cattle? And then what?*

As she walked onto the veranda to look out over the gloomy landscape, she saw two German vehicles approaching from the direction of the center of town. Her chest tightened and her head began to pound at the ominous sight. The first vehicle, an open bed truck, was filled with soldiers, who sat facing each other. The other vehicle was massive, propelled by a half-track. The back of that vehicle was also crammed with soldiers.

"Mama, papa, they're coming! Hurry, the Gelmans have to hide now! Hurry, hurry, the Germans are coming!"

Vladislav pulled back the carpet over the trap door of the cellar, yelling at Suzanna to remove the extra plates and food from the table. The Gelmans scurried into the cellar.

"Don't make a sound," Vladislav shouted down to them as he and Slava hurried to replace the carpet and move the table.

Slava looked out and saw that one vehicle stopped in front of her house. The other vehicle stopped in front of Isaac's house. Armed soldiers jumped down and walked toward their door.

The door shook from the banging. Slava's body trembled. She took short, painful breaths. She wanted to ignore the soldiers, but knew she had no choice but to let them in. After she opened the door, one of the soldiers, a sergeant, pointed Slava toward the living room where her parents stood. She noticed the look of terror in her parents' faces. The veins in her father's temples turned purple and protruded. She feared he might have a stroke. Her chest heaving, beads of sweat poured down her mother's forehead.

The soldiers quickly spread throughout the house and methodically searched every room. She saw one of the soldiers pick up her father's antique ivory smoking pipe and stuff it in his pocket. Her father did not smoke, but he became enamored with this pipe and bought it on one of his trips. Slava realized that the enemy could take whatever they wanted out of the house and they were powerless to do anything. She now understood why her father buried their valuables in the orchard. The soldiers, in the search of the premises, walked past the cellar door many times. Each time one of the soldiers walked past the dining table, Slava stopped breathing. She prayed to her favorite saint, Saint Anthony, to protect them and the Gelmans.

"Identity papers," demanded the sergeant of Slava and her parents. Slava noticed that he stared at the icon of the Virgin Mary hanging on the wall.

"Our passports are in our bedrooms," Vladislav explained to the German, pointing to his bedroom.

At that moment, a soldier came out of his bedroom carrying the documents and handed them to the sergeant. He had all three passports. Slava was horrified to see hers in his hand since she had left it in her handbag on top of the desk in her room.

"You went through my jacket in the wardrobe to get my passport!" Protested Vladislav. "That is my private property."

"Quiet, Vladislav," pleaded Suzanna.

"Listen to your wife, old man," said the sergeant in perfect Russian. "Shut your mouth until you are told to speak. Tell me your name."

"Vladislav Szpakowski."

"Were your grandparents of Jewish origin?"

Beware the Wolves

"No."
"Name?" The sergeant asked looking intently at Suzanna.
"Suzanna Szpakowski."
"Were your grandparents of Jewish origin?"
"No."
"Is your neighbor, next door a Jew?"
"No."
"What Jews do you know in Vitebsk?"
"The ones we were acquainted with left Vitebsk," Suzanna said quickly and nervously.

The sergeant stared at Suzanna, his gaze drilling into her eyes.
"You know something, don't you?"
"No, no, I don't know anything. What do you mean?"
"You are required to report information concerning Jews. Furthermore, you cannot aid or hide the Jews. People who help Jews shall be shot."

Suzanna did not say a word, but looked away from the piercing brown eyes of the sergeant.

"There is something you are not telling me. I can see it in your face. Are you aiding Jews? You are hiding Jews, aren't you?" By now, the sergeant was yelling in her face.

Suzanna remained silent, but appeared completely pale, as though life had just drained out of her. Slava was sure her mother would collapse.

Slava felt weak-kneed. She saw the strain on her parents. Her mother could never hide a lie, and neither could she for that matter. But they would have to this time. It was a matter of life or death. *Be strong, be brave,* she said to herself and prayed that she would hold up under pressure.

"I'll come back to you later, old woman. Maybe this pretty young girl can tell me what you are hiding," the sergeant said turning his attention to Slava.

Oh God, thought Slava, and braced herself for the abuse. The sergeant, with fat droopy lips and protruding jaw, had a smug and arrogant look on his coarse face. He was about to begin his interrogation when a soldier came out of the kitchen. He chewed on a piece of meat while a portion dangled out of the edge of his mouth. In his hands was a large smoked ham from the smokehouse.

"Hey, look what I found. There's plenty more."
At that moment an officer entered the house.
"Put that ham back and everyone out of this house!" ordered the young officer. "Do you hear me? Everyone out!"

The soldiers appeared stunned, and reluctantly followed his orders.
"Get the hell out of here now!"
"Lieutenant, Sir! You are not our commanding officer," the sergeant said.
"No, but I am an officer and my orders to you are to get out, now!"
The officer waited until everyone left the house, then he looked at the three astonished individuals. He was about twenty-two years old, extremely thin with a narrow head. His boots, belt and pistol holster were highly polished.

He appeared more as an office worker than a soldier. He was not a fearful looking man like the sergeant, but he was loud and tried to impress his authority over the soldiers. Slava felt relieved to see him, that is, until he ordered her to go with him.

"What do you want with me?"

"I am Lieutenant Hoffman, the aide to Major Raake. He wants to see you immediately."

"What about?"

"Don't ask questions. You will know shortly."

"What about my parents?"

"They are to remain here. They will not be harmed."

Slava's heart continued to pound. The vice around her chest grew tighter. Her breathing grew even shallower. She felt dizzy. Her temples throbbing, she followed the slight statured officer outside to an open car parked in front of her house. The soldiers milled around their half-track throwing dirty looks in their direction. The vehicle in front of Isaac's house was still there as well.

"You leave that house alone," Hoffman yelled at the soldiers. "Or you will answer to Major Raake."

Behind the steering wheel of Hoffman's car sat a driver who did not look at either Slava or Hoffman. Slava was told to sit in the back next to Hoffman. The officer motioned the driver to proceed and the car made a U-turn and headed toward the bridge and the center of town. It was the first time she had ridden in a car. But under the circumstances, she found no thrill in the experience.

The car turned left prior to crossing the bridge and followed a gravel road adjacent to the tracks to a railroad freight warehouse. At the warehouse, Hoffman told her to exit the vehicle and follow him. There were soldiers sitting on the steps of the building. As Hoffman approached, the soldiers instantly stood at attention, saluting the officer by thrusting their right arms forward as he walked past them. In the empty warehouse she was directed to follow the officer past a door to the office area of the building where the soldiers were setting up desks and chairs. They stopped their work and stared at her. She was told to wait and the officer knocked on yet another door and went through it. Slava waited obediently. She felt like vomiting and her insides trembled. Each minute felt like an hour. Finally, the officer opened the door and motioned her to enter.

"Be seated," said the man sitting behind an old worn-out desk. He spoke in German.

Slava recognized him as the same officer with a cigarette who she had spoken to in German the day before. She studied him carefully. He was a distinguished looking man in his forties. His tall, trim body was dressed impeccably in a gray uniform with a black and silver cross and another medal dangling on his left chest. His silver streaked brown hair was perfectly combed across the top of his long oval shaped head. He stood up and greeted Slava with a friendly smile. Slava realized why she was there. He was going to make her work for him.

"I am Major Raake. You impressed me yesterday with your command of the German language. So I had you brought to me. Here, read this document out loud to me."

Slava did not know what to do. She thought of faking it and telling him she could not read or write in German. But he already knew she spoke German. If she could not read or write German, she would still be used as an interpreter. Perhaps working as a translator would be more advantageous. So she decided to read the document out loud.

"Excellent," the Major said. "Now tell me what you read."

"It is hereby ordered that the city of Vitebsk shall become a stronghold of the German Army in the East. There shall be established a large garrison headquarters with hospitals for the wounded."

"That's enough. Very good, now write what I will dictate to you."

He dictated a short paragraph and Slava wrote down the words. Raake reviewed her writing and circled something on the paper.

"Excellent, again, only one error with the punctuation. I know how you feel about working for the enemy. You have no choice in this matter. You may not like it, but this land and the people here now belong to the Third Reich. Everyone who wants to survive will work for us one way or the other. Believe me, you will be much happier working for me than in some factory producing war armaments. I understand that you have elderly parents. You certainly do not want them, or yourself for that matter, shipped out to one of our labor camps. Regardless, you will be working somewhere and right now you shall work for me. You will be paid five marks per day and will be able to buy some food. No one will eat unless they work."

She wished so much to tell him to go to hell, but she understood that she had no choice. Vladimir's parting words were that she must do whatever it takes to survive. Maybe this was the way for her and her parents to survive. After all, the alternative would be unthinkable. *The officer seems pleasant enough, and maybe I'll be able in someway to undermine the German invaders.* She took a normal breath and the knot in the pit of her stomach eased.

"Do you know how to type?" Raake asked her.

"No, I don't. I have never seen a typewriter."

"That's all right. You'll learn. Now follow me and I'll show you what to do."

Raake led her out of his office into the larger office area and showed her a desk in the corner. On top of it sat a box of ledger books and a shiny black typewriter. Next to the desk stood a dilapidated wooden chair.

"I want you to translate the contents of those books into German and type the entries on this typewriter."

"But, I don't know how to use the typewriter."

"I'll have my clerk, Heinrich, show you how. You will find it simple."

"Do you want me to begin right now?"

"Yes, immediately. You have much work to do."

"But I need to tell my parents that I am all right. They must be frantic with worry."

105

Victor Moss

"They will have to wait. You will work here until 1800 hours. At that time, you may go home."

Raake left and Slava sat down on the squeaky chair with a loose back and began looking at the books from the box. They were vital statistic ledgers—births, marriages and deaths. Slava wondered if her marriage to Vladimir was listed in those books. She began leafing through the book on marriages to find her name when Heinrich walked up to her desk. With his baby face, wavy blond hair and large green eyes, Heinrich came across as a young boy playing dress up in a soldier's uniform. Slava thought he could not be more than sixteen.

"Herr Major wanted me to bring you some bread and sausage. You will find tea on that table next to the window. I'll come back and try to show you how to type. Herr Major thinks anyone can learn to type in a few minutes, but it's not that easy, you'll see."

Grateful to receive the food, Slava realized how famished she was now that her nerves had calmed. Pork sausage, the meat ground up and interspersed with large chunks of fat, was placed on a piece of a buttered dark rye bread. She gulped down the food and wished she had more. She walked across the large room to the tea table, but felt uncomfortable as the eyes of the soldiers in the office followed her. She hurriedly drank the tea and returned to her desk.

Heinrich showed her where to place her fingers on the keyboard and patiently pointed out each letter and told her she would have to memorize their positions in reference to the other letters. He told her she needed to practice before she began her work.

After an hour of practice, Raake came up to her desk.

"I have to leave now, and I'll drive you home. You are right. You need to tell your parents that you are safe. Come back tomorrow morning at 8:00 o'clock."

Slava could not believe her ears. *Is this officer actually a decent and caring person? He seems so different from the other Germans I've met so far.*

It was a short drive, only about 1.5 kilometers to Slava's house and no one said a word during the ride. The car stopped in front of the house.

"So this is your house. It looks very nice. It would have been a shame to burn it down. Maybe someday, I could be your guest for tea."

Slava was surprised by the comment. It was certainly unusual. But as a polite response, a totally reflexive action, she said, "Oh, sure, any time."

As she walked up the steps to her home she thought how stupid she was for saying that. After all, he was the enemy. *What was I thinking? He is an invader of my homeland.*

Her mother met her at the door and threw a frown at the German vehicle. She grabbed Slava and hugged her so tightly that it knocked the wind out of her daughter. She kissed her on the cheeks over and over again.

"What happened to you? Where did those bastards take you? Are you all right? Oh, Mother of God, I prayed nonstop that I would see you again."

Beware the Wolves

"Mama, settle down. I'm all right. Where is Papa? I'll tell you both what happened. Are the Gelmans still here?"

Her father was right behind Suzanna, all dressed up in his suit and shoes ready to go out. Upon seeing his daughter, his eyes filled with tears and he hugged her, kissing her cheeks.

"Where are you going, Papa, so dressed up?"

"Your father could not wait any longer. He insisted on looking for you. I asked him where would he go? But he was so restless, paced up and down the floor. He kept glancing out of the windows towards town. He then walked out onto the street, waited to see if you were coming back. He thought if he had his suit on, he would get more respect and a better chance to find you."

"Never mind about me," Vladislav said. "What happened to you?"

Slava related her experiences of the morning to her parents. They were horrified that she was required to work for the enemy. She tried to explain to them that everyone would be ordered to work for the Germans in one form or another.

"And this Major Raake seems very nice. I actually think he likes me. He treats me with respect. I could be forced to work in a horrible place with horrible people. Believe me, it could be much worse. But, Mama, where are the Gelmans? Are they still down there in the cellar?"

"No, they left shortly after the soldiers drove away this morning," Vladislav answered. "They were afraid the Germans would come back and find them. When they heard those heavy boots stomping above their heads, they were sure that they would be caught. They thought it best to take a chance and try to get to their relatives."

"We gave them enough food for the next several days," Suzanna said. "I just hope that they will be safe. I always liked her."

"Well, we were very, very lucky this morning," Slava said. "I feel everything will turn out all right for us. I just pray that Vladimir was safe today."

CHAPTER 14

"Column forward!" Savitski gave the order and the wagons and soldiers began their march toward Yelna.

Vladimir sat quietly on the lead medical wagon. His eyelids closed and he dozed off, his chin resting on his chest. His body craved sleep. He had spent too much time talking with Tanya and reminiscing about Slava. He should have slept.

The column stopped and Vladimir opened his eyes.

"Why have we stopped?" Vladimir asked the driver. The driver, Timofei, was a rough-looking individual who worked in the stables at a collective farm near the city of Orsha before he was drafted into the army. Even though Timofei was more than twice his age, Vladimir enjoyed talking with him. There was something in his mannerism that reminded Vladimir of his grandfather. Perhaps it was his quiet, easy-going nature that belied his appearance. He admired how skillfully Timofei handled the horses at the time the Panzers pursued the column.

"Don't know for sure, Comrade Captain. I imagine it has something to do with us leaving the woods and moving onto the open field. I'm glad it's still dark, but the sun will be coming up soon."

"How far do you think we are from Yelna?"

"Not far. If we continue at this pace and the road is half-way decent, we should be there by noon."

"Well, I need to stretch a bit. I'll walk ahead to see what the holdup is."

At the head of the column, it was just bright enough from moonbeams for Vladimir to see Savitski and the other officers smoking cigarettes on a fallen log.

"Comrade, come and join us for a smoke," Savitski said offering Vladimir a cigarette.

"Thank you, I'll be glad to join you, but I'll pass on the cigarette."

Vladimir knew that the cigarettes the officers smoked were not the cheap quality makhorka smoked by the soldiers. Instead, they inhaled the factory-made cigarettes with a more pleasant scent. *The privilege of rank,* Vladimir thought.

"Why have we stopped?" Vladimir asked.

"We're waiting for our scouts to return," his friend, Ivanov said. "That is, if they come back."

"Ivanov, I've had it with your negative attitude!" Savitski bellowed. "You are a defeatist. You are sabotaging the morale of everyone around you. I am bringing you up on charges, you worthless son of a bitch."

Beware the Wolves

"We're all tired, Captain Savitski," Vladimir said, trying to help his friend. "In times like these we say things we do not mean."

"Yes, Comrade Captain Savitski, I did not mean anything by what I said. That is just my personality. I'm just a fool."

Savitski gazed at Vladimir, then at Ivanov.

"All right. I'll let it go this time. But no more defeatists talk from you. Next time, I won't bother to bring you up on charges. I'll shoot you. Do you understand? Well, where are those blasted scouts? I sent them out more than one-half hour ago to see if it was safe for us to proceed. They should've been back by now!"

The officers sat with no further words exchanged. Each had his eyes fixated on the ground. Vladimir felt the tenseness in the air, became uncomfortable and decided to return to the rear of the column with his patients and medics, but remained when he heard the distant galloping of horses. Three riders returned.

"Where is the fourth scout?" Savitski asked.

"Yurchenko, took off to the north," said one of the scouts. "He yelled back to us that he had enough of this war. He wanted us to join him. But as you can see, we didn't."

"Why didn't you shoot that son of a bitch?" Savitski shrieked, clearly agitated.

"Well, we chased him, but he got away. That's why we were gone so long."

Savitski looked suspiciously at the scouts. Vladimir knew what Savitski was thinking for he, himself, believed that all four planned to desert, but for whatever reason, three of them decided to return. He knew that desertion had become a big problem. He thought of his medic, Igor, who had run off rather than go into the trenches near Smolensk. *Was Igor a coward? Was it fear or was it the futility of facing the Germans, who seemed to be so unstoppable? Do men desert because of fear? Maybe some do. But it is more likely because of the feeling of hopelessness that compels a man such as Igor to run. Or perhaps Igor had an overwhelming desire to be near his loved ones.* Vladimir easily shared that feeling, longing to be with Slava. He realized the impossibility of that desire and quickly pushed the thought out of his mind.

"Well, what did you see out there?" Savitski asked.

"Nothing out there. The coast is clear."

"All right. Column forward!" Savitski ordered.

Vladimir walked back towards the wagon, and jumped up on the seat next to his driver as it rolled past him.

"So what was the delay, Comrade Captain?" Timofei asked as he lit one of his foul-smelling makhorka cigarettes.

"We were waiting for the scouts to return. They said it was clear ahead."

"Once we're out of the forest and in the open field," Timofei said, "we had better be careful. We'll be sitting ducks."

Victor Moss

The driver's words put Vladimir on edge as the wagon rolled out of the forest. He felt exposed.

"Why is it that we have to exit the forest at this spot, anyway?" Timofei continued. "We could still follow this trail for several kilometers more before we run out of forest."

"I know that the Captain is anxious to get on the road to Yelna to make better time." Vladimir answered. "He has a schedule to keep."

"What good is a schedule if we're dead?" Timofei answered.

The ride was bouncy. The column came out of the forest at a spot where there was no road or trail. To reach the road ahead, the wagons traveled perpendicular to plowed burrows in the field. Vladimir looked back at the wounded in the wagon. They moaned with pain as the wheels hit the ruts.

"Hang in there," Vladimir told the wounded. "The road to Yelna is just ahead."

Tanya ran up to Vladimir's wagon and informed him that the wounded could not take the agony of the rough jolts.

"We can't stop now, Tanya. We have to keep moving. There is nothing I can do right now. Reassure them that we should be on the road soon."

Shortly thereafter, the column stopped again. This time a portion of the drainage culvert that ran alongside the road had to be filled in with rock and dirt, making it wide enough for the wagons and artillery to cross. This took only a few minutes. Finally, the entire column made its way on the road to Yelna. The unpaved roadway was not much smoother on the wounded than the field they had left behind. The deep ruts carved out by trucks and wagons caused the wagons to sway and bounce. In some places wild grass grew between the ruts. Electric and telephone lines, held up by wooden poles, followed the path of the road.

The sunrise was spectacular. Brilliant streaks of red and orange interspersed with layers of gray yellow and violet painted the sky. Vladimir had never before seen such a beautiful array of colors in the early morning. As the column traveled in an easterly direction the colors became more magnificent with every passing moment. *It must be the smoke in the air from the many days of bombing, shelling and gunpowder that is the source of this striking daybreak.* His grandfather told him that there was always some good to go with the bad, but when he thought about all the bad he had seen, this sunrise was of minor consequence. *What good could possibly come out of this dreadful predicament?*

He thought of Slava and how much he missed her. He took her picture out, once again, from his shirt pocket and studied Slava's face.

"Is that your wife, sir?" The driver asked glancing at Slava's photograph.

"Yes, it is."

"That girl, the medic, is kind of sweet on you, isn't she, sir? What's her name, Tanya?"

"What do you mean?"

Beware the Wolves

"I've seen how she touches you, and tries to stand close to you, sir. Haven't you noticed her sparkling eyes and wide smile whenever you are near? I've seen how she looks at you. It's especially obvious when she plays with her hair when you two are talking."

Vladimir could see that Timofei was enjoying this conversation. Timofei's stern face softened with a light, teasing smile.

"All right, all right, I get the picture. She should realize that it's of no use. I love my wife and would never want to hurt her."

"Let's hope you'll see your wife again, Comrade Captain. I also have a wife. I don't know where she is. I left her with her parents at Orsha, but the Germans ran it over a few weeks ago. I have a feeling, deep in my gut, that I will never see Orsha or my wife again."

"You never know what fate will bring," Vladimir said. "But I believe that I will see my wife again someday. I need to believe it."

Suddenly, from the west came the low menacing drone of airplanes. At first the sound was faint, but became louder with each passing second. Vladimir stood up to look over the canvas covering the wagon and saw two planes bearing straight for the column. They were enemy planes.

"Stop the wagon and get under it!" Vladimir yelled at the driver as he leaped off the wagon and dove underneath.

The German Stukas, like swooping hawks after prey, tipped into their dives and began spitting bullets onto the surprised column on the open road. Soldiers tumbled into the ditch along the side of the road and fired their rifles at the planes strafing the ground below. A hailstorm of bullets pounded the ground and the wagon above Vladimir. Vladimir laid on his stomach with his elbows close to the sides of his chest, his hands covering his ears from the raucous clamor.

As suddenly as they appeared, the Stukas disappeared toward the sunrise and Yelna. Vladimir crawled out from underneath the wagon. The driver did not budge. Vladimir called to Timofei, but received no response. Vladimir looked under the wagon and saw the motionless body lying face down on the ground. His head was drenched with blood. Timofei still held the reins from the horses tightly in his hand. Their horses lay in a spreading pool of blood. One horse was wounded and thrashing, the other dead. Stunned survivors milled around assessing the damage.

Vladimir looked inside his medical wagon and could not stifle a gasp of horror when he saw that every one of the wounded in it appeared dead. He ran over to the other medical wagons and saw that those wagons had escaped the barrage. Only one of the horses hitched to the third wagon had been shot. Vladimir was stunned and breathless as he pondered the fate of people. He was the only survivor in the first wagon, yet his was the only wagon that had come under a direct hit.

Vladimir immediately began to search for his medics. He saw Stepan standing motionless a few meters from the wagon, out in the open field. Vladimir approached him.

111

"Where are the others?" Vladimir asked.

Stepan did not respond. *The fellow is in shock.* Vladimir grabbed his arm and shook Stepan.

"Stepan snap out of it. You'll be all right. Pull yourself together."

Stepan gazed at Vladimir. He rapidly blinked his eyes and rubbed his forehead with his trembling right hand.

"I'm sorry, Comrade Captain. I don't know what came over me. I'll be all right."

"No need to apologize. It was, after all, a vicious attack. But now you're needed. Get to work."

"Yes, Comrade Captain. What should I do?"

At that moment, Vladimir saw Evgeniy drag a soldier out of the ditch.

"Go help Evgeniy. Have you seen Tanya?"

"No sir. When the planes came, Evgeniy and I hid underneath the last wagon. Tanya was with Boris. I don't know what happened to them."

Vladimir ran toward the ditch and noticed Misha sitting with his head in his hands alongside the ditch. There was no sign of Tanya or Boris. A chill ran through him. His stomach clenched tighter as a wave of trepidation coursed through him. He backed to the side of the wagon and grabbed it for support. *They must be dead.* Unable to move for a few seconds at first, Vladimir finally made his way toward Misha.

Vladimir placed his hand on Misha's shoulder as he glanced into the ditch. He cringed at the sight of several lifeless bodies. Among them Tanya laid face down with her hands on the back of her head, still covering her ears. Boris' body laid next to her, with his left arm outstretched over Tanya's shoulder in a feeble attempt to protect her from the bullets.

Vladimir clenched his teeth. His breath solidified in his throat. He wanted to vomit. His heart threatened to jump out of his chest. Vladimir reached down and placed his hand over Tanya's and held it for a few seconds, staring at the corpse. He felt drained. She meant something to him. She was his friend. He had confided more in her than anyone else since he left home. *Oh God, why this misery and sadness?*

"Well, Misha. This seems to be our life. One minute we're alive and the next we're dead. It's all a matter of fate. Only the Almighty determines who lives or dies. I hid under the wagon and survived, but Timofei took cover under the same wagon and was killed. Boris and Tanya were good people and we'll miss them, won't we, Misha?"

"I know I will," Misha said. "But at least they will no longer have to suffer from this hellish nightmare."

"Comrade Captain," Evgeniy ran up to Vladimir. "We need you. There are many wounded."

"Well Misha, let's work. Maybe we can save some others. There is nothing we can do here."

Vladimir followed Evgeniy who, along with the other medics, carried all the wounded to one section of the field for triage. Many of the injured had already been bandaged. Vladimir treated the wounds as best he could in the field, but jumped nervously at the rifle shots that put down the wounded horses. Many of the victims were in such desperate condition that he could do nothing for them. He was generous with morphine with those that he thought had hope of surviving until his supply ran out. There were twenty surviving injured, some serious, some with minor flesh wounds. Seventeen were dead including Lieutenant Lavrientev, Boris, Tanya, those in the first medical wagon and some of those sitting or laying on boxes in the supply wagons. While the wounded were looked after, the men dug a shallow mass grave in the adjacent field. It would have been impossible to transport the bodies to Yelna. Most wagons and artillery pieces did not have the horsepower they needed. The surviving horses had to be repositioned to pull the wagons.

Vladimir looked up just as Tanya was placed in the grave along with the others. He thought of her parents. How tragically her life ended, without a decent burial. *Perhaps Tanya and the other poor souls would be properly buried after the war.* After the grave was covered, one of the soldiers took a shovel and inscribed the Russian Orthodox cross in the middle of the grave. No one objected. *The communists had tried to remove religion from our hearts. In some cases they were successful. But in battle, everyone is religious.* Some of the soldiers prayed out loud. *I imagine that even the Soviet political commissar prays secretly.*

"I've waited long enough," Savitski bellowed. "With fewer horses, it will take us longer as it is."

"Comrade Captain, let's go back to the forest and wait it out until nightfall," Ivanov said. "No, if we wait any longer we will be cut off by the Germans. We have to get to Yelna as soon as possible."

Overhearing the conversation, Vladimir agreed with Ivanov. They could be annihilated with another Stuka attack. But then, he also saw Savitski's side. The artillery and the remaining soldiers would be of no use to the defense of Yelna should they fall behind. He was actually amazed that Savitski allowed as much time as he did for the treatment of the wounded and the burial of the dead. He reluctantly admired Savitski for that.

In the distance, towards Yelna, Vladimir heard the distressing roar of waves of Stukas dropping their payloads on the unfortunate town. One explosion followed another. *Oh God! Will there be anything left of Yelna? Those attacks are a precursor to those dreadful Panzers. At least the fascists are preoccupied with the attack on Yelna and may ignore us for awhile,* he thought. But then it occurred to him that the railroad tracks might be destroyed with the bombings. The wounded soldiers would not be able to be transported to the hospital in Moscow. *We'll just have to wait and see.*

The column stumbled on, crippled by the lack of horses. A new driver, another soldier, sat next to Vladimir. Only one horse pulled each of the medical wagons. And even though the wagons had rubber tires, the horses struggled. The weight of new casualties coupled with the weight of the wounded from

Smolensk, overburdened the animals. Vladimir jumped off to relieve the horse of some weight. He ordered anyone able to ambulate off the wagons, including the drivers who had to walk along side their horses. Some of the supply wagons were cut down to two horses from the four. Only four horses pulled the artillery pieces.

There was no rest in sight. Both men and horses were exhausted. Savitski refused to stop, and so they plodded on. Vladimir was thirsty and hungry. He was relieved that the cook and his horse survived the attack. He was ready to eat anything, even that awful mush. *Surely Savitski would give us an order to rest soon. We need to refuel the horses and ourselves. Savitski, himself, must be famished.* One kilometer after another rolled by. Smoke from explosions in Yelna had been visible for some time, and now, acrid smell filled the hot, humid July air. The terrain had turned from flatlands to hills. Yelna could be seen a few kilometers away. *So close and yet so far,* Vladimir sighed as he watched the sweat roll off the men and horses. *Without rest, they're not going to make it.* Just as Vladimir finished that thought, Savitski finally guided the column towards a large hill situated a few meters off the road. With the hill used as protection, he ordered the column to rest.

"All right men. I have a treat for you today," the cook announced laughing.

"What are you laughing about?" One of the soldiers hollered at him. "What are you going to do, give us a choice of cold buckwheat mush or warm mush again? We know your damn tricks."

"Oh, you think you're so damn smart, don't you, you fool?" The cook answered. "Well, you know nothing. I'm going to serve you horsemeat that I've butchered from a dead horse. I took it off one alongside the road while you were digging graves."

The men suddenly perked up. Vladimir's mouth was dry, but nevertheless the thought of meat made it water. He had never tasted horsemeat before, but as hungry as he was, any meat was a Godsend. He imagined chewing the food and felt his stomach rumble.

"Ha, ha, ha. You all should see the looks on your faces," the cook said laughing so hard that his face turned bright red. "No one paid any attention to me and I was able to surprise you. I can't believe no one noticed me butcher a horse and carry the meat to my wagon. Now help me set up some fires and lets start cooking."

Vladimir looked at Savitski for his reaction. Roasting the meat, even in thin pieces would take longer than he thought Savitski would allow. But to his surprise, Savitski sat down on a rock and lit a cigarette.

After the meal, the column moved forward. Closer to Yelna, Vladimir could see two old bulldozers digging out a defensive trench. The soldiers, older men, women and even children did most of the work by hand using shovels and rakes. Something had to be done to defend the town, but Vladimir knew that if the trenches were anything at all like those outside of Smolensk, they would not stop the Panzers. *But perhaps those steel monsters could be slowed down long enough for more reinforcements to arrive.*

Beware the Wolves

The garrison headquarters was a crumbling two-story building surrounded by a brick and stucco fence that needed repair. A bomb had damaged one corner of the building, part of it still smoked as the soldiers were putting out the fire. The soldiers and artillery pieces entered through a beautiful large wrought iron gate. *The place must have been an estate of a wealthy family before the communists took over Russia.* Savitski stopped the supply wagons and medical wagons outside the gate, but allowed the cook wagon to proceed.

"Comrade Captain Moskalkov," Savitski said after riding up to Vladimir. "Follow this road to the railway station. As ordered, unload your wounded for the train to Moscow. You and your medics must get off at Vyazma and report to the Garrison headquarters there. The drivers will bring the wagons back. Do you understand?"

"Yes, Captain, I understand. What if the tracks are bombed out and the trains aren't running? What am I to do with the wounded?"

"That's your problem. You are resourceful enough. For your sake, let's hope there will be a train. Now proceed and good luck to you."

The two men saluted each other and Vladimir hopped on the wagon and proceeded toward the center of Yelna.

The train depot was an anthill of activity. A train, crammed with soldiers, arrived from the northwest. Vladimir watched in amazement at how quickly the soldiers poured out of the railroad cars and ran, full speed ahead, toward the defensive lines. The train for Vyazma, had not yet arrived. Vladimir was told that a large section of track was damaged and repairs were underway. He sent his medics to find water and food for the wounded.

As Vladimir tended to the injured, he once again heard the awful, unforgettable whine of approaching Stukas. His heart pounded. Almost instantly, the booming racket of antiaircraft guns was heard. It was music to his ears. One of the Stukas was hit and he could see the trail of smoke as it fell from the sky. Then another. He counted six planes that survived the defenders' barrage. The ground shook with each explosion as the bombs fell from the sky. The railroad depot was spared; however Vladimir could see smoke billowing from the direction of the garrison headquarters where the attack seemed to have been concentrated. A chill came over him, as he feared for the safety of the officers and men he had just left behind. He felt he should rush over to the garrison to help, but knew his orders were to proceed to Vyazma. Besides, he was told that Yelna had good medical facilities for the soldiers. *Doctors on front lines always need help. There is never enough. But I also have my orders.*

After several hours of waiting, the train from Vyazma finally arrived. Once again, it disgorged the soldiers sent to the front. They jumped from the cars and rushed toward the lines. Vladimir was given priority for his wounded over the throng of locals jamming onto the train for evacuation.

115

It was a relatively short trip to Vyazma, about 150 kilometers. Vladimir found a seat in the crowded train. He slouched, let his head fall against the back of the seat, and fell into a deep slumber.

CHAPTER 15

The train bounced and swayed on the hastily replaced, damaged tracks. Vladimir awoke, rubbed his eyes and looked around the car. Most of his exhausted patients were asleep. Those that were awake gazed blankly into space. The medics also dozed off, except for Misha, who was changing bandages on one of the soldiers. Evgeniy, propped up against the toilet wall, snored with his mouth wide open as drool ran down the side of his mouth. Vladimir glanced at the few civilian travelers in the car. Most were asleep, clutching their few belongings on their laps. The remaining passengers had a desperate, anxious look on their faces.

Vladimir closed his eyes and remembered his first train ride. The day was spectacular. It was late April 1941 and the snow in the forest had melted. Everything had come to life after a dreary cold winter. The family had packed a picnic and gone to a quiet resort at the edge of a forest. Brilliant green leaves sprouted from the trees and bushes. Two squirrels frolicked in the thick, tall green grass. Each breath of the crisp, fresh and fragrant air was a delight. It felt wonderful to be alive. He and Slava were so happy. They had not a care in the world as they frolicked between the trees holding hands and stopping for an occasional kiss under the leafy canopy. *Who would have dreamed that in two months the bedlam of war would bring our contentment to a devastating halt?*

The train rocked as Vladimir tried to remember every detail. There they were, he and Slava, her sister, Maria, and her brother-in-law, Feodor, their eleven-year-old son, Vova, and Vladislav lounging on an olive colored blanket spread out on the ground at the edge of the forest. A large woven picnic basket filled with bread, cheese, and sausage sat lop-sided on the edge of the blanket. A bottle of wine stood prominently in the middle. There were hard-boiled eggs, a loaf of bread, a brass container of salt and a tin pot of tea. Broad smiles lightened their relaxed faces. The laughter was infectious. Vladimir wore white pants, a white shirt and a blue blazer. He thought how foolish he was to wear white pants on a picnic. Slava wore a blue dress with a white flower pattern, white socks, white shoes and a black jacket. But what he remembered most of Slava that day was her round yellow straw hat resting on the back of her head. It looked like halo around her short hair. *My little angel,* he thought to himself.

Vladimir's reminiscence of the picnic, which now seemed of another world, was interrupted when Misha came up and crouched down next to him in the aisle. The strong smell of makhorka tobacco on his breath made Vladimir nauseous.

"Comrade Captain, oh, I'm sorry, I forgot that you don't like to be called comrade. Out of respect for you as a physician, may I call you by your name and patronym? What was your father's name?"

"Of course. My father's name was Grigori."

"Then Vladimir Grigorovich, may we chat for awhile? I feel so alone right now. The ones I worked with the closest are no longer with me. Igor is gone, and God knows what happened to him. Tanya is gone. Boris is gone. Of our original medics, only Stepan is left and he is too quiet for me. Talking to him is like talking to this chair. He just does what you tell him with hardly a word exchanged all day."

Vladimir looked at Misha's kind, gray eyes outlined by his round slightly pock-marked face. How he had misjudged Misha. That day in the abandoned village, near Smolensk, when he disobeyed orders and went in to retrieve the medicines, Vladimir thought Misha was slow and lazy. However, in the days that followed, Misha impressed Vladimir with his dedication to the wounded. He was a quick learner and always anxious to help. A pleasant looking individual, in his mid thirties, Misha was probably well educated. He was a social creature in need of companionship.

"You know, Misha, I don't even know where you are from?"

"I'm from Roslavl."

"It's south of Smolensk, isn't it?"

"Yes, more southeast, then due south."

"What did you do before the war?"

"I was a teacher. I taught eighth grade history."

"That's a good profession. How did you become a medic in the army?"

"After my short, almost non-existent basic training, I asked to become a medic. I thought that I could do more good by helping the wounded. You see, I don't like guns much. So they gave me a few days of simple medical training and told me that I'd pick it up as I go along. I've learned a lot from you and from Tanya. She was such a fine girl. I miss her."

Vladimir could see that Misha's thin lips pressed together and his eyes moistened over as he mentioned Tanya. Vladimir saw redness etched in Misha's face.

"You were in love with Tanya, weren't you, Misha?"

"Vladimir Grigorovich, do you believe in love at first sight?"

"Yes. I believe I fell in love with my wife the moment I saw her."

"Well I felt the same about Tanya. But it was all one sided. She was friendly to me all right, but I could tell she wasn't interested in me. Frankly, I think she was interested in you. But with time, I believe we could have had something between us."

"I still can't believe she's gone. She was a fine person. Unfortunately, Misha, in this war there is little time to build a relationship. Just take the day as it comes along and hope that the next will be better."

"I guess you are right," Misha mumbled. "We have to go on."

Vladimir could see that Misha was becoming maudlin so he thought of changing the subject.

"It's interesting that you were a history teacher. I have always loved history. We have been assigned to Vyazma and it's always good to learn something about the place you are to visit. Tell me what you know about Vyazma. I'm trying to remember what I've read about its history. I know that it was the site of a big battle with Napoleon in 1812."

"Yes, there was a big battle at Vyazma between the Russian defenders and Napoleon's forces. The city is only about 180 kilometers west of Moscow. It's on the main road between Western Europe and Moscow. Historically, the people of this town had to deal with many foreign invaders since it's founding in the ninth century."

"A decisive battle occurred in the early part of November 1812 when Napoleon was retreating, leaving Moscow. The Russians deprived the French army of stocks of food and supplies. They were constantly harassing them as they marched back to France. The Russians finally engaged them near Vyazma and almost wiped out the whole French army."

"Interesting how you said that Napoleon retreated from Moscow," Vladimir said. "I'm trying to remember how he was able to get to Moscow anyway."

"The Czar ordered the evacuation of the inhabitants of Moscow, leaving Napoleon in an empty city with no supplies or support for his troops. The Soviets will use the same technique today. If we can't stop the enemy at Vyazma, just watch how many Moscovites will flee, especially those in the government. Hitler will enter almost a deserted city just like Napoleon did in 1812. We allowed the French to drive their forces deep into Russia, and then let them starve to death. Later, 'General Winter' assisted in finishing them off. Our boys cut them off from supplies and at the same time we attacked the enemy on its flanks and rear, wearing them down. And likewise, if the war continues into late October and November, 'General Winter' will immobilize the Germans just as he stopped the French."

"General Winter? Are you referring to our climate?"

"That's how some of the history books describe the effect our severe winter had on Napoleon's troops. The soldiers and their horses literally froze to death. The same fate will follow the Germans. Their machinery will freeze up and so will their artillery. It could get to be so cold that even their gun barrels would freeze. Because we're accustomed to our winters, we will be able to function while the enemy will not."

"It took Napoleon weeks, if not months to travel deep into Russia," Vladimir said. "The towns and cities had time to evacuate. The Germans move at a lightning pace with their tanks. If we can't stop them in Vyazma, Moscow will have to defend itself this time. There is no possible way that the entire city can be evacuated. I am sure the Germans are aware of our winters and plan to take Moscow before the deep freeze snares them."

"You're right, I'm afraid. Thank you, Captain, for talking with me. I have to go change some more bandages. We should be at the junction soon. Strange, isn't it, we had to go south to go north?"

"What do you mean?"

"Well, there is no direct route to Vyazma from Yelna. We need to travel south to Sukhinichi then transfer to another train that will take us north to Vyazma."

"Yes, I discovered that at the station. Savitski assumed there was a direct connection and was wrong in his instructions to me."

"It will be a hassle again to carry the wounded onto another train."

"Misha, everything is a hassle. We just have to do it."

"I know, that's life. Well, I better go."

Misha left and Vladimir began his rounds. He was examining a soldier's wound when the train came to a standstill. They had arrived at Sukhinichi. The conductor told Vladimir that he had to get his people off the train. They had only five minutes before the train would depart again. Vladimir and the medics worked feverishly to get the wounded and their gear off the train. Finally, Vladimir and Stepan were carrying out the last wounded. Vladimir held his legs while Stepan held him under his arms. Vladimir was down the metal steps of the train, standing on the cement platform, next to the track, when the train started to move. Stepan was still on the train with two steps to descend. The wounded soldier started to holler. Vladimir pulled on the soldier, thus pulling on Stepan.

"Jump! Hurry!" Vladimir yelled at Stepan.

But Stepan seemed to panic, and froze for a second. Vladimir pulled harder and Stepan, still holding on to the wounded soldier, fell out of the train as it gathered more speed. Vladimir fell backwards as the soldier fell on top of him and Stepan fell on top of them both. Evgeniy and Misha ran up, both laughing at the sight of the three men lying in a pile.

"Are you fellows through playing games?" Evgeniy said, still laughing.

"You son of a bitch," the wounded soldier yelled out. "I'm in severe pain and you think it's funny."

"I'm sorry, Comrade Captain," Evgeniy said to Vladimir paying no attention to the wounded soldier after he pulled Stepan and the soldier off Vladimir.

"No need to be sorry," Vladimir said, now also laughing at the incident. "At least no one was seriously hurt."

"Oh, yes I was," the soldier cried out. Vladimir remembered his name to be Vitali. "My chest feels as though it's on fire."

Vladimir removed the bandage around his chest and noticed that the stitches over an incision had come apart and the wound bled slightly. He quickly repaired the wound just as the train bound for Vyazma steamed in. Unfortunately, he was on the wrong side of the tracks with Vitali. The platform for the train to Vyazma was on the other side of the two tracks and the long train blocked his passage. He realized that he had only a few minutes before the train left again and he had to carry Vitali to the other side. All the other wounded soldiers had already been transferred on foot to that side of the tracks. He would have to carry the wounded soldier up to a footbridge above the tracks and then down the steps. And he would have to hurry, for the train would not wait for him. He looked around for help, but no one was around. Everyone was on the other side, including the medics who were busy helping the other injured onto the train. Vitali was unable to use his right leg. A bullet had damaged some nerves and he was in excruciating pain. Regrettably, Vladimir had no morphine to relieve his pain.

"Come on, Vitali, you are going to have to help me get you over that bridge to the other side. The medics have already taken our gear. I know it will hurt, but you will have to walk. I'll hold you up."

As Vladimir tried to lift him up, Vitali started to scream from the pain.

"I can't make it," Vitali moaned. "Just leave me here, you go on ahead, doctor."

"Don't be so dramatic, Vitali. Now, try to get up again. Both of us will make it. Get up now. We don't have much time."

Vitali made a valiant effort and finally stood up. Vladimir grabbed Vitali's right arm and placed it around his shoulder propping him up as they took a few steps toward the bridge. His left arm was around Vitali's back and in his right hand, Vladimir held onto his medical bag. The three-meter walk to the steps was absolute torture for Vitali. Sweat poured at such a rate that Vladimir feared that his patient would pass out. Just as Vladimir was about to pull Vitali up onto the first step of the stairs to the bridge, Misha and Stepan came running down the stairs. Vladimir was relieved to see them.

The medics grabbed Vitali, lifted him and carried him over the bridge, down the steps and onto the platform. Vladimir ran in pursuit. Misha was already in the railroad car and Stepan was just about to jump on the first step when the train started to move. He landed on the step, but there was no room for Vladimir. As the train picked up speed, Vladimir jumped onto the next car and made it. That car was packed, so he inched his way into the car with the medics and wounded. There, again, he found near bursting conditions. He pushed his way through the packed cars until he reached a sleeper car. The hallway was on the left side while sleeping compartments were on the right. Each contained four bunks, a window and a little table attached between the lower bunks next to the window. All the lower bunks in the compartment were filled with as many as five people sitting on each bed. The upper bunks were too close to the ceiling, and only very small children could huddle there.

Vladimir kept walking down the hallways of the sleeper cars looking for a place to sit down. In some sleeper cars, the compartments contained two beds rather than four. He understood that in normal times, passengers paid more to travel in a two-bed compartment. Since there was no place for him to sit, he decided to stand in the aisle and leaned on the window for support. Soon a conductor approached Vladimir. A well-fed individual with silver hair protruding from her cap, she carried herself as though she owned the train. She must have been past middle age, but her face did not have a wrinkle.

"What are you doing standing in the hallway here, General?" The conductor asked of Vladimir.

"There doesn't seem to be any place for me to sit down. And I'm not a general, but a captain."

"Come with me, General. I'll find a place for you. I see by your insignia that you're in the medical corps. Are you a doctor, General?"

"Yes."

Vladimir followed the conductor to the front of the car. Across from the toilet, the conductor took out her keys and opened a door marked "Off limits." Inside was a bed with a little table next to it. On the opposite wall from the bed was a cabinet with a giant highly polished brass samovar filled with boiling water. Next to the samovar, a wooden box held tea glasses and brass holders.

"You look like you've been to hell and back, General. Help yourself to some hot tea. The tea is in the brass pot to the right of the samovar. And here let me give you a piece of black bread I bought in Ukraine yesterday. I have some salt, so sprinkle it on the bread and you'll think you are in heaven, General. Where you going?"

"Vyazma."

"Use my bed and I'll wake you up shortly before we get there. It's about a three hour trip."

"I can't take your bed. Won't you need it?"

"No, I'll be up on my feet most of the trip to Vyazma. Besides, General, you need the rest more than I do."

Vladimir could not believe his luck. He looked at the tea and grabbed the bread as the conductor left the compartment. A second later the conductor opened the door and came back into the compartment.

"Oh hell," she said. "I'll give you something else to eat."

She unlocked and opened another door of the cabinet and took out a package wrapped in cloth. Under the cloth, waxed paper covered a slab of bacon. She took a knife from the shelf and cut Vladimir a fourth of the slab.

"You'll need the energy, General," the conductor said laughing as she left the compartment.

Vladimir devoured the food and laid down on the bed. He fell asleep instantly and only awoke when the conductor shook his shoulder.

"Vyazma in ten minutes, General. Looks like you had a good rest."

"Thank you so much for your kindness and generosity. I wish I could repay you."

"No need. Just keep saving our boys."

Vladimir went back to the car that held his people. He briefly checked each wounded man, said good-bye, and gave them words of encouragement. Two of Evgeniy's original medics would accompany them to Moscow. He worried how they would get to a hospital. Everything seemed so disorganized that he suspected they would wait for hours before receiving help. With his gear in hand, he stood by the door ready to step into yet another adventure. Misha, Stepan and Evgeniy joined him. His orders from Savitsi were to take three sanitars with him to Viazma. Originally he had planned to take Tanya, Misha and Stepan. Now he ordered Evgeniy to accompany him because, even though he was obstinate, he had more experience and was more resourceful than the others.

The train arrived at a beautiful two-story green building with large white columns holding up vast arches. It looked a bit shabby, but still proud of its past. After Vladimir exited the train, he paused for a moment just to admire the architecture. *It's a crime, that the enemy would destroy beautiful buildings such as these.*

In the station, Vladimir and the medics waited under a large clock for several minutes. They had no idea where to look for further orders. None knew which direction to turn. The place was noisy, crowded with soldiers and civilians. Vladimir decided to walk around to see if he could get some information. On a wall he saw a sign that read "All military personnel report to the sergeant at the main entrance." Vladimir returned for the medics and they followed him out.

At the main entrance a sergeant, puffed up with his responsibility, ordered all soldiers onto a short line of trucks that was a transport to the Vyazma Garrison headquarters. As an officer, Vladimir was given a seat next the to a driver of one of the smaller and older trucks. The driver had a difficult time placing the transmission into gear. After several attempts and much swearing, the stick shift finally slid into first gear. The truck lumbered along the street, turned right onto a bridge over the railroad tracks and down another street until it came to a stop sign. After being unable to shift into first gear, the driver shifted into second gear and attempted to proceed. The engine died. The driver, swearing louder with each passing second, went to the front of the truck, lifted the hood and fiddled with the carburetor. Then he sat back in the truck smiling broadly, and shaking his head in approval when the engine came to life. He tried the first gear again. This time, it clanked as metal hit metal, but gave in and worked. The truck made its way down another street until it stopped again at the guardhouse of the garrison. As soon as it stopped, the engine died once again.

"We'll walk from here," Vladimir said.

The guards waved Vladimir and his medics through and pointed to an old three-story red brick building to the left of the gate. Parked in front of the building were several military automobiles painted a dull grayish color. Above the door was a sign that read "Administration." Vladimir looked around the garrison compound. *All of these buildings are ancient. They must have been around since the days of Napoleon,* he thought.

He and the medics entered the building through a low, narrow, wide-open door. The wooden floor creaked as the four men approached a corporal who sat behind an enormous desk.

"Papers, please," the corporal said. "Oh you are Comrade Captain Moskalkov. We received a call that you were on your way here. Comrade Colonel Markov is waiting to see you. The medics can wait here."

Vladimir followed the corporal into the lieutenant's office. Reading a book, his feet propped up on his desk, the lieutenant jumped up quickly and stood at attention as Vladimir entered the room. After the corporal informed him that Vladimir was to see Markov, the lieutenant knocked on the door to another office, entered that room, and closed the door behind him. In less than a minute, he came out and told Vladimir to enter.

Markov sat behind his desk, the top overflowing with randomly scattered papers. A half-full bottle of vodka and an empty glass sat on the side of the desk. Markov was overweight and sweat poured down his extremely round, reddened face. Sweat also stained his shirt. His pug nose and cleanly shaved head gave the appearance of a full moon at harvest time. He gave Vladimir a wide smile and reached for the bottle of vodka. He took another glass out of an open drawer, wiping it clean on his shirt.

"Comrade Captain Moskalkov," Colonel Markov said. "We have been waiting for you. Come, come. Sit down. Here, I'll pour you a glass. I am sure that you can use a good stiff drink."

Vladimir took the glass and waited for the customary toast that followed. He was not a drinker and knew the full glass would affect him. However, he learned long ago not to turn down a drink or the drinkers would think him a weakling. He especially did not want to appear weak to his commanding officer. Markov filled his glass full and held it up.

"To our success against the damn fascists," Markov said. "May they all rot in hell."

With that said, he tipped his head and drained the glass. He looked at Vladimir.

"Well what are you waiting for? Drink up, fellow."

Vladimir knew he had no choice but to follow suit. He quickly drained the contents in one big swallow. Markov, again opened the drawer and pulled out a fresh cucumber and a knife. Slicing off two thick pieces, he kept one for himself and gave the other to Vladimir.

"Did you bring any trained medics with you, as ordered?"

"Yes, Colonel. They are downstairs, and like me, waiting for further orders."

"My aide will show you where to eat and get some rest. Tomorrow at 0600 hours you and your men will be driven to a field hospital west of Vyazma where you'll work with another physician. The more serious cases, or ones that you won't be able to handle, will be transported to the Vyazma hospital or maybe on to the Moscow hospitals. Not all the medical equipment has yet arrived. Hopefully you'll get it before the bastards attack. We do expect a major attack soon. You are now part of the Reserve Front, fellow, and will be close to the defensive lines. I anticipate many wounded, so you will have your work cut out for you. Any questions?"

"Yes, sir, how much time do we have before the Germans attack?"

"How about another drink," Markov said as he picked up the bottle to pour.

"No, thank you, Colonel. I am fine."

"Well, I'll have another one."

Vladimir watched as Markov finished off the bottle, cut another piece of cucumber and stuffed it in his mouth. Vladimir could see that he was high. His eyes were glassy, and his complexion even redder than before.

"Now where were we? Oh yes, you asked about an attack by the damn sons of bitches. Those bastards! Our intelligence is a little confused at the moment. Our valiant warriors have stalled the Germans at Yelna and Roslavl. But, those bastards are too strong. Our positions will likely fall. Then they'll turn their attention on us here, along the Vyazma-Bryansk front. It could be any day now that we'll fight them here. We already had their reconnaissance planes flying. We've even shot one of the sons of bitches down. But, they will be here soon enough, swarming on us like locusts. Stavka, you know, our military brain thrust in Moscow, is sending us garbage as far as fighting men go. They are remnants of other units, too few of them and not well trained. Unless we get the crack troops from Siberia, those that protected our borders from the Japanese, well, quite frankly we don't have a chance. We may slow the enemy down some, and maybe, by then, the crack troops from the east will come in time to defend Moscow. You know, I'll tell you a secret. Stavka does not really believe we can stop the German Army here on this front. They are throwing us in to slow the bastards down and allow more time for the reinforcement of Moscow. We are expendable. We will all be killed and they could care less. Does that answer your question?"

Vladimir nodded in the affirmative. Markov slurred his words and talked incessantly. The liquor had loosened his tongue. Vladimir was surprised by his indiscreet conversation with Markov. It was not professional. *Surely, if he were sober, he would never had expressed his thoughts to a junior officer. And to one that he had just met.* Vladimir felt uncomfortable, and was glad that a political commissar was not present. Otherwise, both of them would have been arrested or executed. But, he realized that even though Markov was under the influence of vodka, what he said made sense. Markov was worried and scared about the impending invasion. Vladimir told himself that he would get through this one way or another. After all, Slava waited for him. He reflected upon his grandfather's wise words, "Never be afraid or show fear. The wolves sense fear."

CHAPTER 16

A third of the old collective farm school was repainted. The remainder of the restoration work had been abandoned. It was middle of July 1941, and there were no children around. It would have been their summer vacation, but Vladimir knew that they had been evacuated. An hour's drive to this school from the Vyazma military garrison and Vladimir was once again in a danger zone. The defensive lines were only a few kilometers away to the west. He sensed the peril. If the defensive lines were to be overrun by the Germans, as they were in Smolensk, he would be killed or taken prisoner. He had escaped encirclement once. It was unlikely he would be lucky enough to do it again. Nevertheless, he was anxious to start his new assignment.

Markov had told him that his new assignment would be a physician at the old farm school that had been converted to a field hospital. It was a sad looking one-story structure with old brick showing through the yellow stucco, except for the area that had been repaired and painted. The tin roof had suffered from corrosion and rust. The school building stood at the end of a row of small wooden homes. They faced each other on a road that was no more than a wagon or truck trail with deep ruts. On the other side of the school, about 500 meters away, were several barns for the animals. The barns appeared in better shape than the homes of the workers.

Vladimir grabbed his gear and led the medics up the four chipped cement steps to the entrance. The driver who had brought them turned his truck around and headed back to Vyazma. As they walked into the foyer leading to the long hallway a young nurse ran up to them. A pretty girl with jet-black hair and blue eyes, she had pale white skin. The khaki uniform hugged her body, and the black leather belt circled her small waist.

"Hello, are you our new doctor and medics?" The nurse asked excitedly.

"Yes, I'm Vladimir Moskalkov, and this is Misha, Evgeniy and Stepan."

"Very pleased to meet you. I'm officially Lieutenant Irina Plutskayia, but just call me Irina. I am the head nurse here, and they tell me that I run the place. Of course, that is not true. You doctors are always in charge. Now, let me show you where all of you can stow your gear until we figure out where you'll sleep. That is, if we'll have time to sleep." Irina said laughingly.

"How large of a staff do we have here?" Vladimir asked as the group walked down the hall.

"I'll be glad to introduce you to everyone. We have another physician and, besides wonderful me, two more nurses. Leave your bags here and follow me to the unknown, I mean to that room over there that reads, 'Third Grade.' I believe everyone is in that room. Its been converted to a ward. We already have patients in it. And so far it's the only one we could furnish. So let's surprise them."

Vladimir did not know what to make of Irina. She seemed nutty and was mouthy. Perhaps that was her true personality. Or perhaps she was trying to mask her anxiety in the face of the eminent attack. At any rate, she did not come across as a serious woman to him. She seemed flippant and he wondered about her qualifications.

"Everyone listen up," Irina said giddily as the group entered the room. "We have additions to our little family here."

Vladimir looked around the room and was shocked to see his old friend, the best man at his wedding, standing next to the bed of a patient.

"Dodik!" Vladimir exclaimed. "What are you doing here?"

"Volodya! You're a sight for sore eyes. I'm so glad to see you. I can't believe this."

"Dodik?" Irina spoke up as the men gave each other a hearty hug. "What kind of name is Dodik? I thought your name was Dimitri?"

"Oh, that's just a nickname. My little sister couldn't say Dimitri when she was a toddler so she called me Dodik. After that, my family and friends began to call me Dodik."

"Well for those that don't know, this is Captain Dimitri Kirkovsky," Irina said looking important as though it was her duty to do the introductions. "The new physician is Captain Vladimir Moskalkov. And the other nurses are Ludmilla, the tall, blood-headed one, and Galina, the brunette." She turned abruptly to Evgeniy and said,

"Now it's your turn to tell us your names and something about yourselves. And, you two doctors should go to the vacant classroom next door and catch up on old news. Go, Go!"

As Irina spoke, Vladimir noticed that that she tucked her hand in Misha's arm and sidled closer to him.

"I especially would like to get to know this man. He's kind of cute," Irina laughed. Misha blushed.

Vladimir and Dodik followed Irina's suggestion and walked into an adjacent room. The student desks were gone, but there were two tables in the corner. One was against the wall, and held a tin teapot and a few cups and plates. Six chairs surrounded the other table, a meter away.

"Here, let's sit down around this table," Dodik said. "We use this room as our break room. We're still waiting for more beds, pillows and blankets to arrive. Once they get here, this room will become another ward. The last classroom on the left is set up as our surgical room. We're also expecting another table, instruments and lights to set up a second surgical room across the hall. I've requested, and was promised, an x-ray machine, but I know we won't get it. They've told me to treat as many as we can here without sending them to Vyazma. But in reality, we are really nothing more than a first aid station. Are your medics any good?"

Victor Moss

"I think they are the best. They know their stuff and work well under pressure. Don't worry about surgical instruments for me. I brought a bag full that I took from the trenches. I think we should consider this field hospital more than a first aid station if we have the equipment to treat the wounded. But tell me about yourself. The last time we talked, you said you were going to join the army, and that was shortly after our graduation."

"Yes, I guess I followed in my father's footsteps. As you know, he was an army doctor, and I guess I always wanted to be one."

"So where have you been for a year?"

"I did my residency in internal medicine at an army hospital in Minsk, then they transferred me to a hospital outside of Moscow. A week ago, I was assigned to set up this hospital out of this old school building. I hope that is all they want me to do. But I have a feeling that they will keep me here once the battle begins."

"You haven't seen any battle casualties yet, then?"

"No, I've been lucky. How about you?"

"Yes, unfortunately. We came under fire in Smolensk, then in a village west of Smolensk, then again on the way to Yelna, and again in Yelna. I have seen injuries that they didn't teach us much about in school. It has been horrible."

"Well, the wounded will be here any day now," Dodik said. "I can't imagine what to expect. How will I be able to diagnose and treat each injury? We are too close to the front lines. What if we get blown up?"

"You will do just fine, Dodik. You are very bright. After all, you were the smartest one in our class. Besides, once the wounded start pouring in, your adrenalin will kick in and you'll work on impulse and do the right thing. You won't have time to worry about how to treat the injured or whether a bomb will hit us or not. You have patients now. Who are they? Surely they are not wounded from battle?"

"No, a couple were shot in friendly fire during training. One has shrapnel from a grenade that exploded near him. But most of the patients are just plain sick with the flu. One has pneumonia. One had tuberculosis, so I sent him on to Vyazma."

"How is our stock of medications?"

"It is adequate. Perhaps you could take a look and tell me what you think about our medical supplies. They put me in charge here, but I really don't want to be. I guess that is why Irina thinks she can run the place. Actually, you should be in charge. At least you have seen the war and dealt with the wounded of battle. I don't know if I'll be able to handle it. Just because I have seniority in the army, I have to be in command of this hospital. Ha! That's a joke, isn't it?"

"Dodik, you'll be just fine. Did you ever marry Anna? I thought you liked her."

"No, after I left, we wrote to each other for awhile. The last letter I received from her told me that she was getting married to some engineer."

"Well, is there anyone in your life now?"

"No. I am still looking."

Dodik had changed, Vladimir decided, although he still looked the same with his slight build, frail round face with large eyes and ears. He had always liked to be with Dodik, who was full of jokes, had a fun loving disposition and generally laughed a lot. He was the life of any gathering. But since the first smile at their meeting that day, Dodik had not smiled again and definitely had not laughed out loud. *Did he really change that much,* Vladimir thought. *Or is he just plain scared of the imminent attack and not himself? Maybe, the stress of war and the responsibility of setting up a hospital brought Dodik down?*

"So where do you want me to start?" Vladimir asked. "Do you want me to look over the drugs first?"

"Ah, well, I guess that will be all right. I hope the beds and other supplies come in today. I was told that you should set up your own surgical room and make more wards from the empty classrooms. Will that be all right with you?"

"Sure, that's all right. Actually, I'll call Colonel Markov regarding those supplies we need. He seemed like a cooperative commanding officer. You know, Dodik, I haven't been in the army long, but I discovered that you have to push and pester to get anything you need. So where is the telephone? Let's call Markov."

"We don't have a telephone yet. Supposedly they are working on running a line from Vyazma to here. They will lay it right on the ground, so it shouldn't take too long."

"Since we expect an attack at anytime, we can't wait for our inefficient army to get us what we need," Vladimir said. "The medical corps and the wounded soldiers always seem to be an afterthought. When the wounded start coming in, this building will not be big enough even if it were filled with beds. We have to put pressure on Markov to supply us with what we need. That truck we came over on, how often does it come here?"

"It comes once per day to bring us supplies, and to pick up any patients that we need transferred to Vyazma."

"I'll be on that truck tomorrow to see Markov," Vladimir said. "We must push him. By the way, I'm sure Slava would say 'Hello' if she knew you were here."

"Oh, I meant to ask you what you've heard from Slava. Is she still in Vitebsk?"

"Dodik, I have no way of knowing. I pray that she is all right no matter where she is."

At that moment, Irina came in and insisted that she show Vladimir and the medics where they were to sleep. They followed her to the row of houses that Vladimir passed earlier on the way to the hospital. The houses were actually huts or "izbas" built of wood with a few narrow windows and thatched roofs. Some looked a little nicer than the others, especially the ones made of logs, but overall, each showed considerable wear and tear. The village appeared much poorer than his grandparents' village of Jazwino, but somehow it reminded him of that village. And even though the summer heat and humidity had sweat running down his forehead, the sight of this village took him back to the winters of his childhood.. He remembered how the villagers piled snow against the outside walls for insulation. As a small boy, he enjoyed the first snows of the season. He played in the snow and helped his grandfather scoop the snow against the wall. As the snow piled high against the wall, even higher than the window, he slid down the slope.

And, just as in Jazwino, there was the typical wooden outhouse and a wooden tool shed and a barn for the animals in the back. Since the communists took over, very few animals were kept in the barns behind the houses. The animals were moved to a central location like those large barns at the other end of the school. But chicken, ducks and geese were allowed as personal animals of the farmers.

Vladimir was to share the first house, closest to the hospital, with Dodik and another officer. The nurses shared the house across the street, and Irina made sure that the medics shared the house next to the nurses. She told them that food was to be served twice a day in the break room at the hospital. A local woman who refused to evacuate and lived in one of the huts agreed to be their cook. Vegetable gardens, outlined by stick fences, surrounded the huts. The gardens had not been destroyed and the cook also volunteered to take care of the gardens, and to use the produce for the workers and patients at the hospital. The other huts housed officers from the defensive lines.

The hut's only room contained a massive brick stove in the middle. The stove was designed not only for cooking, but also for the warmth of the house and a bed for the family. People were able to sleep on the thick top of the stove and stay warm during the cold Russian winter. The sight of the stove once again reminded Vladimir of his childhood at his grandparents' house. He recalled lying on the stove with his grandparents and his sister, Anna. *Those were the good old days,* he thought to himself. However, there were big differences between this hut and his grandparents' house. The house in Jazwino was much bigger with several rooms wallpapered in beautiful colors. His grandfather had built several nice pieces of furniture. In this hut, old newspapers lined the walls. The ceiling was made of rough-cut birch boards. The floor was worn and uneven from the many years of use. There was a crudely built table and bench along the wall and three chairs made from tree branches. Three shelves lined the wall, where pots and pans along with dishes and glasses were stored. Three metal beds with metal springs and saggy mattresses stood on the opposite wall. Two of the beds were made up with an army blanket and a pillow, while the third stood unmade, with a blanket and a pillow piled to one side. Vladimir assumed that was his. There were no sheets or pillowcases and the mattress looked filthy. He decided there and then that he would not use the blanket or the pillow. He would sleep on his greatcoat and use his arm for a pillow, or better yet, sleep on top of the stove.

"Well, what do you think?" Irina said. "Just like home, no?"

"No," Vladimir said. "But it will do."

Beware the Wolves

"Well, we had better get back to the hospital," Irina said. "I hear a truck approaching. It might be bringing more sick from the front."

"Yes, let's get to work," Vladimir said. "Although, I hope it's the equipment we need."

Unfortunately, the truck did not come from Vyazma, but brought more sick from the front. Each side of the truck's canvass cover had a large red cross painted on a circular white background. The two sick soldiers were sappers who had become dehydrated and had passed out as they dug defensive trenches. At the hospital, Vladimir asked Ludmilla to give the soldiers water and rest. As he was leaving the ward, Irina arrived. He heard her yell at the soldiers:

"What a way to get out of work. Just don't take any water and get a ride to the hospital. Let someone else do your work. Was that your plan? Well, now you boys can just get a ride back to the lines. I don't want to see you here again or wonderful me will just have to tell your commanding officer that you are slackers and have you shot. Now get out of here, you goof-offs."

Irina had once again surprised Vladimir. She was seething with anger. *What happened to her bubbly, happy-go-lucky personality?* He wondered if he should say something to her. Surely, she heard that he ordered rest for the soldiers. But it was not critical. The soldiers could go back to work. He decided to let it go this time, but knew that should a similar situation come up again, he would have to deal with it.

Throughout the rest of the day he explored the old school building. Vladimir talked to Dodik about the "good old days" in medical school and their days in Vitebsk. He longed to tell Slava about his experiences since he last saw her and particularly of his meeting with Dodik. Slava liked Dodik and would enjoy hearing about their conversation. The desire to hold Slava in his arms, squeeze her tight and kiss every square centimeter of her body became overwhelming. He went into the break room, poured himself a cup of tea and sat down at the table. Not only was he homesick, he was bored. He needed to work. He had always worked, even as a child. He worked while attending medical school; after graduation he held down three full-time jobs. He smiled, recalling how he was quick enough to work at three clinics in the course of a day and get paid from each. Slava was a full-time student and did not mind the extra hours he put in. He made good money compared to the rest of the population. Since being drafted, he did not seem to have a moment for himself. He should appreciate the downtime considering the tragedies he had witnessed in the last few days, the lack of sleep and extreme exhaustion. *Relish it, Volodya,* he thought, *for soon this idleness will only be a memory.*

He heard the rumble of a truck, jumped to his feet, and ran out the door to meet it. It was a supply truck from Vyazma. They quickly unloaded five twin beds, mattresses, pillows, blankets and a sack of potatoes. There were no medicines or surgical apparatus. The driver had no idea what Vladimir was talking about when he asked about a surgical table or a light to go above it. He chuckled, while rolling his cigarette, when Dodik asked about the x-ray machine.

Victor Moss

"Comrades, I was told that what I brought to you today is all you are going to get," the driver said. "You should know there is a shortage of everything. There are battles and wounded all over the place. You are damn lucky to get what I brought you."

"I'm going back with you to Vyazma," Vladimir told the driver. "I need to see Colonel Markov."

"Volodya, you shouldn't go," Dodik said. "It won't do any good. You heard the driver. He said we're lucky to get what we got. We'll make do."

Finally convincing Dodik that he should go back and talk to Markov, Vladimir hopped into the cab alongside the driver. He had no idea if it would do any good. But he felt he had to try something.

◆ ◆ ◆ ◆

Markov sat behind his desk when an aide showed Vladimir into his office. He smiled broadly at Vladimir and seemed genuinely pleased to see him.

"You're just in time," Markov said. "I was ready to open a fresh bottle of Armenian cognac. We can wash the dust off our lips."

Markov went through the same routine of taking a glass for Vladimir out of his desk drawer. His glass was next to a stack of papers on the desk. Vladimir could see that he had already had a few drinks as his nose and checks were reddened. Markov walked to the door and called out to his aide to find Tamara to bring them some cheese.

"Nice girl, that Tamara," Markov said. "She cooks for us officers here. We have a game. I chase her and she runs away. One of these days, I'll catch her. So how is it going at the field hospital?"

"Well, Colonel Markov, that's why I'm here. We need another surgical table, lights, medicines, beds—everything. An x-ray machine would be good. What we have now will not be enough once the battle begins. I've seen the overwhelming number of wounded outside of Smolensk and how quickly the wounded accumulate in the trenches. We need to be prepared. I'd rather have everything set up, ready to go, than to beg you later for more."

"Here, Comrade Captain, have a shot of Cognac. Tamara will be here soon with the cheese."

Markov took the glass and in one swallow downed the cognac. Vladimir took a sip, for this was not a shot glass, but a large glass used for water or juices.

"No, no, no, Captain. You must chug the whole drink at once. That's how we do it in the Army."

So Vladimir did. He felt a burning sensation all the way down his throat and had to catch his breath. Markov looked satisfied and poured himself and Vladimir another full glass. *This is getting serious. Another glass like this and I will end up under the table.* At that moment there was a knock on the door and Tamara came in the room with a plate of cheese laid out on pieces of dark rye bread. Vladimir was happy to see the food. At least now he would have something in his stomach to fight off the effects of the Cognac. Tamara, a plump, buxom girl in her mid-twenties, was not overly attractive. A quick glance at Markov and Vladimir decided that, actually, both of them fit each other. He noticed Markov pat Tamara on her rear as she set the plate on his desk. Both of them smiled.

"I don't have anything more that I can give you." Markov said with his mouth full of food, smacking his lips as though he had not eaten for days. "You see, Moscow has not sent me any more hospital supplies. I think they are hording it for themselves."

"Well, what about medicines. We need morphine. We have only a small supply. We need more sulpha drugs. When the battle starts, we'll run out of medications in a week."

"Here, drink up. I like you and I'll tell you what. I have no medicines in my warehouse. But the hospital in Vyazma may have more than it needs. Why don't we go there tomorrow and see if we can free them of some of their supply."

"That would be terrific. What about a surgical table, lights and more beds."

"Don't push it, comrade. I can show you my warehouse and you can see how empty it is."

Vladimir excused himself after being forced to drink the second glass. He insisted that he did not want the third. Markov didn't protest and drank his third. The aide showed Vladimir where he could sleep for the night in the officer's quarters.

The next morning, Markov, his aide and Vladimir drove to the Vyazma hospital that was converted for military use. Markov, and the hospital's administrator, a major in the medical corps who appeared to be in his late forties, carried on a heated discussion whether or not any medicines were to leave the hospital. Vladimir's head was pounding from the Cognac of the day before and the argument resonated in his head. Markov acted perfectly normal. The alcohol did not faze him at all. After more shouting, Markov pulled his rank and ordered that several boxes of medications be loaded in his vehicle. The Major complied but was furious, sending a deathly look in Vladimir's direction.

When Vladimir went down into the storage room, he was astonished to see the large supply of medications. They won't miss some of these at all. He looked through some of the boxes and then Markov's aide and he carried them into the waiting car. They filled up the trunk and the entire back seat, leaving only a small space for Vladimir to sit.

The warehouse turned out to be fruitful as well. Vladimir found an old cooking table from a restaurant that he decided could double as a surgical table. There were no beds, but in a room in a cellar of the warehouse he found forty-three folding cots. There were dozens of drab-looking blankets that the soldier in charge of the warehouse told him were used during World War I. He could not, at first, find anything he could use for a surgical lamp until he noticed a light hanging over the entry door that had a wide reflective cover. After convincing Markov's aide that the light could be replaced with a hanging bulb, he was allowed to take the light fixture. That afternoon Vladimir sat in the truck loaded with medicines, a table, a light fixture and cots. *Now we may be ready for battle,* Vladimir thought.

CHAPTER 17

The expected attack against Vyazma had not materialized even though it was already the end of July 1941. Every room of the old school, transformed into a field hospital, was equipped with beds and cots, except the two rooms used for surgery. The break room was left intact. There were not enough cots to use it for a ward. The little hospital could treat many of the wounded, but Vladimir knew that it would be overwhelmed once the battle began.

"If those rat bastards are going to attack, then let them do it now," Evgeniy complained. "This waiting around is driving me crazy. I'm not alone. The nurses and even you and Comrade Captain Kirkovsky are on edge. I can see it. Every time the boys at the front shoot practice rounds from the artillery we almost shit our pants."

"Evgeniy, what's your hurry for battle," Vladimir said. "Unfortunately, it will come sooner than later. Let's put it out of our minds until such time that we have to deal with it. In the meantime, we have a few sick soldiers to attend to."

"You are right, Comrade Captain. We have just a few sick soldiers. Stepan and I have been talking about asking for a transfer from this hospital detail to the front. Until the attack begins, medics will not be very busy there either, but at least we may feel a little more useful. With the nurses around here, there isn't a damn thing for us to do except to move beds around."

"I think that is a good idea. I would authorize the transfer. But you have to get permission from Captain Kirkovsky. As a matter of fact, now that the hospital is set up, I'm ready to be transferred as well. I don't think the Germans are ready to attack us just yet."

Vladimir suddenly thought about what he just said. *Would I really want to go back to the battlefield? I am no hero.* He, like everyone else, wanted to survive. Evgeniy was right. Each time practice artillery or mortars went off, it unnerved him. He still had flashbacks of the deadening sound of battle. His nights were filled with the nauseating images of arms, legs and heads blown off men, or the sight of intestines hanging out of abdomens. The overwhelming suffering that he had witnessed was indescribable. He could not put Ilya out of his mind. He was the poor boy whose leg he had to cut off under those primitive conditions in the forest. Who in his right mind would want to go back and relive the nightmare? *Yet I am here for a purpose. And that purpose was to save lives in battle. And no matter how much I dread the thought of going back to the front, I have a duty to do. Surely, I could be more useful somewhere else.* So he decided that if an attack on Vyazma was not imminent, he would ask Markov for a transfer to a battlefield.

135

Victor Moss

Vladimir left the break room to check once again on the patients in the wards. As he passed by an empty ward, he heard grunting sounds coming from that room. He stepped into the room and saw Irina on one of the beds with her skirt raised and Misha on top of her, his pants down. Vladimir instantly turned and left the room in disbelief. *What am I supposed to do about this?* He thought to himself.

Shortly thereafter, Irina ran out of the room with one half of her tunic hanging out of her skirt and, catching up to him, said, "Vladimir, what in the hell were you doing walking into an empty ward? Are you spying on me? You better not tell Dodik about this. Promise me you won't tell."

"Irina, I am not going to tell anyone, unless this happens again. You know the rules. You are not allowed to fraternize with the soldiers. Especially as a nurse and an officer. That is so unprofessional."

"Well, let the devil deal with the rules. I have my needs. Actually, go ahead and tell Dodik. He won't do anything about it. Just watch."

Vladimir walked away. The more acquainted he became with her; the more he decided that he wanted very little to do with her. Instead of apologizing, she was itching for a fight. He sensed that any working relationship with her would be a stormy one.

A few more days passed by and Vladimir became extremely bored. There was not enough work for one physician, let alone two. He was homesick and thought much of Slava and his mother and sisters. *If only I could write and let them know that I am alive and safe. If only I could receive some kind of message that they are safe or whether they are still in Vitebsk.* He and Dodik spent more time together, but most times ran out of topics to discuss. Irina avoided him and began bad-mouthing him to the other nurses. Then, on other occasions, she would once again be bubbly, complimenting herself with a task that in her opinion, was well done. Five minutes later, she threw daggers with her looks at Vladimir.

Their roommate in the hut, Timoshenko, a tall, thin straight-backed captain in charge of a sapper brigade, was not present very often. Many times he did not come in from the trenches even to sleep. When he did, Vladimir enjoyed hearing about the preparedness at the front. In his last conversation, Timoshenko, described how his men were busy cutting trees into logs with sharp pointed ends and digging them into the ground at approximately a five degree angle in an attempt to stop the Panzer advance. Timoshenko was very thankful that the invasion had not yet begun. This gave the sappers more time for defense preparations and additional time to train the raw recruits that flooded into the Vyazma front. Unfortunately, there was a dire shortage of equipment. The shortages were such that three soldiers had to share one rifle. He also told Vladimir that several thousand soldiers were being sent to Yelna and many more may be sent to Roslavl. Fierce battles were raging around Yelna and Roslavl and that, in fact, on the 19th of July the Panzers had entered Yelna after a twelve-hour battle. The defenders were decimated, including regular units of

Beware the Wolves

the garrison along with the workers' battalions. It was Timoshenko's opinion that the heroic resistance delayed the attack on Vyazma.

Since that conversation, Vladimir could not help but think of Captain Savitski and his friend, Ivanov, who he left behind at the garrison at Yelna. He assumed that, if they had not been killed in battle, the enemy probably executed them. Timoshenko informed him that officers, particularly political commisars, were the first to be shot whenever prisoners were captured.

◆ ◆ ◆ ◆

The first week of August 1941 arrived and there was no indication that Vyazma would be attacked soon. Vladimir decided that he had too much time to think. He discussed a transfer with Dodik, who objected and thought Vladimir was crazy to even consider it. Nevertheless he allowed Vladimir to talk directly to Markov.

Colonel Markov was not in his office when he arrived. Vladimir sat in the aide's room and waited. Markov arrived about an hour later and was surprised to see Vladimir.

"Come in, come in Comrade Captain. How is everything at the field hospital? Kirkovsky tells me that all of you are very busy with the sick from the incoming troops."

Vladimir did not know how to respond. He was stumped. He wanted a transfer because they were not busy enough. Yet if he told Markov the truth, it would show Dodik in a bad light.

"We do have patients, Colonel Markov. But I'd like to talk to you concerning a transfer."

Markov's smile faded, but again lightened up as he opened his desk drawer and pulled out a half full bottle of vodka and two glasses. *Oh, no, not again,* thought Vladimir. *We have to go through this again.*

"Here you are. I'm always happy to have your company. I'll ask Tamara to bring us some ham," Markov said as he rubbed his big round stomach. "Now drink up, son. It's good for you."

Markov lifted his glass, swallowed the contents in one gulp, wiped his mouth with the back of his hand and looked intently at Vladimir to see if he did the same. Vladimir knew what was expected of him, so he also gulped down the vodka as Tamara came in with a plate of ham on rye bread and butter. Vladimir expected Markov to pour himself another glass, but this time he did not. Instead, with a frown on his big round face, he asked what Vladimir had in mind with a transfer.

"Well, Colonel, I feel that I can be of more use treating wounded soldiers. I've heard about the heroic resistance at Yelna and Roslavl. I am sure more physicians are needed and I'd like to volunteer. It doesn't look as though the Germans will attack Vyazma any time soon."

137

"My boy, you do not want to go to Roslavl. The fierce resistance by our troops continues outside of Roslavl. This week alone, reports are coming in that 38,000 of our men were encircled and taken as prisoners by the Fritzes at Roslavl. And where you were stationed, Smolensk, the Germans took more than 300,000 prisoners from the second encirclement there. The situation at Yelna is no better. The German strategy is to encircle our positions with an overwhelming force. We have no mobility. They have tanks and personnel carriers. What do we have in battle? Farm tractors and a few horses, if we are lucky. You can imagine how angry Comrade Stalin is with our men for giving up and surrendering. After all, his orders are that each is to die fighting and not give up. You know, 'Save the last bullet for yourself' philosophy. Giving up is a crime against the State. But, and this is between you and me, it is human nature to protect yourself and surrender rather than die. Of course, you are just as likely to die in captivity with the Germans as to fight it out. So who knows what's better?"

"But Colonel, surely, there would be a need for me to be with the troops in battle?"

"Here, have another drink of vodka. And take some more ham. It is a luxury you know. I am lucky that I know the right people. This ham is delicious. Here, here, drink up. We won't always have vodka around. Now where were we?"

"About my transfer?"

"Oh yes. Transfer denied. I need you here. The Nazis may not be on our doorstep this instant, but now that the resistance around Smolensk, Yelna and Roslavl is diminished, Vyazma is next on the road to Moscow. I send you away, and then when I need you, I may not get you or another doctor. Forget it. Anyway, we are probably going to start receiving wounded from those areas. They have to go somewhere, don't they? I believe you will be very busy soon once the wounded are transported here."

"You think they will bring them to our field hospital?"

"They will go wherever there is room for them and a doctor to treat them."

◆ ◆ ◆ ◆

Markov was right. A few days later, wounded from Yelna and Roslavl arrived by train and started to fill up the Vyazma hospital. Markov ordered Vladimir to Vyazma to treat the wounded. He was given a room in the officer's barracks at the Garrison, but rarely spent time in it as he worked around the clock at the hospital. Occasionally he napped wherever he found space. His favorite spot was the floor of a supply closet. Dodik remained at the field hospital with the nurses. The medics were transferred to the front.

In the middle of August 1941 the flow of wounded diminished as the battles on the German Central Front around Vyazma ceased. Vladimir still could not fully understand why the Germans had not yet attacked the defensive posi-

Beware the Wolves

tions west of Vyazma as the summer was quickly coming to a close and "General Winter" would be a factor. *Surely, the Germans are aware of this tactical mistake? What do they have in mind? Are they going to wait until next spring?*

While treating the wounded, Vladimir asked whether they heard of the fate of Savitski and Ivanov. No one seemed to know of them. The injured soldiers from the Yelna front were from a group sent in to recapture the city from the enemy and were unable to do so. They were fortunate that they escaped the German encirclement around Yelna. He admired the soldiers. *They lay in pain, yet hardly complain.* But they did complain about the military strategy that led so many of their comrades to their deaths. Several soldiers told Vladimir that they were part of the twenty-one divisions that charged the enemy in an unprepared attack in the last few days of July. The result of that action disseminated the troops to only twelve divisions.

"It was a damn massacre," one of the soldiers told Vladimir. "We were thrown into battle as fodder for the enemy. We were sent into battle unprepared, completely exhausted, with no ammunition and totally disorganized against the coordinated armor of the Germans."

"Yeah, we had no artillery and not a single tank that worked," another soldier in the adjoining bed chimed in. "Except for our own feet, we had no mobility. Even if we had the tanks or the artillery, there was no way to get them where we needed them. I saw a dilapidated farm tractor pull a Howitzer until it broke down, too. I didn't even have a rifle to fight with. We were told to pick up rifles from fallen soldiers. They better get their act together or we will all be annihilated by those sons of bitches."

"Yet, you soldiers did your jobs," Vladimir said. "Look how long you had held off the Germans in Yelna and Roslavl. They still have not attacked Vyazma. You have worn them down. Good job, men!"

Vladimir continued his rounds and treated the injured. However, after a week, fewer wounded arrived at the Vyazma hospital. And after another two weeks, many were eventually discharged, died or were transferred to Moscow facilities. The long, tiring days of surgery and care of the wounded for now ended, and Vladimir had extra time on his hands. The hospital had ten additional army physicians, and at least thirty nurses and numerous orderlies. Vladimir thought that his help was no longer needed and once again asked Markov to transfer him where he could be of more use. Markov reassigned him to the field hospital once again since Dodik had complained that he was overworked with the sick, and accidentally injured soldiers, that were accumulating at the defensive lines.

◆ ◆ ◆ ◆

The motor overheated in the 1936 GAZ truck as Vladimir sat next to the driver on his way back to the field hospital. The driver apologized to Vladimir for the delay, but they had to wait for the engine to cool off before he could add water. Vladimir noticed that this was probably not the first time the engine overheated. The driver was prepared with a container full of water. After a half hour wait, the truck trudged on. The going was slow. The dusty dirt road was filled with a never-ending column of soldiers marching toward the front. There were thousands of them and the driver drove the GAZ off to the side blasting his horn and yelling at the soldiers to move over. Many times, he had to drive in the ditch to get around the throng.

"Where are all these men coming from?" Vladimir asked the driver.

"Like us, they are all part of the Western Front and Reserve armies. The Army is scraping them up anywhere it can. Many are remnants of units that were able to escape the German encirclements around Smolensk, Roslavl and Duhoshina. They keep coming and coming. I make this trip to the field hospital daily, and each day it's this bad."

"How many men do you think we have here at the Vyazma front?"

"Oh, I don't know for sure. But if I had to guess, it's over a million."

"Can you imagine? Over a million men concentrated in one area right here west of Vyazma. You would think they would spread them out along a line."

"Well, maybe they will," the driver said.

"Maybe they will. But they didn't do it around Smolensk."

The column of soldiers kept on marching. The driver had to make a left turn through the column. He honked his horn, motioned with his hand and yelled at the soldiers to let him through. As the soldiers were reluctant to let him pass, he edged into the column, almost running into the crowd and proceeded. Heated words flew between the driver and the soldiers. The driver looked at Vladimir and laughed.

"I love to do that," he said. "A foot soldier can't argue with a truck and win."

Vladimir saw the familiar village adjacent to the field hospital. But the scene now was different. To his immediate left, the crop of wheat was replaced with T-34 tanks, their guns pointed toward the west. They were neatly lined up in row after row. *There must be five hundred,* Vladimir thought. On the right side were artillery pieces, some attached to ordinary farm tractors. A little further down the field were corrals filled with horses. Around the village hundreds of soldiers were milling or sitting beside rows of tents.

Vladimir took a deep breath. His soul ached. The sight of acres of once beautiful rolling fields replaced by weapons of human destruction, and so close to the field hospital, constricted his stomach. *Oh God! Did they bring the front to the hospital? They must have just stored the weapons here. Surely they will move them toward the defensive lines once the attack begins. But if you have over a million soldiers, you have to put them somewhere.*

With a heavy heart, he walked into the field hospital. Irina and Ludmilla stood by the door. Vladimir's smile faded once he saw Irina. He remembered how unpleasant it was to work with her. He hoped that in his absence, she had changed.

Beware the Wolves

"Look who finally decided to show up," Irina smiled sarcastically. "You know that you have no place to sleep. Your bed was taken over by another officer. As a matter of fact, they moved three other officers into your hut while you were gone. Of course, you can probably sleep with Ludmilla. Isn't that right Luda?"

Ludmilla's face turned bright red. She turned and hurriedly walked away shaking her head and muttering something to herself.

"Irina, please, I'm your superior officer. You need to show some respect. You have embarrassed both Ludmilla and me for no reason whatsoever. We have to keep discipline here or our organization at the hospital will be in shambles."

"Well, what are you going to do about it? Fire me! You are not even in my chain of command. But maybe someone should do me a favor and fire me. I'm too good of a nurse to be stuck in this hellhole. Just because you have a doctor's degree you think you are superior. Well you're not. I worked in the finest hospitals in Moscow and where are you from? You're from some provincial town in Byelorussia. Ha!"

Having exploded on Vladimir, she turned around and stalked out of the building slamming the door behind her. Vladimir stood there in amazement.

"What's all the commotion about?" Dodik asked as he walked up to Vladimir. "Welcome back. I missed you. Markov said he would send me some help. I was hoping it would be you. So what happened here?"

"I see Irina has not changed much while I was gone. She was speaking nonsense and after I criticized her, she lost her temper and stormed out."

"I know," Dodik said. "I don't know what to do with her. She can be the friendliest person one moment and then the rudest person the next. The staff and the patients complain about her constantly. She does not work. She tries to do everything but her assignment. For example, last week I called her to come in and assist me with a surgery. Instead she yelled back to me that she was busy. After the surgery, I found her busy in the supply closet alphabetizing medicines and moving them onto another shelf."

"She does seem to be insubordinate."

"I punished her with house arrest and confined her to quarters for three days."

"Didn't seem to have helped," Vladimir said.

"No, she even disobeyed me with that. I had to go to her house on the fourth day to tell her to get back to work. I even threatened her with a court marshal."

"You did! What did she say?"

"She has friends in high places who will 'take care' of me."

"And you believe that? Vladimir laughed.

"I'm still hoping to get transferred back to Moscow. I really don't want any trouble."

"Where should I bed down, or at least find a place for my gear?"

141

Victor Moss

"That's a good question," Dodik said.

"A thought occurred to me that while you're away from your office, I could grab a few blankets, lay them out on the floor and stretch out next to the desk."

"Good, that will solve that problem," Dodik replied.

◆ ◆ ◆ ◆

By September 27, 1941 Vyazma still waited for the expected attack. Some said that the Germans would not attack until spring. But rumors persisted that the Germans were building up their forces west of Vyazma. The field hospital was full of patients despite the lack of combat. Misha and Evgeniy were reassigned to the hospital. With hundreds of thousands of soldiers stationed at the defensive lines, accidents and illnesses, such as severe diarrhea with dehydration, were common. Vladimir had convinced Dodik to send as many of the sick as possible to the Vyazma hospital as the field hospital was designed for the wounded in battle. Markov agreed, and sent two trucks daily to transport the patients that needed additional care. Irina refused to work. She sat mostly in her quarters and usually showed up at the hospital when meals were served. Dodik notified Markov of her behavior and asked her to be court marshaled.

"Captain, Comrade Colonel Markov is here." Misha found Vladimir in a ward speaking to a patient. "He wants to see you. He is in the break room."

Vladimir was surprised to hear that Markov was at the field hospital. It was the first time Markov had visited the place. As he walked down the hallway to the break room, he wondered what this visit meant. *It must be important enough for him to be here,* he thought. As he walked into the room, Markov sat behind the table, leaning against the back of the chair with his arms crossed over his enormous stomach and his feet stretched out under the table. His face was red, as always. On top of the table sat Markov's hat and a tattered brown leather briefcase bulging on its sides. Across the table from him sat Dodik. His back was ramrod straight as though he was at attention. Markov smiled broadly to Vladimir. Vladimir, as usual, saluted, and, as usual, Markov returned a salute that looked more like a wave.

"Come and join us," Markov said while opening his briefcase. "I brought with me my kind of medicine. Vladimir, get three glasses. I have some good Armenian Cognac. You'll get a treat."

Vladimir picked up the glasses from the opposite table. He saw Markov pull out a bottle followed by a large stick of hard salami from the briefcase. Markov poured each a full glass of Cognac and made a toast to victory. The three clinked their glasses.

"Gentlemen," Markov said. "Soon, very soon, any day now, the Germans are going to attack."

Beware the Wolves

"But why have they waited so long?" Vladimir asked as Markov again topped off each glass. Vladimir was determined that he would slowly sip his drink.

"Well, perhaps Hitler was afraid to attack Moscow. Maybe it's the ghost of Napoleon that he fears. On the other hand, maybe he is trying to pick us off, one at a time, before he attacks Moscow. Vladimir, why aren't you drinking? How often do you get good Cognac as this? Now drink up, son. You are not keeping up with Dimitri and me. Here, at least have some of this sausage."

Vladimir took another sip of Cognac and took a thick piece of salami that Markov had cut with his shiny red pocketknife.

"Anyway, as I was saying," Markov continued. "Hitler, that fascist swine, moved most of the Panzers and soldiers from the Center Front, that was progressing toward Moscow, onto the North Front toward Leningrad beginning on August 17$^{th.}$ And about the same time, he moved several divisions from the Center Front to the South Front toward Kiev and the Crimea. This month has been horrible for us. On September 8th Leningrad was surrounded and on the 12th Kiev was encircled and then captured on the 19th. Of course, STAVKA, our joint chiefs of staff, doesn't keep me informed, but my sources tell me that Hitler gave the go-ahead to attack Moscow under a huge operation known as 'Typhoon.' Comrade Captain, you are not drinking your Cognac. You are holding us up. We are ready for another drink."

Markov, nevertheless poured himself another drink, and made a toast to "our gallant warriors," and downed the drink while Vladimir, and now Dodik, took sips from their glasses.

"So, what about the operation 'Typhoon'?" Dodik asked.

"Well, as I said, or maybe I didn't say it, after Kiev was captured, Hitler has and still is transferring divisions from the South and North to Center. Also the delay in attacking us gave them the opportunity to rest the remaining soldiers and equipment. It gave them a chance to repair their tanks, those sons of bitches!"

"So why didn't we attack them," Vladimir asked. "Why do we always take defensive positions all bunched up, waiting to be encircled?"

"Ah, that's not for me or you to decide. You better ask that of Comrade Stalin, who is telling our generals how to run this war. But you did not hear that from me. Understand? Now, back to what we were talking about. Their Center wing is stronger now than it was on June 22nd. They have increased their strength by twenty divisions. I read a report that says that they may have fifty infantry divisions, fourteen armored divisions, and eight mechanized, just to name a few. And they are all out there, those wolves, those demons. They are ready to pounce on Bryansk and Vyazma on the way to Moscow."

"How do we stack up compared to them?" Vladimir asked.

"Our commander, Comrade Lieutenant General Lukin, is not optimistic. But we have a sizeable army of 1,250,000 soldiers, 7,600 guns and mortars and 990 tanks. As you've heard, our T-34 tanks are superior to the Panzers. The

Victor Moss

German 37- mm. and 50- mm. guns can't dent the T-34 with its sloping frontal armor. Actually, I know for a fact that the Germans retooled and mounted our captured 75-mm. guns on the Panzers. It helped against the T-34, but really to stop one you need a 105-mm. gun. Sounds good, doesn't it? But in reality, they were prepared for this war. We were not. They are better trained. They are the professionals with more equipment. Now I propose another toast. This one for the glory of our people, may they endure."

All three raised their glasses, clinked them and repeated the toast. The bottle was empty and Markov stared at it for a few seconds, picked it up and poured the last three drops into his glass and drank it. Vladimir could not believe how much liquor Markov could consume and still function. *Perhaps it was all the food he ate along with the drinks?*

"Let me tell you something else," Markov continued with a more noticeable slur to his speech. "I like you fellows and I'm going to give you some advice. If those criminal scoundrels capture you, as officers you need to protect yourselves. Your chances of being shot on the spot are strong. I never thought much of our uniforms looking the same as the regular soldiers. After all, according to the communist propaganda, we are all equal. But this could be to our benefit. Get rid of your documents, weapons, belts, medical corps insignias and, of course, any indication of your rank. Hopefully, you'll fool them that you are not an officer."

"But if they know we are medical officers, surely they will leave us alone?" Dodik asked.

'I don't think it would make a shit of a difference to them that you are doctors. As a matter of fact they might kill you so that you couldn't render help to your soldiers."

Vladimir sat quietly, stunned. He looked at Dodik whose face was pale staring into space with his mouth wide open.

"Of course, you fellows need not worry about being Jewish, but if you were, information we have is that they shoot Jews on the spot as well. We have not verified if that is true or not; however, a few soldiers who have escaped captivity have said the same thing. Well, now that the cognac is gone, I better get back to Vyazma. Oh yes, as far as Lieutenant Irina Plutskaya is concerned, you can do whatever you want to punish her for her insubordination. As far as I care, you can shoot her. I believe she wants out of here. But I think keeping her here is punishment enough for her. What do you think about that?"

"Then we are all being punished." Dodik said.

"What was that, Comrade Captain?"

"Nothing, sir. I will deal with Plutskaya."

Markov staggered down the steps as Vladimir and Dodik saw him off. "Volodya, I have something to tell you," Dodik said. "My mother is Jewish and under Jewish law, that makes me a Jew. I grew up in the Jewish tradition. I am really worried about the German attack now."

Beware the Wolves

"Dodik. I never knew that you're Jewish. And if I, your friend, wasn't aware, how will the Germans know? Assuming, of course, that the Germans will capture us. The Colonel said to get rid of our passports. What does yours say as far as nationality?"

"Byelorussian. But that's because my father is one. My mother's says 'Jewish'."

"Dodik, don't worry about it. How could they find out?"

◆ ◆ ◆ ◆

October 2, 1941, was a beautiful autumn day. Vladimir operated on a patient who broke his leg when his horse threw him. Ludmilla assisted with the surgery. Vladimir liked working with Ludmilla. She was a good, hard-working nurse. She anticipated Vladimir's every move and supplied the right surgical tool without him asking for it. Ludmilla reminded Vladimir of Tanya. Perhaps that was why she was his favorite nurse and they worked so well together. Dodik still had not punished Irina. She continued to avoid work. The third nurse, Galina, did not have Ludmilla's experience, nevertheless was a hard worker and a fast study.

Vladimir had just closed up the incision to the leg after setting the bones of the soldier when suddenly he heard planes flying in the distance. He had heard that drone before. His heart dropped to the ground. For a second, he lost his breath. Those were Stukas. A moment later, his ears pained with the explosion, the ground shook, the lights went out and Ludmilla screamed.

CHAPTER 18

The sky fell, the earth collapsed, and the gates of Hell flew open. The devil greeted the victims with the firestorm of incessant pounding of bombs, artillery shells and tank barrages. There was no place to run or hide from the ear splitting clamor. Vladimir felt the world had come to an end.

Ludmilla sat, with her knees to her chest, ears covered with her hands, in the corner of the surgical ward. She sobbed with fright. The patient lying on the surgical table with a broken leg awakened screaming to the chaos of explosions.

"Ludmilla, help me get this man under the table," Vladimir yelled out over the racket. "Ludmilla! Get your rear over here! Now move! I need your help!"

Ludmilla looked up and stared at Vladimir. She took her hands from her ears, but did not seem to comprehend what was said to her. Vladimir motioned for her to help him. She sat there motionless and appeared to look through Vladimir. In anticipation of Ludmilla's help, Vladimir had lifted the patient's neck and shoulders, but laid him down again and walked over to Ludmilla. He grabbed her hand and began pulling her up. She suddenly understood what he was doing and jumped to her feet. Under a snowfall of plaster they were able to lift the patient and shove him under the table for protection. Ludmilla immediately returned to the corner and huddled once again with her head between her knees. Vladimir sat down next to her without saying a word.

Vladimir heard another wave of Stukas approach followed by a whistle, then a scream of a bomb falling to earth. The bomb detonated. The building shook, the center of the ceiling caved in, shards of window glass and pieces of metal flew in all directions. Smoke filled the room. As suddenly as it came, so abruptly the air raid stopped. The planes were gone, but the battle could be heard in the distance. Vladimir stood up, coughing from the smoke. Ludmilla remained coughing in the corner.

"Ludmilla, let's get out of this room. The smoke is heavy. There is probably less of it on the other end of the building. Come on Luda, get up! We need to move the patient out of here."

Vladimir again grabbed Ludmilla's hand and pulled her up. Once up, she again came to life and helped Vladimir get the patient out of the room into the hall. Vladimir noticed that a large shard of glass was embedded into the table upon which the patient had laid. *It's lucky we moved him,* he thought.

Patients fled into the corridor where the smoke was lighter. Evgeniy took charge of getting them out of the wards. Galina began to bandage a soldier who had been cut by flying glass. Ludmilla rushed over to another soldier to render help. For the most part, the patients were not seriously injured. Vladimir looked around for Dodik, Misha, or Irina. When he did not see them, he searched the wards, one at a time. He found one bedridden soldier whose neck had been severed by a glass shard. Everyone else had been dragged out of the wards.

"Evgeniy, have you seen Captain Kirkovsky or Misha or Irina?" Vladimir shouted over the ever-increasing artillery fire to the west. "I can't find them in the building."

"Kirkovsky was here somewhere. But I think Misha and Irina are in their quarters."

"What did you say?" Vladimir shouted again. His ears felt stopped up and ringing.

"I said Kirkovsky is in the building. Misha and Irina are not."

Vladimir once again began his search. In the break room, he looked closer at the pile of rubble from the collapsed ceiling. It moved. He ran over to the pile. Dodik emerged, shaking off chunks of plaster. Vladimir helped Dodik brush off the pieces and helped him up.

"Are you all right, Dodik?"

"I guess so. I must have had the wind knocked out of me. I hid under the table when the planes came. After I thought that the raid was over, I was crawling out from underneath the table when more planes came and a bomb went off. The ceiling fell on top of me. Did we take a direct hit?"

"I don't think so. But a bomb exploded close by. The concussion from it damaged our hospital. If we had known, we should have closed the shutters prior to the attack. But it came up so suddenly, without warning. It's the shrapnel and glass that have caused the most injuries. Are you in good enough shape to help me close the shutters now, before another attack?"

"You mean to go outside? Isn't it too late now? The glass is already shattered."

"From what I could see, not every window was broken. Besides, the shutters will protect us from the shrapnel and the smoke. Let's go."

Dodik followed Vladimir out the front door. In the distance, they could see a lightning storm caused by flashes of light from continuous explosions within a dark cloud of smoke. The ground under their feet quaked. Vladimir had seen battle before, but this view of the devil's artistry froze him in place for a few seconds. His breathing had been shallow from the first moment of the attack, but now he felt his heart beat erratically. Dodik could go no further and sat down on the top step. Then they saw, with the battle in the background, Irina and Misha running towards them. They stopped, out of breath, in front of Vladimir and Dodik.

"My house, my house was destroyed," Irina yelled out to them. "I would have been killed if I had been in it. This is horrible. Someone should have warned me."

Dodik, still sitting on the step with his right hand on his head, yelled back at Irina. "Well, you bitch. You better take it. We all have to take it. Now get in there and start cleaning up and act like a soldier in this army. I've had it with you. As for you, Misha, help Captain Moskalkov with securing the shutters. Then get inside and help with the cleanup. As soon as this battle is over I'm going to do everything in my power to get you two court marshaled."

"Big deal. I'm not worried," Irina snapped back. "You will need me."

Irina stormed off into the building followed by Dodik. Vladimir was amazed at Dodik's response. It was rare to hear him lose his temper. Perhaps the battle made him realize that there was no time to play. It was the real thing and he had to get a grip on himself and command.

"Misha, were you with Irina at the time of the attack?" Vladimir asked.

"Yes, we were in my quarters. We had the place to ourselves." Misha answered Vladimir reluctantly. "I'm sorry, Captain. It will never happen again."

Vladimir shook his head, waived his hand in disgust and quickly proceeded to secure the shutters with Misha's help. They noticed most of the stucco was stripped from the bricks on the south side of the building. The brick was pockmarked from the shrapnel. Approximately one hundred meters away was a large crater in the field. Vladimir realized that the bomb was meant for them.

With everyone's help, including patients able to work, the field hospital came to order. Glass, metal and plaster were swept and washed away. No sooner had they finished than the first truck filled with battlefield wounded arrived. More trucks and even horse and wagon teams followed. This constant stream continued for five straight days. The field hospital overflowed with needy injured. All beds and cots had been occupied following the first few hours of battle. Patients were placed on floors in the break room, in Dodik's office and in the hallway. Later, when there was simply no room left, the wounded were placed outside. The two doctors worked around the clock performing surgeries. Galina assisted Dodik and Ludmilla assisted Vladimir. Even Irina worked tirelessly taking care of patients. Misha and Evgeniy worked alongside her assisting the wounded. Nine orderlies, who had been sent by Markov, assisted the staff. When he found that he was simply too tired to function, Vladimir took little catnaps for twenty minutes to an hour. They needed more help, but realized they had to make do with what they had. Dodik and Vladimir tried to send some of the wounded to the Vyazma hospital, but travel became impossible after the third day because Vyazma had undergone regular attacks by the Stukas that disrupted any semblance of order in that city.

Sounds of heavy fighting now surrounded the field hospital. Vladimir realized that the wolves were circling, ready to pounce. His grandfather's warning, "Beware of the wolves," revolved in his head. His grandfather had scared them off with a shot from his old rifle. But these wolves would not scare off as easily. There were too many of them and they brought their own rifles. They may be frightened, but kept coming back in larger packs. He felt it was a matter of time before the end for him would come.

Beware the Wolves

Five days after the attack on Vyazma, the weather turned cool and rain drizzled intermittently. A month earlier, the army had issued heavier woolen underwear and winter tunics with long sleeves and caps with earflaps. Vladimir received his when the supply truck from the Vyazma garrison came.

Since early morning on October 7th, Vladimir felt uneasy. Wounded soldiers had told him for days that the army was collapsing and that the entire area will be overrun with German troops. He had a strange feeling in his gut that today was the day. He needed to prepare for something—either capture by the enemy or evacuation.

He left his summer uniform in a pile in the corner of the office where he had been sleeping. He took inventory of the contents of his duffel bag. He kept the civilian woolen coat Slava had insisted that he take with him. He had two packs of cigarettes, gifts from appreciative soldiers. He thought of giving them away, but decided that he might need them later. He had dried salami wrapped in waxed paper that was also a gift from a patient. He placed the salami in the sleeve of his civilian coat. In addition, his bag was stuffed with a change of underwear, his razor, the mess bowl he had kept since the trenches in Smolensk, a spoon, extra woolen socks, the greatcoat, field cap, winter cap and his revolver. He touched his breast pocket to make sure his most precious possession was with him, Slava's photograph. He pulled it out and sadly studied it for a few minutes. He touched his lips to the picture and pressed it against his right cheek. He briefly daydreamed of holding her once again.

At that moment, Dodik stepped into the office. Vladimir told Dodik that he feared the Germans would be on their doorstep shortly.

"I feel the same way about it, but what should we do?" Dodik asked. "I have tried to reach Markov, but the damn phone lines must be severed."

"I think everyone should get their gear together and be prepared for evacuation now. I really believe that we should get out of here. But there are two difficult problems. One is, what to do about the two hundred or more bedridden patients that can't be easily moved? There are no vehicles around. I've talked to the supply officer in the village about trucks or carts. He only laughed. He, himself, is concerned about his men, lamenting that they are supply soldiers and not warriors. He said they are sitting ducks, but his orders are to hold the village. There were but a few rifles among them and they could not be seriously expected to hold off an army."

"And what's the second problem?" Dodik asked.

"We are surrounded. So where would we go? At any event, I think you should tell everyone to prepare for something and have their knapsacks close by."

"You're right. It won't hurt to be ready."

Dodik left to issue the order and Vladimir took his duffel bag and his great coat and placed it near the entrance behind the open second set of doors.

He learned to live and work under the constant artillery and tank barrages in the distance. He performed surgeries under the often-quaking ground of explosions and occasional air raids. So, when in a few hours after his conversation with Dodik, it became suddenly quiet and the ground stopped shaking, he noticed immediately. The silence seemed eerie. His chest began to thump. Irina ran up to him smiling and happy.

"Do you hear how quiet it is?" Irina said. "The battle must be over."

"Our battle is just beginning," Vladimir said.

"What do you mean by that?"

"I do not think that we are the victors. We will be overrun soon."

"What do you mean?"

"Irina, the Germans won. And we, most likely, will be captured. Do you understand now?"

Irina's eyes widened and her mouth fell open. She looked astonished. Vladimir could not believe that she never considered being captured. *Where has she been? Surely she was not so absorbed with herself that she did not consider that possibility?*

"How do you know the Germans won? We had all these men and equipment. We must have won."

"Irina, don't you ever talk to your patients?"

"No way! I do my job and I prefer that they keep their mouths shut. Besides, all they do is complain about their troubles. Who needs that?"

"Well, if you had listened, you would have heard how combat was going. We have been overrun. Haven't you heard of Dodik's order to prepare your gear in the event of capture?"

"No. I was at my quarters. But I'm not worried. Even if those Fritzes come here, they wouldn't dare harm me. They better not touch me. I'll show them. Besides, it might be better to be under German rule anyway."

Shaking his head in disbelief, Vladimir absorbed Irina's treasonous words. *How can anyone be so stupid,* he thought. Under normal conditions, Irina would have been locked up long ago. He walked away from her and into the surgical room where Ludmilla waited for him. A patient had shrapnel in the corner of his eye and needed to have it removed. As he picked up his instruments, he heard rifle fire nearby. He realized that combat had moved closer or possibly within the collective farm itself. The rifle fire was returned by heavy machine gun fire. He finished the surgery, Ludmilla bandaged both eyes and Misha, whose face looked white as a sheet, came in to wheel the patient back to the ward. The gunfire seemed closer. Then the booms from exploding tank shells shattered the air. Total silence followed the shelling.

Vladimir and Ludmilla followed Misha into the hall. There was barely enough room for Misha to navigate the gurney through the wounded lying in the hallway. At the entrance to the corridor, Vladimir saw Evgeniy dash inside the hospital. He was frantically waving his arms and screaming at the top of his lungs that German armored vehicles had surrounded the village and had exchanged fire with the Soviet supply troops. He barely got away, but the Soviet soldiers surrendered. Vladimir knew, as well as most of the patients and staff that the day they most dreaded had, indeed, come. Vladimir felt weak in his

Beware the Wolves

legs. He was frozen to the floor. At first there was silence in the hospital from a collective gasp. Later, panic and fear set in. He saw some cross themselves and a few prayed out loud. Most cursed the enemy. Those who could walk scurried about with no particular plan. Vladimir thought of grabbing his handgun and fighting to the end. He realized that it would do no good. Not only would he be killed, but so would everyone in the hospital. *The gun, the gun,* he thought. *I need to get rid of it.*

Dodik grabbed Vladimir's arm and pulled him off to the side.

"Remember Markov told us to remove all evidence that we are officers. Do as I did, rip off the officer and medical insignias from your collar. Where's your cap?"

"Its in my bag. What did you do with your sidearm?"

"Go get it and take off the officer insignia. I already took mine off. I threw my weapon out the window."

Vladimir did as Dodik suggested. As he opened his bag to get his cap, he heard the rumbling approach of heavy vehicles. He looked out the blown out windows of the door and saw halftrack trucks approaching the hospital. A crowd bunched up behind him. He took his bag and made his way through the crowd toward the back of the building. There he removed his captain's insignia from both caps and grabbed his holstered revolver. He did not think he had enough time to go to a window and throw it out. *Besides the enemy may see him.* He had no idea what to do with it. He could not be found with it or close to it, as that would give away his rank. His body was shaking and he could not think straight. Everyone in the building was agitated and the mood added to his panic. Suddenly he had an idea. He saw a large bucket used to dump bedpan waste into on the way to the latrine. He threw his revolver, officer belts and insignias into the bucket. The contents splattered onto the floor. He did not care. The noise from the crowd by the door and from the wards warned Vladimir that the enemy vehicles had approached the hospital.

"They are jumping off the trucks!" He heard Galina scream. "They have surrounded the hospital!"

"They have dropped to the ground!" A patient yelled out. "They're going to open fire at us! Don't they see the big red cross on top of the roof?"

Without warning there was a crash of machine gun and sub-machine gunfire. Bullets flew into the windows and doors. Blood oozed out of fallen victims. Vladimir, like everyone else, dove to the floor. Bullets from the doorway whizzed over his head. Choking plaster dust filled his lungs. The shooting stopped followed by the grinding sound of tanks growling toward the hospital.

"Why were they shooting at us?" Asked a young patient, no older than eighteen, lying next to Vladimir.

"Probably to see if we will return fire at them," Vladimir said. "They fear that we have snipers waiting for them in the building. Stay down, we'll be all right."

A moment later some German soldier, in a broken Russian language, yelled out, "Everyone out with your hands on your head! You have three minutes. If you are not out in three minutes, the building will be leveled. You now have two minutes."

Vladimir realized that there was nothing he or anyone could do to stop them. Yet no one complied with the order.

"You now have one minute!"

"I'm coming out; I'm your friend!" Irina yelled, as she walked out of the front door.

At that instant, Dodik gave the order for everyone to comply. Vladimir's heart pounded so hard that he thought it would break through his chest. He put on his great coat, grabbed his duffel bag and hung it on his right shoulder and waited in line to exit. A patient ahead of him was too weak and had difficulty walking. Vladimir grabbed him and held him up as the line slowly proceeded out the door. As they passed by wards, bedridden patients pleaded for someone to help them.

"Don't leave us behind. Help us. God save us."

Vladimir had to put it out of his mind. There was nothing he could do. The medics, orderlies and several stronger patients helped those that could walk out of the hospital.

Fierce looking soldiers, each helmeted and holding rifles or sub-machine guns pointing at the captives, stood several meters outside the door. The captives were herded into a group about fifty meters from the hospital and told to stand silently.

Irina broke loose from the captives and approached a German soldier.

"I want to talk to whoever is in charge here," Irina demanded.

The soldier pointed for her to get back with the others. She continued toward the soldier yelling to see his superior. Another soldier grabbed her by the arm and started to pull her back to the group of captives.

"Let go of me, you bastard!" Irina screamed, swinging her other arm at him. She struck him on his chest as she tried to pull away. The soldier let go of her arm, yelled at her and struck her with the butt of his rifle knocking her to the ground. As she laid on the ground, he pointed his rifle and shot her in the head.

"No, God, no!" Misha cried out. He lunged forward to run to her. "I'm going to kill the scum."

Vladimir grabbed him and held him back. The shooter heard the yelling, turned toward the captives and saw Misha and Vladimir wrestling. Vladimir could feel the evil emanating from the shooter directed at him. The German soldier began walking toward him. Cold sweat covered Vladimir's brow as the shooter approached. They were told to be still and silent. He already saw Irina's fate. It was of no consequence for the soldier to shoot Misha and him. Above all, he did not want to bring attention to himself.

An approaching vehicle distracted the shooter. It was a gray open car splattered with mud. It stopped a few meters from the group of captives. In the

Beware the Wolves

back sat two officers. The older officer was in a black uniform while the younger one wore gray. The younger officer exited the vehicle and the shooter stood at attention. The older officer remained in the car and carefully scrutinized each of the captives. The shooter saluted the younger officer. The officer barked some order to him and the shooter scurried off to join a sergeant standing next to a half-track. The sergeant slowly walked up to the officer. Vladimir exhaled deeply. He felt relieved that his life was spared, at least for now. But Irina's body still lay on the ground. The Nazis did not seem to be concerned about it. Misha stood sobbing, continuously hitting his head with his hands.

"Simmer down, Misha," Vladimir whispered. "Get a grip on yourself."

"I've lost two women I loved to those sons of bitches," Misha answered softly. "But now I can't take it any more," Misha raised his voice. "I'm going to kill those demons."

Vladimir quickly placed his hand over Misha's mouth.

"Misha, you're going to end up like Irina, if you don't shut up. Now keep your mouth shut. You're a soldier. Act as a soldier, damn you."

Misha squirmed for several seconds, but Vladimir continued his grip over his mouth. He finally settled down and Vladimir let go.

The sergeant left the officer and yelled something to the soldiers. A moment later the Germans rushed into the field hospital. Vladimir knew that the fate of the bedridden wounded would soon be sealed. A moment later, his body quivered when an outburst of rifle and submachine gun fire came from within the building. Screams from the hospital were heard as the shooting continued for what seemed an eternity. Vladimr knew that that was the end for those poor individuals.

The wind came up, followed by a cold driving rain, as though God was angry. Vladimir reached into his bag and put his winter cap over his field cap. The German officer dressed in gray joined the officer that remained in the vehicle. He barked an order to the driver and the vehicle drove back to where a row of huts once stood. Vladimir watched as the officers entered one of the huts. It was one of the three that survived the Stuka bombings. On the other side of the village, Vladimir could see another, much larger, group of captives herded together.

"Move out!" A German sergeant gave the order to Vladimir's group of sixty or so captives rounded up at the hospital. The group followed the soldiers past the village to a compound, already filled with other prisoners. The Germans had the compound surrounded with barbed wire held up by posts made of small tree logs. Armed German soldiers, stationed every few meters apart, totally encircled the captives. *Fast work,* was a fleeting thought in Vladimir's mind. The captives were allowed to sit on the wet ground, but talking was not permitted.

Vladimir sat down on some wet grass and placed his duffel bag on his lap. He noticed that the guards ordered a group of four captives to follow them into the same hut that he saw the officers enter. Another group of four captives was taken and ordered to wait by the door. After five to fifteen minutes, the first group exited the hut and marched off to another compound on the other side of the village while the second group entered. And so this process continued, one group after another

"What do you think they're doing in that hut?" a fellow prisoner, sitting next to Vladimir asked.

"Silence, we told you!" A guard barked at Vladimir's neighbor in German.

Vladimir knew that they were interrogating the captives inside the house. The process was slow. Suddenly, the guards hauled a lone captive out of the hut. He was forced to kneel on the ground and quickly shot in the head in full sight of the other detainees. Vladimir's insides trembled. One of the nurses screamed. A few minutes later, another captive was shot in the same manner, followed periodically by others.

"Do you think they are shooting officers?" Dodik whispered softly under his breath.

Vladimir shrugged his shoulders, indicating he had no idea. He sat in the rain, cold and thirsty, next to Dodik. *What fate awaits me?* he thought, as his head and heart pounded. A bitter taste of fear filled his mouth. *God, please help us.*

CHAPTER 19

The day of death and desperation finally turned into night. Vladimir had no idea what transpired in the hut, but at the rate the process was going, he knew it would take days before all the captives were processed. He looked around at the mass of captured humanity, that bleak brown blob penned in by barbed wire. There were thousands of soldiers. The number seemed so large that he could not even estimate. And all the while, new groups were brought in.

Vladimir stretched out on the wet ground as he waited his turn and tried to sleep. The great coat kept him dry and fairly warm. He had not had anything to drink since mid morning. He was hungry, but focused on his thirst. He remembered he still had that stick of salami in his bag. But he decided that eating the salty sausage would aggravate his thirst. Besides, he thought, *I'll save it for later, when I really need it.*

Falling asleep was difficult. Intermittent shouts and screams followed by gunshots and worries about what to expect once in that house with the Germans twisted his insides. His head continued to pound. He could feel his temple veins protrude. He remembered Markov's words that the Nazis shot Soviet officers. *What are they going to do to me? Are they going to shoot me if they find out I'm an officer? What are those gun shots all about? Who are they shooting?* After a few hours, the lack of sleep and the mental stress of his predicament had weakened him to the point that he finally dozed off.

He awoke to feel a pain in his side. Then another.

"Get up you pig!"

He rolled over onto his back and saw a German soldier about ready to kick him again. Quickly, he jumped to his feet. Dodik was already standing up, wincing in pain and holding his side. Vladimir, Dodik and two other captives waited outside the hut for the group inside to exit. It was early in the morning and Vladimir glanced at his watch. It was 5:43 a.m.

"Give me that watch," the guard said as he grabbed Vladimir's left arm and forcibly removed the watch from the wrist, placing it quickly in his pocket. Vladimir was sorry to see it go. It was an attractive stainless steel watch, *Zenit*, with a black leather band. Slava had given it to him as a graduation present. *Oh, well,* he thought. *I should have gotten rid of it. It could easily reveal my status as an officer.*

Inside the house, the air was permeated with sweat. Brown blankets served as shades over the small windows. Five kerosene lanterns illuminated the room. Behind a table sat two officers in black uniforms, and another officer in a gray uniform. Also seated at the table was a soldier with a pen and a tablet of paper. Vladimir recognized two of the officers from the previous day. On each side of the table stood three German soldiers. Of the three on each side, one had a submachine gun aimed loosely at the prisoners.

"Take off your coats and hats and lay them on the table. Empty your pockets and lay your bags on the table," the officer in gray barked out in broken Russian.

Vladimir and the others did as instructed, except that he did not remove Slava's picture from his breast pocket. Meanwhile, the three officers and the soldier at the table gazed, almost with disinterest, at all four men. They picked up and examined any papers that were laid out by the soldiers. Vladimir could see that they had been through this procedure before numerous times and would rather not be there.

"Name and town you are from."

Each gave his name and town while one of the soldiers wrote down the information.

"Any of you political commissars?"

All shook their heads in the negative.

"Any of you officers?"

Again all shook their heads.

"Any of you Jews?" The older officer dressed in black asked through a translation from the gray-uniformed officer. He looked directly at Dodik.

Again, all shook their heads in the negative. One of the guards began looking through the coats and caps. Then he opened each duffel bag and emptied the contents. Vladimir's civilian coat fell out. Immediately, the coat generated great interest. They discovered the stick of salami tucked in the sleeve and two packs of cigarettes fell out of the duffel bag. The officers conversed in German, but Vladimir understood much of the conversation. They each wanted the coat. While the other officers argued over who got the coat, the officer in gray grabbed the salami and placed it in a bag next to his chair. One of the guards picked up a pack of cigarettes and sniffed it.

"This is shit," he grumbled, throwing the cigarettes back on the table.

"Why do you have a civilian coat with you?" The older officer asked with suspicion.

Vladimir pretended not to understand the question.

"Translate my question," the officer directed the younger officer.

"My wife gave it to me in case I needed it."

"It's a fine coat. It's too good for just a plain soldier. You are an officer, aren't you?"

Vladimir's insides knotted up even more. Blood palpitated in his veins. His knees shook and his hands trembled.

"No, no. I promised my wife that I would keep it with me. It was a cheap coat that a neighbor sold her. My wife always worries. She wanted to make sure I was warm. Now I have to lug it around. You know women, they make you do crazy things."

Beware the Wolves

Vladimir did not know whether he said too much. He realized that his voice shook with fear and he must have appeared stupid. But after his statement and its translation, he noticed a slight crack of a smile from the older officer.

"The coat is probably full of lice. Let him have it"

"No, I'll take it," the officer in gray said.

"Let him have it, I said. Give him all of his stuff back."

A soldier threw everything back into the bag, except for the salami.

"Each of you lower your pants," the officer ordered.

Vladimir could not understand what that was about. However, he heard Dodik gasp. He glanced at Dodik whose face became white as a sheet. All four men did as they were told and stood there naked from the waist down. One of the soldiers picked up a kerosene lamp. He approached each of the men and directed the light at each man's crotch. Vladimir was second from the right. Dodik was third from the right.

"Well, what do we have here? A circumcised Jew," said the second black-uniformed officer who so far had been silent. "Take him out!"

"No! No! I'm only half Jewish," Dodik pleaded. "My father is a Christian. No, please, please. Don't do this!"

Vladimir was stunned. He knew that Jews circumcised their sons because he had some as his patients. But he never had given it much thought. His eyes filled with tears and he gasped. He watched as two soldiers dragged out his best friend. There was nothing he could do to stop them. Dodik yelled and pleaded for his life. The Nazis continued to examine the captive's papers. Vladimir pulled up his pants and stood frozen, fearing his body would explode. He heard Dodik's screams and felt each as a stab of a dagger in his heart. Then, he heard a gunshot and Dodik's shrieks ceased. He knew that bullet was for Dodik.

"Get the scum out of here," the older officer in black ordered.

Vladimir and two other men were led to another compound, also surrounded by barbed wire. Armed German soldiers guarded the captives inside the enclosure. Vladimir walked in a daze, feeling numb. He did not recognize any faces. He just wanted to find a spot to wallow in grief for his friend. At that moment, he did not care if he lived or died. He felt hopeless as he sat on the ground for hours in despair, surrounded by the sheer melancholy all around him.

After many hours feeling sorry for himself, his thoughts turned to Slava. He pulled out her picture and gazed at it for twenty minutes. His depression began to subside. *What am I doing, giving up like this? I need to gain control of myself. I have to see Slavochka again. By God, I'm going to do it! Besides, grandfather always told me to be tough, to be strong, and to never be afraid.* His pep talk to himself helped. He held up his head, took a deep breath and convinced himself that he would endure. *No matter how thirsty, hungry, cold, tired or miserable I'll be, I'm going to survive!*

Rain began to fall. Vladimir took out his mess pot and held it up in the air to catch rainwater. The soldiers sitting around him did the same. It

Victor Moss

was difficult to drink without choking because of his parched throat. He took small sips at first and let the swelling in his throat diminish before he took larger swallows.

He felt hunger. No matter how hard he tried to avoid thinking about that stick of salami, he could not. His thoughts were on that sausage. Even reminiscing about Slava or his family could not erase his fixation on his hunger. He continued sipping the water as the rain turned into a downpour. He covered his head with the greatcoat. After one half hour the rain let up and Vladimir removed his coat. As he did so, he saw red cross badges on two approaching soldiers' sleeves. He looked closer and recognized Misha and Evgeniy dragging their feet, searching for a spot to sit down. Vladimir waived to them. Evgeniy saw him and they made their way towards him. He motioned for them to sit down next to him.

They sat about ten meters away from the barbed wire as German guards patrolled the perimeter. There was a guard that passed by every fifteen seconds. As soon as a guard walked past them, Misha whispered to Vladimir,"Captain, we're so glad to see you; let's see if we can stay together."

"I'm happy to see you both as well. But, Misha and Evgeniy, don't call me Captain or doctor and use the familiar 'you' rather than the formal 'you.' Here, I am just one of the soldiers. Call me Vladimir or Volodya."

"Oh, I'm sorry," Misha said. "I heard rumors that they shot officers. Volodya, so where is Captain Kirkovsky? I mean, Dodik. Wasn't he with you?"

"Yes, Volodya," Evgeniy asked showing obvious pleasure in calling his captain by his diminutive name. "What do you know of Dodik?"

"I believe they shot him."

"For being an officer?" Misha asked.

Vladimir saw the guard approach and kept his mouth shut. As soon as the guard passed, he told them that Dodik had been shot because he was a Jew. Misha and Evgeniy looked at each other with astonishment.

"He was Jewish?" Misha asked. "I had never suspected. You mean that the only reason they shot him was that he was a Jew? God forbid! Just like that? Who would have thought? What has civilization come to? I just don't understand mankind anymore."

"Well, as far as I am concerned that's just one less Jew to deal with," Evgeniy said. "You know, they ruined our homeland."

"You son of a bitch," Vladimir raised his voice. "Dodik was my friend. He, like us, was a hardworking individual who was just trying to get by. He was one of the nicest and kindest persons I had met. He would give the shirt off his back if you needed it. Get out of my sight, you bigoted fool! You fool. I don't want to hear or see you!"

The German guard stopped and looked their way.

"Shut up you pigs!" The guard yelled at Vladimir and the medics. "Any more noise from you and you'll be shot."

Beware the Wolves

Evgeniy turned red in the face and heaved his chest. His nose flared. He stared briefly at Vladimir, then picked up his coat and duffel bag and walked away yelling, "Jew lover!"

Vladimir looked to see if a guard had heard Evgeniy. Fortunately, the guard kept walking without turning his head.

"Don't mind Evgeniy," Misha said to Vladimir, consoling him. "He doesn't mean half of what he says. He is just an uneducated idiot. I know that Captain Kirkovsky was a good man and a good friend to you."

Many more hours had passed. Night fell again. Rain, driven by strong gusts of wind, battered the captives. Vladimir, bundled in his greatcoat, laid on the soaked, muddy ground. He felt weak and miserable. Misha slept most of the time and remained by his side. He looked at Misha's sleeping body and thought how ironic it was that he had consoled him twice over the loss of Tanya and later Irina. Now, Misha tried to comfort him in his grief over Dodik. *Life has so many twists and turns,* he mumbled to himself.

As the hours passed and more prisoners were forced into the compound, there was little room for anyone to lie down. Vladimir had no choice, but to sit in the mud. If he stood up, another prisoner would take the space. His legs were cramping, his bottom was numb and his lower back and shoulders felt as though they were on fire. He tried to move around, but there was no room as the bodies squeezed together. After several more hours the captives agreed to stand in unison and stretch.

The days dragged on. No food was provided the captives. Vladimir lost count of the exact number of days that he had been confined in the open in the cold with wind, rain, slush and snow. One of the fellow prisoners had been keeping track of the days by marking the daylight with a line in the mud on his boot. Nine days had passed. Vladimir knew that a healthy human being could last nearly two months without food. He was grateful that he had rainwater to drink. Without water, he would die in a matter of days. He barely moved, knowing it was crucial to conserve energy. But if he did not have nourishment soon, this incredible abuse to his body would leave him permanently damaged. He tried to remember his medical school lectures concerning the effects of hunger. There would be permanent damage to the bones and muscle tissues in two weeks. Hallucinations would set in after three weeks. He seemed to recall that after four-five weeks, brain and internal organs would be injured. His immune system would be destroyed and cold weather could lead to hypothermia.

He tried not to dwell on his hunger and its effects, but with each passing day he felt uncomfortable dull pain in his stomach, followed by severe sharp pains. He recalled that it was about the fifth day of his captivity, that he no longer felt any pain. He was no longer hungry. As the days went by, he became dismayed at the hundreds of dead bodies that were carried out because they starved to death. *Surely, someday, they'll have to feed us or we will all die. But that's probably what they want,* he thought.

Victor Moss

Misha had been by his side throughout. Evgeniy found a spot to sit on the other side of the compound and avoided Vladimir. There were women in the compound, mostly medics from the front lines. He thought he saw Ludmilla and Galina led in by the Germans. The only time he was allowed to walk about was to the latrine, a ditch dug out in the open field. While he walked to it, he looked around hoping to see Ludmilla and Galina, but he was not able to find them in the mass of humanity. Vladimir was concerned for them, hoping that they were not in the groups of corpses carried out hourly. Suddenly, he felt chilled either from the stress of his environment or from the penetrating wind. Quietly, hoping that no one would see him, he took out the coat Slava had insisted he take and put it on underneath the great coat.

Early on the morning of the tenth day, Vladimir heard the rumble of trucks and halftracks. He looked up from underneath the greatcoat and snow hit his face. It was again a dank, dreary day with low visibility. He saw a closed car followed by a convoy of trucks filled with German soldiers. The trucks surrounded the compound. Soldiers, armed with submachine guns and sticks, jumped off the trucks. A few began to dismantle the barbed wire while the rest aimed their weapons at the captives.

"Everybody up!" yelled the Nazis as they gestured for the prisoners to rise.

"Move out! Move your asses, you pigs!"

Vladimir grabbed his duffel bag and fell into line as the prisoners were funneled into a long column. Vladimir was in the middle of the line. The captives were forced to walk in a northwesterly direction through muddy fields. The muck was so thick that each step was weighted down by accumulated mud that grew heavier with each stride. After a few meters, some of the prisoners fell, either from the slippery sludge or from extreme weakness caused by starvation and the cold weather. Vladimir quickly discovered that he had better stay on his feet because the German guards kicked those that were down. If they did not rise up immediately, a rat-tat-tat from the submachine gun was their fate. He saw that some of the guards took boots off of the dead. It was slow going.

The Nazis tried to hurry the column along, but they too had trouble walking in the mud. Sporadically, Vladimir would see a German fall. He would have laughed, but knew that would be instant death for him. In the fields, he saw destroyed artillery canon, trucks and tanks, belonging to both the Germans and the Soviets. Here and there as he trudged along, he saw pieces of bone scattered about and decomposing bodies of dead warriors. It did not faze him any longer. He had seen so much death and destruction that he became immune to it all. His only goal was to concentrate on his walking and surviving.

After an hour in the field, the miserable column of prisoners turned onto an unpaved road. Most of the roads in Russia were not paved. Vehicles and tanks left deep gouges in the mud. Vladimir tried to avoid the ruts, as the footing was extremely slippery. On several occasions, he almost slipped, but managed to catch himself. Misha also began to slide, but Vladimir caught him

Beware the Wolves

and held him up as they moved along. Only a few moments later, Vladimir could not avoid a side of the rut. His foot slid out on the slick mud and he fell squarely on his back.

He saw the German approaching. He tried to get up as fast as he could, but was unable to get a footing. The column did not stop, but went around him. Misha remained by Vladimir's side, grabbed his hand, as did another Soviet soldier passing by, and lifted him up. The German guard approaching Vladimir also slipped and fell as he raised his dark brown oak stick to strike him. Vladimir kept walking, knowing that once he went on, that guard would never be able to recognize him in the drab, mud covered blob of humans. He was not alone. Many fell that day. And many of the fallen were never able to get up and were shot down like mad dogs. He and Misha walked holding each other up when necessary.

Vladimir's ankles hurt and his right big toe developed a blister. *When are we going to stop? Keep your strength; keep your strength,* he repeated in his mind over and over. He saw vehicles stranded in the mud that were pushed and pulled by captives taken out of the line. The convoy of trucks kept bogging down in the mud. The Germans used the prisoners to pull them out. He was so grateful to have escaped that grueling task. He saw several motorcyclists stuck in the mud. The motorcycles and their drivers were caked with the muck. They looked like bizarre statues displayed in the field. Captives were ordered to lift the motorcycles out of the mud and place them in trucks.

Then Vladimir and the group around him were ordered to pull a Mercedes vehicle, with officers inside, out of the mud. As Vladimir approached the vehicle, the mud was so deep that it came up to his knees. They were directed to pull the vehicle onto higher ground on the edge of the road. He, Misha and five others pushed from the back, while ten prisoners pulled the ropes that were attached to the frame. The guards yelled and screamed at them to work harder. Vladimir felt a blow from a guard's baton across his left shoulder. It stung for a minute, but the pain could have been worse. Either he was numb or the civilian coat underneath the greatcoat shielded him.

After the vehicle was pulled from the mud, Vladimir glanced toward the front of the column. He could not see the beginning. It stretched for kilometers. He looked back and could not see the end. *There're thousands here,* he thought. He was ordered back into the column with Misha sticking by his side.

As darkness covered the ground, the captives were herded into a specially prepared pen surrounded by barbed wire. On each corner was a crude guard tower made of tree trunks. A machine gun, mounted on a platform, stood approximately three meters off the ground. The guards used a ladder made of tree branches to climb the tower. Flares illuminated the compound throughout the night. Vladimir prayed for water and food. But as the hours passed by, nothing was given. He looked at his duffel bag, all caked in mud. *Why am I dragging this around with me.* He took out his mess kit, razor, extra socks, spoon and cigarettes. His boots were so caked with mud that he did not dare to leave the spoon in the side of the boot as was the custom. He placed it with the other items in his coat pockets. He left the mess kit next to him on the ground, hoping to catch some rain. He knew he would miss the duffel bag as a pillow, but carrying it in his weakened state would be impossible.

"They call this *rasputitsa*," Misha whispered to Vladimir.

"What's that?" Vladimir asked, surprised by Misha's comment. Vladimir was dozing off and really was too weak to carry on a conversation.

"It's that time of the year, in the autumn when rains come and dissolve the roads into mud and they become impassable."

"Well, right now, I pray that we get some rain. We're thirsty and need to fill our mess kits with water."

Misha did not answer. Vladimir looked at him and saw that he was sound asleep. In the next minute, Vladimir was snoring.

Vladimir was awakened by submachine gun fire. It was the enemy's alarm clock. He quickly glanced at the mess kit to see if it had rained. The pot was empty. Vladimir's lips were parched. He craved water. His tongue was thick from its lack. He grabbed the mess kit, unbuckled his belt and hung the container on his belt. After a latrine stop, the captives were ordered to move out. Vladimir barely stood up. He was sore, his back hurt as well as his knees and feet. But he proceeded. He looked back and saw what appeared to be hundreds of bodies that did not rise. They did not survive the night. He tensed up when he heard the shots. The Nazis made sure the bodies left on the ground were indeed dead.

Since it had not rained the night before, the road was not as slick, but was stickier. Walking was still difficult because the boots stuck to the mud. Vehicles still had to be pulled out of the mud, but not as many as the day before. More and more prisoners fell from hunger, cold and exhaustion.

At mid morning, the column reached a section of road that was paved with tree trunks and branches laid out by the Germans for motorized travel on the muddy road. Walking became even more treacherous and many tripped on the uneven surface. Again, those that could not rise or continue after other prisoners helped them up were summarily shot.

The Germans found a new use for their prisoners as mine detectors. They forced a group off to the side of the road and ordered them to walk on both sides of the column. When a mine exploded, the prisoners were either killed or maimed. Those that survived an explosion were shot. Some mines, laid out by the Soviets, were designed for the weight of a heavy truck or tank. A tank that accompanied the column blew up on one of those mines. As retaliation, the Nazis opened fire on the column. Vladimir was further back in line and avoided the random shooting. He stepped over at least a hundred bodies as the column moved forward.

At the end of the day, the column reached the main highway M1 and they proceeded in a westerly direction toward Germany. The highway was paved with stone. The walk should have become easier, except that Vladimir's feet

Beware the Wolves

bled from raw blisters. Every step was painful. His whole body was stiff and sore. He hurt all over, particularly in his knees, the backs of his calves and his lower back. His shoulders burned with pain.

Finally, an hour after dusk, the prisoners were once again herded into another compound similar to the one in which they spent the night before. Again no food or water was given. Vladimir sat quietly in the cold air. He covered himself with his greatcoat and removed his boots. His socks were drenched in blood. His feet were raw. He pulled the extra pair of socks out of his pocket. His feet were on fire, yet his toes felt frozen from the cold. He put the clean socks on and slipped the old socks over those for added warmth. He then reached into his pocket and pulled out a raw potato. He and Misha each caught a potato thrown to them by some boys as they passed through a village. He had never eaten a raw potato before. But at that moment, it was the best food he had ever eaten.

Once again, submachine gun shots awakened the prisoners. Vladimir was surprised to find six inches of snow covering him. His mess kit was full of snow. He grabbed the snow around him and started to eat it. *Oh, the pleasure of the cool, wet slush on my lips and throat.* He scratched his head as it had been itching for a second day, put on the cap and headed out with the column. Again, he saw the same scene of bodies unable to rise. Only this time, there were many more. Again he heard the shots of the captors as they finished them off.

On the third day, after an hour of walking, the guards yelled out, "Run, run, everyone, run!"

As the prisoners ran past the guards, they beat on the prisoners with their sticks. After ten minutes of the forced run, Vladimir was breathless. He had severe pain in his sides, his chest hurt and he felt as though he could no longer go on. Around him, men fell like flies. Constant shots were heard. As he ran, he had to leap over fallen bodies. Finally, the Nazis stopped the prisoners. They were allowed to sit down on the cold stones of the road. Vladimir was hot, breathless and covered with sweat. He needed to take his coat off, but knew if he did, he would never see it again. Cold sleet struck his face as he sat there with the others for close to an hour in the cold, penetrating wind. Without warning, the same order was given again. He was forced to run for at least twenty minutes, and then told to sit on the ground. The captives sat for another hour. As before, the dead bodies of those who did not make it were left out in the open for all to see. Vladimir dwelled on the roar of laughter and delight the captors exhibited. *Was this a sport for them? Or was it a premeditated method of annihilating the prisoners?*

The captives trudged on for the rest of the day. Vladimir limped from the pain in his feet. Vladimir sensed that Misha was struggling more than ever. Misha had slowed down and was about to stop all together when a guard walking near him took his stick and beat him on the shoulder.

"Keep moving, you pig!"

Misha began to fall. Vladimir grabbed him, but was too weak to hold Misha up much longer.

"Help him," Vladimir yelled at the captives around Misha. "It's almost dark and we will be stopping soon. Help him!"

No one helped; there were too many that were falling for anyone to worry about. Everyone was barely able to stand on his own, let alone hold another one up.

"Leave me. I want to die," Misha whispered to Vladimir. "Save yourself. It's too late for me."

Vladimir and Misha fell behind, as the column moved around them. Guards yelled at them to keep moving. Vladimir did not know what to do. He could not let his faithful medic fall and be shot. But yet he thought of Slava. He yearned to see her again. He needed to survive. He knew that he scarcely had the strength to walk on his own. He could not hold Misha up by himself. *What should I do? I must survive,* he thought. He decided that he had to drop him. But before he did, he again begged those around him to help. Again no one even looked at him or Misha. Suddenly, a big soldier came to the rescue and grabbed Misha's other shoulder. Vladimir looked at him in bewilderment when he recognized Evgeniy. Vladimir felt so relieved that his eyes filled with tears. The three walked together holding each other up for the next twenty minutes until they were herded once again into another compound for the night.

Still no food or water was provided. But it had snowed and each filled his mess kit with snow and placed it under his coat so that the body heat could melt the snow into water. When Vladimir laid down, his fatigue was so severe and his body was in such pain that at that moment he did not care whether he lived or died. He thanked Evgeniy again for his lifesaving help. He felt so relieved that Evgeniy saved the moment and Misha was still with them. He closed his eyes and wondered if Misha would rise up in the morning and for that matter, if he, himself, would make it through the night.

Sleep helped. Vladimir, Misha and Evgeniy survived the night. All three were able to get up next morning and were determined to proceed. The fourth day of walking brought them to Yartsevo. Early in the day, as they passed by several villages, Russian peasants threw potatoes, pieces of bread and apples at the captives in the column as they straggled by. Vladimir was on the outside of the line and an elderly lady all wrapped up in a warm coat, felt boots and a scarf, slipped a cabbage head into his hand. It was somewhat stale, but Vladimir was overjoyed. He immediately broke off a chunk for himself and gave a piece to Misha and Evgeniy.

"It's amazing, Misha," Vladimir said. "How some rotten cabbage can be the most important thing in life isn't it?"

Vladimir knew Yartsevo was approximately 150 kilometers from Vyazma. He found it unbelievable that he had walked such a distance under such miserable conditions. In Yartsevo, Vladimir thought he heard a train. He hoped that wherever the Germans took him, if they took him anywhere else, that it would be by rail. Every muscle and bone in his body ached, especially his feet. Every step was torture. He felt that he could not last much longer if he had to walk another day. Above all, he prayed that he would get something to eat.

CHAPTER 20

The early morning of July 12, 1941 was hot and muggy. The black typewriter with its round silver keys stood undisturbed on the desk. Slava shuddered as she looked at the machine. It represented the enemy that invaded her homeland. Because of them, the Red Army had snatched Vladimir from her to defend the mother country. She deeply resented the Nazis and could not believe that she was forced to work on their behalf. She had no choice. The alternative was some labor camp for her and her parents, most likely in Germany. There they would be expected to work until they dropped dead. And considering her parents' age and state of health that would not have taken long.

Slava smelled the mildew in the large room in the old potato warehouse next to the railroad tracks. The Nazis used it as an office since the building was one of the few still standing. On the left were six wooden non-matching desks placed in a row, facing each other. A uniformed German sat behind each desk, either reading sheets of paper or busy writing. On the right hand side of the room, standing apart from the others, was the desk of Lieutenant Hoffman, the aid to Major Raake. She remembered how relieved she was when he saved her from the soldiers searching her house the day before. Next to Hoffman's desk was a much smaller desk where Heinrich, the baby-faced soldier, sat typing.

Everyone stopped whatever he was doing when Slava entered the room. Not a word was said, but she felt their eyes drilling her. She was self-conscious and uncomfortable. She walked up to her assigned desk, which stood alone in the right corner of the room, and sat down. The yellow-green walls next to the desk were badly cracked with peeling paint. Even though her back was to the Germans, she knew that they watched her every move. The thought of their eyes on her made her skin crawl.

Out of the corner of her eye, she saw Heinrich approach her.

"Good morning, Vladislava."

"Good morning," Slava said curtly, unable to hide her anger.

"Let's practice on the typewriter," Heinrich said with authority. "I'll show you where to place your fingers on the keys."

Heinrich patiently worked with Slava for over an hour. After Heinrich decided that she was familiar enough with the keyboard, he gave her a letter he had typed and told her to retype it. The letter was only three short paragraphs, but it took her almost an hour to type it with ten mistakes. Heinrich reviewed it and told her to try again. The second draft was done within twenty minutes and only contained three mistakes. The third draft was done in fifteen minutes and had no mistakes.

Beware the Wolves

"Good," Heinrich said. "You learn fast. Major Raake wants to see you in his office. I'll show you in."

Slava's breathing was short and choppy as she followed Heinrich into Raake's office. *What's this all about,* she thought. Major Raake immediately stood up, smiling pleasantly, and asked her to sit down.

"Heinrich told me that you have already mastered the typewriter."

"No, not really. I need much practice. I'm still too slow."

"With time, your speed will increase. I trust your parents were all right and didn't worry about you too much yesterday."

"Yes, thank you."

Slava was taken aback that Raake asked about her parents. *Surely his concern was not legitimate?* Just the mention of her parents made her cringe even more. She wished that he would forget about them altogether. He just might remember to send them away.

"I want you to begin with the vital statistic ledgers that are on your desk. Translate the most recent ledgers from Russian into German on the sheets of paper that Heinrich gives you. I want the information typed. That's all, you can now return to your desk."

Raake stood up as Slava left the room. She was amazed how courteous he was. It was obvious to her that he was a gentleman. However, Slava wondered why Raake called her into his office. He gave her the same instructions the day before and as far as she could see, there was no purpose for another meeting.

At her desk, she opened the book on marriage registrations in the Vitebsk area from 1938 to 1941 and began typing the names and addresses into German. After a slow start, her speed increased. She could not understand why the Germans needed this information. Most of the people had left Vitebsk. Her work seemed a useless waste of time. *Could it be that this translation has some military or administrative purpose and I'm helping them?* With that thought, Slava's head began to ache.

An armed soldier entered the room followed by four older men carrying an old oak desk. It was obviously a heavy desk as the men strained, dripping with sweat. Behind them was an older heavyset man, and like the others, he was dressed in a soiled, wrinkled gray suit, grubby white shirt and tie. He carried a wooden chair with a cracked brown leather seat. He was breathing heavily and appeared ready to collapse. Slava jumped up from her chair and attempted to help the man put the chair down. Another armed soldier, one that followed the men, yelled at Slava to sit down and mind her own business. The man with the chair gave Slava a nod with a strained smile and managed to put the chair down. Wrapped around the sleeve of each man was a black six-pointed star drawn on a piece of yellow fabric. The men were glum. Resignation showed in their almost lifeless eyes. Lieutenant Hoffman ordered that the desk be placed next to Slava's. As soon as the desk was placed, another five men, similar to the first group with armed guards brought another desk and chair and placed it behind Slava. Tears prickled Slava's eyes at the thought that these men were now forced by the fascists to do menial labor.

The room suddenly felt smaller with the addition of the two desks. Slava kept working until she realized that it was mid-afternoon. She was hungry. Food was not offered to her, as the day before. She walked to the tea table and poured herself a cup of tea. Unfortunately, there was no food in sight to satisfy her hunger. Nevertheless, the hot tea felt good, and temporarily filled her empty stomach. At six o'clock she was told by Hoffman to go home.

At home, she was surprised to see Vladimir's sister, Anna, and her two toddler daughters, Tamara and Galina.

"Anna, what are you still doing in Vitebsk?" Slava asked wearily. "I was sure you had gone with your mother and sisters to Jazwino. But you've heard my opinion before. I don't think that your escape to the village would be much safer than here. The Nazis are all over. Agafia should have taken you all east, beyond Moscow."

"My mother was stubborn. She wanted to go back to her home village, and now I have no choice but to follow her. I thought we would have more time to evacuate. Tamara was sick and I wanted to wait a few more days before leaving. The only way to get there was to walk and Tamara was just not strong enough. The Nazis came so quickly. Now our apartment building is burned to the ground and we have nowhere else to go. We still want to go to Jazwino. I think it will be safer there and with all those fields around the village, food may be easier to find. Your parents so generously allowed us to stay here until we can make it to Jazwino."

"Of course, you can stay," Slava sighed. "Stay as long as you want to. We have a fairly decent supply of food. We'll be all right."

"Oh, that's wonderful. But I want to rejoin my mother as soon as I can. Your parents said that you haven't heard anything of Volodya. No word, at all?"

"None whatsoever. I worry so much. I just pray he is alive."

"We all do," Anna said. "With God's grace, we will see him again."

◆ ◆ ◆ ◆

The next morning, as she arrived at work, Slava saw two other young women that sat at the desks next to hers. Each desk was also equipped with a typewriter. *I'm so relieved that I won't be the only female in the room. Now the Germans have someone else to stare at,* she thought. The new women, she soon found out, were in their twenties and were also Byelorussian. They had studied German in school or by private tutor, as had Slava, and were now forced to work for the invaders. The three began to chat quietly.

"Quiet!" Hoffman yelled out. "You are to remain silent unless an answer is expected of you. There will be no talking to each other."

Slava quickly turned toward her typewriter and began the tedious and boring translations while Heinrich taught the new women to type.

Beware the Wolves

Later in the afternoon, Hoffman came up to Slava and told her that Major Raake wanted to see her in his office again. Slava felt her heart rate accelerate as she entered his office. Raake stood up again as she entered the room. His smile was so infectious that Slava, for the moment, forgot that he was the enemy as she smiled back. It was her first smile in days. It was her nature to laugh and smile, but since the war began in June, her laughter and smiles became rare.

"Please sit down and rest for a few moments. Lieutenant Hoffman has complimented you. He said that you are a fast learner and have become very proficient with the typewriter."

Slava sat quietly wondering what his compliment would lead to. She wanted to thank him as a matter of courtesy, but decided it would be best to keep her mouth shut.

"He said that you type very quickly. Do you play the piano?"

"Yes, I have had lessons since I was six."

"I've heard that those that play the piano are also good on the typewriter. Your fingers are nimble. I would love to hear you play someday."

Slava did not know how to respond. *Does he want to come to our house and hear me play for him? That is absurd,* she thought.

"I am not very good," Slava answered timidly. She was an excellent pianist, but she would not want him inside her house. "You do not want to hear me play."

"Well, that's just a thought. I have prepared written orders for the community. They are in German. Please translate them into Russian."

Relief washed over Slava. The orders sounded simple enough. *But why did he have to call me into his office for that? Hoffman or Heinrich could have given them to me and told me to translate the papers.*

"Do you have the documents here?" Slava asked.

"No, Lieutenant Hoffman has those that have been typed by Heinrich. Ask him for them."

Slava started to get up. She was beginning to feel uncomfortable and wanted to leave. Raake gazed at her as if he was taking her measure.

"You don't have to go back yet," he murmured. "Sit and rest. It's always a pleasure to look at a pretty face in this war torn hellhole."

Slava's muscles tightened. That remark knocked the wind out of her lungs. *First of all, it was his kind that caused Vitebsk to be a hellhole. And secondly, what is he getting at? Is he just being complimentary or is there something more calculating in his words?* Whatever the meaning, she knew she had to get out of his office instantly.

"Major Raake, I'm not tired. I really need to get back to work, there's still much to be done."

"Very well." Raake answered, sounding surprised. "You are excused to return."

This time, he did not rise and open the door. As Slava walked out, she felt his intent stare on her back. Her unease continued throughout the afternoon.

169

She dreaded more than ever the thought of returning to work the next day. And it seemed as there were many more days to come.

◆ ◆ ◆ ◆

Three weeks passed and Slava had settled into a routine. The days were long. She sat at her desk, with barely a break, from eight in the morning to six in the evening translating endless documents. Slava had no contact with the outside world and had no idea what was occurring on the war front. Her impression, judging by the occupation of Vitebsk and the volume of equipment, supplies and troops moving in and out of the town, was that the war was proceeding vigorously. Vladimir was constantly in her thoughts. *Where is he? What is he doing? Dear Jesus, please protect him and bring him home to me.* But then she looked around and wondered, *what home? How could he possibly come home when the Germans had taken control of our lives?*

One morning Slava was combing her hair, preparing for work when the sound of engines interrupted her moment of tranquility. It was different from that of a car or a truck. The sound was a buzz, then a whine and then a roar. The windows rattled and the floor shook from a burst of explosions. Blood drained from her face. She could not move even if she wanted to. The panic that gripped her held her glued to the floor, a comb clenching in her hands. A second later, her mother's screams and cries from her tiny nieces forced her body into motion. She dashed into the dining room. Her mother, Anna and the girls stood huddled in a corner. Her mother was chanting prayers. Tamara and Galina were screaming at the top of their lungs. A few seconds later, Vladislav ran into the room from the outside. He yelled over the sound of the racket that Soviet planes were bombing the city.

"Shut up, all of you!" Vladislav yelled. "You are worse than the explosions. Control yourselves! Now hurry, get under this table."

"Are you crazy, you think this table will protect us from a bomb?" Suzanna whimpered.

"It will keep debris from hitting us directly. Get under the table now. We don't have time to climb down into the cellar. Besides, if the house falls on top of us, we would never get out of the cellar alive."

Suzanna saw Slava, Anna and the girls crawl under the table, so she got down on her knees and joined them, still praying to Saint Barbara for Divine protection. Another blast shook the house. *This was a close one,* Slava thought. The windows rattled against the sash as though they, too, were trying to escape. Plaster dust fell from the ceiling. Slava and the others held their hands over their ears from the intense turmoil. Whistles and screams of bombs amplified the mayhem as they showered the town. Gunfire and artillery fire added their ominous sounds to the explosions.

"We're going to be hit," Anna yelled. "We're just one of two houses still standing here and we're a target!"

Beware the Wolves

"You're right. The house could be a prime target. Quick," Vladislav yelled. "Grab some pillows and run outside. We'll hide in the ravine next to the orchard. Use the pillows to cover your heads."

Bending at the waist, the feather pillows over their heads, they ran out of the house and hid in the back waiting for the bombardment to cease.

"How awful, how awful," Suzanna lamented as all were lying on the ground. "God save us!"

Slava's heart raced. It was good, she thought, that the Soviets were attacking and attempting to retake Vitebsk. On the other hand where would they go if the house were destroyed? She was torn between patriotism and their personal safety.

The air raid ended. Slava could see that most of the bombing was in the center of the city where plumes of fire and smoke filled the air. Their house was spared. The worst damage was cracked windows and large fractures in the ceiling and walls.

She was late for work that day as were most of the people working in the office. There were no usual jokes and laughs from the Germans that day. Slava saw that the Soviet attack had shaken them.

From that day on, bombing raids continued sporadically. If Slava was home, the family dove under the dining room table. Or, if time permitted, they scurried out to a ditch in the orchard. At work, she would slide under her desk, knowing full well that if the building took a direct hit, the desk would not save her. Over time, the raids diminished. It was a bittersweet feeling for Slava. The air raids petrified her, but once the raids ceased, the realization struck her that the Soviets have been unable to recapture Vitebsk. They were stuck with the Germans. *It can't be forever,* she consoled herself.

◆ ◆ ◆ ◆

Raake left her alone. Her back was always to the door as she worked so she never saw him enter or leave his office. But on several occasions she sensed him stop and watch her work. The women around her made remarks that he liked her and asked on several occasions why he called her into his office that time. They looked at her with disbelief when she said it was for a new assignment. She hoped that she would not have to go through that again.

Weeks of drudgery dragged on. Every day was the same. Slava worked daily except for Sunday. She walked to work in the early morning and straight home in the evening. The walk was dismal. Where houses, apartments, stores and schools once stood, there were now charred remnants. Only two houses in the section of the city where she lived remained—theirs and their neighbor Isaac's. In the distance, she could see a third house, now occupied by German officers. The neighborhood was unrecognizable. When not at work or walking to and from work, Slava stayed at home. To occupy her time, she began rereading the many books in her father's collection.

Victor Moss

Summer was almost over and the first week of September 1941 was a day away. Six more Byelorussian women were brought in to work as clerks for the Germans. The old warehouse room was filled to capacity. It became a very noisy place with women chatting with each other. Hoffman threatened all of them with a hard labor camp if they did not keep quiet. But that threat only quieted them for a few hours before the gabbing began again.

On September 1st Hoffman approached Slava and told her that Raake would like to see her in his office. Slava, tensed up. *What does he want now? It can't be for any good.* As she walked toward the door of Raake's office, all the women stopped their work and watched. Hearing the whispers behind her back, she could only imagine what they were saying.

Raake again stood up as she entered the room.

"Please sit down, Vladislava. Here, let me pour you some tea."

Slava was stunned at the offer. It was so unusual. She did not want to fraternize with the enemy. Working for them was bad enough, but drinking tea with Raake was too much. Without waiting for her response he poured tea from a teapot with a rose dotting its white surface into a matching cup and saucer. She immediately recognized the set. It was a Dmitrevski Porcelain Factory set that she admired at a store shortly before the war began. *So he stole this set from the store,* she thought. *I could not afford the set, but he took it.*

He offered her the cup of tea and a piece of apple strudel.

"This strudel just arrived today from my wife in Dresden. She baked it and sent it to me through an engineer for the railroad. It is delicious. Please have a piece. I don't know how much longer I will be able to receive supplies from my wife. Your partisans are trying to disrupt the flow of trains. I am sure it's just a temporary nuisance."

Slava heard of the partisans that hid in the forests. She heard there were thousands of them, both men and women, civilians or soldiers separated from their units, and who managed to escape the Nazis. They fought the Germans any which way they could. They often attacked the enemy columns from the rear. They also sabotaged railway lines and cut off German supply to their troops. She also heard from the women at work that the Germans tortured and hung persons suspected as partisans, their bodies swinging in the open for days in the center of the city. Many of those executed were not even partisans, but the Nazis considered them as sympathizers. She always tried to avoid that part of town and she personally did not see the hangings, for which she was grateful.

"I am sorry, Major Raake, but I can't accept the tea and cake. Thank you very much for your generous offer but I must return to my work. Besides, if you give me a piece, to be fair you need to give some to the women I work with."

"Please excuse me. I thought I could do something nice for you. I did not mean to make you uncomfortable. It is that I just want to have a decent conversation with a lady. Your German is excellent and I feel that we could talk. There is something about you that reminds me of my daughter, Marlene. She is about your age and also very smart. For instance, Lieutenant Hoffman told me that you have a piano in your house and you told me that you play the piano. You must love music as I do. It would be so nice just to discuss with someone life's little pleasures such as opera or a symphony. I studied the violin. Unfortunately I'm not that good with it. But my wife is an excellent pianist."

Slava started to relax. Her breathing became regular and she smiled. She suddenly realized that he was lonely. He was isolated from the civilized world he knew and he missed his family.

"There, you see, I made you smile. I love your smile. You, again, remind me of my daughter. You should smile more often."

"It is difficult to smile much under the circumstances."

"It will get better. I promise you. Once the Soviets are defeated, life will return to normal."

Slava's smile faded quickly. *Who is he kidding. The Soviet people will never give in to foreign occupation. The struggle will go on until the invaders are out of my country,* she thought to herself. She wanted to make her thoughts known, but bit her lip. She knew that she probably would be shot if she voiced her thoughts.

"Thank you for your generosity," Slava said as Raake placed the strudel on the desk in front of her. "But you must realize that if I spend time talking to you in this office, the women will eat me alive. I do not want to be the center of their gossip. I really need to get back to work."

"Fine, perhaps we can talk later. By the way, how are your parents doing? Do you have enough to eat?"

"Thank you, they are doing fine and we are getting by."

In reality, the situation at home began to look grim. To conserve their now meager supplies, the adults in the house ate small meals twice a day. Vladimir's little nieces were fed three times per day until Anna and the girls left for Jazwino in late August. There were some jars of home-canned vegetables, fruit and smoked meat, but that provision would be gone before long. Slava was worried, as were her parents, about running out of food. She earned a small salary, but food was scarce. One of the women at work said that she had found a food vender on the other side of town. But he was very expensive. A loaf of bread cost five marks. Slava's wages for a day were one mark.

She often marveled how her brother, Leonid, who lived by the Black Sea, had the foresight to deliver to them a cart full of sacks of wheat flour shortly before the war. He exchanged his gold watch to buy the goods for the family. Her mother, very sparingly, made bread from the flour. *How did Leonid know that there would be a war and a food shortage?* She wondered. She could not ask Leonid because all communication with the outside world had been terminated. *Is Leonid even alive?*

Slava was also worried about her desperate countrymen who readily turned to thievery and murder to provide for their hungry families. Her own family had been victimized. At night, her father heard noises emanating from their storeroom. Vladislav grabbed his shotgun that was hidden under the bed. He snuck into the kitchen and looked out of the peephole in the door. In the light of a full moon he saw two scraggly men attempting to break open the padlock to the door of the storeroom. He stuck the shotgun into the peephole and shot into the air. The thieves fled. The thunder of the shot was loud and Slava and Suzanna ran shaken into the kitchen.

"What's the matter with you?" Suzanna yelled at Vladislav.

"There were thieves trying to steal our supplies."

"Now the whole world knows you have a gun," Suzanna said.

"At least the thieves will know better than to mess with us."

"What about the Germans? I'm sure they heard the shot. They'll be here again and we will be taken away. You know it's illegal to have a gun, you fool."

Slava tossed and turned all night for fear that the Nazis would come at any minute and drag them away.

◆ ◆ ◆ ◆

One late Sunday afternoon, Slava heard a knock on the door. The whole family was startled. Slava tensed up as she approached the door. To her surprise, she saw Richard, her friend from medical school. He held a covered metal pot.

"Richard! I can't believe it is you! I'm so delighted to see you," Slava said as tears of joy streamed down her cheek. "Let me give you a hug. I think of my friends so often. My girlfriends left before the occupation, but I never knew what happened to you or Oleg. The three of us were there, that awful day, when the Germans were already in the hall. I see you weren't able to get out of Vitebsk? Where is Oleg? Come in, come in. We have lot of catching up to do."

"No, I can't stay. Here, I brought you and your parents some beef and barley soup. Everyone is hungry these days and I knew you could use it. I'm so glad to see you too. I've been meaning, now, for a long time to come and visit you. But as you know, it's not as easy to move around under the occupation. Everyone is a suspect. And it's certainly impossible to leave Vitebsk."

Slava noticed that Richard was jumpy, looking nervously around as though he thought someone might be watching.

"Are you and your parents all right?" Richard asked hurriedly.

"Yes we are fine. But won't you come in. To carry that soup all the way here, you must have been sure we're still here."

"I wasn't sure. I thought your house was destroyed like most of the others and had no idea where to look for you. Until yesterday, that is. I spoke to Masha. We were talking about her work and she mentioned names of women she worked with. When she mentioned Vladislava, I immediately asked her to describe you and what she knew of you. She told me that you live in the same house with your parents."

Beware the Wolves

"Yes, I did tell them at work that our house survived. They seemed surprised. I wish you had come weeks ago. I have so many questions to ask you and so much to tell you. For example, what are you doing now?"

"I'm a cook for the Germans. At first they were nasty to me, but now as long as I do what they tell me, they pretty much leave me alone. I can even sneak out with a pot of soup and even if they saw me, I don't think they'd care. So I'll be over every so often with some food from the kitchen. It's great to see you! You look as good as ever."

"Please come in, Richard. We have a lot of catching up to do."

"No, I really need to go. It's a long walk back and I need to return before dark. If I'm out past curfew, they'll arrest me. Or worse, they may think I'm a partisan and hang me. Enjoy the soup. I made it myself."

"Well, then you better go. Next time come earlier. By the way, have you seen Oleg?" Slava yelled out as Richard was on the street.

"Yes, I see him everyday. He also works for the Germans. He cleans up their messes. I'll tell him I saw you."

"Please do and come back soon. Bring Oleg with you if you like."

The visit was brief. But Slava was elated. It was a refreshing breeze that blew through her humdrum life. The thoughts of medical school and all her friends revolved in her head. She wished she could spend more time with Richard and reminisce. She, once again, felt giddy as a schoolgirl. And even though Richard seemed nervous about their meeting, she hoped that he would return again. Any break in the monotony of her life was refreshing.

Slava rarely left the house other than to go to work. She feared the Nazis and there was nowhere to go. Every morning and night Slava prayed that she would see Vladimir again and life would return to normal. She studied photographs of Vladimir and of the two of them together at family gatherings. Her favorite was the one at a picnic by the river. She tried to remember every detail of each photograph, as tears flowed down her cheeks like the river Dvina that ran through Vitebsk. Her eyes swelled and bags above her cheeks. She hated the idea that she might be helping the enemy and hoped that she would never be forced to translate a militarily sensitive document. She planned what she would do if faced with the dilemma. Would she have the courage to alter it, if given the opportunity? She knew that a German officer with Russian skills arbitrarily spot-checked her work and that of the other translators. They were warned that if the translations were not accurate, they would be severely punished.

◆ ◆ ◆ ◆

The weather in September had been beautiful. But by October, the cold winds blew through Vitebsk. Light drizzle turned into wind driven rains that chilled Slava down to her bones. Her father had gathered a good supply of firewood for their stoves. He also had stashed a supply of coal. He was sure that he had enough fuel to last through the winter, but Slava feared that he was too optimistic.

Victor Moss

Slava appeared at work one morning drenched from the walk in the rain. She sat at her desk shivering in the cold warehouse. She walked over to the tea table and, as she did, she saw a document on one of the desks that caught her eye. It was a requisition form for barbed wire and lumber for a prisoner of war camp in Vitebsk. She felt a pit in her stomach as she studied the document. *Is there a chance she could see Vladimir if he had been captured?* Her heart began to beat faster at the thought of seeing Vladimir. *Even under those circumstances it was better than not seeing him at all.* She tried to imagine what it would be like to be a German prisoner. She had no idea, but knew it would be atrocious.

That evening, Slava and her parents sat down to a meal of bread, pickled green tomatoes and a thin slice of smoked mutton for each of them.

"I saw a paper at work today," Slava said. "It requisitioned material for a prisoner of war camp in Vitebsk."

Her parents said nothing.

"I told you before what the women told me. They said that the fascists have captured thousands of our soldiers and have taken them away. There was also talk that thousands of prisoners were killed."

"What are you saying?" Vladislav asked. "Do you think Vladimir was captured?"

"There is a good chance. And, if he was, and they bring him to Vitebsk, I have to find a way to see him."

"You're talking nonsense," Suzanna said. "A prison that will accommodate that many will not be in Vitebsk, but somewhere outside of the city. You are going to go searching for him and only get into trouble. You think that they'll allow you in to search for your husband?"

"Mama, you're always against everything. I need to find out. Wait! Do you hear a truck?"

Slava ran to the window and saw the narrow-slotted headlights of a car. She felt a chill pass through her body and her stomach tightened into knots at the sight and the sound of the car. Her parents were next to her and as the gray German officer's car with a black cross on the door stopped in front of the house, her mother cried out, "Oh no! Now what. The bastards have come for us. Dear Jesus. Save us all!"

CHAPTER 21

Machine gunners, perched on guard towers, fixed their eyes on the throng of depleted and bedraggled war prisoners as they hobbled into an abandoned brickyard at Yartsevo. The lines of prisoners were ordered to halt and stand in place. The day's brutal walk sapped every ounce of Vladimir's strength. He was hungry and thirsty. It took all his energy just to keep his exhausted legs together. His only desire, at the moment, was to collapse onto the ground. But he did not dare. He watched as others fell, only to be poked in the ribs with a stick or kicked with a boot. Those who did not rise with the prodding or those who were not helped up by fellow captives were summarily shot, their lifeless bodies dragged away carelessly. Thus Vladimir stood still, praying for inner strength to survive a few more minutes. He looked at Misha. Misha's eyes were closed, his head slumped onto his left shoulder. Evgeniy held him up.

"Hang on, Misha," Vladimir said, in a hoarse whisper. His mouth was dry. It hurt to talk. His throat and lips were swollen from the lack of water.

Vladimir sidled closer to Misha, trying to help hold him up. But then he realized, if Misha started to fall, he had no strength to stop him. *How much longer do we have to stand here? What's the hold up? Let's get moving.*

He gazed around slowly. A wooden shed stood next to several large brick structures in the brickyard. Vladimir saw groups of prisoners funneled into the buildings. The column finally moved a few steps forward. *Perhaps, they'll give us shelter from the wind and cold for a change,* Vladimir thought. He had been out in the open for days. Just a covering over his head would be a luxury. *Why am I thinking about a roof? What I need is water and food. Besides, it's impossible to fit all of us inside those buildings.*

The brickyard was divided into several sections, each separated by rows of barbed wire. Finally, the guards herded Vladimir's section of the column through a narrow gate and into an area surrounded by several strands of barbed wire with a gate at each end. On the other side of the gate was an old red brick building with smoke billowing from a tall round chimney. Twenty large black kettles with piles of wood stacked underneath hung in a row adjacent to the structure. A surge of energy ran throughout his body as he realized that they might finally be fed. He assumed that the building was a kitchen and the kettles lined up outside of it were for food preparation.

He waited for his column to proceed through that gate toward the kitchen and the buildings for shelter. His hopes were dashed when the gates shut and they were told to stay put. Fellow captives spread out, falling to the ground

Victor Moss

wherever a space was found. Misha and Evgeniy still stood at his side, wavering on their feet.

"Well, Captain, I mean Vladimir," Evgeniy said. "Let's find a spot so we can plant ourselves down. Those sons of bitches are going to keep us out in the open again."

"Let's stay close to the gate," Vladimir said. "That's closer to the food."

The three men inched their way to the gate, but others had the same idea. Finally, they found a spot, next to the barbed wire fence about fifty meters from the gate. *God, it feels good to lie down,* Vladimir sighed with relief. His legs and feet burned with pain. Spasms grabbed his lower back. A patch of snow caught his eye. He quickly scooped it into his mess kit and stuffed some into his mouth, letting the cold liquid seep down the hot swollen tissue of his throat. It was a tickling sensation. He grabbed more snow and stuffed that in his mouth. As the snow melted in the mess kit, he drank what he could from there. His thirst somewhat quenched, he closed his eyes and slept solidly until dawn.

Shouts and yells from guards woke him.

"Get up! You pigs go to the trough for tea!"

Vladimir could not believe what he heard. *Tea? I must be hallucinating.*

He glanced toward the kitchen. The sun had not yet risen. Bundles of wood he had seen the night before were now ablaze, the flames hugging the kettles. Smoke mingled with the early morning fog, gave an eerie vision. Darkened shadows of men appeared to be floating around the fires. *I must be in Hell,* Vladimir thought. He rubbed his eyes. It was difficult to comprehend what was happening. He was groggy, awakened from deep slumber. The chilling cold numbed his toes. He wiggled them trying to get the circulation going again. *Oh God, let them not be frostbitten,* he prayed. Finally, life seeped back into his toes. With a tired gaze, he glanced over the other captives. *How many more have died from the freezing temperatures,* he wondered. His thoughts turned to Slava. He was so grateful that she insisted that he take along the civilian coat as he left home. He had it under his greatcoat. No one knew he had it, and he wanted to keep it that way. *Slava, through this coat, keeps me warm.*

"Tea time! You're invited to tea," said a German guard, laughing out loud.

It was an ordeal to get up. His body was slow to respond. He felt stiff and still deadly tired. The short sleep was not enough to rejuvenate him. Evgeniy pulled Misha up and extended his hand to Vladimir. Gratefully, Vladimir grabbed his hand and pulled himself up.

"Where do you get your strength, Evgeniy? You're like an ox."

"Hey, considering that I've been deprived of my daily ration of vodka for all these days, I'm doing pretty well."

"Well, at least you can joke about it."

"No joke. If I had a bottle right now, I could mow down all of these damn bastards."

Beware the Wolves

The three men shuffled toward the gate. Once there, they were funneled through the gate and then into lines formed in front of each of the kettles. Vladimir looked back. The field he had left was littered with bodies. *They didn't make it,* he thought, almost apathetically. He was more concerned about his own survival. He could almost feel the hot food slide into his mouth, warming his stomach. He could hardly wait his turn. He saw what looked like fellow prisoners ladle out a brown liquid into mess kits. Vladimir took his out and held it tight. At that moment the little metal bowl was his most precious possession. *How we take the simple, most basic things in life for granted,* Vladimir mused as he inched toward the pots. *Can't they hurry? What's taking so long?*

Suddenly he was shoved from the back and almost fell to the ground as several men in back of the line pushed their way forward toward the kettles. Others joined in. Shots rang out as the guards discharged weapons in the air to restore order. Vladimir was swept forward with the crowd. The warning shots did not quell the stampede. Men fell to the ground. Vladimir almost tripped on one, barely able to remain standing. His heart was racing. *What are we doing? This is dangerous. We have to stop.*

The guards had enough and cut down a multitude of prisoners with machine guns. Vladimir could not believe what he saw. A pile of bodies lay in front of him. He was only a few meters away from the spray of bullets. His insides quaked. His ears rang from the staccato of gunfire. Not all those on the ground were dead. Men lay all around in agony; some screamed. One, close to Vladimir, had blood gushing from his leg. Vladimir felt a need to help. He knelt beside the man ready to attempt to stop the bleeding, even if he had to use his hand to do so. From the corner of his eye he saw a muddy boot in his line of vision. Suddenly, a forceful kick knocked him to the ground. A rat-tat-tat of gunfire followed. His insides shook. His breathing stopped. *I've been shot,* was his first thought. Then he realized that the Nazi was moving down the line firing his weapon, finishing all those that were still alive. The poor captive Vladimir tried to help lay riddled with bullet holes.

Vladimir was stretched out on the ground enveloped by shock. Physically and emotionally drained, he attempted to rise. He saw Misha and Evgeniy sidling up to help him up. A guard shoved them back into line. *I have to get up. I have to get up. If I don't, I'll be shot. It can't all end here.* He painfully rolled over onto all fours. He raised his torso standing on his knees. Walking so many kilometers with hardly any sustenance for almost two weeks left his legs feeble. He needed food and rest to rejuvenate. He saw a guard approach. *Oh my God. He's coming for me. Please God, give me the strength to get up.* The guard stood over him and pointed his gun at Vladimir.

"Get back in line now!"

Vladimir looked into the gun barrel. It seemed as big as a canon. He gazed into the eyes of the German soldier. His piercing cold eyes reminded him of those of the wolf that he saw as a child in the forest with his grandfather. A vision of his grandfather appeared in his mind. "Always be strong. Never be afraid."

Then briefly, he saw Slava's smiling face. *This can't be my end?* He had to see her again. With all the strength he could muster, he pushed hard with his legs and arms. Another push and he stood up. The guard watched with a smirk as Vladimir dragged himself up. It hurt to breathe. He held his bruised and throbbing ribcage. Each deep breath sent excruciating pain throughout his body. *He must have cracked my ribs,* he told himself. He glanced at the captives waiting in line. They appeared emaciated, their eyes sunken into their skulls. *God, what are they doing to us?*

As Vladimir attempted to regain his place in line by Evgeniy and Misha, the other prisoners objected. They cursed and shouted at him.

"Get in the back, you bastard," one yelled.

"Don't let him in," someone else shouted.

A tall, gaunt prisoner was just about to shove Vladimir away when Evgeniy pushed him back and pulled Vladimir into line. This caused the captives to swear at both Evgeniy and Vladimir. *They barely have strength to walk, but their mouths are still strong,* Vladimir thought, shaken even further by the hatred he saw in the faces surrounding them.

"Quiet! Or you will be shot!" A guard bellowed. "Now, you men drag the corpses out of here. Put them along the fence!"

Vladimir's effort to rejoin the line was in vain. He knew that, in the general weakened state of the captives, moving the mound of at least fifty bodies even a few meters would be a horrendous task. *We are as weak as flies in winter.* Vladimir grabbed a leg of one of the dead. Another prisoner grabbed another leg, and two others pulled on the arms. Winded and with his ribcage stinging with pain with every breath he took, Vladimir helped pull one of the corpses to the side. It was a young soldier, a boy no older than seventeen. *Will his parents ever know what happened to him?* The boy's eyes were open. Blood poured out of his mouth soaking his already grimy uniform. Vladimir reached over and closed the soldier's eyes. Even with four individuals to move the body, it was a great effort. Once moved, Vladimir wondered if he would have to bury them somewhere. *Unless I get nourishment, they'll be burying me.*

The column formed again. This time the prisoners proceeded in an orderly fashion. Vladimir was saddened that death of fellow prisoners had become of no consequence. Death was all around them. To the captives it became part of their miserable lives. Each expected to die at any moment. They, themselves, felt like the living dead.

Finally, Vladimir's little mess kit was filled with a brown liquid. Vladimir still clutched it tightly with both of his trembling hands. He, like the others, immediately attempted to drink from it, but the guards shoved them out of the area and back to their compound. The bowl was almost too hot to hold so Vladimir pulled his sleeves out and held it tightly. As he walked he lifted the bowl to his face. His skin felt raw from the many days battered by the elements. The steam from the bowl felt wonderful. He smelled the brown water. Its odor was that of boiled water. As soon as they crossed the gate to their area, Vladimir and the medics took a sip. It did not taste like tea.

"It tastes like shit," Misha said.

"Well at least it's hot," Vladimir said. "And it's a liquid."

"It's just plain boiled water with some kind of brown crap," Evgeniy proclaimed.

"Now, food is what we need," Vladimir said. "This stuff won't keep us alive."

"Look, over there," Evgeniy pointed. "They have men pulling a horse in a cart."

"That's a switch," Vladimir said. He wanted to laugh but was unable. The best he could do was slightly curl his swollen lips into a grimace.

The horse was a casualty of the war. Vladimir watched as ropes working as a pulley lifted the horse and suspended it on a crossbeam held up by poles. Some of the prisoners butchered the horse into small pieces and threw the horsemeat into several kettles of boiling water.

"How do you think those men got kitchen duty?" Vladimir asked of anyone around that listened. Most everyone around him was asleep.

"They have been here for awhile," a voice from behind answered. "I heard that those men have been here for two weeks already."

"Vladimir's heart pounded with the thought that he might be fed. Above all, he hoped he would get a chunk of meat. A gust of cold wind intertwined among the prisoners. He laid down on the chilled ground. His eyelids again began to close. He fought sleep, forcing his eyelids to remain open. He felt that he had to watch the kettles. He was afraid that if he fell asleep he might miss out on the soup.

Hours went by. He watched a detail of prisoners shuffle by. They loaded the corpses onto hand pulled carts and wheeled them away. Vladimir moved his arms and legs, and rolled from side to side as his toes were numbing from the cold. The leather boots and two pairs of socks were not enough. Evgeniy told him that he had on six pairs of socks and his feet were kept warm. *How could he fit six pairs into his boot?* Vladimir wondered. He finally decided that he had to move around to keep warm even though he would expend more energy. It did not appear that they would be serving food any time soon.

"Evgeniy, Misha, let's walk around some. It will be good for us."

You and Evgeniy go," Misha said weakly. "I'll stay here."

Evgeniy rose up, although Vladimir noticed that the task became more difficult for him as well. Evgeniy stretched his hand out to Vladimir. Vladimir grabbed it and pulled himself up. They slowly walked toward the wooden shack about thirty meters away in another compound separated by barbed wire. Near the shack stood three officers with medical insignias. They were fellow prisoners. Vladimir was surprised to see them. *The fools,* Vladimir thought.

Victor Moss

How did they escape being shot as officers? Could it be because they're doctors, their lives were spared. Was I misled when I was told to remove all evidence of being a medical officer? Vladimir suddenly felt ashamed that he masqueraded as a soldier. But then, he was certain with the interrogation he received in Vyazma, by the German officers in that house, that they would have shot him just like they shot Dodik. *Maybe it depended on who you got? Surely, there are many decent Germans. I've only seen the worst.*

"What's in that wooden shack?" Vladimir asked one of the captives standing close by and looking in that direction.

"I looked inside when they left that door open. It appears to be a room filled with wounded. They're on bunks three rows high. The stench from there is awful."

"They brought our wounded here?" Vladimir asked, very surprised that they made it without being summarily executed.

"They were here when we came. Don't know where they came from or how they got here. Don't think they will be leaving though. Those poor bastards, they might as well shoot them now and put them out of their misery."

"I see they have doctors here," Vladimir said.

"They were here before us. I've been watching them. They and a few medics go in and out. One of the medics has a bag, probably with medicines. It's no use. There is not much they can do."

It is so ironic, Vladimir thought. *The Germans prevented me earlier from helping a soldier who was quickly shot. They went about and finished off the wounded. Yet they have allowed wounded to remain in the shack, protected from the elements and allowed doctors to treat them.* He was confused by the irrational behavior of the Nazis.

"Evgeniy, let's get back and join Misha. Hopefully, we'll at last get something to eat soon."

When they returned, Misha was still lying on the ground. But near the gate a throng gathered to be let out into the kitchen area. The aroma of cooking permeated the air, stirring everyone into frenzy. Evgeniy and Vladimir helped Misha up and all three joined the crowd at the gate. Vladimir knew that as soon as the gate was opened, it was going to be a repeat of the morning "tea." *A prudent person would wait,* Vladimir thought. But their hunger was so severe that no one thought of being rational. Passion for sustenance held everyone in a firm grip and the sooner they got to it, the faster they could eat. *Besides, they might run out of it if I am not there first.*

At long last, the gate opened and the swarm pushed itself out. Bodies once again fell as a mass of emaciated humanity shoved itself forward. The German guards yelled for the captives to stop. They ignored the shouts. Gunfire was heard. That did not deter the hungry. This time, however, the guards did not shoot into the crowd as it propelled itself toward the kettles. Vladimir was in the horde. He had to keep up. Even in his desperately weakened condition, the thought of food ahead pumped adrenalin into his system and gave him the strength to proceed.

Beware the Wolves

The mob overturned the kettles in their eagerness to get the food. Vladimir saw liquid spill out. His heart sank. *Oh my God! There goes our food.* Men dropped to the ground and picked up bits and pieces. He quickly made his way closer to where the spill occurred. The ground was steamy and muddy from the hot water hitting the surface. It was also oily from the fat in the horsemeat. Vladimir did not care. He, too, fell to the ground. He saw little kernels of barley, tiny blades of cabbage and tiny pieces of potatoes. He picked them up and shoved them in his mouth. *Where's the meat? I know there must be meat.* Like a bird pecking on the ground, he picked up whatever he could get his fingers on. As he crawled along, he saw something dark an arms length away. He realized that it must be a piece of meat. He saw that another captive was even closer. *Don't touch that piece. It's mine.* Vladimir threw out his arm and grabbed it. The other captive tried to wrestle it out of his hand. Vladimir pulled back with all his might and quickly shoved the piece in his mouth. *We're a pack of wolves fighting over a scrap of meat.* He stopped pecking for a second, closing his eyes in the sheer delight of chewing on the petite piece. He looked for more, but there was none. He continued to pick up bits and pieces. He spit out chunks of mud and rocks until he saw no more food.

All this time as he crawled on the ground on all fours, he heard laughter from the guards. The German soldiers repeatedly referred to the captives as subhuman. Because they were so, they could be treated like animals. Vladimir called them Hitlerites. It seemed that the Nazi officers, from the lower ranks and all the way up to Hitler, sanctioned the behavior of the brutality of the soldier in the field. The enemy's laughter made him realize how he and all the others must have appeared. *We're dirty, smelly, unshaven and infested with lice. We're crawling on the ground picking up grains from the muddy, oily ground. Their torture turned us into subhuman beings,* he thought angrily. *And now they laugh at us and even take our pictures as if we were animals in a zoo.*

He picked himself up and leaned on another prisoner who was still foraging, trying to find more food. Evgeniy and Misha had already returned to the compound. Vladimir joined them and sat on the ground.

"Well, that was something," Vladimir said.

"Something what? It was nothing but a disaster," Misha said. "I barely got anything, maybe a kernal of grain or two. What was in that soup? It was nothing much but boiled water."

"I saw with my own eyes that they were throwing horsemeat into the kettles," Evgeniy said. "But what happened to it? I didn't see any on the ground. Someone took it out before it got to us, those sons of bitches."

Vladimir did not have the heart to tell them that he found a small chunk of meat. He was lucky, he thought. That meat tasted so good. He only hoped that it was enough to give him some strength.

"How long do you think they'll keep us here?" Evgeniy asked.

"I think we'll be moved out soon," Vladimir said. "I think this is just a stopover until we're placed in a permanent camp."

Victor Moss

"I won't be able to make it if we have to walk somewhere again," Misha said. "I might as well die right here."

"I don't think we'll have to walk," Vladimir said. "Didn't you hear that train whistle as we came into town?"

"No," Evgeniy said. "There was no whistle. You must have been hallucinating. Have you heard a train since we've been here?"

"I didn't hear anything either," Misha said.

Vladimir was sure that he heard a train. *Maybe they're right. I was in no condition to be sharp. They're right. I haven't heard a whistle since we've been here. Oh God! They're going to make us walk again.*

"Well, you're probably right," Vladimir said. "If we have to walk, we'll walk. We'll make it. Do you know why?"

"Why?" Evgeniy asked.

"Because we're tough, right Misha?"

At that moment the three managed a laugh. Even some of the prisoners around them, overhearing their conversation, joined in the laughter.

"And to be stronger, let's sleep. Sleep cures everything. So I'm turning in. Wake me up if there will be more food."

Vladimir turned on his side, brought his greatcoat over his head and feet and tried to fall asleep. His scalp itched. He was afraid to scratch it. A day ago he scratched it so hard that his skin bled. He decided that he would have to bear the annoyance and let the itching continue under his cap and earflaps. He knew that in these filthy conditions the lice could lead to Typhus fever. To take his mind off the lice, he took Slava's picture from his tunic pocket. He opened up his greatcoat a little, enough for the early evening light to reflect on her face. *Slavochka, I miss you so. I love you so much. You are my treasure. Please be alive. Someday we will see each other again where I can look into your bright eyes and then kiss you all over. I'll make it out of this Hell. I have to make it. I'll see you someday. Dear Jesus, please, save me and save Slavochka. Please protect us so that we'll be together soon.*

He kissed the picture, put it back in his pocket, covered himself up again and fell asleep.

He felt someone shaking him. He opened his eyes and saw daylight.

"Look, Volodya," Evgeniy shook him once again. "They lit up the kettles again. We might get some breakfast."

Vladimir looked out toward the kitchen. Through the fog, he saw flames licking the sides of the kettles. Towers of smoke and steam rose into the crisp autumn air. Vladimir smacked his lips from the expectation. Saliva flowed. He sat up alert but uncomfortable. He was stiff and ached all over. The lice seemed to have spread down his body. For the first time in many days he had the urge to go to the latrine. He'd seen it the night before. It was just a hole dug in the ground. He could smell it, too.

He hurried back and rejoined Misha and Evgeniy. Their turn still had not come. A whitish liquid was doled out to captives located in other sections of the brickyard.

Beware the Wolves

"Just watch," Misha said. "By the time it's our turn, there'll be nothing left."

"Yeah, those sons of bitches," Evgeniy said. "It's just our luck."

"Those are big kettles, boys," Vladimir said. "Let's just wait and see. Maybe we should wait closer to the gate."

After thirty minutes, the first groups of captives had received their portions. Fellow prisoners who ladled the liquid into mess kits still stood at their posts. The guards opened the gate and again a throng of prisoners shoved their way forward. This time, the Germans closed the gate and stood with their weapons pointed at the captives. The shoving stopped. The Nazis allowed a few at a time to proceed through the gate toward the kettles. A guard directed them to a line in front of each kettle.

Vladimir stood in line for the third kettle. Misha and Evgeniy were in line moving toward the fourth kettle. Vladimir had twenty fellow captives ahead of him and again his eagerness to be fed was overwhelming. He understood why the men rushed the kettles to get the food the night before. The body took over the mind and in its instinct for survival it craved the nourishment instantly. Vladimir's heart pounded the closer to the kettle he shuffled. He clutched his bowl tightly with both hands. *I'm almost there,* he told himself. *Just three more men and it will be my turn.* Finally his turn came and he saw the server pour a ladle full of soup. He hurried back to the compound, and still standing took a sip. The soup was hot. He burned his lip and the roof of his mouth. He blew on the bowl to cool it off. He knew he should wait, but couldn't. He took another sip, then another. It tasted like boiled water with a few grains and vegetables floating about.

"This is not soup," a fellow prisoner complained. "There's nothing here to nourish us. Where is the horsemeat? The cooks took it out for themselves. Those bastards. If I get my hands on any one of those sons of bitches, I'll strangle him."

Vladimir had seen them butchering horses. *They must have used the horsemeat as stock, but then removed it. Of course, it's a valuable commodity and they could get anything they wanted in trade.*

"Oh well," Vladimir said. "At least it's hot and may fool our stomachs."

Misha and Evgeniy joined Vladimir.

"What awful soup, Evgeniy said. "Some of the captives called it *balanda.*"

"What's balanda?"

"Misha, it's crap. A very thin soup that has little nutrition."

Vladimir sat down and watched as more captives walked through the lines for their meager portion of soup. After an hour, the fires underneath the kettles were extinguished. The early morning fog had drifted away. *Vladimir wondered, what's next. How long are we going to be kept here?* He hoped that wherever they took him there would at least be a shelter over his head.

Another thirty minutes went by and Vladimir saw many German soldiers approaching the captives. He knew that they would soon be on the move again.

He still hoped that they would be transported by rail, but he realized that he was mistaken about a train at Yartsevo. He wondered how far he would have to walk today and more importantly, if he would be able to walk. *The sleep and a little bit in my belly should help, but was it enough?* All his muscles in his body still ached from the long, grueling forced marches he had undergone.

"Get up you pigs! Everyone move out, you bags of garbage."

Vladimir stood up, still with difficulty but able to get up on his own power. Evgeniy had no problem rising, but Misha was still weak and unable to get up without help form Evgeniy and Vladimir. Vladimir and Evgeniy helped several weak ones to rise up as well.

"Prisoners," another guard yelled out. "Help those unable to get up. Those still on the ground will be shot."

Even though that guard threatened to shoot those still on the ground, Vladimir sensed some sympathy in the guard's voice. After a column was formed, those unable to walk were shot on the spot. The guard, who Vladimir thought was sympathetic, took part in the shootings. *Murderers just following orders,* Vladimir thought.

Vladimir was once again walking west on the Yartsevo-Smolensk highway. He realized that he'd have to walk all the way to Smolensk, approximately thirty kilometers away. *How ironic,* Vladimir thought. *I'm going back to where I started.* Vehicles on the road forced the column to walk in the semi-muddy, semi-frozen ditch running alongside the highway. As the vehicles lumbered by, mud splattered from the tires and half-tracks. German soldiers laughed and yelled obscenities at the prisoners. Some took pictures.

It was apparent that the guards had a schedule to keep and they hurried the column along. After an hour's walk, Vladimir's legs and feet throbbed with pain. He felt his blisters bleed. Every step was a stab of a knife in his back. His breathing became irregular from the pain. To keep his mind sharp and divert his thoughts from how miserable he was, he counted the number of fellow captives that fell to the ground and were shot. He had counted three hundred twenty-nine before he gave up. There were constant gunshots, both ahead and behind. Each shot caused Vladimir's body to tremble.

"Keep moving, step over the fallen," one of the guards shouted as Vladimir tried to help a prisoner who fell two rows ahead of him. Vladimir saw the guard approach so he left the man on the ground. He knew that to disobey, meant instant death. In fact, he was in such a weakened condition, that he did not have the strength to help anyone. *Oh God! When is this nightmare going to end? When I'm dead, I suppose.*

At midday, the column was allowed to rest on a grassy field, next to a forest. Vladimir heard whispers among some of the prisoners that they were going to make a run toward the forest. Evgeniy was one of them.

"Men, don't even think about it," Vladimir told them. "You're too weak to make a run for it. That's at least two hundred meters. They'll shoot you down like fish in a barrel."

Beware the Wolves

"We have to do something to save ourselves," Evgeniy whispered back. "One or two more days of this and we'll all be dead anyway. At least we'll have a chance if we make it into the forest."

"No, Evgeniy," Vladimir countered. "You do not have a chance. You will die in that field. They can't keep herding us forever. Who knows what tomorrow will bring. We may be able to survive, whereas running through that field is suicide."

"Sorry, Volodya, if you want to die marching in the column, go ahead, but I'm going to take a chance. Who's coming with me?"

Several men nodded and started to edge their way toward the forest.

"Men, I am ordering you to stop this foolishness."

"What does he mean, 'ordering us'?" one of the men said.

"Well, Comrade Captain, we no longer have to take orders from you," Evgeniy sneered. "You gave that up when you took your insignias off. It was nice knowing you, though. See you in the afterlife. You coming, Misha?"

Misha hesitated and Vladimir grabbed him and held him tightly. Evgeniy and fourteen others rushed out toward the forest. Within seconds it was all over. Machine gunners on the ground, and machine gunners on motorcycle sidecars mowed them all down. Vladimir closed his eyes and lowered his head. *Those fools! It was suicide.* He would miss Evgeniy. Evgeniy was a rough individual, a career army person and a bigot. It was obvious that he did not like officers. He had no use for them. But Vladimir had liked him and he felt that Evgeniy had liked him as well. He looked over at Misha who was, especially at the end, very close to Evgeniy. Misha was devastated. He expected tears, but instead saw a numb look. Misha's mouth was wide open. He had a glassy look in his eyes.

"I want to die," Misha muttered. "Why did you hold me back?"

Vladimir looked away sadly. He did not answer, and he did not believe Misha expected one. They sat a few minutes in silence. Vladimir stared at the forest. He tried to avert his eyes from the bodies sprawled on the field. Evgeniy's death left him reeling. It should not have. He had seen so much death around him. He needed a mental escape. He forced his mind back to his childhood. He recalled the good times he had with his grandfather. He saw images of his mother and sisters weeding the garden. He pictured his lips as they pressed against Slava's, then gently covered her mouth. Even in remembrance he could capture the intimacy of her kisses.

Suddenly, he heard the command to move forward, and was hurtled back to reality.

CHAPTER 22

Darkness fell as the pitiful column of war prisoners struggled into Smolensk. At first, Vladimir could not recognize the city. All was in rubble and ruins. The destruction was incredible. Only piles of bricks and twisted metal remained of what were once functioning structures. Those that were not completely transformed into a heap of wreckage stood like ghostly skeletons. Vladimir's heart sank even lower. *These buildings represented peoples' lives— their homes, their work. It's all ruined. The city is destroyed. Was it the same fate for Vitebsk? My God, what about Slava and my family? How could they survive anything like this?*

Vladimir heard a train whistle. He realized that starvation leads to hallucinations, but this time he was sure he heard the sound. *At least maybe they'll put us on a train. My body will not hold out for any more walking without water, food or rest.* Misha was still beside him. With Vladimir's help and the help from another prisoner, Misha limped into Smolensk. Vladimir knew that while Misha talked about dying, he was tougher than he looked. He held on to life.

The captives were herded to what was once a beautiful railroad depot. It was the same one Vladimir visited when he reported for duty. That day seemed so long ago now. The depot was barely recognizable. Half the structure was in ruins. The portion of the old train station, still standing, had sustained heavy fire damage. On the tracks, a train with a string of bullet-ridden wooden freight cars awaited them. Vladimir shuffled along following others in the column toward the boxcars that were being filled with prisoners. He realized that it would take some time to board the cars with the long line of captives, although there were now significantly fewer prisoners than there were at the start of the long trek to Smolensk. The general consensus among the captives estimated their original population at 40,000 prisoners. Now, fewer than half survived. *Those bastards! By the time we get anywhere, we'll all die,* he thought angrily as he fixated on the devastation around him while the line inched along.

Another train rolled in. It pulled more wooden freight cars. Most were open cattle cars. The second train stopped behind the first train. Vladimir and his group were diverted to the second train. The guards ordered the prisoners closest to the door of the car to set up a wooden ramp that lay on the ground. Once the ramp was set in place, the captives were forced into the boxcar. Vladimir ended up standing one person away from the side, toward the end of the car. Misha stood next to the heavily splintered wooden side.

"Look," Misha whispered to Vladimir. "I have this wall to lean on."

"You're lucky" Vladimir whispered back. "I barely have room to move."

Beware the Wolves

"Some luck," Misha said. "If I were lucky I wouldn't be here. Besides, I have no room to move either. We're packed in here like sardines in a can."

"Don't talk to me about sardines," Vladimir answered. "At this point, I could eat the can."

"Volodya, are you sure you have no more cigarettes? I need one badly."

"I've given you the pack that I had. You asked me the same question yesterday and the day before. I don't have any more. Cigarettes should be your last concern. It's water that we all need. We're dying from thirst."

"If I'm going to die, then I want to die with a cigarette in my mouth."

Vladimir kept quiet. His throat was parched and his lips were swollen. Conversation was difficult.

The door slid shut and locked. Vladimir was anxious for the train to start rolling. Instead minutes and then hours dragged by and the train stood as though it was frozen to the rails. *Maybe they are not going to take us anywhere. Maybe this boxcar is only used as a holding cell. And in the morning they'll let us out and we'll have to walk again,* Vladimir pondered as he stood there in one spot. The temperature in the wagon rose from the body heat of the prisoners. Vladimir was in a closed boxcar and at first, the warmth felt good. For the first time in days, Vladimir was warm. But as the hours crept by, and the train stood still, Vladimir began to sweat. Slava's coat, coupled with the great coat became unbearable even after he unbuttoned both coats. *I need to take off a coat, but I can't move.* Vladimir tried to position himself to remove the coat. He was unable to lift his arm over his shoulder. He wiped the sweat off his forehead. He took off his cap exposing his perspired, lice infested, matted hair. The itching was unrelenting. He noticed that some of the prisoners were able to sit down with their legs crossed underneath them. He thought he would try it as well. *But how will I be able to get up in my weakened condition. And if I sit too long, my legs and feet will go numb. No, I better continue to stand,* Vladimir decided, although his whole body ached. After another hour, the wind gusts came up, forcing cold air to circulate through the cracks and holes in the floor and walls. Vladimir felt relief from the heat. His exhaustion overwhelmed him and he leaned on a fellow solder and fell asleep.

A jolt awakened him. It was daybreak and the train began to move. Then he heard shots fired. *What the devil? Now what is going on?* The gunfire came from both rifles and submachine guns. Interspersed among the shots, Vladimir heard laughter and howls coming from the German troops outside the train. The blasts grew louder as the boxcar rolled down the tracks. Suddenly, a shower of bullets hit the side of his boxcar. It was as if Vladimir was trapped in a hailstorm under a tin roof. The ruckus was ear splitting. Splinters of wood flew overhead as bullets penetrated the side of the boxcar. *I can't believe this. Those bastards are shooting at us. We're just sitting ducks, trapped in this box. They've done this before. It's another game for them.*

Captives screamed from pain, some from fright. Those along the wall either collapsed in place or fell onto their neighbors. Misha fell toward Vladimir.

Vladimir tried to hold him up, but was unable. Misha's weight forced Vladimir to be shoved into his neighbor. Those around pushed on Vladimir and in turn, Vladimir pushed Misha forward, causing Misha to fall onto a slumping body in front of him. The person behind him toppled onto him. The whole row next to the wooden side of the car tumbled like a row of dominoes.

"No! No! No!" Vladimir cried out. "Misha, Misha!"

Misha did not answer. Vladimir maneuvered around to grab his arm. His hand shaking, he attempted to feel his pulse. He could not feel it. He next felt Misha's neck. Again, there was no pulse. The train lumbered on. The only sound in the boxcar was the click clack of metal wheels on rails. The captives were silent except for an occasional moan from a dying wounded. Those closest to the corpses stripped them of their mess kits, jackets, caps and coats. Some stripped the boots and chewed on the leather. A fellow captive sat down on the pile of bodies in which Misha was in the middle, sandwiched between two others. Vladimir grabbed that soldier and somehow mustered the strength to pull him off.

"What are you doing? Have a little respect for the dead. You're sitting on my friend."

"What's it to you?" replied the captive. "I'm tired and need to sit down. You think the dead care?"

Vladimir still held on to him, squeezing his arm tighter as though he was taking his anger out on the poor captive.

"Hey! Let go. All right, I won't sit on him. Just let go. You're hurting me with your grip, you bastard."

Vladimir let go of the captive's arm. He glanced down the car and saw others sitting on the lifeless bodies.

"Oh shit! Do what you want. I don't give a damn anymore."

Vladimir's boots felt sticky as he shuffled around in place. He realized that he stood in a pool of the seeping blood of the dead. Misha's blood was commingled with the others. *How many more men will die at the hands of the damn Nazis? Since Vyazma, it has been a journey of death with no end in sight.* Thousands of prisoners had died. Death had become commonplace. But Misha's death was personal to Vladimir. He lost his loyal medic, his friend. As Vladimir thought of the loss, he could feel every artery and vein throughout his body pound as if his blood was trying to escape. His breathing was laborious and deep. Tears filled his eyes and ran unchecked down his cheeks. He finally broke down and sobbed as he had never sobbed before. He felt alone surrounded by a sea of misery. *Dear God,* Vladimir prayed. *Please, please protect Slavochka so that, at least, she will be safe. And protect me so that someday we'll be together again. I need her so.*

Vladimir felt depressed and discouraged. He knew his remedy was to seek strength from his grandfather's words, "Life is tough. You have to be tough." He repeated those words to himself and then thought, *I have to survive. I have to be strong.*

Beware the Wolves

♦ ♦ ♦ ♦

The train moved slowly with many stops. Each time the train stopped, Vladimir hoped that they would be let out. But the captives remained locked in the boxcar. A stench of death permeated the foul air. With great effort the weakened captives, working together, dragged the bodies to one side of the car. Some were loaded on top of each other. With the many that either had been shot or died from thirst and exhaustion, there was more room for the survivors to sit down or even to stretch out. Vladimir tried to find a spot to lie down, but hesitated when he saw the condition of the wooden boards below him. The floor was filthy with a combination of blood, urine and defecation. If he stretched out, he would have to recline in that bacteria-laden refuse. He saw how many of the captives were sick with diarrhea. *It must have been the balanda soup they ate,* he thought. He knew that they would be sick just because they had not eaten for many days. The sudden intake of food was too much on a human's digestive system. When he thought about the floor, he knew why so many tried to sit on the corpses. He finally found a spot that he thought was cleaner than others and sat down. He leaned against another prisoner for back support and his body immediately felt the relief.

Vladimir had no idea how long he had been cooped up in the rotten boxcar. The fellow prisoner he leaned against had not moved for hours and did not complain. Vladimir became suspicious about his motionless friend. He turned around and as he grabbed his right shoulder, the body fell over onto another sitting soldier.

"Hey, get off of me!" A fellow captive yelled as he pushed the body away.

"Can't you see he's dead," Vladimir said.

"Well, who cares, he shouldn't be doing that."

"Let's pull him over with the rest of the dead."

"No way. If you want him out of here, you do it. I don't have the strength even to get up."

Vladimir tried to get some of the other captives to help him drag the body, but they waved him off. Vladimir knew, that by himself, he didn't have the strength. In addition, he felt nauseous. *It must be from the stench in the car,* he thought. He needed fresh air. He was feeling faint. He stood, using another captive for support. His legs were wobbly, but he walked over to the side of the car and standing over a sleeping captive, he stuck his nose as close as he could to one of the many bullet holes in the wall. The little bit of fresh air was cold and crisp. But, it was not enough to fill his lungs. The smell in the car overwhelmed what little fresh air the small hole produced. And his nausea did not go away. The train moved slowly. The day had turned once again to night and back to daylight. *When are they ever going to let us out?*

Finally, at midday, the locomotive came to a halt. After a few minutes the door slid open. Cold air from a gust of wind burst inside. Vladimir took deep breaths to force the stale air out of his lungs.

"Out! Out! Quick, quick," the guards on the ground yelled to the captives inside the boxcar. "Out! Now!"

This time there was no plank on which to walk down. The prisoners had to jump down from the car onto the ground. It was only a distance of about one meter; nevertheless, in their weakened condition, it was as though they were leaping off a cliff. The first few captives that hopped down from the car collapsed to the ground, as their legs simply were not strong enough to hold their weight. Vladimir expected the guards to beat them or shoot them, but instead they motioned for those still in the car to help them up once they were off the train. Vladimir was so used to the Germans shooting anyone down on the ground and unable to get up, that he was stunned for a moment. *What do we have here, a bit of humanity?*

Vladimir followed the others and slid off the train car by backing out as he lay on his stomach. Once on the ground, and in fresh air, his nausea disappeared, he felt better. The prisoners were told to stand away from the train in an area surrounded by German guards with German Sheperd dogs. He could see men, dressed in civilian clothing with six-pointed stars painted on yellow armbands wrapped around their sleeves. They stood next to large handcarts. As he stood in place, he could see them board the rail cars, drag bodies out and load them onto the carts. He watched intently for Misha's body to be removed. He thought he saw the corpse thrown on the cart. *Good-bye, my friend, I hope that wherever you are, that you are happy,* he thought sadly to himself.

The railroad depot looked similar to the one in Vitebsk, but much smaller. It had evidence of chipped bricks from flying bullets, but basically it survived any attacks. He had no idea where he was. He did not see any civilians other than the Jewish workers. *Am I in Russia, Byelorussia, Poland or Germany?* Vladimir tried to find writings on signs to give him a hint, but he could not see any.

After a few minutes, Vladimir sat down with the others and waited, as it appeared that the prisoners were not going anywhere. Sometime later, they were ordered up on their feet, and once again funneled into a column and told to walk. *How far are we supposed to walk? There is not much daylight left. They won't want us to walk in the dark as we could escape. On the other hand, who has the energy to run? When are the cruel bastards going to give us water?* As soon as he thought that, he saw men pulling several handcarts loaded with a wooden barrel on each cart. They were placed on each side of the column as it proceeded forward. The column slowed down. Vladimir looked ahead and what he saw he could not believe. As the men walked past, water was ladled into their mess kits. Vladimir's turn finally came and after he received his share, he gulped down the water, knowing he should drink it sparingly after so many days without. But he could not help it. His body shook as he felt the liquid flow down his esophagus to his stomach. The water was a Godsend. At that moment, he knew he would survive at least another day.

The column turned onto a street and as Vladimir walked past the front entrance to the railroad depot he finally saw a sign above the tall wooden

Beware the Wolves

doors. It read "Baronovichi." *What do I know of Baronovichi?* Vladimir thought. He believed it was in Byelorussia. But he thought it might be in Poland. At any rate he was either in Poland or close to it in Byelorussia. As he continued his march he glanced around and saw that Baronovichi was a fairly large town, with many buildings and houses now burned to the ground. He also saw many that withstood the battles. He assumed there were battles because the Germans were now in control of the area. *Surely, they didn't give in without a fight?* Vladimir thought. *Of course, this close to the border, the Germans must have executed a surprise attack and had taken this region quickly.*

His eyes fell on a white bell tower. It had a blue spire and a cross on its peak. His first thought was that it was a Catholic cross, so he must be in Poland. But as he approached the church, Vladimir saw that the bell tower sat on a larger bell tower and the cross was the traditional Orthodox cross. *Now I am positive this is Byelorussia since Byelorussia is mostly Orthodox, while Poland is Catholic.*

Not far from the outskirts of town, possibly five kilometers, Vladimir saw what once was an army base. He saw rows of drab wooden barracks with pealing gray paint surrounded by two separate rows of barbed wire. There was a space of at least five meters between each row. Eight guard towers stood around the perimeter of the outer fence. The captives were led first through the wooden gate of one fence, then through the gate of the second fence. They were ordered to stand in rows in a large parade area in front of several barracks. Vladimir glanced at the barracks and saw other captives peering through the small windows. Across the field, there were brick buildings with Nazi flags prominently displayed on each structure.

Thirty minutes dragged by. It was almost dark, but the captives were required to remain standing in place. Vladimir stood in the fifth row. As soon as someone tried to sit down, the guards poked him in the ribs with a stick. Nevertheless, from sheer exhaustion, some fell to the ground. Vladimir again anticipated that they would be shot on the spot. Instead, the guards yelled for those around them to pick them up and hold them up. Vladimir, himself, felt as though he could not last much longer. He was still thirsty and thoroughly exhausted. The walking sapped whatever strength he had left and the standing around was almost more that he could bear. He craved to sit down. Then something totally unexpected happened. He saw other prisoners pull handcarts loaded with wooden barrels. Each cart had three barrels rather than one as back in Baronovichi. Vladimir was overjoyed as he thought he would get more water. Instead his heart started to pound when small loaves of bread were distributed to the captives. He watched as men dug into the bread and devoured the loaves. As crumbs fell onto the ground, they dropped to the ground to pick up every piece. Not a speck of bread was wasted. This time the guards allowed the captives to fall to the ground. Vladimir's mouth smacked and salivated as the barrels came closer to him. The bread was dark rye with a hard crust.

Victor Moss

Vladimir's loaf was burned on the bottom, but that did not bother him. Like the others, he tore the loaf apart and bit into the bread. He almost fainted from the shear joy of the food.

After every captive received his loaf of bread, four Germans came out of the largest brick building that Vladimir assumed to be the administration offices. The officer walking in front of the others toward the captives was a short older man, probably in his fifties. Gray hair was visible under his cap. His fat belly protruding, the officer's coat with insignias billowed around him. He looked like a walking tent. Two other officers, one of them in a black coat and hat, and a corporal, followed him. Each had a scowl on his face. The field was covered with prisoners standing in muddy snow, aligned in neat rows by the guards. A guard brought a wooden box to the officer, who stepped on it and began to speak, while the corporal translated:

"My name is Colonel Klaisle. I am the commandant of this prisoner of war camp at Baronovichi, in the new territory of the German Third Reich. If you survive, you will be here a long time so I do not want any trouble from you. If you cannot follow discipline, you will be punished severely. Do not even try to escape. It is impossible. The guards have an order to shoot anyone attempting to escape. They will beat or execute anyone refusing to follow one of their orders. Before breakfast is served you are to report in formation, as assigned by the sergeant in charge of your barracks, for roll call. Every man must be present at the assigned time. If you are late for roll call, you will not be fed that day and will be placed in the cooler. Bread may be furnished to you, such as the loaf we generously gave you today, once per week, if the supplies hold out. So it is suggested that, if you are fortunate enough to get a loaf, that you make your bread last a week. Cigarettes will be issued to you, one pack per week. You will be fed in the morning and in the late afternoon. You should receive enough calories to get you through the day. Some of your fellow prisoners are barbers and they will cut your hair. After you are settled in your quarters, you will be called for interrogation. That is all. Heil Hitler."

Vladimir stood and listened sadly to the commandant. There was no emotion in the German's voice. His tone did not vary. He looked straight ahead. It was obvious he and the interpreter had made this speech time and again and they were bored with it. They sounded like robots that had a job to do and they did it. As soon as Klaisle finished, he extended his right arm toward the sky, then turned around and walked back to the brick building. The interpreter remained. Vladimir knew he was in for a long, hard experience at the hands of the Nazis. At that moment, he was not afraid. He had already been in Hell. *How much worse can it be?* His only thought was to survive. At any rate, he would have a roof over his head. *But what did he mean by interrogation? What is that all about? Do they think we know military secrets?*

Next, the officer in black stepped onto the box. He carefully reviewed the miserable, pathetic tide of humanity that had flowed into the camp. Vladimir now estimated that of the forty or so thousand war prisoners that had been captured at Vyazma there remained less than a fourth. *The sons of bitches did a good job in eliminating us. Now they won't have as many to feed.* The officer began to speak,"I am Major Kimmer. Are there any political officers or officers in the group?"

Vladimir's blood drained from his face. *Are they after officers again?* He remembered, once again, Colonel Markov's words about not letting the Germans know that he was an officer.

"I said, are there any political officers or other officers among you? Because if there are we want to treat you with the respect that you deserve, assign you to better accommodations and provide the same meals that we receive."

"Who are they kidding?" a fellow prisoner whispered to anyone in earshot. "Their 'respect' will be a bullet to the head."

Unexpectedly, three men in the front row stepped forward and announced that they, indeed, were officers.

"Well, good for you," Kimmer said. "Sergeant Klumpf, take these men to the officer's mess hall and give these men a full meal immediately." With that, the men marched away.

"What do they think we are, stupid?" another prisoner said under his breath. "Those men are their agents."

Vladimir never thought that the Germans would use spies among the captives. It made sense to him. He stood still, almost holding his breath.

"Don't be afraid," Kimmer continued. "There must be more of you in this crowd. Come forward now!" It was obvious that Kimmer was losing his patience, but no one else stepped forward. "I'll give you one more chance. If you do not identify yourselves as officers, you will be treated like the others, even if you come forward later."

Kimmer waited a few minutes staring at the captives. With no response, he turned in a huff, and walked back to the brick building. Vladimir felt that he had escaped the bullet, at least for now. His breathing returned to normal. But his legs, particularly his left leg, were in severe pain. He continuously moved his ankle from side to side to give his leg some relief. He needed to sit down, or at least take a few steps. But he did not dare. The third officer remained silent, but made a waving motion with his hand to the Sergeant. The Sergeant gave the order to the guards, and the prisoners were ordered to follow the guards, row by row, beginning with the back rows, toward the barracks.

The shabby, rickety barrack No. 37 with its crumbling stone foundation became Vladimir's new surroundings. It was located in the fourth row of a long string of such barracks. The rough wooden plank floor was worn down by many years of use. In the middle of the long rectangular room a black potbelly stove immediately caught Vladimir's eye. Adjacent was a wooden box, filled with evenly cut small tree branches. A two-liter dented metal bucket filled with water stood next to the heater. Atop was an equally dented large teapot with a missing lid. A rusty brown exhaust pipe that protruded from the stove to the pitched wooden ceiling seemed to divide the space. The inner wall and the outer wall were one and the same, supported by roughly sawn lumber. Rows of three-tiered wooden bunks lined the sides of the room. A narrow aisle, just wide enough for a person to pass separated the bunks.

Prisoners who had arrived earlier occupied several of the bunks. They stared at the new arrivals, protecting their bunks from the invasion of the newcomers. Vladimir could care less where he bunked as long as he could lie down. From the moment he entered the barrack, he fixated his mind on the bucket. He had his mess kit ready. As he walked by he scooped some water into it. Other prisoners followed his lead. Vladimir continued toward an empty bunk on the first tier.

"Hey you!" a captive behind him yelled out. "I want that bunk. I had my eyes on it since I walked in. Go up higher."

"That's all right with me," Vladimir said. "I'd rather not be peed on from above."

"What do you mean peed on? No one had better pee on me. I'll kill him."

Vladimir lips broke into a slight smile as he climbed the crude ladder all the way to the third tier. *I'll have more privacy on top than the bunk in the middle.* Besides, he remembered from his physics classes that heat rises to the top and the cold air stays at the bottom. Also, with the pitched roof he had more space than the first or second bunk, he figured.

None of the bunks had mattresses or pillows. They would rest on wooden slats. Even so, Vladimir was elated. He finally had a roof over his head and the boards were far better than sleeping in the snow on the cold hard ground. *It's all relative,* he muttered to himself. He drank the water in his bowl, slacking his thirst once again. He laid down on his stomach and placing his arm under his right cheek, fell asleep.

A shrill whistle wakened the prisoners. The fact that the sun had not yet risen did not deter the sergeant from rousing the captives out of their bunks and ordering them to proceed outside. As Vladimir began descending from his bunk, a person in the lower bunk next to his row looked familiar. *It can't be? But it is, its Sergey Ivanov.* Vladimir rubbed his eyes to make sure he was not mistaken. Sergey looked straight at him with a blank stare. *He doesn't recognize me. Of course he wouldn't with this beard and grime.* Vladimir had not bathed or shaved since his capture, almost three weeks before.

"Sergey Ivanov, is that you?"

Sergey focused on Vladimir. "Yes, who are you? How do you know my name?"

"Sergey, it's me, Vladimir."

Vladimir could see Sergey's eyes open wide in astonishment. A smile broke through his sullen face.

"Everyone shut up and keep moving!" The guard shouted to the captives.

Vladimir held back, allowing time for Sergey to walk around the bunk. Vladimir and Sergey hugged each other and followed the others outside into the narrow courtyard between the barracks.

"Everyone line up in two rows," the guard yelled out.

Vladimir stood in the second row, next to Ivanov. The sergeant stood in front facing the captives, while a guard walked past each prisoner and shouted out a number. Vladimir's number was 58. The same corporal who interpreted the day before, ran up to the Sergeant who then proceeded to give instructions.

"Remember where you are today. See who is on both sides of you. You must be in the same position every day as long as you are breathing. The latrine is at the end of this row of barracks. Now follow the guard to the kitchen. That is all. Dismissed! Heil Hitler."

"What about new clothes or washing our clothes," one of the captives yelled out.

"That's not my concern," the Sergeant answered. "Now move out, or you'll get no breakfast."

The captive began to say something else, when some of the other prisoners yelled at him to keep his mouth shut.

Vladimir walked on with the others, Ivanov behind him. He was so glad to see his old friend and he was especially elated that he would be fed.

CHAPTER 23

Slava watched from behind a curtain as Major Raake and Lieutenant Hoffman exited the car. They stood by the car, gazing intently at the house. Even though she knew them, the sight of the two German officers left a pit in her stomach. *What are they doing here at our house,* she wondered. Her mother's rising panic compounded Slava's anxiety.

"They're going to take us away, I tell you," Suzanna wailed. "Vladislav, what shall we do?"

"Calm down," Vladislav said. "Let's find out what they want. Suzanna, you have to control yourself. Here, give me your hand."

"Hand? Can't you see we have to do something? But, dear Jesus, Blessed Virgin Mary, protect us! They're going to take us away. Slava, it didn't do any good for you to translate for those bastards."

"Mama, I had no choice. Now, settle down!" Slava said with irritation and fear in her voice. "It can't be what you think it is. Raake, himself, would not be here to haul us off to the labor camps. He would have sent soldiers in a truck. Mama, what happened to you? You used to be tough, now you're driving yourself crazy and us crazy as well. Oh, oh. They're on the steps now. I better get the door."

With those words, Suzanna appeared to calm down. But Slava could hear Suzanna's deep breathing as she opened the door.

"Major Raake and Lieutenant Hoffman. We're surprised to see you."

"Good day," Raake said, brushing off the snow from his hat. He had a small bag under his arm. "May we come in?"

"Yes, come in."

Both men entered the room, smiled and nodded a greeting to Suzanna and Vladislav.

"I would like you to meet my parents, Vladislav and Suzanna Szpakowski."

"Very pleased to meet you," Raake said, bowing his head and clicking the heels of his highly polished black leather knee-high boots.

Slava's parents barely nodded back. Vladislav managed a fake smile, but Suzanna just stood there terrified.

"We've met already," Hoffman said, unbuttoning his coat. "You have a nice home. It reminds me of my home in Rudesheim."

"I don't know where that is," Slava said.

"It's a medieval town in the romantic Lorelei Valley on the Rhine River. To this date, it is still surrounded by an ancient wall that was used for fortification. Actually, I live about 20 kilometers from Rudesheim, very close to the famous Lorelei Rock. It's a magnificent site. The rock rises up vertically 132 meters above the water. At that point the river narrows and legend has it that the siren named Lorelei bewitched the sailors and when they looked up at the rock, their boats crashed and sank."

Slava could not understand why Hoffman appeared so talkative. He was overly friendly and, more importantly, why? Hoffman rarely spoke to her before. He had been cordial, but very formal. Now, he acted as though they were old friends. Raake placed the bag on a table and both men hung up their coats and hats on the coat tree that stood next to the door.

Slava did not know what to do next. Everyone stood around awkwardly for what felt like a very long minute. Finally, she asked the officers to sit down. She wondered if she should offer tea to them, even though the family's supply of tea was almost gone. Suzanna was particularly careful with it. She had rationed their tealeaves since the occupation. On many days they drank plain, boiled water instead of tea.

Raake picked up the paper bag he brought and with a wide grin on his face, gave it to Suzanna. She appeared startled by his action.

"Here, Frau Szpakowska," Raake said. "I know that times are rough for the civilians in Vitebsk. But believe me times will get better. In the meantime, we brought you a little something from our commissary."

Slava translated what Raake said.

"Tell him," Vladislav said, throwing a dirty look at the officers, "Times will get better once they leave our land."

Slava's breath froze. They must have understood her father—not in words, but in body language. *Oh my God! My father should keep his mouth shut.*

"Papa, please don't cause any trouble. Now smile at them and make them feel comfortable. These are not people you can discuss your politics with. They can hang you on the spot. Now give them a smile and pretend that they are welcome. We must hide our feelings. You too, Mama."

"Is there a problem," Raake said with annoyance. "I don't understand."

"Oh, my parents are very proud, and don't want to accept a gift that they can't repay."

"Oh, we certainly do not expect anything in return."

While Slava and Raake talked, Suzanna unwrapped the package. As she pulled out the contents, a beaming smile overtook her long frown.

"Look, Vladislav and Slavochka. Look at this. We have a kilogram of butter. Look at these two pieces of cheese, a box of tea and this loaf of bread. Slava thank them for the food and ask them to stay for tea."

When Vladislav saw the food, his smile became more genuine, but Slava could see he was agitated and certainly unhappy that the Germans were in his house. He managed to say "thank you," as he walked out of the house through the kitchen door muttering quietly that, "A little food cannot buy our loyalty."

"Your father must feel uncomfortable with us here," Hoffman said.

Victor Moss

Slava did not know what to say. Thoughts fleeted through her head. *What can I say to save the moment? I can't tell them that they are the enemy. They have invaded our homeland, and caused Volodya to be removed from us. Their occupation has caused indescribable misery. But Raake and even Hoffman seem like decent people. All the other Germans in the office are respectful. They don't want to be here any more than we want them here. And they did bring us that food. I must be tactful.*

"No, he's just upset today. It's nothing personal. He likes to work in the barn. He has been spending much time there since his retirement. Think nothing of it. Your gift is very appreciated. Food is so hard to come by."

"We sneaked it out," Hoffman laughed nervously.

Raake gave him a stern look as though to say, shut up, you idiot.

"Well, so there is the piano I heard about," Raake said. "May I?"

"Of course," Slava said.

Raake sat down and started to play a tune that Slava had not heard before. She decided that small talk should be avoided and did not ask what the tune was called.

"I really missed the sound of the piano," Raake said. "Music has always been my love. Now Vladislava, won't you play something for us."

I knew that would be next. Where's mama with the tea. They'll have me playing the piano all night, Slava thought.

Slava sat down and played the *Turkish March* by Mozart.

"Bravo, bravo," both Raake and Hoffman called with approval.

"It is so wonderful to hear the music," Raake said. "You play well, I could listen to you all night."

Slava tensed up. *Oh, no, I won't play the piano all night. We have to give them tea and get them out of here.*

"Please excuse me. I'll see if my mother needs some help with the tea."

As she rose from the piano bench to go to the kitchen, both men immediately stood up. *Their gentlemanly behavior makes me nervous,* she thought. At that moment, Suzanna entered the dining room carrying a teapot. She had already set the table with plates, dinnerware, cups and saucers. In the center of the table, she laid out slices of bread, a stick of butter and thin slices of cheese.

"Tell them to come to the table," Suzanna whispered to Slava.

"Ask papa to come in and join us."

"No, he won't sit at the table with them. Actually, neither should I, or you for that matter."

"I don't have a choice. They are dangerous men to upset."

Slava walked up to the Germans and invited them to the table.

The men stood and unsnapped their holsters. They looked around the room briefly and put their weapons on a table in the covered veranda. Slava was surprised to see them without their weapons. *They must feel pretty cozy here,* she thought. They followed Slava into the dining room and sat at the table. Slava offered them tea with the food that they had brought. They drank the

200

Beware the Wolves

tea with pleasure, but ate very little food. *Are they simply not hungry, or are they trying to leave as much of the food for us? They are not bad people. Its too bad that they are our enemy.*

"Please, help yourselves to more cheese. This cheese you brought is delicious."

"Its from France," Hoffman said. "The bread and butter are from Germany. Do you think it tastes different from your bread, Mrs. Szpakowska?"

Suzanna was startled to be addressed. She just put a piece of buttered bread in her mouth and felt awkward. She understood her name and understood the word "brot" for bread, but did not understand the gist of the question.

"Slava, what did he ask?"

"He asked if our bread tastes different from German bread?"

Suzanna tried to smile, but it was strained.

"I think German bread is delicious. Actually it is similar to our Byelorussian bread. I really can't tell a big difference. Maybe it's my imagination, but maybe the rye tastes a little differently."

The strained conversation continued. Slava steered clear of anything dealing with the occupation or the military. It also soon became obvious to her that the officers shied away from any unpleasantness. The topics were of music and literature. Raake explained that he was from Dresden, along the Elba River in eastern Germany. With great pleasure, he described the magnificent buildings, particularly the opera house a few meters from the Elba. Suzanna sat with them, determined not to leave Slava alone with the uninvited guests. Vladislav did not come into the house while the Germans were there. Slava was somewhat taken aback by her father's behavior. In the past he had always been mellow and let bygones be bygones. But she also understood her father. This was more than a dispute between neighbors. The people in his house were the invaders and no matter what was said or what happened, they had the upper hand. *Should I be like my father and ask them to leave? I can't do that. If we are not cordial to them, we could all be in big trouble. Although they seem nice, who knows what's underneath their skin and what they would do? Maybe it's all an act. But why would they act? They can get anything they want as occupiers.*

"Vladislava, you seem to be deep in thought," Raake said. "What is on your mind?"

"Oh nothing at all. I must be tired."

"Well, we do need to go and let you rest," Raake continued. "But before we leave, please play one more piece for us on the piano. Do you know any Brahms?"

Slava went to the piano bench and opened the seat that contained music of various compositions. She shuffled through the contents until she found the book containing works of Johannes Brahms. She opened to the page of Sonata No. 2 and played it for the officers.

"Bravo, bravo," once again the officers applauded. "That was absolutely wonderful."

201

Victor Moss

"Well, with that," Raake said. "We have to leave. We will carry that melody with us to our quarters. Thank you, Mrs. Szpakowska, and thank you, Vladislava, for your hospitality. We had a splendid evening."

"Yes, thank you," Hoffman said. "Next time we'll bring some cognac."

Next time, they'll bring cognac! They plan to come back. Oh God! What can we do? Why? What do they want?

After the Germans left, Slava looked at Suzanna and shook her head.

"Mama, they said next time they'll bring cognac. They're going to be back. How can we stop them? They make me nervous. What is papa going to do?"

"He's not going to do anything," Suzanna said. "Neither are you or I, as though we could. Obviously, they like you and that may be useful. They are pleasant and courteous. They are not warriors, but office administrators. I saw their eyes as you played. They are homesick for their families and for their country. They want to talk to someone in their language. I now realize that those two individuals do not mean to do us any harm. I'll talk to your father and explain to him that we should not fear those men. He'll come around. Besides, if they bring food when they come, what's wrong with that? We must survive."

After her mother's words, Slava felt better about the evening. Her father entered the room and asked what happened. While Suzanna filled him in on the details, Slava's slight headache dissipated and she was beginning to wind down from the visit when there was a knock on the front door. The knock startled the three of them.

"Who could that be?" Her father muttered as he looked through the window of the door. "It's our neighbor Isaac. I wonder what he wants?"

Vladislav opened the door, and a short, balding man bustled into the house.

"What the Hell is going on? Those Germans were in your house a long time. What did they want?"

"Those damn Nazis wanted some entertainment, that's all," Vladislav explained. "Slava had to play the piano for them."

"I thought they were taking over your house. I still can't believe that the Germans have allowed us to live in our houses. You know, our houses are the only ones left. I'm old and alone. All they have to do is put a bullet through my head and they have my shelter. Frankly, every time one of the soldiers comes to my door, I think it is the end. But they left me alone until now, at least. All they've done, so far, was ask for water out of my well. They even thank me for the drink. It doesn't mean they won't change their minds and take our homes."

"I know. I'm very nervous around them," Vladislav continued. "But I must admit that the ones we dealt with have been decent to us."

"Well, don't jinx it," Isaac said. "Spit over your shoulder three times."

Both Vladislav and Isaac laughed nervously before the old neighbor shuffled back to his house. It was the first time in months that Slava heard her father's laughter.

Beware the Wolves

♦ ♦ ♦ ♦

Her duties at work continued as normal. Weeks had gone by and neither Raake nor Hoffman made any comments that they had been at Slava's house. Slava was relieved knowing that, if the girls in the office found out, she would have much explaining to do. She was glad to avoid that discussion and the gossip that would follow. Raake had not mentioned that he would come over again. And, she was relieved about that. *Maybe my father's reaction to their visit gave them a big enough hint that they were not welcome,* she rationalized.

One Sunday afternoon in late June 1942, Slava and her parents were startled once again by a knock on the door. Visitors were so infrequent since the occupation that anyone approaching their house could mean trouble. Only Richard had been coming over on occasion to bring them food from the German kitchen where he worked. It had been several weeks since his last visit and Slava hoped that the knock was Richard's. Each time he visited, he stayed a little longer and it was pleasant to talk to him about the "good old days." She felt that Richard, since school days, desired to be more than a friend. She discouraged any romance between them. She made sure he knew of her deep love for Vladimir and that she awaited his return. She hated Richard when he reported to her of the severe battles between the Germans and the Soviet troops. Especially those battles where the Germans were the victors. He told her of rumors that thousands of Soviet soldiers had been killed. The stories so upset her, that she understood the meaning of "killing the messenger" of bad news.

"The fact that you have heard nothing of Vladimir since he left means that he was either killed or is a prisoner of the Germans," Richard had said each time he saw her. "And if he is a prisoner, chances of his survival are poor."

I refuse to believe that Vladimir is dead. He's just trying to make me forget Vladimir, she told herself. And she refused to pay any attention to Richard when he started on that subject.

"Who's at the door now?" Vladislav asked as he looked through the window. "Slava, its Richard. He brought someone else with him. I think its Oleg from your school."

Slava ran up to the door as her father let Richard and Oleg inside the house. She hugged both of the men, kissing each on the cheek.

"Richard, Oleg! It is so good to see you. Oleg, I haven't seen you in months. You have lost a lot of weight, like we all have."

"You didn't have any weight to lose," Oleg replied. "But, as always, you look gorgeous."

"And Richard," Slava said. "Where have you been? You haven't been around lately."

"I haven't been able to get away. But you have always been on my mind."

"Oh, you're so kind. Both of you always know what to say to make me feel better. Come in and have some tea. We have some German tea that is special. Later we can have dinner. Mama was going to boil some potatoes."

Victor Moss

"We'd love to have some tea," Richard said. "But we won't be able to stay for dinner."

"Yes, we have to get back soon," Oleg said. "We came to discuss something very important with you."

Both men suddenly looked grave and Slava's heart skipped a beat.

"Well, maybe it could wait until we have tea," Richard said. "Important discussions are best around the table."

"I'll put a pot of water on the stove," Suzanna said. "It won't take long."

Both Suzanna and Vladislav went to the kitchen while Slava and the men caught up with their lives since last they saw each other. Slava carried on the conversation, but her mind was on the mysterious purpose of their visit. She hoped that the tea would be ready and they could finally discuss what it was they wanted.

In the meantime, Suzanna set the table for tea. The day before she had baked a loaf of bread from what was left of the flour her son, Leonid, had sent them. She sliced up the remaining portion and placed the bread on the table along with a small dish of strawberry preserves she had canned the autumn before.

"We're ready," Suzanna announced. "Please, to the table."

Finally, after a few sips of tea and a few bites of bread and preserves, the conversation turned to the purpose of their visit.

"Slava," Oleg said. "We have some great news for all of us. Through some contacts here in Vitebsk, I was able to get in touch with the medical school in Riga, Latvia. They wrote back that they would accept the three of us in their class in September."

"Isn't it wonderful," Richard said. "The three of us will be together, like the three musketeers. We can finish our degrees."

At first, the news elated Slava. She now had the opportunity to complete her medical education. Then she realized that it would be impossible for her to leave for Latvia. Besides, she had so many questions.

"First of all, what do you mean the three of us? How would they even know about me?"

"Well, we took the liberty of submitting your name along with your transcripts," Richard said.

"How could you possibly get my transcripts? The school had been shut down since the occupation."

"Oleg knew someone that got them for us. Let's leave it at that, all right?"

"Why do you look so upset?" Oleg said. "We were doing you a favor."

"I would think you would ask me first what I thought about it."

"No time," Richard said. "We had to act fast."

"Even if I could leave here," Slava said. "How would we get to Riga?"

"Riga is also occupied by the Germans," Oleg said. "I can get permission to leave Vitebsk and move to Riga. That's no problem as long as the travel is within occupied areas."

Beware the Wolves

"Well it was good of you to think of me. I am very touched. I would love to finish my schooling and get that degree. It's a shame that I'm so close to it, yet it seems out of reach. But I can't leave."

"What do you mean, you can't leave. Is it because of your parents?" Richard asked. "Because if it is, you can take them with you."

"No, it isn't because of my parents, although it's certainly a big consideration. You know the reason. I need to wait for Vladimir. When he comes looking for me, and I'm not here, we may never see each other again."

"Slava, you have to be realistic," Richard said. "I hate to be so blunt, but you may be waiting for a dead man."

"No! Don't say that. Don't even suggest it. I know that somehow I'll see him again. I won't give up that notion."

"Richard is right, Slavochka. The chances that he has survived are slim to none. If he has not been killed on a battlefield, or bombed out in a hospital somewhere, he must be a prisoner under the Germans. His chances of survival will be nil. We know how the Nazis treat the Jews and partisans. Do you think they treat prisoners of war any better?"

'I don't care what you say. I'm staying here to await my husband's return."

"You're making a big mistake, Slava," Richard said. "One more year or so, and you'll get your degree. We've set everything up for you. All you need to do is start to attend classes. You have a chance to leave Vitebsk. It is very dangerous here and only will get worse. The Germans battle the partisans continuously. They suspect all Byelorussians to be in cahoots with the partisans and eventually they'll get to your family. And think about it, what would happen if the Soviets retake Vitebsk? They'll prosecute or even execute anyone who remained behind in the occupation area and use the excuse that we were German sympathizers, even though we're not."

"I know everything you say is probably right. I dream of the day when I finally receive my degree. But I can't leave. Vladimir will look for me in Vitebsk, and in Vitebsk I must stay. I'm sorry, Richard and Oleg. Go to Latvia and be successful. I know you will. With much regret, I can't join you."

"You're making the mistake of your life, Slava," Oleg said.

Slava trembled as she watched the men leave. Tears filled her eyes. *Oh God, why is life so difficult?* She wanted so badly to go to Latvia and finish her schooling. She watched her opportunity walk away. Her parents joined her. Suzanna hugged her child and held her tight.

"We heard everything from the kitchen," Vladislav said. "Are you sure you're not making a mistake? We know how important it was for you to finish school. You dreamed of being a doctor since you were a little girl. It's been over a year since Vladimir left. I know you hate to hear this, but he may never come back. You have to think of what's best for you. We have relatives in Latvia who, under the circumstances, will take us in."

Victor Moss

"Papa, stop! I can't leave Vitebsk as long as there is a chance I'll see my Volodya. My dream will have to wait."

◆ ◆ ◆ ◆

The following Sunday afternoon, Slava heard a vehicle approach. She looked out and saw two men in an officer's car. Since the top was down, she was able to recognize Raake and Hoffman. They stopped their vehicle and approached the house, Hoffman carried a rather large package.

"Mama, Papa! We have company. The German officers are here again."

"Oh, Saint Barbara, what do they want now?" Suzanna rushed up to the window to peek at the men as they stood on the steps.

Vladislav opened the door even before they had a chance to knock and motioned for them to come in. Slava saw the veins on her father's forehead protrude. She knew what it cost her father to invite the enemy inside.

"Hello, once again, Mr. and Mrs. Szpakowski," Raake said. "And hello to you, Vladislava. I hope we're not disturbing you too much. But we'd like to visit for a few minutes."

"Lieutenant, please give our gift to the mistress of the house."

Once again, as in the previous visit, Suzanna opened the package and Slava watched her eyes light up as she unwrapped two loaves of bread, half kilogram of cheese, two sticks of butter, and half a stick of hard salami. Slava's mouth watered from the sight of the sausage and cheese. The cheese the men brought before had long since been eaten. Her diet consisted mainly of potatoes, eggs, canned vegetables and fruits and bread baked by her mother. Because of the shortage of salt and sugar, the bread tasted bland. But it was edible. Fortunately, the truck garden produced fresh vegetables and the family's supply of smoked meat, if rationed once a week, could last for several more months. But once the meat was gone, it would not be replenished because their pigs and most of the chickens had been stolen. The family suspected a group of partisans that frequently sneaked into town from their hideouts in the forests and took whatever food they could find. The family lived in fear that the partisans would, one night, break in and kill them.

"Slavochka, ask the officers to stay for tea," Suzanna said. "Vladislav, come and help me. You can slice the cheese and bread."

"We would be very pleased to have tea," Raake said as the two officers removed the holsters containing their pistols and placed them on the table next to the door.

"But first, would you play something on the piano. We miss the wonderful sound of beautifully performed music by an accomplished virtuoso."

"You are so kind," Slava blushed. "I only wish that I could play as you think. You must have forgotten how I play."

"Not at all," Raake said. "I can't put out of my mind the wonderful evening we had experienced when you played for us. You are selling yourself short. Please play a classical piece for us. Music is food for the soul, you know."

Beware the Wolves

Raake gently took her hand, held it tightly and escorted her to the piano.

"Can you play some Beethoven, Vladislava?"

Slava's heart began to beat rapidly. *What's he doing, holding my hand? He better not have anything in mind. It must be just a friendly gesture.* Sometimes Raake's polished manners and the many compliments that he bestowed on her made it difficult for Slava to regard him as a foe. Even though he was dressed in the uniform of the oppressor, she began to see him just as an individual caught up in a situation in which he did not want to be. His occasional flattery made Slava again feel appreciated as a young, pretty woman. It was an escape from the drab, humdrum existence of the occupation. Slava sat down and played several Beethoven selections before her mother announced that the tea was ready. Suzanna also served thin slices of salami and cheese with the bread and butter.

This time, Vladislav joined the group for tea. He sat quietly and did not participate in the conversation. Slava knew it was not the language barrier. She could see that he was tense. Suzanna was more involved and, through Slava's interpreting, she interacted somewhat with the visitors. After two cups of tea, Hoffman reached into his breast pocket and pulled out a flask.

"Cognac," he said. "Perhaps, Mrs. Spakowska, you could bring us each a glass?"

Slava and her father refused the alcohol. Her mother drank her glass. The Germans continued drinking, one shot after another, until the flask was empty. Slava could see that they were feeling the effects of the alcohol. Their laughter became more frequent and boisterous. Their jokes became more risqué. The speech was not as precise. One joke in particular made her blush. She could see the concern on her parents' faces. *The cognac is gone, and they seem all right—maybe just a little high.*

Out of the corner of her eye, Slava thought she saw a bearded face look into the side window of the veranda. She stiffened and gazed intently at the window, but did not see anything. *I must be imagining things,* she thought. But the more she thought about it, she became convinced that she had, in fact, seen someone look into the house. She excused herself from the table to go into the veranda and look out. As she stood up, both officers stood as well.

"I'll be right back. I need to check on something."

"Is there anything wrong?" Hoffman asked, a lopsided grin, affected by the cognac, splitting his face.

"No, no, not at all. Please sit down. Here, have some more sausage."

The officers sat down and dug into the sausage and cheese. Slava looked out the window but saw no one. The darkened street was quiet. Only the German car stood alone on the street in front of her house.

As Slava returned to the dining room, her mother was rising to fill up the teapot with more hot water.

"Mama, since I'm up, let me do that for you."

Slava took the teapot and walked into the kitchen. She just began to pour the boiling water from the kettle into the porcelain teapot when she heard a noise on the back porch. She set the pot down and flung open the door. She just opened her mouth to scream out when a man grabbed her, placing one hand behind her head and the other hand over her mouth. Slava trembled as she tried to push the filthy and smelly hand away. The man applied even more pressure causing his index finger to slide underneath her nose cutting off her oxygen. Slava jerked her head back and forth trying to free herself from the hold.

"Now shut up. I'm not here to hurt you. I actually have helped you all these months. Now will you keep quiet if I let go? If you don't, we're all in trouble."

Slava nodded her head in the affirmative. The man let go. Slava took several deep breaths. He was thin and scraggly. A dirty tan shirt and grimy dark blue pants loosely covered his body. The blue eyes staring at her appeared sunken into their sockets. A long pointed nose did not seem to fit his face. Through the slightly opened mouth, his teeth emerged, brown and crooked. She continued to shake, taking deep, sporadic breaths. *Oh God! I have to get away from this madman. If I cry out, they'll save me.* Slava stared into his eyes, and somehow, even under these frightening conditions, she saw something in his eyes that calmed her. Her intuition guided her that he was not there to harm her. She thought of what he said, "I actually have helped you." *What did he mean by that?*

"Now, keep quiet," he whispered.

"Who are you? Slava whispered back. "What do you want?"

"They call me Igor. I knew your husband, Captain Moskalkov. I used to be his medic."

Goose pimples covered Slava's arms. Blood rushed to her head.

"You knew my husband? Is he dead?"

"I don't know for sure. Unfortunately, I assume so. Not many have survived. I'm sorry, miss."

Slava stood still. She felt strength drain from her body. Her breathing strained.

"Where did you last see him?"

"He was on his way to the trenches outside of Smolensk."

"How long ago?"

"Oh, that was in July last year."

"That was a year ago. Didn't you go with him into the trenches."

"Well, no. I'm no fool. I could see that we stood no chance with the German forces against us and I chose to leave."

"You're a deserter, then."

"Call it what you want, miss, but I'm a survivor."

Slava looked at him, repulsed. *He's a coward, a stinking no good for nothing coward that should be shot.*

"So you really don't know whether my husband is alive or not. For all you know, he could still be alive, right?"

"Well, yes, but sorry, I doubt it."

Beware the Wolves

"How did you know who I was?"

"Wasn't hard to find you. The captain told me you were from Vitebsk and some of the partisans from here knew of you and your family. You know there are two types of partisan groups. There are those that fight the damn Nazis and those that mostly steal. For many months I was with the group that stole. They had your house targeted for anything they could carry away. But I liked your husband. He was decent to me. So I talked them out of stealing from you or harming your family. Now our group wants vengeance against the Germans for the brutal torture. We are all fighters now. We fight the bastards and attack and disrupt their rear. I'm proud of the work we're doing. If we can keep the Germans from getting their supplies through, we're helping our boys on the front lines."

This confrontation with Igor and the revelation that their house was a partisan target left her speechless for a moment. Her mouth hung open.

"I suppose a big thank you is in order. But what do you want?"

"Slava! Are you all right? Where are you? We're waiting for more hot water." Slava heard her mother's voice behind the closed door of the back porch.

"Wait here, Igor. I must answer my mother."

Slava opened the door, stepped back into the kitchen.

"I'll be right there, mama. Just a minute."

She stepped back onto the porch and again shut the door.

"Well, Igor, what are you doing here?"

"I want those German pistols sitting on your table."

"Are you insane? No! You can't be serious?"

"Look, unlock the front door. Then somehow divert the scum. I'll grab those pistols and use them to shoot the sons of bitches, all right?"

"No, you'll get us in trouble. You kill them in this house, you'll be long gone, and my parents and I will be tortured and hung. Are you out of your mind?"

Igor stood, deep in thought. Slava's mind spun. *He can't be serious. Surely, he can't expect me to agree to such a mad scheme. We'll be killed. I have to get him out of here immediately.*

"Igor, you can't do that. Don't you understand? You'll kill us as well."

"Ah hell, out of respect for your husband, I'll let those sons of bitches live, if that's what you want. But do you realize what a prize it would be to kill two German officers. I could brag about it for months. Oh well, I'll find another opportunity later. At least unlock the front door so that I can take their weapons."

"No! I can't do that either. They'll arrest us on the spot once they discover the door open and the pistols missing. No, Igor, I appreciate everything you have done to help us, but please go before they discover you're here. Now, please, leave."

"Give me something to eat, enough for a few days?"

"That's fine. I'll be glad to do so. I have to get back to them before they come here looking for me. Wait here and I'll see what I can do."

Slava filled the teapot and returned. The officers were deep in song. She sat down for a minute and kept them company. Again she excused herself to return to the kitchen. As she stood up, so did the officers. She paid no attention to them and quickly walked back to the kitchen and into the storeroom. She looked around. *What can I give him, what can I give him?* She grabbed a loaf of her mother's bread, a jar of pickled beets, and cut off a piece of smoked bacon. She had nothing to wrap them in so she took the items, returned to the porch, shut the door and handed the provisions to Igor.

"I'm sorry that I have no more to give you. We're worried that we'll be out of food ourselves."

Igor smiled, stuffed the jar into his pocket and held the bread and the bacon in his hands.

"Thanks. Do you have any cigarettes I could have?"

"No, Igor. Go."

"All right, then. But once I leave, I'm not sure I can protect you or your house from partisans."

Her head pounded as she watched Igor run down the hill into the orchard. She locked the back door and leaned against it exhaling deeply. *Vladimir, you better be alive.*

CHAPTER 24

Once again the morning meal was that foul tasting thin soup the captives called *balanda*. Vladimir did not give a damn about the taste. The hot liquid pouring down his gullet was heaven. And, if he could sink his teeth into an occasional cabbage leaf or some undistinguishable chunk of vegetable, it was an added bonus.

"We get that shit twice a day, day in and day out," Ivanov said as the men marched back to their barracks. "They promised us a loaf of bread once per week, but rarely do we get it. I don't know how much longer I'm going to last. Vladimir, I'm starving to death. I wish I had died in Yelna back in July. It sure would have saved me a lot of misery."

Vladimir did not say a word. Sergey Ivanov was a walking skeleton, but then so were all of the captives. Vladimir's lingering hope of being fed a nourishing meal faded as he listened to Ivanov and looked around at the prisoners that had arrived before him.

"How long have you been here?"

"Since August."

Ivanov pulled out a pack of cigarettes and a small box of matches. He lit a cigarette with one of the matches, took a deep drag and exhaled with a cough.

"Those are German cigarettes, how did you get them?"

"They don't give us food worth a damn, but at least, they give us these," Ivanov said pointing to his smoke.

"Sergey, you'll have to tell me what happened to Savitski."

"Ah, good old Captain Savitski. As the Germans approached Yelna, we were setting up our artillery battery outside of the garrison, you know the place we said our goodbyes before you went to Vyazma."

Ivanov took another deep drag on the cigarette and watched as a cloud of smoke drifted toward the sky.

"Well, what happened?"

Ivanov coughed. One cough led to another, then another. His hacking continued until his face turned red. Vladimir readied to help him when the coughing fit stopped. Ivanov took a quick ragged breath.

"Are you all right now?"

"Yes, I've had this nasty cough for days. Seems to be getting worse."

"You should give up those cigarettes."

"What else can I do around here? Look around you. Everyone smokes. Besides, it calms my nerves. Just watch, before long, you'll be smoking."

"Everyone line up according to the numbers assigned to you this morning," The guard yelled at the captives as they approached their barracks.

After roll call, the men were ordered inside. There was nowhere to go but back to the bunk. Vladimir scooped up water from the bucket with his mess kit and climbed up to the third level to his bunk with great difficulty. He felt weak. Ivanov laid in the middle bunk, one row over.

"So Sergey," Vladimir yelled down to him. "What happened to Savitski?"

"He was behind an artillery piece that took a direct hit from a low flying Stucka. I watched as his guts exploded and splattered onto the howitzer."

"Where were you at the time?"

"We were setting up another cannon, unhooking it from the horses, when the plane flew straight for us. We fell to the ground. The Stucka could have hit us, but instead it took aim directly for Savitski and the men around him. You know, it's all fate. Why did Savitski take a direct hit and not me? Why does one person survive, when another just a few meters away doesn't? That has always been a mystery to me."

"I don't know. You see it every day, don't you? There must be a divine scheme for all of us. But why God allows us to suffer so much baffles me. It's as if our planet is hell. But then, when I'm with my dear heart, Slava, I am in heaven. How did you get captured?" Vladimir asked.

"The Germans moved their tanks and infantry so rapidly that in no time at all, they had Yelna surrounded. We used up our last shells. Their bombardment was endless. To escape the shelling, my men and I ran for the nearest ditch and hunkered down. We had no rifles to defend ourselves. We laid glued to the ground. Clods of dirt covered me. Suddenly the melee stopped. I looked up and saw the enemy running toward us. They must have seen me peering out of the ditch because they shot at us and before we knew it, they were on top of us with their rifles pointed at us. I was positive that I'd be shot right there in the ditch. I mean, we all have heard rumors that the stinking Nazis shot and killed soldiers cowering in the trenches. It is easier than taking prisoners. We quickly raised our arms to surrender. But to my surprise, they actually took us as prisoners. And here I am today, suffering a slow death. I wish they had shot me. What about you, Volodya? How were you captured? By the way, on the way here, they held us for several wretched days outside of your home town, Vitebsk."

Vladimir suddenly perked up with the mention of Vitebsk. His heart raced

"You were in Vitebsk? How did it look?"

"Devastated. Fire gutted most of the structures. The railroad station was half destroyed. The streets were in ruins."

Ivanov's words sent icy shivers down Vladimir's back.

"Did you see any of the inhabitants?"

"No, not really—maybe a few old people sobbing as they watched us led through town. A couple of women threw a few vegetables at us. Some of the women held up pictures of their sons or husbands in case someone had seen them. Actually, except for the Germans, the city looked devoid of life."

Beware the Wolves

"So where did they take you?"

"It was an army base right outside of Vitebsk."

"Oh, I know exactly where it is," Vladimir said.

"Well, you wouldn't recognize it now. It's surrounded by several rows of barbed wire, guards with dogs everywhere, including guards on towers with machine guns. It was the first place that we were fed something. It's the same crappy mixture they call soup that we get here. But they also gave us some bread."

Vladimir did not say a word. His thoughts at the moment were of Slava. *Could she still be in Vitebsk? Did she survive the devastation that Ivanov described? What about my mother and sisters?*

"Volodya, so how did you get captured and where did they take you?"

Vladimir related to him the story of his capture and the miserable journey to Baranovichi.

"You know," another captive listening to their conversation began to speak. "We are now men without a country through no fault of our own."

"What do you mean?" Vladimir asked.

"We're obviously not Fritzes. And, we can't return home. At our great father Stalin's whim, we are considered traitors for being captured. If we go back we are likely to be shot. Our country has abandoned us." The captive spit on the floor.

"When did Stalin come up with that insanity?" Ivanov asked. "But then, that's typical of Stalin."

"Hey, didn't you listen to the sons-of-bitches, also known as political commissars? What's the first thing they drilled into our heads?"

"What, to be a good communist? So?" Ivanov asked.

"No, we were told over and over that we have to fight to our deaths. They didn't want us to surrender. We had to die for our motherland. Surrender was absolutely forbidden. And if we were captured, we would be executed. Actually, it's all part of Stalin's paranoia. He distrusts anyone that has had contact with any foreigners. And now that we are in German hands, he thinks we can't be trusted."

"Well, I never heard it put quite that way," Ivanov responded angrily.

"That's probably because you were captured early in the war."

"I can't believe what you're saying," another captive lying in a bunk next to Ivanov said. "You're telling fairytales, that's horseshit. That's insane."

"I wish it was horseshit," the first captive continued. "We can't go back. They have even threatened that our wives will be sent to gulags in Siberia."

"Why?" yet another captive from a bunk two rows over asked.

"Because they're married to a prisoner of war."

Vladimir's body stiffened as he listened to the conversation. He had not thought much about his status with his government. He just assumed that captured soldiers were common in any war. *How can Stalin penalize us for following the human instinct for survival? Is there really no way back? What*

213

about Slavochka? A tremor went through him. His sole hope was to survive and go home. *I know no other life. My wife, my family all wait for me.*

"Well you have to survive first to worry about it," yet another captive said. "No one is getting out of this hellhole alive."

Vladimir laid back in his bunk and closed his eyes. He was tense. The implication that Soviet prisoners were traitors was beyond belief. The enormity of the suffering the captives had undergone and would yet undergo, only to be finished off by their own government, was too much for him to comprehend at the moment. A tight band of pressure encircled his head. *Well, no matter what the consequences, I'm going to see Slavochka one way or another. I'll find her and my family,* he decided with determination as he laid wide awake in his bunk. Then his mind swung to another concern.

"Sergey, have you gone through what the Commandant called 'interrogation'?"

"Yes, I'll tell you about it later."

Vladimir understood. Ivanov did not want to discuss the interrogation or mention that he was an officer. There were too many ears eager to listen and maybe to pass on the information.

◆ ◆ ◆ ◆

The *balanda* ladled out for the evening meal did not surprise Vladimir. He expected it. What did surprise him was that the captives were allowed to stand around for a few minutes outside the barracks. The weather was bitterly cold, but Vladimir took pleasure in breathing the crisp air into his lungs. It was a respite from the putrid atmosphere of the barracks. The meals did not deviate from one day to the next. On the fifth day, the soup seemed to have a few more vegetables. Vladimir was sure he swallowed a small piece of potato. On the sixth day, dinner was a tiny portion of watered down oatmeal mush.

Vladimir realized that the portions and the quality of food were not enough to sustain life. Some of the captives were so weak from starvation that they would not last much longer. Another concern to Vladimir was the high incidence of dysentery and the deaths from dehydration. Everyone was infested with lice. The itching drove several berserk. Vladimir felt the bites. He gritted his teeth and knew he would have to live with it. When he scratched his head, the itching became more intense, so he tried to avoid touching his scalp. *The parasites get more to eat than I do,* he joked to himself. Somehow, that thought alleviated his discomfort. Vladimir was deeply concerned that he and his fellow captives would contract Typhus Fever, a disease spread by lice. He knew that once the disease spread, with no medicines, the death toll would quickly escalate.

After seven days, the captives were given more time in the yard. Vladimir attempted to perform some feeble exercises such as stretching or running a few steps in place. But with the severe frigid temperatures and the lack of calories

Beware the Wolves

in his body, he was quickly fatigued. While still in the yard, Vladimir saw two guards approach the barracks. They held bags in their hand and had rifles slung over their shoulders. They ordered the men to stand as if for roll call. Shivering, they lined up and stood in place. One of the guards walked past the line of the prisoners and handed out packs of cigarettes. Vladimir did not smoke, yet he gladly grabbed the cigarettes. He saw how the craving for a cigarette became more crucial than food to some men. When the packs were distributed, the other guard took out a loaf of bread and dangled it in the air taunting the prisoners. With a cruel smile, he tore off a chunk of bread and threw it up in the air toward the captives. The captives lunged at the piece of bread. Each pushed the other away at the chance to grab the chunk. The guards stood laughing, greatly enjoying the "show" in front of them.

"Look at the pigs, fighting over a scrap of food," one of the guards shouted. "Karl, throw them another piece."

This game went on for several minutes while three loaves were thrown to the men like pieces of bread to ducks in a lake. Vladimir attempted to snatch a piece of bread. He was shoved aside on the third attempt and fell to the ground. But while on the ground, he saw a piece lying close to him. He quickly grabbed it and thrust it into his mouth. He thought of getting up and trying to grab another piece, but decided against it after he saw how many of his comrades laid limp on the ground.

At dinner, Vladimir was pleasantly surprised to receive a small loaf of bread with the watered down soup. This time, he did not finish off the entire loaf, remembering to eat a little and to save the rest. After their meal, the prisoners were allowed to stay outside the barracks for a few minutes. Vladimir looked for the opportunity to talk one-on-one with Ivanov about the interrogation that Vladimir had yet to face. Finally, they found themselves standing next to the barracks. There was no one else around.

"Sergey, now tell me, what's your experience with the interrogation the commandant talked about?"

"Well, after three weeks here, the guards took several of us to one of the buildings where the top brass keep themselves. We were told to stand in a hallway. They took us into a room one at a time and with an interpreter, three officers started to ask us questions."

"What kind of questions?"

"What unit we were in? How many men in the unit? What types of weapons? What were my duties in the army? What kind of work I did before I became a soldier? Was I an officer? Did I know of any officers in our barracks? You know, questions like that. They were fishing for military information and looking for officers, particularly, political officers. Whatever you do, don't admit you're an officer. I saw what they did to officers in Vitebsk. They pulled them out and the next thing we heard were gunshots. Never saw them again. It was a good thing I pulled off my insignias and quickly buried them in the dirt while still in that ditch."

"I certainly don't have any information to give them," Vladimir said.

"Remember, when they call you in, don't tell you're a doctor. Didn't you once tell me that you worked as a shoemaker?"

"Yes."

"Well, tell them that. I told them I was a clerk in a store."

❖ ❖ ❖ ❖

Three months had gone by. The routine was the same each and every day. Two captives from the barracks were required to bring in the water and the firewood from a handcart that came around daily. Vladimir took his turn with the others. The winter was colder than any Vladimir remembered. It was brutally frigid. *How could the armies battle each other,* Vladimir pondered throughout the cold months. *The guns and tanks must be frozen shut. But then, under these conditions, our boys should have the advantage.* The snow on the ground and on rooftops was a meter high. The prisoners shoveled walkways from their barracks to the latrine and mess hall. Some days, there was not enough firewood to heat the stove. More prisoners died from the cold. Portions of food diminished each week. Loaves of bread for the prisoners were sporadic. The cigarettes were still handed out, though not as often. Always pleased to get his pack, Vladimir used it to trade for extra portions of bread. He knew if he did not, like so many others, he would die of starvation.

No matter how cold the weather, the captives had to stand outside the barracks after the meal for a few minutes before they could go back in. The Germans called it, "exercise time." One evening, as both men stood huddled waiting to go back inside, Vladimir mentioned to Ivanov how surprised he was that no one in his group of prisoners had been called in for the interrogation. Ivanov did not answer and appeared to be in pain.

"What's wrong with you? You look as though you're going to collapse."

"I don't know. My head, it feels like its busting open."

"You do look feverish. Here, let me feel your forehead."

Vladimir touched Ivanov's forehead. Even in the severe cold, Ivanov's head was burning up. *He has a high fever—so suddenly, too. That's not good,* Vladimir thought to himself.

"I don't know what's happening to me? Suddenly, I don't have the strength to stand up. All my muscles ache."

Vladimir grabbed Ivanov and helped him into the barracks. Another captive came up to help.

"What's wrong with him?" The man asked.

"I don't know yet. Let's get him up on his bunk."

As they heaved Ivanov up into the middle bunk, Vladimir felt a tug on his left shoulder.

"Vladimir, my friend Boris is sick," a fellow, whose bed was on the other side of the barracks, said. "He complains of a severe headache and can't move his muscles. We can barely make out what he is saying. We also had to help him into his bunk. Can you do something for him?"

The request did not surprise Vladimir. Since he moved into the barracks, he tried to help his fellow prisoners. For the many with diarrhea, he made sure that they drank water to keep them hydrated. On one occasion, he made a splint for a broken arm of one of the prisoners beaten by the guards. For the splint, he used a small but stiff branch from the firewood box and strips of material from a shirt of one of the dead. On another occasion, Vladimir put back in place a dislocated shoulder another prisoner received from a beating. It soon became evident that Vladimir had knowledge of medicine. When the prisoners asked if he was a doctor, he never acknowledged it, but smiled slightly. He knew that Ivanov would not give away his secret.

"There is not much I can do right now without any medicine," Vladimir answered the man. "Let me examine Sergey, then I'll be over to see your friend."

Ivanov laid on his bunk, burning up with fever and holding his head with both hands. He shook uncontrollably, coughing incessantly. Boris exhibited the same symptoms. Shortly, more prisoners began to complain of the onset of severe headaches, weakness and high fever.

Vladimir shook his head quietly. He had a pit in his stomach. His fears of typhus fever had materialized. He had no thermometer or stethoscope, but knew that the body temperature was extremely high, maybe 40 or 41 degrees Celsius (104 degrees Fahrenheit) and feared that the blood pressure was low. He knew that the men would soon become delirious, would experience severe muscle aches and extreme fatigue. A severe dry cough, difficulty breathing, vomiting and more dehydrating diarrhea would follow. Later, a rash would appear on the chest and spread to the rest of the trunk and then to the extremities. Tiny areas of superficial bleeding would appear under the skin. In some, the spleen would enlarge and the kidneys would fail. Some would develop pneumonia and would be unable to breathe. He knew that in the horrible condition of the camp and with the lack of medication, death was more than likely. He realized that he, too, would probably come down with the disease.

The concerned, grave-looking captives surrounded him. Several had questions.

"I need to think about it," Vladimir said. "We need medications."

He realized that an engagement in conversation about what had befallen them would distress the men even more. Their prognosis was not good. Besides, even simple talking drained his energy and became too much of an effort. He wanted to just think things through in his mind. *Sulfa will help. I'm sure the Germans have it here for their troops. But then, why would they want to help us? They're trying to kill off as many of us as they can.* The supply of food was scarce even for the Germans. He overheard the guards complain about feeding the captives while their own rations were getting skimpier. It made sense to Vladimir. *The fewer captives survived, the more the Germans* had left to eat. Typhus plays into their hands because the more of us die, the better it is for them. And with typhus, you won't be eating much anyway as the body shuts down to preserve itself. So why would they help by giving me medicines? But, somehow I'll have to try.*

Vladimir tore another strip of material from a shirt, dunked it into the bucket of water and gave it to Boris's friend.

"Here, keep this compress on Boris's forehead," Vladimir said. "Try to keep him cool. It should help his fever."

Vladimir prepared a compress for Ivanov. As he placed the wet cloth on Ivanov, several other captives started complaining of similar symptoms. Vladimir went to the door, opened it and yelled at a guard to come to him. The guard seemed surprised by this request. He approached with a stern face and with his rifle pointed at Vladimir, motioning for him to get back inside. Vladimir did not budge.

"Get back inside! You are violating rules. Now get back before I place you in the cooler."

"We need help," Vladimir explained with his limited German vocabulary.

"What do you want?"

"We're sick here. Typhus fever. We need medications."

The guard began to laugh.

"You prisoners are entitled to shit. There's disease in every one of the barracks. Now get back inside, you lice infested scum."

"Get the sergeant or an officer?"

The guard laughed even harder. At that moment another guard approached, also pointing his rifle at Vladimir.

"What does he want?"

"He wants medications. He wants to talk to our sergeant or an officer."

Both men stood there laughing. Vladimir saw that he was getting nowhere with his request. Once they stopped laughing, if he was still there, they could punish him. So he closed the door behind him and went back and applied cold compresses to the sick.

"Those bastards!" Vladimir cursed in frustration. "I need medications!"

There was a deafening silence from everyone. Even the moaning of those with fever stopped. He crawled up the wooden ladder to his bunk and laid down. He was exhausted, both physically and mentally. *Except for cold compresses, there is nothing more that I can do, but lie here and await my turn.*

There were fewer men at roll call the next morning. The guards stopped entering the barracks to check on those missing. They were afraid. Typhus was raging in the camp. After the morning meal, as had become the custom, the prisoners were ordered to carry out the dead and load them on handcarts pulled by other captives. Vladimir, again, was ordered to help pull the carts, under heavy guard, to a field outside the camp. Mass graves, dug out by a bulldozer awaited the corpses. He thanked God for the extra bread he had traded for cigarettes. The bread gave him the energy to accomplish that task. On the walk back, Vladimir became chilled. His legs barely held him. He felt a sudden, unexplained weakness. Each step became more painful.

"Keep moving," the guard yelled.

Vladimir forced himself to keep up with the others. His head felt as if someone grabbed his brain inside his skull and squeezed it like wringing out a wet cloth. Fever burned him up. *Oh God! I have the typhus.*

◆ ◆ ◆ ◆

Vladimir tried to open his eyes. They seemed glued shut. He rubbed the muck off his eyes and with the help of his fingers opened his eyelids. With his vision blurry, he rubbed his eyes once again. He was able now to see a little clearer, but did not recognize his surroundings. The room smelled of death. Gray light filtered through the small windows. He heard voices, but could not make out the words. His eyes focused on the potbelly stove. It finally came to him that he was in the barracks and in his bunk. Someone approached him.

"You're finally awake."

"What happened?"

"You've been down with typhus fever for nine days now. You sure had it bad. No one thought you'd survive. Don't you remember talking to me during that time?"

"No. I don't remember much of anything."

"Well, no wonder. You had really high fever and some strange hallucinations. You helped us, so the few of us that miraculously didn't get sick, cared for you."

Vladimir tried to soak into his brain what he had just heard. He was groggy.

"I don't even know your name," Vladimir said.

"It's Kiril, you know, I asked you to help my friend, Boris."

"How is he?"

"One of the few that survived."

"How did I get here? I don't remember crawling up to my bunk."

"You collapsed while on a work detail. The men lifted you, put you on a cart and brought you here. We lifted you up on your bunk."

Vladimir felt overwhelming gratitude, but was unable to express it. He closed his eyes. He wanted to sleep.

"Hey, don't fall asleep on me now," Kiril said. "I've saved some bread here for you. Here, eat some. I'll get you some hot water."

Vladimir took a bite of a small chunk of dark rye bread. Then another. He gulped it down. He was famished.

"When is the last time I ate?" Vladimir asked Kiril when he came back with the water.

"I kept giving you water all along, but whenever I tried to feed you a little bread, you refused it. I even talked the fellow in the kitchen to fill your mess kit with some soup. You took only a few sips. On that day I had a double portion," Kiril said laughingly.

Vladimir rubbed his eyes and massaged his face.

"I don't remember much of anything. Thanks for your help."

"No thanks are necessary. You helped so many of us here."

Vladimir looked around the barracks again and it occurred to him that the room looked empty.

"Where is everyone? Are they outside?"

"What you see is all that's left. The rest are all dead."

Vladimir grabbed the side of his wooden bed and turned towards Ivanov's bunk. It was empty. He looked around the room, but Ivanov was not there.

"What happened to Sergey?"

"He died two days ago."

Vladimir swallowed hard and sighed. He laid on his bunk and stared at the ceiling. *I lost another friend. When will this misery end? Dear God, why have You forsaken us on earth? So many have lost their lives. Both heaven and hell must be crowded with souls. Is there hope for us here on this planet?*

"Are you all right?" Kiril asked. "Can you get up? Soon it will be time for our meal. You would think that with so many of us gone, they would increase our portions. Instead, we get even less."

"I don't think I can get up. I can barely move."

"You have to get up."

Vladimir forced himself down from the bunk. His muscles did not function, and he fell off the ladder onto the floor. Kiril and another captive helped him up and steadied him as strength, bit by bit, returned to his body. He still needed their assistance to walk to the kitchen. Vladimir was surprised that roll call was no longer required. He assumed it was because there were fewer captives. After his portion of watered-down oatmeal, with help from Kiril and others, he returned to his bunk. The next morning he felt better. Gradually, as the days went by, his muscles strengthened. Portions of food had increased as the cold winter days were replaced by the new life of spring. And on occasion, small pieces of meat showed up in the soup.

The summer was hot and humid. Even with the windows open, it was an inferno inside the barracks. Vladimir was so uncomfortable that he wished for a return of the cold winter. The months dragged by, and his determination to survive grew stronger. He still had the picture of Slava, now worn and wrinkled from being pulled out of his pocket frequently. *Slava, where are you? What are you doing? Have you given up on me? I want you so much and someday we'll meet again.* He imagined what she looked like and what he'd do once he saw her again. *Don't despair, don't despair. I'll get out of here some day. God is protecting me,* he told himself.

The color of the leaves changed from green to gold and red. The winds turned cold and leaves fell to the ground. *How long are we to be kept here?* Vladimir lamented as melancholy and desolation flowed into his mind. He fought hard to maintain an upbeat attitude, that soon he'd be released. But in the gray, rainy days of autumn it was difficult to stay positive. *What a waste of humanity? Will we have to survive another winter here? Can I do it this time?*

One afternoon in late October 1942, two armed guards entered the barracks and ordered Vladimir to follow them. Vladimir's chest felt as though someone had stomped on it, as he was led away with a guard on each side. They entered the large brick headquarters building and Vladimir was told to stand still and wait in the hallway. One guard knocked on a door and went inside, while the other stood next to Vladimir. *This must be the interrogation that I had been expecting. But why did they wait a year to do this? And why am I alone?*

Vladimir entered the large room with a worn hardwood floor and drab green, cracked plaster walls. His teeth clenched from anxiety. His hands and knees trembled while his heart pounded erratically against his ribcage.

"Sit down!" Colonel Klaisle barked.

Seated next to Klaisle at a highly polished table that looked out of place in the dingy, smoke-filled room was Major Kimmer, all dressed in black. His jet-black hair and round black wire-rim glasses gave him an ominous look. On the other side of Klaisle was another officer in a gray uniform with a string of medals across his chest. Vladimir remembered Klaisle and Kimmer, but had not seen the third officer. The interpreter sat at a desk to the side of the officers' table.

"Name?"

"Vladimir Moskalkov."

"Nationality?"

"Byelorussian."

"What city or region?"

"Vitebsk."

"What is your rank in the army?" Major Kimmer asked staring intently at Vladimir in an obvious attempt of intimidation.

Vladimir hesitated. Throughout the long months of captivity he had thought how to answer their questions. The easy way would be to lie and follow Ivanov's advice. *I'm nothing in the army, just a shoemaker in civilian life.* But now, a twist to his story, had surfaced. The need for medications in the barracks continued. With winter fast approaching, typhus or other diseases would strike once again. Medicines could make the difference between life and death. He faced a dilemma. Once again he had to take a risk for the benefit of his patients. *I'm a fool if I tell them I'm a doctor. But they may give me drugs if, I, as a physician, request them. What am I saying? If I tell them I'm a doctor and therefore an officer, they'll just execute me.*

"I said, what is your rank?" Kimmer bellowed.

I'm going to do it. Oh, what should I do? I have no choice. Deja vous all over again. Vladimir thought. *I've been through this with Popov. Somehow I've survived. Besides, I'm just a medical captain and have nothing to do with military strategy. They'll understand. I'm going to do it.*

221

Victor Moss

"Speak up! You want us to beat the information out of you?"

Vladimir took a deep breath. His knees trembled. His heart banged against the ribcage and his head was about to explode.

"I'm a medical doctor and therefore they assigned me the rank of captain."

Oh my God! What did I do? Vladimir sat still, unable to breath as he watched the three German officers. No one said a word for a minute. Instead all eyes glared at Vladimir. The minute felt like an hour.

"You just saved your life," Klaisle said with a smile.

"Yes, we have known for some time that you are a doctor," Kimmer said.

The trembling in Vladimir's body intensified. *Oh God, they knew I was a doctor. Who squealed on me? Now what?* But he said, "You just saved your life." *Maybe, it's not as bad as I think? Now is the time to ask for medications for the prisoners.*

Vladimir opened his mouth to request medications for the captives when the third officer sitting at the table asked him where he went to medical school.

"Vitebsk Medical Institute."

"Any particular specialty?"

"Yes, ears, nose and throat."

At that answer, the three officers looked at each other. Klaisle smiled thinly once again. Vladimir noticed that the third officer's facial expression seemed to soften.

"Had you ever performed brain surgery?"

"Yes, when it concerned the ear."

"How often."

"Quite often."

"You can step out now and wait in the hallway until called," Kimmer said dismissively.

Vladimir waited in the hallway. The tension in his body remained taut. Even though the door was closed, he heard voices as a serious discussion ensued in the room that he just left. He recognized Kimmer's booming voice that drowned out the voices of the other two officers. The pit in his stomach seemed to grow with each passing minute. To ease his anxiety, he tried to think positive thoughts. *They must need me for something. They must have a patient for me. Otherwise why would they ask those specific questions? I'll be all right.*

After several minutes, Colonel Klaisle opened the door and told Vladimir to come back into the room. Vladimir followed him in and was told once again to sit down. Kimmer looked upset and glared at Vladimir. The third officer began to speak, "Listen, doctor, we have a fellow officer who needs immediate surgery. Unfortunately, there are no doctors available for him right now. It will take days for one to be brought in from Minsk. You must perform the surgery immediately."

"Yes, captain, it's an order," Kimmer snarled. "You might have survived up to now, but know this, it will be your life or his. If he dies, you die. Do you understand?"

CHAPTER 25

Stunned, Vladimir stared back at the three German officers. He shuddered as he drew a sharp breath, his hands trembling as he mulled over Major Kimmer's threat, "Either he lives or you die." He knew nothing of the condition of the ill officer. *He could be in such a state that saving him would be impossible.*

"Well, do you have anything to say?" Kimmer asked impatiently, with open hostility.

Vladimir opened his mouth to speak, but words stuck in his dry throat. Instead, he coughed.

"May I have some water, please?" Vladimir asked. "My mouth is parched."

Klaisle poured water out of a pitcher into a glass and handed it to Vladimir. After several sips, Vladimir asked, "Who is this officer?"

"It's not important for you to know," Kimmer answered. "The fact is that he is an officer of the Third Reich, a hero and therefore, very important."

"Major Kimmer, please, let me speak," the third officer said. "My name is Captain Schwartz. The officer in need of your service is my friend, a major stationed here at Baranovichi."

"What's wrong with him?" Vladimir asked.

"For several days now, he has had severe headaches and high fever with chills," Klaisle answered. He is acting strangely and wants to sleep all the time. The other day he tried to stand up, but lost his balance and fell. He seems to be very sick and we are concerned that he won't last much longer."

"How long has he been sick?" Vladimir asked.

"For over a week now."

"Is he delirious?"

"Well, yes," Schwartz said. "He's not himself. He's even had fits."

"You mean like a seizure?"

"Yes, I suppose so."

"Can I see him?"

"Well, what do you think you're here for?" Kimmer snapped.

"He's in our infirmary," Schwartz said. "We'll take you to him."

"Not so fast, Captain," Kimmer said. "Before you let this prisoner see one of our officers, he has to be cleaned up and deloused."

"Yes, that is an excellent suggestion," Klaisle interjected. "We'll have the guards take him to their showers."

"So, you, prisoner of war!" Kimmer bellowed at Vladimir. "Yes, go see our sick officer. But remember, you must make him better or I will personally have the pleasure of shooting you."

223

Victor Moss

Vladimir had just begun to relax a little when Kimmer threatened him again. A huge, painful knot inside returned with a vengeance. *The man must be close to death. Otherwise, why would they have called me in? It must stick in their craw to have an enemy doctor work on one of their own. They are desperate, but is he too far gone for me to save him?*

Klaisle stood up, approached the guards that stood by the doorway and whispered something to them. He turned to Vladimir and told him to follow the guards. Vladimir rose and walked out of the building with them. The guards led him down a cobbled walk past the brick buildings and to the barracks that housed the Germans soldiers. A tall brick fence separated their quarters from the captives' camp. After walking past several of the long, narrow wooden structures, they came upon a small grassy field lying between two barracks. A few German soldiers were kicking a soccer ball back and forth. At the sight of a Soviet prisoner, they stopped their play and glared at Vladimir incredulously.

"Hey, what's the pig doing in our area," one of the soldiers yelled out.

"Never mind," one of the guards yelled back. "It's all right. Mind your own business. Keep playing."

The soldiers did not resume their play. Instead they approached Vladimir and the guards, quickly surrounding them.

"What's the subhuman scum doing here?" another soldier shouted while the others heckled Vladimir. Some fisted their hands as if to strike.

Vladimir gritted his teeth and tried to avoid direct eye contact with any of the soldiers. *They can't be serious? I have to keep my cool and not look afraid.* The young soldiers' taunts did not surprise him. After a year as a prisoner-of-war he had heard all the threats and insults before. *Just another pack of wolves trying to intimidate the prey.*

"I tell you, it's all right," the guard responded. "We have orders from Colonel Klaisle. Now back off. Go back to your game now."

The soldiers did not budge, enjoying themselves at Vladimir's expense. The guards slipped the rifles off their shoulders and, holding them to their chests, began to push forward. The soldiers backed off, but continued their verbal abuse, as Vladimir walked toward a barrack converted into a shower house for the German soldiers.

They entered a large room lined with rows of wooden benches. Through the open doors ahead Vladimir saw a sequence of showerheads. One of the guards motioned for Vladimir to remove his clothing. Embarrassed by his emaciated condition, with legs that looked like twigs and bones that protruded through his skin, Vladimir sat naked on the bench. A guard took a small stool and a large metal gas can from a storage closet and placed them underneath one of the showerheads. *Good, I will finally get rid of my lice.* He was directed toward the shower area and told to sit on the stool.

Vladimir kept his eyes shut tight as one of the guards poured the liquid over his head. The kerosene smelled and stung his scalp, but Vladimir rubbed his hair vigorously. With his eyes closed he reached out for the faucet and felt warm water pour out. A guard yelled out and threw him a piece of soap. *This must be ecstasy,* Vladimir thought. He had not showered since his capture. He could have stayed under the water for hours, but the guard instructed him to turn off the water and get out of the shower.

When he returned to the bench area, he saw a towel and, to his surprise, a clean Soviet uniform waiting for him. *From which corpse did they take that uniform? At least they washed it.* The underwear and the socks were German. The uniform was loose, but adequate.

The shower was his rebirth; with clean clothing Vladimir felt human again. They walked past the same soldiers playing ball, and once again he was the butt of their verbal abuse. It did not bother him in the least as he now felt on top of the world. For the moment, even Kimmer's threat had left his mind.

The guards brought him back down the hallway adjacent to the room where he had met with the officers earlier. One of the guards knocked on the door. An assistant to Klaisle opened it, and motioned for Vladimir to wait. Within minutes, the interpreter rushed into the building and both were escorted into the room.

All three officers were still seated in the same positions. The table was covered with documents and a half full bottle of cognac sat in the middle of the table.

"Ah, that's much better," Klaisle said. "Come with us."

Klaisle and Schwartz walked toward the door. Kimmer remained seated. His fury that a prisoner doctor could hold a German life in his hands was obvious. Vladimir knew that if Kimmer had it his way, Vladimir would be taken out back somewhere and shot. *Who knows, even if I save their friend, they might still execute me,* Vladimir thought as he followed the two officers and the interpreter. The two guards that escorted him around the camp walked alongside. After a short walk, the group entered the infirmary. Seven German patients lay in steel-framed beds in a large room. They stared as the group walked passed them into a private room where a rather thin, tall man, in his forties slept with his feet protruding from under the blanket. The matted blond hair on his balding head framed an elongated face with a protruding jaw. He was white as a sheet and the sweat beaded his face.

As Vladimir touched the patient's shoulder, he felt dry heat radiate even through his shirt. The patient did not move. Vladimir shook his shoulder lightly. The man's eyes rolled open, but then quickly closed again. He appeared to be semi-conscious.

"Can you hear me?" Vladimir asked in Russian. The interpreter repeated the words in German. Not getting a response, Vladimir shook his shoulder and in a louder voice asked again if he could hear him, this time in German. The man mumbled, repeating the same incoherent phrase over and over.

"Do you have any instruments here?" Vladimir asked generally of the group of people standing behind him and around the patient's bed.

"What do you need? We have some here," said a nurse standing in the doorway.

"I need a head mirror and if you have an otoscope, it would be very helpful."

The interpreter was unable to translate the word for otoscope, so the nurse asked what he meant.

"It's a lighted cone-shaped instrument to examine the ear canal."

"Yes, yes, I know what you need," the nurse said with the help of the interpreter. "I'll be right back."

As Vladimir waited for her return, he examined the patient. Redness and swelling was visible behind the left ear. The ear also was turned forward. He surmised that the ear was pushed frontward by a large buildup of pus in the back of the ear. As an ENT, he knew that there could only be one diagnosis at this time. He was convinced that his patient had a mastoid infection that had gone untreated for too long. The instruments would verify his diagnosis. He needed to look inside the ear canal. *Where is that nurse? I need those instruments.* The nurse, a small framed shapely woman with auburn hair and a pretty face, returned with the instruments a few minutes later.

"I found them," she said excitedly.

Vladimir took the head mirror, adjusted it for the most light and through the hole in the middle looked inside the canal. The eardrum was red and swollen. He took the otoscope and through the cone and the light he was able to see past the pus behind the eardrum into a portion of the middle ear. The cavity was filled with pus. He opened the eyelid of the left eye. The pupil was dilated, indicating excessive pressure on the optic nerve from the infection.

"Well, what's your diagnosis?" Klaisle asked.

"I believe he has a serious middle ear infection that has abscessed."

"See, I told you," the nurse said proudly. "And he needs surgery immediately, doesn't he?"

At that moment, Kimmer entered the room. Just his mere presence sent a chill down Vladimir's spine. After all, Kimmer may soon be his executioner.

"So, can you help him?" Schwartz asked.

"I believe so. The nurse is right. He'll need surgery immediately so that I can drain the abscess."

"Again, I object to this Soviet scum performing surgery, especially on our own," Kimmer said in a voice loud enough for everyone in the infirmary to hear. "My suggestion is that we take Herr Major Mann to Minsk immediately, as we should have done days ago."

"Herr Major Kimmer, we have already discussed this at length," Klaisle countered. "It was our opinion that in his condition he would not make it to Minsk. Do you agree, Herr doctor?"

Vladimir was shocked to hear himself addressed as a doctor. It had been such a long time. He was even more surprised to hear that his opinion was requested. And with this question, he saw a chance to remove his risk of death by avoiding the surgery. *What should I say? I can tell them that he needs to go to Minsk. But I can't do that. This poor man will die within hours. I need to tell them the truth, even if it kills me.*

Beware the Wolves

"In his state, the intracranial pressure is extremely high. Any delay at this point is unadvisable. There may already be perforations of infection into the brain that continue to grow. As the area swells, tissues in the area begin to die and he will die."

"Well, you better do it then," Schwartz said. "But, you heard Major Kimmer, you must save his life or else."

Vladimir did not have to be reminded of the threat. He felt his body wind up like a mainspring of a watch. *How will I be able to operate if they keep scaring me? The bastards! Don't they realize that I need steady nerves? What do they think, that I would kill him on purpose?* Vladimir took some deep breaths and closed his eyes for a few seconds. *I've done this procedure before, but anything can go wrong. He is in really bad shape and I may not be able to save him.*

"We have a surgical room down the hall," the nurse said. "But no one has used it since I've been here. Come with me."

Vladimir followed the nurse to a room three doors down from his patient's. The exuberance and confidence that the shower and clean clothes provided faded with every step. The officers, including Kimmer, and the interpreter lagged behind. The guards were sent away.

The surgical room had not been painted in many years. Dust clung to the walls and ceiling. The surgical table had boxes piled on top of it. The light bulb above the table was out and a layer of dust covered the hanging green fixture.

"We need to clean up this room before I can operate," Vladimir said. "Where are the surgical tools?"

"What do you need?" the nurse asked, appearing to be overly helpful and eager. "I haven't seen a surgery since I left nursing school in Bavaria."

"Corporal," Klaisle barked to an orderly who entered the room. "Get some men together and clean this room. Remove all boxes and wash down everything. Replace the bulb above the table immediately."

"I believe that there are some tools in that drawer," the nurse pointed to one of the drawers in a row of cabinets along the wall.

Vladimir looked inside and found a metal box containing a scalpel, several clamps of various sizes, a chisel, surgical scissors and several 4 mm curettes (small little scoops). It was apparent that the instruments had not been used for months. They were filthy. The scalpel and chisel even had blotches of rust on the metal.

"Do you have any other instruments?" Vladimir asked.

"What's wrong with these?" Kimmer asked with hostility.

"They're too dirty and rusty," Vladimir answered.

"No, these are all the instruments we have," the nurse answered quickly.

"Well, you better make do with these instruments," Kimmer snapped.

That son of a bitch does not want me to save this life. He wants me to fail.

"I don't see a surgical hammer. But if you don't have one, any hammer will do as long as we clean it up."

"I can find you one," the nurse said after listening to the translation. "What else would you need?"

"I need a small rubber tube for a drain and dressing over the ear like a large pad of some kind of absorbent material. I also need sulfa powder and pills. And ether. If you don't have it, bring me some vodka or cognac."

"For you to drink," the nurse said, laughing heartedly.

"No, it's for the patient," Vladimir said, irritated.

"Don't get upset, I'm just trying to lighten things up a bit. I see how miserable you look."

"What do you need a hammer for?" Kimmer asked suspiciously, looking for any reason to prevent Vladimir from performing the operation.

"I need to break into the bone with a hammer and chisel."

Vladimir noticed the Germans glance at each other. They did not trust him. The idea of an enemy doctor working on one of their own with a hammer and chisel, breaking open the skull was frightening to them. Although his life was in danger, Vladimir felt good knowing that he would be in charge and that they had to listen to him.

"You see," Kimmer said. "You want this prisoner of war working on our officer's head with a chisel and hammer? You must stop this insanity now, Colonel."

"Major Kimmer," Klaisle said. "The decision has been made. Please do not interfere."

Kimmer squinted his eyes and compressed his lips. He wanted to say something else, but turned and stormed out of the building instead.

"I will find everything that you need," the nurse said. "Except, of course the vodka or cognac. But I'm sure one of the officers can bring us a bottle. By the way, my name is Helga. I want to assist you. What else can I get you?"

"Can you bring me something to clean these instruments? Alcohol, soap and rags?"

Helga started rummaging through the cabinets and drawers in the room, while Vladimir carefully inspected the instruments he needed. The scalpel was in particularly bad shape. Rust covered the blade as well as the handle. *Some fool left it wet in the box,* Vladimir thought. He also took out the curettes and the chisel. The curettes were dirty, but not rusty. Helga brought Vladimir a bottle of rubbing alcohol, two cloths and soap in a wide metal bowl and a pitcher of water.

The young interpreter with a thin face and narrow black-rimmed glasses stood next to Vladimir, watching his every move. Two other men washed down the room and wiped it clean. The officers stepped out of the room, but Vladimir heard their voices in the hallway.

Vladimir poured some water in the bowl and with a cloth and soap scrubbed the instruments. His mind boggled at the thought of performing surgery under the present conditions. After scrubbing with soap, the rust spots still remained.

Beware the Wolves

"Helga," Vladimir said. "Can you get me a plain knife?"

"What for?"

"I need something to scrape off as much of this rust as I can. And I still need a small hammer."

Helga ran out of the room. Vladimir heard her asking someone in the hallway if it were all right to bring the prisoner a knife. He heard an affirmative answer and in a moment, Helga brought Vladimir a knife with a short blade. A few minutes later, a soldier brought a carpenter's hammer. Vladimir worked on the tools, including the hammer, for several minutes. He scraped them, washed them and rubbed them down with alcohol.

"Please throw these instruments into boiling water and boil them for at least five minutes. Did you find the rubber tubing?"

"Yes, here it is, on the table."

"Good. It will do. Throw the tubing into the boiling water with these instruments. When they're through boiling, bring them to me on a heated pan."

Vladimir looked around the room. It still looked dingy and grimy, but considerably cleaner than when he first saw it. He walked out to the hallway and gingerly approached the German officers.

"Well, Herr Doctor, are you ready to proceed?" Klaisle said. "I sent Captain Schwartz to find a bottle of vodka for your patient."

"I'll be ready soon. When the liquor arrives, give the patient a good stiff drink, if he's able to drink. It will ease the pain."

As Vladimir washed his hands with soap and water, his patient was carried in on a stretcher and placed on the table. The instruments were in the pan as requested. He was impressed with the work that Helga performed. He admired her efficiency and enthusiasm. But, she was also his enemy. He could not forget that he was in the wolves' den, and his life was at stake. *One slip of the knife or too much pressure on the bone and I'm a dead man.* He had operated on brain abscesses before. It was a delicate operation. He knew he had to concentrate in order to avoid damaging the brain. But the pressure to succeed had shaken him. The tight knot within him begged for release. He swung his mind home to Slava. Her face swam in front of him. Slava's gentle, smiling image usually put him at ease. He felt better, but still remained on edge. *Oh well, I might as well begin.*

"All right," Vladimir declared, exhaling sharply. "I'm ready, let's proceed."

"So what do we do now?" Helga asked. "Will you explain to me everything that you are doing?"

"All right," Vladimir said, thinking all along that she was just another watchdog.

"So where are you from?" Helga asked following Vladimir's instruction to shave behind the patient's left ear.

"Look, I've explained all of this to the officers."

"No, no, you don't understand, I'm asking you not as an official. It's just small talk. I admire a man who holds a life in his hands. I just wanted to know a little more about you."

229

"Vitebsk, do you know where that is?"

"No, I assume that it's in Russia."

"It's actually in Byelorussia."

Turning the patient on his side, Vladimir swabbed the back of the ear with alcohol. He could hear the loud beat of his heart as he picked up the scalpel. As he did so, he felt power and life surge into his veins. The familiar weight of the scalpel eased his mind. The walls of the prison, the surly faces of guards and the threatening presence of the Nazi officers ceased to exist. Above all, fear for his life dissipated. It was a moment, not unlike when a maestro picks up a violin, and all else fades away. The struggle against disease and time was now solely between the patient and his doctor.

Vladimir gently cut the skin and the underlying soft tissue in the back of the ear over the mastoid bone with the scalpel. The patient did not move, and seemed to be out cold. He scraped the skin and tissue back, and took the chisel and hammer and with a quick blow punctured a hole in the bone. With the curette, the bone fragments and copious amount of pus were removed. He scraped the bone with the curette, widening the hole and inserting the instrument into his patient's head.

"Why did you enter in that location?" Helga asked.

"Because an uncontrolled middle ear infection spreads into the mastoid, you know, this triangular shaped bone behind the ear. If the opening in the middle ear gets obstructed and untreated it ruptures externally and drains behind the ear. The infection spreads from the mastoid to the brain."

Vladimir continued to scrape away the diseased bone with the curette, removing as much of the bone and pus as he could.

"Hand me the tube and the sulfa powder."

Helga handed him the tube and the powder. Vladimir sprinkled the powder on the tube and on the wound. He then inserted the tube into the opening. Immediately yellowish pus poured out. He allowed it to drain for a few minutes and placed a large, soft pad over the area.

"How long are you going to leave the tube there?" Helga asked.

"I need to keep an eye on him, but most likely a week to ten days. He'll be fine."

"Good job, Herr Doctor," Helga said. "I'll tell Colonel Klaisle that you have finished."

Vladimir exhaled deeply. Sweat poured out of every pore in his body. His head throbbed. *I did it. He'll live and maybe so will I?*

As he cleaned up, Colonel Klaisle came into the room.

"I want you to go back to your barracks and get whatever possessions you have. The guard will take you to new quarters at least for the time that your patient is recovering. Do not tell anyone what you have done or explain why you are being moved."

Vladimir returned to the barracks accompanied by a guard. The men looked worried, but no one said a word. He knew they were surprised to see him in a clean uniform and wondered what was up. Vladimir scooped up his few possessions that laid on his bunk, including the civilian coat that Slava insisted he take and his great coat and followed the guard out. The men waived goodbye, still in a shocked state. He glanced at Kiril. Kiril's eyes were glassed over with tears. *I wonder what's going through his mind. I wish I could tell him what I've done.* He waved goodbye to his fellow captives, the men he had lived with and had suffered with for a year. Vladimir, at that moment, knew nothing of his fate. In the men's eyes he saw the knowledge that they would never see each other again.

CHAPTER 26

The guard escorted Vladimir to a brick building next to the infirmary. The building served as the kitchen and mess hall for the Germans. Vladimir followed the guard through the kitchen. The aroma of cooking food overwhelmed him. At that moment, he realized he was starving. The adrenalin that gave him the energy to perform surgery, had run out. His stomach cramped from hunger. He slowly followed the guard into a hallway. Small storage rooms lined each side. Through one ajar door, Vladimir could see that it contained sacks of flour. A strong odor of onions emanated from another room. The doors to the other two rooms were closed. The guard opened the door to the room on the left and motioned for Vladimir to step inside.

Immediately, a moldy smell assaulted Vladimir's nostrils. The guard pulled a string on the lone bulb overhead and Vladimir saw a small portable cot sitting on the warped wooden floor. Across from the cot were shelves filled with empty glass bottles. A pillow and a blanket lay on the cot. The guard pointed toward the cot and left, leaving the door open. Vladimir glanced at the cot again. He quickly pulled back the blanket and for the first time in a year, his head touched a pillow. Granted, it was a hard pillow filled with straw, but to Vladimir it was pure luxury. He closed his eyes to try to sleep, but the aroma of food emanating from the kitchen was too intense. He got up and walked to the kitchen and saw an older German soldier stirring a pot. The soldier was startled at the sight of Vladimir in the Soviet uniform. He pulled the heavy, iron ladle out of the pot and held it up as if to strike Vladimir. He backed up behind the large wooden table in the center of the room. Vladimir saw fright in his face. Holding his palms open and waving his hands in front of his chest to indicate that he meant no harm, Vladimir advanced further into the kitchen.

"I'm very hungry. Can you give me something to eat?"

At that moment, a sergeant came in the room. With a quick glance, he assessed the situation, and his face broke into a grin.

"It's all right, Otto. This prisoner is on some kind of special status. He is going to sleep in one of the storerooms. Give him something to eat. He's harmless."

The sergeant walked out, still laughing. Otto, with suspicion still in his eyes, picked up a bowl from a stack on the table and ladled out some soup for Vladimir. Vladimir grabbed it and tried to drink it directly from the bowl, as was his custom with the *balanda*. However, this soup was thick, more a stew than a soup. He needed a spoon for the large chunks of meat, potatoes, cabbage and other vegetables. Otto cracked a smile and handed him a spoon. Vladimir devoured the contents and asked for more. *I can't believe how good this tastes. I have forgotten what real food tastes like. Oh, God, thank you for this meal.* His spirits lifted considerably. *If they plan to execute me, they wouldn't have given me this food,* he mused.

For the next three days, Vladimir ate well and slept well. Helga always smiled when she saw him and on one occasion even gave him a small piece of dark chocolate. Vladimir savored the taste of chocolate. He closed his eyes and lightly smacked his lips, enjoying each bite. But aside from the smiles and the chocolate, Helga kept at a distance, as did Vladimir. After all, they were enemies. He was a prisoner of war whose future was uncertain. Vladimir hoped that he would be allowed to treat fellow prisoners, now that they knew he was a doctor. He would even agree to treat German soldiers as he missed the environment of the infirmary. But no one came forward with that notion, and he did not volunteer. In the meantime, he spent much time with his patient, Herr Major Franz Mann. Mann did not talk much, but when he was able to, he thanked Vladimir profusely for his help.

"You saved my life. I'll return the favor," Mann told him on numerous occasions. "You'll see. You'll be a free man soon and have a good position."

Vladimir was elated to hear those words. *What does he mean by them? What does he have in mind?* A week after the surgery, Mann was ready to have the tube removed and be released. The abscess had drained well. He did not have to cut away the soft tissue that could have grown into the tube and pinched the drain. Vladimir was pleased with his success. *But, now what? What's going to happen to me now? Was Mann serious? Will I be released?* His breathing became labored and his insides twisted as he thought of his fate. *Or now that I finished my job, will I be executed?*

After Vladimir told Mann that he could leave the infirmary, Vladimir went back to his little room and laid down on the cot. He stared at the ceiling. He counted the cracks in the plaster. Anything to take his mind off what would come next. *Well, no matter what happens, I might as well have a full belly.* He went into the kitchen and asked for something to eat. The cook gave him a large piece of boiled pork and three pieces of boiled potatoes. *He actually gave me a smile today, and this is the most meat he ever gave me. What's going on? Is this my last supper?*

Vladimir thanked the cook and went back to his room. Once again he laid down on the cot. The large meal settled in his belly and made him sleepy. The thud of heavy boots approaching his room startled him. Vladimir jumped out of his cot and as he stood up, two armed soldiers, scowls marring their young faces, entered his room. They motioned for him to follow them. Vladimir tried to grab his few belongings, but one of the men took hold of his arm and pulled him out of the door. Vladimir left his possessions and followed the soldiers out of the building. *Is it over for me? Those bastards! I've done my job, and they're still going to shoot me. But no matter what happens, I won't be afraid. I have to be strong.*

The guards led Vladimir to the administrative offices. He was taken once again to the same room where the three officers met with him. The guards told him to sit down at the table. Vladimir complied. An inner torment gripped him. His heart thudded as he waited. Minutes felt like hours. Finally the door opened and Klaisle, Schwartz and his patient, Major Mann, walked through the door. Vladimir stood up immediately. He watched intently the expressions on their faces to see if there was a hint of his fate. As soon as he saw the broad smile on his former patient's face, his tension eased. Vladimir's heart jumped back into place. *It will be all right. They are not going to execute me. Surely, Major Mann would not be smiling.*

"Vladimir Moskalkov," Klaisle began after all three sat down at the table. "Because you have saved the life of our officer, in gratitude, we will release you from the prisoner of war camp."

Vladimir's heart leaped out of his chest, this time the leap was one of disbelief and joy. He glanced at Mann who was beaming. *Thank you, dear Jesus, you have answered my prayers.*

"In addition," Klaisle continued. "We will send you to Slonim to open your own practice. Slonim, a city of about fifty thousand people, is in dire need of an ENT specialist."

Astonishment struck Vladimir once again. *I will have my own practice!* Vladimir felt air whoosh out of his lungs. His heart sang with delight even though he had no idea where Slonim was.

"Unfortunately, Herr Doctor," Klaisle continued. "The main medical commanding officer for this region, Colonel Neusbaum, will not release you until such time as you prove to him that you have the training. He needs to see a diploma from your medical school, proving you are a graduate. Also, any documents to prove you are proficient in Ears, Nose and Throat would be helpful."

Vladimir felt he had been punched in the gut. The euphoria disappeared, giving way to despair. *How can I obtain my diploma and other documents here in Baranovichi? Vitebsk was burned to the ground. Slava must have been evacuated. And if not, how could I get word to her. Does she still have my diploma? She may not even be alive. Oh God, no!*

"Well, Herr Doctor, will it be possible for someone to obtain those documents and bring them to Colonel Neusbaum in Minsk?"

"Can you help me?"

"Unfortunately, no. That, my good doctor, is your responsibility."

"Colonel," Mann intervened. "Maybe, if I can get some civilian clothes for Vladimir, perhaps we can release him for a few hours into Baranovichi so that he can make some arrangements. I am sure if he promises he won't run away, and without papers, it would be hard to get far, he can be trusted to return."

Vladimir promised. The next day Mann brought Vladimir a box containing civilian clothing. Vladimir was delighted to see a gray hat with a wide black band, a white shirt, a dark blue double-breasted suit, brown socks, a pair of slightly oversized black shoes and a light blue tie.

"These are yours to keep. Here is also a pass for the afternoon. You will need to show it to the guards when you leave and when you return. If you're stopped in town, show them this pass as well. You'll be all right. Sorry, I couldn't find a coat for you."

"I have a civilian coat," Vladimir said in a state of exhilaration. "I don't know how to thank you."

"No, I am the one who thanks you. Now get ready and go. Maybe you can come up with something when you're in town."

Vladimir dressed and ran out of the building. As he walked past the infirmary, Helga happened to be going up the steps.

"Vladimir! I heard about your conditional release. I have an idea for you."

Vladimir stopped. He wanted to hear more. He could use all the help he could get.

"Go to the railroad station. Trains run in all directions, including Vitebsk. I specifically asked about this for you. Find someone who can take a message. You probably have someone in Vitebsk waiting for you."

"If that is only so. Thank you for your suggestion."

"Good luck."

Vladimir had no problem walking out of the camp. Everyone seemed to know his status. As he proceeded to Baranovichi, the miserable journey to the camp ran through his mind. He shuddered at the thought of his weakened condition on the verge of starvation and death. He gritted his teeth at the thought of his torment at the hands of the Nazis.

Not much had changed in Baranovichi over the year's time. Some houses remained, but many of the buildings were still in ruins. The day was cold and windy. The dreariness of the cloud cover coupled with muddy streets and buildings lying in rubble could have depressed Vladimir. However, that afternoon, away from the prisoner of war camp, Vladimir walked with an overwhelming feeling of freedom. He felt liberated. He even hummed a tune, the first time in over a year. Vladimir strode on with a spring in his step from the excitement. *On a wonderful day such as this, Slovochka, I'll get word to you somehow. I feel that you are still there waiting for me. You'll find my diploma, I know it,* Vladimir told himself.

The railroad depot was finally in sight. As Vladimir approached the station, his mood became somber. The mission seemed impossible. He had to find someone to deliver a message to Slava. Slava had to still be in Vitebsk. If she was, could she find the needed documents and then deliver them to Minsk? It seemed an insurmountable task. And if any one element were missing, he would be locked up, as an animal, for only God knew how long. But his task was to find a way to get a message to Slava. After that it was all in Slava's hands. *If Slavochka is there, she is resourceful enough to get me out. She'll get it done.*

Having been bolstered by the thought that Slava could get him out, he walked into the station and asked the clerk behind the window whether any trains ran to Vitebsk.

Victor Moss

"Only troop trains. Civilians are not allowed without special permission."

"Can you at least tell me which train goes to Vitebsk?"

"Well, I guess there is no harm in telling you the number of the engine. It's Number 47. But I tell you, unless you have an official pass, you can't get on it."

"Is it on the tracks now?"

"No, it should be here anytime."

Vladimir thanked him and walked out on the tracks. German soldiers waiting to board filled the area adjacent to the tracks. Vladimir walked among them to find a strategic spot to observe trains as they rolled into the station. He felt strange walking freely among the armed and helmeted soldiers. He imagined that all eyes were on him, but in reality, no one seemed to care of his existence. The trains finally left, the area became deserted. Vladimir sat down on a bench and watched for engine No. 47 to arrive.

After an hour, Vladimir heard the whistle of a train. He quickly stood, anticipating that it was Engine Number 47. To his disappointment, it was Number 39. A small group of soldiers gathered to board. *What if this is the train to Vitebsk? I better check.* Vladimir walked up to a soldier at the edge of the group and asked where that train was bound. To his surprise, the soldier told him, "Vitebsk." *Should I perhaps give him the note to take to Slava? No, I don't want the military involved. I need to find a civilian. But who?*

The train stood still. The soldiers boarded. Vladimir's heart raced, *Who can I give the note to, who can I give this note to?* He felt a panic come over him. He took some deep breaths to calm himself down. Suddenly, he saw an older man with a wrench climb down off the engine and walk back toward the third car. He stepped onto the tracks and began checking hoses between the cars. Vladimir ran up to him, startling the man.

"Please, can you help me?" Vladimir asked in German.

"What do you want?" The man answered in German.

"Are you going to Vitebsk?"

"Yes. Look, I don't have much time. I need to fix this and be on the way."

"It will only take a minute. I desperately need to get a message to my wife in Vitebsk. I really need your help. It is very, very important. Please. You're the only one that can help me."

"I can't help you."

"Please, it's a matter of life or death. Please do me this favor."

The man looked at Vladimir for a long minute. He saw the desperation in Vladimir's face.

"So, what's the message?"

"Here, I have a little note for her, Vladimir said as he handed him a piece of paper provided by the cook in the camp.

"All right, how do I find her?"

"Thank you, thank you. Her name is Vladislava Szpakowska. Her name and address are on the note. She does not live far from the station. On the back

I drew a little map of how to get there from the depot. I wish I could pay you, but I have no money."

"I don't need your money."

The man took the note and stuck it in the front pocket of his overalls. Vladimir watched as he tightened the clamp. The man glanced back at Vladimir as he went back to the engine and said, "I'll do it, all right."

That was too easy. Can I really trust him to do it or was he just trying to get rid of me?

CHAPTER 27

The Nazi occupation dragged on. Days turned into weeks, and weeks into months. Slava heard nothing of Vladimir. For all she knew, he was dead. Yet she never gave up hope. She had no information of the outside world other than what was provided by the fascists. She recognized their propaganda. Was she to believe that the Germans were there to liberate the people from Stalin and communism? The Germans were reporting their military successes on the front. Stalin would surrender any day. Slava knew that if the reports were true, the war would have concluded months ago. And as the months went by, she saw the tide turning. She noticed the Germans in the office were becoming increasingly concerned about their losses, and the length of the war.

At work, Slava's relationship with the Germans remained amicable. But she could not say that about most of the occupied. She had witnessed public hangings of partisans and suspected sympathizers. Bodies were left hanging for days and gave her nightmares for weeks. She resented the Nazis for invading her land and imposing such dire misery on the population. She hated being forced to work for them against her will but knew that the slightest misdeed could land her and her parents in the labor camp.

Although she had her parents, she felt alone and desolate. A bitter cold despair dwelt in the caves of her lonely soul. Her misery was an anvil weighing on her heart. She missed Vladimir and longed for his company. She needed his calm reassurance and his strong protective arm around her. Every night she pulled out the album of pictures and perused them until tears filled her eyes, overwhelmed by the torment of separation.

For months, Slava held out hope of finding Vladimir. Then she heard the Germans gloating over the thousands of Soviet prisoners that had been brought to the military base at the outskirts of Vitebsk. She decided to go to the base in search of Vladimir. Although the base was six-kilometers away, she made the long trek after her work hours regardless of the weather conditions. She anxiously circumnavigated the perimeter of the compound peering at the captives. They all looked the same—dirty, unshaven and lifeless, huddling together on the mud or snow. They were too weak or perhaps indifferent to communicate with her. The dilapidated old barracks housed some of the captives. Slava wondered if Vladimir was inside.

Slava's feet were often bloodied and blistered. Months of weekly walks to and from the base drained her strength. Yet, she made the fruitless journeys. Her mother prayed for her safe return and chided her for her dangerous walks, especially through the city's cemetery. The path through the cemetery was a substantial shortcut to the base. Although the lonely cemetery instilled terror in her, Slava felt it worthwhile to pass through it to save time and energy. The wind howled between the headstones, making her skin crawl. She believed she saw ghosts behind each monument as she ran alone in the darkness of night. All her attempts were in vain. As far as she knew, Vladimir was not among the captives.

◆ ◆ ◆ ◆

Slava had not seen Vladimir for more than sixteen months. She began to believe that she might never see him again. One evening, in late October 1942, she walked home from work wrapped up in her black coat, rabbit fur hat and a brown scarf. The stiff cold wind nibbled at her face. The sun had set an hour earlier, but the full moon reflecting off the snow lit up the night.

She was used to the lonely walks to and from work. Seldom was anyone else on the street. And she preferred it that way. If an occasional German patrol drove by, her heart stopped. At first she was stopped each time to have her papers checked. The soldiers verbally harassed her, but for the most part left her alone. Now as the patrol went by, they recognized her and did not bother to stop. The devastation of burned out buildings and houses, now part of the landscape, no longer bothered her. That night, the walk was as dreary as always, except that Vladimir was more than ever on her mind. She suddenly felt overwhelmed with the thoughts of how much she needed him. *Volodya, are you alive? Dear Jesus, please, please give me a sign that he is alive.*

As she approached her house, she saw the silhouette of a man walking towards her. As the figure came closer, she saw that the man was bundled up in a heavy jacket and a railroad cap. A bright red scarf covered his ears and part of his face. A few meters away, the man pushed the scarf down to his neck and lifted his hand in salutation.

"Do you live in that house?" The man asked in German as he pointed to Slava's house.

"Yes," Slava answered in German. She studied him briefly. He was elderly and looked tired. He had a kind round face with deep creases on his forehead. His jowls hung. The narrow white mustache appeared frosted from his breathing into the scarf. Whitish-gray hair protruded from underneath his cap.

"I knocked on the door and rang the bell. Someone was inside, but no one answered."

"What do you want?"

"Are you Vladislava Szpakowska?"

"Yes."

"Good. I have a message for you."

He took off his glove and reached into his pant's front pocket and pulled out a little piece of paper. It was crumbled up into a ball.

Victor Moss

"Here. Good luck, miss," the man said as he handed the paper to Slava and without waiting for a reaction, walked off toward the depot fiddling with his glove.

Surprised, Slava held the piece of paper in her hand. She took off her gloves, unfolded the note and tried to read the message. It was too dark to make out the text, but she recognized the word, "Volodya." Her hands began to tremble. A suffocating sensation tightened her throat. She ran to the house clutching the scrap of paper in her hand. She fumbled with the key and had trouble finding the keyhole. Her father opened the door.

"What's the matter with you? Calm down, what happened?"

"Oh, papa, wait!"

She rushed to the light of the lamp and stared at the note. Both parents stood gazing at Slava in bewilderment. Slava gulped hard as tears blinded her eyes. A warm glow filled her.

"Slava, what is it?" Suzanna asked. "Bad news? What happened?"

Slava did not answer as she was breathing in shallow quick gasps.

"Slavochka, my darling daughter," Vladislav said. "What's on that paper?"

Slava turned toward her parents. She was beaming. She was radiant. Happiness and merriment flowed from her eyes.

"It's a message from Volodya," she whispered with her chest heaving from the excitement. "He's alive and I need to go to him. Oh, dear God. Oh, dear God. Thank you, thank you, thank you."

Both parents' eyes flew open in astonishment at Slava's words. Suzanna grabbed her heart.

"Oh, my God. Oh, Blessed Virgin Mary, Oh sweet Jesus, Oh Saint Anthony," she repeated her prayers as tears flowed freely from her eyes. Vladislav, the quiet one, howled with excitement.

"Where is he?" Suzanna asked. "What does the note say?"

"Here, read it mama, I'm too excited to say anything more."

"I can't either. I'm too wound up. Read it, Vladislav."

Vladislav took his reading glasses out of his shirt pocket. The wire frame became entangled. As he fidgeted with it, Suzanna lost patience.

"Will you hurry it up? How long does it take to put your glasses on, for heaven's sake? Here, let me read the note."

"I have my glasses on now, and I'll read the note. Now give it to me."

Suzanna handed him the note. Vladislav drew closer to the light and began to read:

"Slovochka, I'm here in the prisoner of war camp in Baranovichi. You must go to Minsk and see a Dr. Neusbaum, the chief German medical officer. Show him my diploma and documents that I completed the ENT program. Then come meet me in Baranovichi. I operated on a German officer and saved his life. In gratitude, they will release me if you show them the documents. I will find you. Volodya."

"Mama, Papa, isn't it wonderful. Volodya is alive and we'll see each other soon. My dreams and prayers have come true."

"Slavochka, of course it's the best news we could possibly receive," Vladislav said. "But how can you travel to Minsk?"

"Yes, and would that German officer even receive you," Suzanna said. "Are you sure that note is from Volodya? Maybe it's some kind of a German trick."

"Of course, its from Volodya. It's his handwriting. Why would they want to trick me, anyway like this? I'll find a way to get to Minsk. The important thing is that my love is alive and waiting for me. I'll get there even if I have to walk."

"Don't be silly," Suzanna said. "You think it will be easy to get to Minsk. You know darned well that all travel is restricted out of Vitebsk and only the military can travel. You have no chance to get there."

"I'll find a way, just watch. I have to."

Slava tossed and turned all night. She went from moments of laughter to tears of joy, then back to laughter. She could not wait to snuggle up against Vladimir. But the longer she laid wide-awake in bed, the almost insurmountable task of reaching Minsk began to sink in. Suddenly, it struck her that Raake might help her get on a train to Minsk. *Yes, I'll do it. I'll ask him in the morning. Who knows? He might actually help me. But what about the diploma and other documents? Where are they? Where did mama hide all of our documents?* She jumped out of bed and began searching the house for the papers. Her mother came out of her room.

"What are you doing?"

"Mama, I'm looking for Volodya's diploma. Have you seen it?'

"Yes, I believe I hid it with the deed to our house."

"Where?"

"I hid them in the piano."

"The piano?"

"Here, let me show you."

Suzanna opened the lid and reached down into the edge of the upright section of the piano. She pulled out a package of papers tied with a string. After untying the string, she flipped through the papers and pulled out a small booklet with the word, "Diploma," printed on the cover.

"Is this what you were looking for?"

"Oh, great, thanks mama."

"I also need Volodya's ENT certificate. Here, let me look. I know exactly what it looks like. Oh, here it is. Good, we have what he needs."

"Slavochka, my child, your father and I have been talking. Once you leave here, we will probably not see you again. But you must find Volodya and go with him. Don't worry about papa and me. We'll be all right. As soon as we have a chance we'll try to get back to our old homeland in Latvia. But whatever you do, you must not come back here. Our troops will eventually win. They never give up. But when they retake Vitebsk, anyone that stayed behind will be dealt with."

241

Her mother's words hit Slava like a rock. In her excitement, she had not thought of the future as long as she was reunited with Vladimir. But now she realized that her mother was absolutely right.

"And it's Godsend that you heard from Vladimir now," Suzanna continued. "This is your opportunity to get out of here. We've been worried about it for some time. Find Vladimir and take him as far from here as possible."

"Yes, Slavochka," Vladislav said as he came into the room. "You must not worry about us. Even if we won't be able to leave for Latvia, we'll be all right. We're old and they'll leave us alone. But you and Vladimir could be in danger if you stay here. You must go and not think of us. Find a way to get to Minsk. You are clever. You can do it."

Slava fell into the closest chair. She rubbed her eyes and let her face rest in her hands. The thought of leaving her parents behind was too painful to imagine. But, regardless of the reason her parents gave, all she knew was that she had to find Vladimir. Everything else did not matter. *Once Volodya is with me, we'll decide what to do.*

◆ ◆ ◆ ◆

Slava ran almost all the way to work. She was anxious to talk to Raake. But when she entered the old warehouse, she had second thoughts. *What am I supposed to say to him? Why would he even listen to me? Sure, he seems nice, but why would he do me such a favor? Why would he help a Byelorussian prisoner? Nevertheless, I have to try.*

"Lieutenant Hoffman, it's imperative that I talk to Major Raake." Slava tried to speak softly, but every one of the girls turned her head toward Hoffman's desk.

"Vladislava, you know that he wants me to handle all the issues in the office."

"It has nothing to do with work."

Hoffman had a puzzled look on his face. He raised one eyebrow and looked inquiringly at Slava.

"What do you want with him? He is a busy man."

"I know. I just need a few moments."

"What's this all about?"

"Please, Herr Lieutenant. It is very important and I need to discuss my personal problem with him."

Hoffman again raised his eyebrow. He did not say anything for a moment. Slava could see the wheels in his brain turn trying to guess what her personal problem could be and whether or not he should ask Raake to see her.

Come on, Hoffman, do me a favor and let me see Raake. After all, you have been socializing at my house. I've put up with you. Just let me in to see Raake. "Please, Herr Hoffman. It is crucial that I see him right away."

"Wait here. I'll see if he'll receive you. You know though, this is out of the ordinary, and generally is not allowed. You must first talk to me."

Beware the Wolves

Hoffman reluctantly stood and knocked on Raake's door. Raake shouted, "enter" and Hoffman walked into the office. Slava stood still afraid to glance over her shoulder at the other women in the office. She knew all eyes were on her at the moment.

"You can go in," Hoffman said as he stood at the door, following Slava inside the office.

"Vladislava," Raake said. "What's this all about?"

Slava saw that Hoffman was still in the room. She didn't want to put Raake in a position where he would have no choice but to turn her down if another officer were present.

"May I speak to you alone?"

"Lieutenant, you may go back to work?"

"Yes, Herr Major," Hoffman answered, clicking his heels as he left the room.

"Well, Vladislava, What's so important?"

"I received a note from my husband. He's alive and held as a war prisoner in Baranovichi. He saved a German officer's life and may be released if a Colonel Nausbaum in Minsk verifies his diploma and other medical documents. I need your help to get to Minsk."

Raake listened attentively. He let Slava finish without saying a word. He stretched his arm out to the edge of the desk and opened his cigarette case. He took out a cigarette, tapped the edge on the desk, staring at Slava vacantly. He kept the cigarette between his fingers for a moment, then placed it in his mouth and lit it. After a few puffs, he rose, walked to the narrow window and stared out. The pit in Slava's stomach grew larger by each passing second. After all, Vladimir's future and hers might depend on that man. *What's he thinking about. But it must be a good sign. He didn't say "no" immediately or throw me out of his office.*

Raake took a few more puffs and then turned toward Slava.

"How do you think I can help you, young lady? You know that civilians cannot travel without official authorization. It is impossible to obtain that authorization at this time. Besides, even if I could get you on board a train that would carry non-military personnel, the ticket is too expensive and the bureaucratic red tape is mind-boggling."

"I've saved up a little from what you've paid me here," Slava interjected. "How long would the red tape take?"

Raake shook his head negatively. He looked at Slava, then up to the ceiling, deep in thought.

"I really would like to help you. I've heard you speak of your husband more than I wanted to hear. His name is Vladimir, isn't it? I realize how much he means to you. You're a good person and I've always liked you. As I mentioned to you, you remind me of my daughter. But in this situation, I can't help you. It would be impossible to get you on that train. I'm sorry Vladislava."

Slava felt as if a heavy beam hit her over the head. *Oh my God, what's he saying? I was sure he'd help me. There has to be a way.*

"There's has to be another way then, perhaps a car or truck. Major Raake, I am desperate. There must be a way to get to Minsk. Can you think of anything at all? Please, please help me. I implore you."

"I'm sorry, Vladislava. You have to go back to work now."

Crushed and smothering a sob, Slava hurried back to her desk. She plopped into her chair. The women in the office stared at her, but she paid no attention. One of the women began to approach to console her, but she quickly turned back after Hoffman yelled at her.

After wiping her eyes, Slava decided that she had better attempt to work, or Hoffman may yell at her. But concentrating on her duties was impossible. Her mind was fixated on some plan to reach Minsk. She was stumped. She hoped that Raake would change his mind and help her, but he had left the building shortly after their morning conversation. Soon it was time to quit work for the day and he had yet to return. Besides, she now resented him, although she understood that, maybe, he truly could not help her, even if he wanted. She sat at her desk, frustrated, glancing at her wristwatch waiting for the long day to be over. *Thirty more minutes, and I'm out of here. I need to go to the train station myself and see if I can talk someone into a ticket.*

Suddenly, Raake returned to the office, walked straight to Slava's desk and asked her to follow him into his office.

Slava darted out of her chair. *Maybe he's changed his mind. Maybe, he can help me, after all?*

"Sit down, please."

With a wide grin, Raake sat down in his chair behind the desk.

"A thought occurred to me as to how I can get you to Minsk," Raake said.

Slava's heart pounded. She held her breath.

"Yes, Major, anything."

"I've telephoned my superior in Minsk. I told him that I needed to show him documents concerning the inventory of supplies in person. He authorized my travel to Minsk. This gives me the opportunity to escort you there."

A sob of relief broke from Slava's lips. Her smile broadened in disbelief. She bounced up and down in her chair. Raake saw her reaction and laughed out loud.

"I am so elated and relieved," Slava said. "A load has been taken off me. May I give you a hug?"

"But of course, it would be most pleasant," Raake answered as he stood prepared for the embrace.

Slava hugged Raake and gave him a quick kiss on the cheek.

"I suppose that once you meet up with Vladimir, you will not come back to Vitebsk."

"I don't know. Most likely not."

"We'll miss you here. Go home now. The train leaves in less than two hours. Meet me at the station."

Slava flew home. Her feet sprouted wings, as she did not feel the ground underneath her. The regular one-half hour walk took less than fifteen minutes.

"Mama, Papa, I'm going to Minsk tonight. Major Raake is so wonderful. He will escort me on a troop train. He's arranged it all. I have to pack and meet him at the station. I don't have much time. Oh where is my suitcase?"

"Calm down, Slavochka," Vladislav said. "You need to slow down and rest a minute. You're too excited. Now take a deep breath. How much time do you have?"

"Not much time at all. Mama, what should I take?"

"Slavochka, my darling, my baby girl, here is the suitcase. It's not very big so you can't take too much. I would suggest a couple of summer weight dresses and a couple winter dresses. One you'll wear and the other pack away. Take a sweater and of course several pairs of underwear, and…"

Suzanna could not finish the sentence. She turned around and ran out of the room. Slava heard her sobs. Her father stayed with her as she packed. He approached her and gently petted her hair. He touched her cheek with the back of his hand.

"We'll miss you terribly. But we'll be all right. Whatever you do, don't worry about us. Take care of yourself. Someday you'll have a wonderful life with Vladimir and have beautiful, happy children. And who knows, maybe I'll even get to see them."

"Oh, Papa, life is so hard sometimes."

Slava realized how hard her departure was on her parents. It weighed on her, but she knew she had no choice. Vladimir needed her. For the remaining minutes that the family had together very little was said. The atmosphere was heavy. They sat huddled together on the sofa, with Slava between her parents. Plans for reuniting with each other should have been made, but no one could make those plans because everything was so uncertain. No one knew where Slava would wind up or if her parents would be all right.

"Well, Slavochka," Vladislav said. "You better go now."

"Oh, Papa and Mama, I don't want to leave you. Are you sure you'll be all right?"

"Of course, my little one," Suzanna said. "Don't worry, we'll see each other again, most likely after the war is over. We'll be together. You father is right. You better go now."

Suzanna rose and went into the kitchen. Slava remained on the couch a few more minutes with her father. When she went to her room to get her coat, hat and suitcase, her mother met her in the dining room with a towel, a bar of soap and a package.

"Here, put these in your suitcase. I've prepared some sandwiches for you along with some apples. Don't forget to take your money with you."

"Mama, let me leave you fifty marks."

"No, we'll get by, take it all. God knows, you'll need it all and more."

Victor Moss

As Slava left the house, she took the fifty marks out of her coat pocket and without letting her parents see, left the money on the table by the door. The parents walked her to the end of the block. All three were crying. After several more embraces and kisses, Slava was finally off.

The beautiful train depot of Vitebsk was so devastated that the Germans set up a temporary depot for their troops. Slava found the station, an old warehouse adjacent to the tracks. The platform was crowded with soldiers. She searched for Raake, avoiding the stares and rude remarks of the men. The train arrived. Very few soldiers exited. Those on the platform rushed to board the train. She wondered where everyone would sit.

Almost everyone boarded, but Raake still had not come. Where is he? Did he change his mind? The train whistle blew a warning and Slava began to panic. *Should I just jump on that train, and take my chances? Surely, they won't throw me off? Where is he?* She walked toward the door of the depot in hopes of seeing Raake. *Oh please show up. Come on.*

Suddenly she heard Raake call out to her. He came in from the side of the building.

"Hurry, let's get on the train," Raake said.

Slava rushed to the track and as the train began to move they both jumped on the step and pushed their way inside. There were no seats. All the men stood in place. As Raake walked in, everyone saluted him. He saluted back and pulled Slava from one car to the next, searching for one less crowded. Finally he stopped in one that seemed to have a little more room. On a side of the car, close to the bathroom wall, stood a small wooden chair occupied by an officer.

Raake ordered the junior officer out of the chair and told Slava to sit down. Slava felt awkward and told him he should take the seat. She insisted that she would be all right standing up. Raake was adamant, so she sat down. No sooner was she seated than a conductor came by. Surprised to see Slava, he asked to see her papers, authorization to travel and ticket. Raake showed the conductor his own papers and told him that Slava was his guest and to leave her alone.

The night train traveled slowly. The German soldiers began to sing, tell jokes and broke into boisterous laughter. Several hours into the journey, Slava fell asleep. She awoke to the sound of Raake's voice ordering everyone to stay quiet and tone down on the jokes.

"What's this all about?" The officer dispossessed from the chair asked.

"Can't you see that this young lady is sleeping," Raake said. "Have some decency and let her sleep."

Slava felt embarrassed by the unusual attention and treatment. *I wish he would just pretend that I were not here.* She did not want to impose or be obligated to anyone. And the nicer Raake was, the more uncomfortable she became. Nevertheless, his efforts to help her were truly appreciated. She was overwhelmed by his generosity. *Who would have thought?*

After several stops and almost twelve hours later, the creaky train finally rolled into Minsk. It was daylight and Slava saw some of the city alongside the

Beware the Wolves

tracks. The devastation was disheartening. She had visited her sister, Maria, in Minsk many times before. Maria had studied at one of the universities. She thought the city was beautiful. *What a drastic change? How can one nation cause such destruction on another?* Sadly, she sat in her chair and gazed at the buildings lying in ruins. She was amazed that one building could be totally destroyed, while next door, another could be totally untouched by the ravages of war. The depot also was damaged. She remembered that Maria told her the depot was originally built in 1871 and totally renovated in 1939, just two years before the war began. *Yet look at it now. The renovation was for nothing.*

"You'll never find the chief medical officer," Raake said. "Our administration is huge since Minsk is the main headquarters for Operation Center. It covers many buildings. I'll help you find him. What was his name again?"

"Colonel Neusbaum. But thank you very much. You've already done so much for me. I will take it from here. I will find him. I could never repay you for everything that you have done for me."

"I'm not looking for payment. I'm just glad to help a young lady in distress," Raake said laughingly. "Besides, I like being with you."

Slava never understood Raake's attentiveness. She assumed that he thought of her as a substitute daughter. But she felt if she had given him any encouragement, the relationship would have been much different. She sensed he liked her from the start and feared that he would demand a romantic relationship with her. But he, indeed, turned out to be a true gentleman.

"And furthermore, I can help you get in to see him. It is highly unlikely that he will condescend to see you. I mean, you're a civilian, right off the street."

Slava realized that he probably was right. Her mother told her the same. *Why would he see me just like that? I probably wouldn't be able to get through the front door.*

"Thank you so much, Herr Major Raake. I really would appreciate your help here as well."

Raake had a problem finding the office of the medical administrator. But after a few dead ends and finally asking for directions, Raake and Slava walked into the right building. Just outside the foyer, a soldier sat at a desk. Raake approached him and conversed with him out of Slava's earshot. The soldier nodded his head and walked up the stairs. Raake returned to Slava, took her hand and held it with both of his hands.

"I must leave you now. The corporal assures me that he'll try to get you in to see Colonel Neusbaum. I wish you well, and pray that your husband will be released. You are a charming person and I have always admired you."

"Oh Herr Major Raake. I can't thank you enough for all you have done."

With that said, Raake took Slava's hand and kissed it slowly. He looked a moment at her, clicked his heels, bowed, turned and walked out of the building. Slava stood by the desk with the little suitcase and her purse in her hand. In a way, she was sorry to see Raake go. But, her mind quickly turned to the meet-

Victor Moss

ing with Neusbaum. Her knees shook with the thought of encountering the man who held their fate in his hands. *What if he refuses to see me? What do I do then? I know so little of what I'm supposed to say? Oh what's taking so long? I can't believe what a fine person Raake turned out to be.*

The corporal returned and told Slava to sit down on one of the chairs down the hall.

"Colonel Neusbaum will see you shortly."

Oh my God, thank you Dear Jesus. He'll see me. Oh my God. Her heart beat rapidly and butterflies filled her stomach. She tried to breathe evenly.

After twenty long minutes passed, the phone rang and the soldier came up to Slava.

"Follow me, miss," the corporal said. "Herr Colonel Neusbaum will see you now."

CHAPTER 28

The large area at the top of the wide staircase was covered with a multitude of desks. Seated behind them, a number of uniformed German soldiers had telephones to their ears, while others pecked away on typewriters. Slava followed the corporal through the narrow aisle between the desks into a large room. More desks occupied that space. Here too, a few more soldiers manned the desks, but most of the workers were local women. As the corporal led Slava into Neusbaum's office, they stopped their work. A dark green carpet runner ran from the doorway the approximate ten meters to Neusbaum's desk. To the left of the runner, an extravagant conference table, flanked by red leather chairs, stood on the highly polished oak floor. To the right were several smaller tables surrounded by more red chairs. Red velvet drapes framed the large windows. Slava was already intimidated, and the huge, extravagantly furnished office added to her nervousness.

Neusbaum stood up politely as Slava approached. He was a relatively short, pot-bellied man. His black narrowly trimmed mustache stood out against the backdrop of his silver-white hair. His chubby face softened as a buttery smile widened his generous mouth.

"Please sit down, fraulein. I understand you speak German."

Slava sat in the chair. Her thin fingers tensed as she squeezed the wood of the armrests. She returned Neusbaum's disarming smile.

"What is your name, young lady?" Neusbaum asked, his gray eyes sparkled as though he was playing a game.

"I'm Vladislava Moskalkova," she answered awkwardly, clearing her throat.

"Ah, yes, you're the wife of the prisoner doctor in Baranovichi that I've heard about."

"Yes," Slava said, stirring uneasily in the chair.

"You can't be a wife yet, can you? I mean you're so young looking, probably no older than sixteen."

Slava did look young for her age. And it always infuriated her when people commented on how young she looked. Even when she attended medical school, people thought she was still in gymnasium (high school).

"Herr Colonel Neusbaum, I am married and, actually, at the end of this month I'll be twenty-one years old."

"Well, you look so young. Maybe its because you are so thin."

Slava let the comment go. She was used to it. Besides, she had to get down to business.

249

Victor Moss

"It is my understanding that you need to see my husband's diploma and a certificate that he completed an ENT program, is that correct?"

"Yes. I thought it certainly should be a requirement."

Slava lifted the suitcase, placed it on her lap, opened it and took out the precious documents.

"Here is the diploma and the ENT certificate."

"It's in Russian?" Neusbaum asked, playing with his mustache.

"Russian on one side, and Byelorussian on the other."

"I need to get it translated, then."

Neusbaum lifted the receiver of the telephone and called for a translator to come into his office. While they waited, Neusbaum asked Slava more about herself.

"I met my husband in medical school. He was on the last course of study and I was on my second."

"But you were so young to be in medical school."

"I tested out of several subjects and graduated early from gymnasium."

"So, you have medical training also?"

"Yes."

"That will be useful where you're going."

"Oh, where am I going?" Slava asked, her voice shaking with anticipation.

"Weren't you told? I will assign your husband to Slonim. Of course, provided that I find these documents in order. He is to open a medical clinic, specializing in ENT. I suppose you will be his assistant, then."

Slava was astonished. Her mouth dropped and she took a quick sharp breath. *Oh my God! We're going to Slonim and will work as doctors. Oh my God! But where and what's in Slonim?*

"Slonim? Is there a clinic waiting for us?"

"No, it will be your husband's responsibility to set one up. I'm sure he'll be able to do it. There will not be a lack of patients. I guarantee that. Of course, getting paid for your work is another story." Neusbaum laughed as though he was sincerely amused.

The translator finally arrived and Neusbaum handed him the documents.

"You may wait downstairs. The translator will bring the documents to you. After I review the translation, and if everything looks in order, I will call Baranovichi and order your husband released. He should be released within a couple of days. Good luck to you and your husband."

Slava's mood was suddenly buoyant. She could not hold back her excitement. An overwhelming sense of euphoria overcame her and her broad smile turned into a giggle. Neusbaum saw her excitement and also laughed out loud.

"I'm glad I could make you so happy."

"Thank you so much for everything. But before I go may I ask, where is Slonim?" Slava asked as her heart sang with delight.

"We have placed it in Poland. It's close to the border of Poland and Byelorussia."

"Oh, how can I reach Baranovichi? Could I simply buy a ticket and go there?"

"I will issue a pass to travel as a civilian. You have to purchase your own ticket, however. Do you have money?"

"Yes, I have some."

"Fine, I'll have the translator bring you the authorization as well. Once again, good luck," Neusbaum said as he stood, clicking his heels.

Slava picked up her suitcase and handbag and walked out of the office. She was still in a daze, her heart pounding from the fantastic news. She sat down again on the same chair downstairs and waited for the documents. Various thoughts ran through her head in the excitement of the moment. *Dear Jesus and Blessed Virgin Mary, thank you for everything. This is a miracle. I can't believe our luck. Neusbaum turned out to be a pleasant person. Bless his heart. What exactly did Volodya do to merit a release and to obtain such a position? Whoever he saved, must have been very important. Now I have to get to Baranovichi. I hope I have enough money. Then once I get there, how will I find him?*

A rumble in her stomach reminded Slava that she had not eaten. As she swallowed the last piece of a sandwich her mother sent with her, the translator came down with the documents.

"Here you are, miss. The Colonel says everything is in order. You may go now."

◆ ◆ ◆ ◆

Slava used up more than half of her money to purchase a train ticket. *I wonder if I even have enough marks to buy food or to find a place to stay in Baranovichi?* The concern was only for a fleeting moment. She sat joyfully at the window of the passenger car, a happy smile on her face at the notion of seeing Vladimir. Everything else was inconsequential. The train pulled out of the station and Slava knew that it was taking her to a new life. And what it would be like, only God knew.

The train moved slowly. The car was half empty. Slava and a tall man in his forties, dressed in a dark gray coat and brown hat, were the only civilians. He sat two rows ahead of her and turned and gazed at Slava frequently. The other passengers were military. Half way into the trip, a young soldier sat down and began a conversation with Slava in German. Slava understood him, but shook her head as though she did not. After no response to the numerous questions he asked, he finally left Slava alone.

Suddenly, the roar of the planes startled her. Out of the window she saw two planes heading straight for the train. *Oh my God! Are those planes attacking this train?* The soldiers in the car began shouting for everyone to take cover. They squatted between the seats. At the same time, the only civilian man yelled at Slava to get down. Slava quickly slid down under the seat and edged herself toward the aisle. In an instant, with a loud racquet, the planes flew overhead.

"They're ours," one of the soldiers yelled out.

Everyone stood, relieved. Slava, also stood up with them. After brushing herself off, she returned to the seat. The civilian man walked over to Slava and in Polish asked her if he could join her for a few minutes. Slava was still shaken by the incident. *What does the old goat want? I want to be left alone.*

"Yes, please sit down," Slava answered reluctantly in Polish, trying to be polite.

"You speak Polish well. Are you a Pole?"

"My parents are of Polish background. But, we're from Vitebsk."

"Let me introduce myself. My name is Yan and I'm from Baranovichi. I take it you're going there?"

"Yes."

"Do you have relatives there?"

"No."

"I don't mean to pry, but it's so unusual to see a young lady traveling by herself. It's such a dangerous time now. You must have some pull to obtain authorization to travel."

Slava did not like probing questions about her life from a stranger. Living under Stalin's paranoia, she learned to guard her tongue and not give much information. *Why is he asking me these questions? Is it just talk or does he have some purpose?*

"Can you tell me a little of Baranovichi?" Slava asked.

"Oh, you've never been to the city before?"

"No, and I'm anxious to hear all about it."

"It began as a railroad center in the 1870's. Belonged to Poland, then to Russia, then in 1920 it was Polish again. A 1939 treaty made it Byelorussian. Now the Germans consider the Brest region to be Polish again. It was a pleasant city in which to live, but you'll see the devastation. Life has become very difficult."

"What kind of work do you do?"

"I'm a baker. I bake bread. I used to bake beautiful cakes, but with the shortage of sugar, that's impossible. Now that I've answered your questions, the curiosity is killing me. What's a young lady doing on this train by herself going to Baranovichi?"

Slava hesitated to answer. *Should I make up a story? Should I tell him that it's none of his business? On the other hand, if he is some sort of spy, or he's with the Gestapo, they probably know why I'm going to Baranovichi anyway. So there's probably no harm. And maybe, he can help me.*

"I'm to meet my husband."

"Oh, he must be important for you to have permission to travel."

"Yes, he must be."

"What does he do? Maybe I know him."

"I'm sure not. He is a prisoner-of-war."

The man looked perplexed and gazed at her in disbelief.

Beware the Wolves

"You like to joke, I see."

"No, I'm serious. They're releasing him and I was given permission to travel to him."

"I never heard of such a thing. Why? I mean, if you're serious, there must be a very good reason for the Nazis to do such a thing."

"I really don't know the details. I hope to discover the circumstances behind his release myself. But, I wonder if you can help me?"

"Yes, of course, if I can."

"Can you give me directions to the prisoner-of-war camp? Perhaps you know of a place where I could stay close to the camp?"

"The answers to both your questions are easy. For the camp, when you exit from the depot, turn to your left and follow the road through town. But it's several kilometers away. It will be almost dark when we arrive in Baranovichi. You would have to go there in the morning. As for a place to stay, I know a perfect place for you. It actually belongs to my sister. It is right on the outskirts of town on the road to the camp."

"Oh, that sounds wonderful. But I don't have much money to pay."

"I'll make sure she doesn't charge you much. I'll be happy to accompany you there."

"Thank you, but I don't want you to go to any trouble. If you please give me the directions, I'll find it."

"Oh, it's no trouble at all. I live not far from there."

◆ ◆ ◆ ◆

It was a two story wooden house, obviously in need of repair and paint. The landlady, a heavyset woman with graying hair, seemed pleasant enough at first and welcomed Slava wholeheartedly. She showed Slava the room upstairs. It was clean with a brass double bed. A large square pillow lay on top of the multi-colored down comforter. A table with a pitcher and washbowl stood in the corner. A wooden chair was used as a nightstand. The room was perfect for Slava. The journey from Vitebsk and the two-kilometer trek from the station to the house had exhausted her. She could barely wait to fall into the bed. She glanced out of the window and saw the road below.

"Is this the road that leads to the war prisoner camp?"

"Yes, yes," Yan said. "That's the same road we've been on."

"If you like the room," the landlady said. "The rent is by the week, payable in advance at fifty marks per week."

"Oh no! I only have thirty marks left," Slava said desperately.

"I'm sorry then. I guess you're not staying here."

"Danuta," Yan said. "Give this young lady a break. You haven't been able to rent that room for months. Take the thirty marks and be happy you got it."

"Oh, all right," the landlady, said disgustedly. "But I'm not going to give you clean towels every day."

253

Slava paid the landlady, realizing that she had no money left for food. *Oh well, at least I'll have a roof over my head and I'll be able to watch for Volodya out of this window.* As soon as the landlady and her brother left, she locked the door and collapsed into a deep sleep.

At dawn, she ran to the window and looked out for a few minutes. An occasional German truck rolled by. *Should I go over to the camp now or wait until later? Maybe it's too early?* She pulled the chair over to the window and sat down to observe the street that led to the camp. A smell of frying bacon drifted from the floor below. She suddenly realized that she had not eaten since Minsk. The aroma caused her saliva to flow. Her stomach ached. *I have no money to buy food. What am I going to do?* She remembered a saved apple given to her by her mother. Reaching into her suitcase, she rummaged until her hand closed on the fruit. She rubbed it clean on her dress and blissfully bit into the small apple. Munching on the apple, she decided to go to the camp right away.

The walk was cold. The camp was further than she thought, and by the time she reached the gate, she felt frozen.

"What do you want here?" A surly guard yelled out from behind the barbed wire gate.

"I need to find out about my husband. He is to be released and I'd like to know when."

"What do you think this is, an information bureau? Move along."

"Is there any way I could talk to him?"

"Lady, I said move along."

"Can I talk to your superior, perhaps he knows of the release of my husband?"

"Lady, get out of here. I see a truck coming. I have to open the gate and you have to be out of here. Now leave before you get hurt."

Slava edged a few meters away and waited for the truck to enter. *What shall I do? There has to be a way for me to ask someone about Volodya.* She glanced at the gate and saw the guard waving at her to keep moving. But instead, she began to approach the gate again. *I have to give it one more try.*

The guard started to shout at her for disobeying his order. A sergeant, witnessing the fuss, walked up and ordered the soldier to quiet down. As Slava turned to the sergeant, she realized that he was livid with anger.

"What do you want?" The sergeant said. "Why aren't you obeying the order of this soldier?"

"All I need is information. My husband is to be released and I want to know if he's still here."

"What's the name of your husband?"

"Vladimir Moskalkov."

"Is he a doctor?"

"Yes, yes."

"I've heard about him. As far as I know, he's still here."

Beware the Wolves

"When will he be released?"

"There is no way I would know that. It all depends on the commandant."

"Can I see him?"

"That is impossible. You have to leave now."

"Could you call him?"

"You think I'm crazy to do a thing like that? I've given you all the information I know. Civilians are not allowed in and that is that. Just go."

Her heart heavy with disappointment, Slava trudged back to her room. *What if Volodya is not released for days or even weeks?* Every step suddenly became more difficult. Her energy depleted, she felt weak and dizzy from hunger. She could still smell the bacon. She could almost see it. As she walked up to the house, she decided to ask the landlady for a scrap of food.

"My dear landlady, you wouldn't have something, just a little left over from your breakfast. I am absolutely famished. Just a bite of anything would be wonderful."

Danuta gazed at her in disbelief. Her face red with indignation, she spat out, "You know, that the money you paid me for rent did not include food."

"I know. But I have no more money to buy food. And even if I did, I wouldn't know where I could buy any."

"There is a store not far from here."

"But I have no more money."

"Well, I suppose, this one time, I'll give you something to eat. Come into the kitchen."

Danuta reluctantly gave Slava two thin slices of dark rye bread, a slice of ham and a slice of cheese. The slices of ham and cheese were so thinly cut that Slava could see through them. She also poured Slava a cup of tea. Slava devoured the food and thanked Danuta for her generosity. Danuta grunted in response. Slava went back to her room and took up her post at the window. *Volodya would be walking this way, and I better not miss him.* She sat at the window until dark. She smelled food cooking again. It reminded her how hungry she still felt.

The daybreak found her once again at the window. Again, the aroma of bacon permeated the air. Slava felt her stomach do summersaults. She hoped that the landlady would take pity on her and give her a morsel of food. But none was offered.

Slava carefully watched the vehicular traffic up and down the street. She studied men as they walked from the direction of the camp. From a distance, one of the pedestrians resembled Vladimir. *It's been so long since I saw him, would I even recognize him?* Her heart began to race when she saw the individual. But the closer he came, she realized the man was not the love of her life. The day went by and again no Vladimir. She went to bed with tears in her eyes. *What if he went by in a vehicle and I missed him. How is he supposed to find me? Maybe, I should go to the railroad station.*

255

Victor Moss

That's the logical place for us to meet. Oh, I'm so hungry. But it kills me to ask for food from that woman. I'll make it. If only Volodya were here with me. He'd think of something.

At the break of day, Slava was back at the window. The smell of food from downstairs tortured her. She knew she had to eat. But the humiliation of asking the landlady was too much for Slava to bear. And to leave the room to search for food was out of the question. If she left her post at the window, she might miss Vladimir as he walked into town. In late afternoon, a knock on the door startled Slava. The landlady grudgingly offered Slava two boiled eggs and a slice of bread. Slava was so overwhelmed by this act of kindness that she hugged Danuta.

"Well, I don't want to find a dead body in my house," Danuta said forcing a smile. "Next time you come visiting, you should bring enough money so you can eat."

Slava gobbled down the food as she peered out the window. Dusk was rapidly approaching and Slava became more distraught by every passing minute. *They must have released him by now and I probably missed him. I'd better go to the station. Maybe he's there. It's been three days. I'll wait a few more minutes, then I'll go,* she thought as she kept her eyes glued to the road.

In the twilight she saw the silhouette of a man approaching. He walked quickly, almost at a run. Her heart began to hammer against her ribs. The gait was familiar. She knew at that instant that it was Vladimir. *It has to be him!* Without hesitation, she flung open the door to her room and raced down the stairs. She grabbed the brass handle of the front door and turned it. The door was locked. Her hands trembled and her knees shook as she twisted the lock open. Gasping for breath, her heart lurching madly, she dashed out of the house and down the road toward the silhouette. The man saw her and sprinted toward her. *That's my Volodya, that's my Volodya. Oh my God!*

"Volodya! Volodya! It's me. Oh my God, Volodya!"

"Slavochka! Slava!"

And there, in the middle of the road, in one forward motion, Vladimir swept Slava into his arms.

EPILOGUE

Vladimir and Vladislava survived the war. As per agreement with the Germans, Vladimir set up a private medical practice in Slonim and Vladislava assisted. For a short period, life for them was fairly peaceful. The Germans occupiers left them alone and the practice flourished.

Meanwhile, the Red Army made great progress in pushing the Nazis first out of Russia, then out of Byelorussia. The author, son of Vladimir and Vladislava, was born in Slonim in 1944. The city was still under German occupation. However, a few months later, with the Red Army approaching the city, the Germans evacuated the Moskalkov family, among others, to refugee camps in Germany. And soon, after several battles, the Soviet army entered Slonim.

The many months of Allied bombings rendered life in Germany dangerous. Devastation was everywhere. Food was scarce and the people were starving. There was a breakdown of civil order. Nevertheless, Vladimir continued his work as a physician in the refugee camps, paid by whatever government was in control at the time. After the war, Vladimir was able to take the train to Latvia where he thought Slava's parents had probably gone from Vitebsk. He found them and brought them back to join his family in Germany.

As the war ended and Germany was divvied up among the conquerors, the area around Munster, Westphalia where the Moskalkov family lived became the British zone and came under the British administration. The change did not affect the lives of the refugees--at least not immediately.

Unfortunately, the Soviet Union demanded the return of its citizens to the Motherland. The demand was unequivocal, regardless of whether these citizens wanted to go back or not. An ugly process of forceful repatriation began with full cooperation of the British and the American governments. If the documents indicated or the officials believed that the person had resided within the borders of the Soviet Union in 1939 or before, then, regardless of that person's nationality, he was deemed a Soviet citizen.

Many were anxious to go home, but those who refused were forcibly loaded on trucks, trains or ships and sent back to the Soviet Union. Those who fought repatriation were killed. Others committed suicide. Rumors spread quickly throughout the refugee camps that the returnees, once on the Soviet soil, were either executed or sent to labor camps in Siberia. Stalin's paranoia was as strong as ever. He believed that any Soviet citizen who had contact with the outside world could not be trusted and was probably a spy for the West.

Victor Moss

Again, Vladimir and Slava had reason to fear for their lives. Fortunately they found a way, on the advice of some good people, to escape the fate of their many compatriots. They avoided repatriation. During that tumultuous time, Slava's parents died and were buried in Germany. They never new the fate of their other children and grandchildren left behind in the Soviet Union.

The fear of repatriation was behind the Moskalkov family and life again surged forward. The Marshall Plan stabilized the German economy and Vladimir and Slava could again live a happy and fairly prosperous life. Vladimir worked as a physician for a state-supported medical clinic. Slava stayed home with her little son. Nevertheless, they began to dream of the far-away America they heard so much about. The American way of life, free of repressions and fear, beckoned them. In 1950 they arrived in New York on board an American troopship.

At the dock, a Methodist minister approached them and asked Vladimir if he would consider a job in Asher, Oklahoma. He had the information that Vladimir was a physician and Asher was in desperate need of a doctor. Vladimir and Slava had never heard of Oklahoma or Asher, but readily agreed. Upon their arrival in Asher, the town's residents came out in full force to welcome the newcomers.

After a few weeks, however, Vladimir was told that he was unable to practice medicine in Oklahoma without a license. To obtain a license, he had to pass several examinations that in English would take him months to study for and pass. Vladimir was desperate. He needed a job to support his small family. Fortunately, the Oklahoma State Hospital in Norman hired Vladimir as a physician's assistant. It was both a relief and a disappointment. Vladimir was a physician and wanted to work as such. Vladimir set himself down to learn English, and as his language skills improved he studied medical texts and eventually passed the required examinations for licensure. In addition, he completed instruction and training to become highly proficient in the specialty of psychiatry. Vladimir and Slava's second child, Mary Veronica, was born in Norman, Oklahoma. In 1956, Vladimir and Slava became United States citizens and shortened their name to Moss.

◆ ◆ ◆ ◆

Vladimir passed away on December 2, 1983, at the age of sixty-eight.

In 1993, after the political changes swept through what used to be the Soviet Union, the author was able to track down Slava's and Vladimir's relatives in Russia and Byelorussia. Slava traveled to Moscow to meet her beloved sister, Maria, her only surviving sibling. For over fifty-two years neither had known whether or not the other was alive. The meeting was very emotional and both women shed many tears both of happiness and sadness. Later Slava met Maria's son and his family. Vladimir's sister Anna and her daughters traveled from Vitebsk, Byelorussia to Moscow to meet with Slava. Maria told Slava of the several nephew and nieces who lived in St. Petersburg and the author took Slava to meet them all.

Slava passed away on July 14, 2005 at the age of eight-three.